ONE
MUST
KILL
ANOTHER

MARCUS ALEXANDER HART

 Canaby Press

Canaby Press, LLC | Sheridan, Wyoming

Canaby Press, LLC
30 North Gould Street | Suite R
Sheridan, WY 82801
CanabyPress.com

This is a work of fiction. Names, characters, places, and events are either a product of
the author's imagination or are used fictitiously. Locales, awards, and public names
are sometimes used for atmospheric purposes. Any resemblance to actual persons,
living or dead, or to businesses, events, institutions, or locales is unintentional.

One Must Kill Another / Marcus Alexander Hart
Print Edition 6

Paperback ISBN: 9781092426657
eBook ASIN: B07BZV1P95

Also by Marcus Alexander Hart

Alexis vs. the Afterlife

Amber's Blind Date
(as Casey Summers)

Caster's Blog: A Geek Love Story

Walkin' on Sunshine:
A Quantum Physics Sex Farce

CONTENTS

CHAPTER ONE

Kimberly
Thirteen Years Ago

I'm going to kill him.

My husband is beside me, behind the wheel of our BMW Sport Wagon. He's humming "99 Bottles of Beer on the Wall." He's been doing it on and off for hours. Under his breath, right at the cusp of being audible. Just loud enough to be abrasive. Every time I'm about to ask him to stop, he stops. And a few minutes later, when my annoyance level has dropped, he starts again. It's like Matty has an internal barometer tuned to my aggravation.

Thank God we're almost there.

The suspension bobs as the car creeps back and forth up the earthen switchbacks of our private driveway. To even call it a driveway is generous. It's just two narrow strips of packed dirt sneaking off an old service road into a labyrinth of ancient oak and pine trees. Impossible to find unless someone tells you where it is.

I've never told anyone but Matty. And this is a secret he's actually managed to keep.

A goofy grin spreads over his face as he begins rhythmically rapping his fingers on the steering wheel. He glances over his shoulder at the backseat.

"Ooh, we're getting close now. I think I hear the tribal war drums. Do you hear them, Bex?"

Our daughter notices him mugging and pulls a white earbud from her head, spilling a tinny warble of boy band into the air.

"What?"

"Duhh, *whut?*" Matty says playfully. "Come on, kiddo. Get on the ball before we all end up scalped. We've entered the deadliest depths of the Forbidden Jungle!"

He leans forward, grunting over his gut, and plucks a piece of yellow construction paper from the door pocket. It's mottled with grime, and strips of masking tape hold it together at its worn folds. Matty flicks it open to reveal a hand-drawn map filled with palm trees and tiki huts, with something like an Aztec pyramid in the center. Some of it is penciled in his own tight hand. The rest is crudely rendered in crayon.

Matty passes it to Bex in the back seat. "We're heading into Sasquatch Country. You're the expert here, so I'll need your help navigating to the safety of Outpost 132."

Bex studies their map for a long moment, silent and devoid of expression. Her round little face is flawless. And it's less round every day. My little girl is growing into her good looks. She casts a glance at her father in the rearview mirror, then at me.

"Dad, I'm too old for these dumb games."

"You're ten. You're not too old for anything." Matty's eyes stop smiling, even as his lips continue the lie. "And you can't give up the expedition now. Last summer we were so close to finding the Lost Temple of Zamrycki. I know this year we'll—"

The thought chokes in his lungs as a tire crashes through a deep divot in the earth, bouncing us brutally in our seats. A sharp kick of pain blasts up my spine, and my reflexes throw my arms and legs into a brace position.

"Whoa!" Matty laughs. "I think we hit a sasquatch footprint!"

I suck a hot breath as the surge of unnecessary adrenalin festers in my muscles.

"Damn it, Matty! Pay attention before you wreck the car!"

He just grins and pats the dashboard. "Relax, hon. A little pothole can't hurt a 5 Series wagon. This sweet baby is top of the line."

I know it is. I paid for it.

I rub my temples and murmur. "Please, just stop goofing around and watch the road. Okay?"

Matty frowns. "Jeez, what a party pooper. Right, Bex?" He looks in the rearview mirror. Bex doesn't make eye contact. She just plugs her earbud back into her head and gazes out the window at the crush of trees.

Matty sighs. "Well, we're almost there anyway." He turns his attention to the last switchback. The steep one. A fifty-foot stretch with an incline like a playground slide. The engine roars and loose gravel pounds the wheel wells as the tires spin and grip against the mossy slope.

"Come on . . . Come on, you big bad Beemer." Matty eases on and off the accelerator. "You've got this."

The wagon fishtails side to side, then bites the earth and hurls itself over the top of the ridge into the small clearing in front of our summer cabin.

We call it a cabin. The realtor called it a "rustic manor." A three bedroom, two-and-a-half bath monster of rough-hewn logs thrusting out of the earth to an exaggerated peaked roof. An oversized chimney of rounded cobblestones slumps against one side like the tower of a medieval fortress. The whole house is still hibernating from the winter, its windows shut tight behind steel storm shutters.

Matty quiets the engine and gives the cabin a long, slow appraisal. "No snow damage. Looks as good as it did that very first summer. Remember that, honey?" He smiles and puts his hand on top of mine, resting on my lap.

I don't answer him. The question is the worst kind of rhetorical. Do I remember that summer? As if I would forget it. As if those happy memories aren't the frayed stitches still holding us together. He turns back to Bex. "You see, your mom was so exhausted after she finished filming the first *Blood Blitz* that she needed someplace to escape for some—"

"She's heard it," I say. "We've all heard it. Let's unload the car."

I pull my hand from under Matty's, exit the vehicle, and slam the door. Regret flares so instantly and deeply I feel dizzy. I should have let him tell the old story again, about when our love was in full bloom. Isn't that why I came here? To remember? To feel that again? I'm trying my best to be open minded, but he's so selfish. The sound of his voice puts me on edge. His touch revolts me.

But I still love him. Deep down I know I do. The emotion is small and it's frail, but it's still there, trying to find a light to guide it out of the darkness. If that light is anywhere, it's here in these woods.

I stretch my arms and legs and back and take a deep, calming breath, filling my senses with the heady smell of the pines. Nothing interrupts the quiet but distant songbirds and the gentle swishing of wind through branches. The tranquility here is so complete it's almost unnerving. This cabin is only eighty miles from Los Angeles, but it's a million miles from the real world.

An earthen path leads up the hillside behind the house, through overgrown grass toward a large shed and the gazebo. The gazebo. Just the sight of it brings a rush of warmth to my heart, fueled by memories of lazy summer days spent with my husband on a little wooden bench swing built for two. The gazebo is a gift box filled with bright, shining moments to be recalled and savored.

The gazebo is my light in the woods.

I pop the station wagon's hatch and grab a flashlight from our cache of supplies. Every summer we have to pack in everything we'll need. The nearest store is forty-five minutes away in Lake Arrowhead. There's no phone in the cabin, but thankfully the previous resident had the place wired for electricity and installed a pump down by the river with a cistern in the attic for running water. The whole system is a temperamental pain in the neck, but it works well enough for a few weeks of roughing it.

Matty plods up next to me, shoulders hunched in a hangdog expression that makes his bowling shirt hang over his round belly like a muumuu. I brush my hand over the ginger fuzz of his scalp and smile. "Hey, I'm sorry I snapped at you. It's just . . . I'm still paying that car off. Take it easy, all right?"

At my touch he brightens with the energy of a puppy wagging its tail. "I'm sorry. My bad. I'll be more careful. I promise." I look for sincerity in his words, but there's none there to find. He gestures at the flashlight in my hand. "You wanna go get the power turned on? Me and Bex will gather up the stuff and bring it in."

"Yeah, okay. Thank you."

I give him a little peck on his ever-expanding forehead and saunter off across the yard. My feet creak the boards of the short staircase leading to the front porch, and I slot my key into the first deadbolt. There are three of them on a reinforced door to keep any mountain psychopaths out during the off season. Although I doubt even a psychopath would want to be up here once the snow starts. I unlock the remaining bolts and push the door open, letting a beam of dusty sunlight spill across the living room.

This cabin doesn't wear rustic as a veneer. The interior walls are all corpulent logs—the back sides of the same logs that make up the exterior. But on the inside they've been polished smooth and varnished to an elegant finish. All the furniture is stout knotty pine covered in hardy leather upholstery fastened with brass tacks in wobbly, hand-hammered rows. Opposite the door is a stone fireplace, still full of ashes from last summer.

The air is stale and heavy with silence. I click on the flashlight and cast it around the room. Inky shadows scurry from my light and slither behind the furniture. This place used to have its own energy. A sense of wellbeing that oozed from the walls like sap. Now it just feels empty and grim. I wonder if this is how the cabin felt to Dr. Cheung in her final days here.

My light glints on the typewriter on Matty's desk in the corner. He used to use it to work on his screenplays the first few summers we came up here, mostly for the novelty value. He said using it made him feel like a "real genuine old-timey writer," but he never seemed to write more than half a page before getting distracted with something else. Usually that something was me.

Usually I was distracting him on purpose.

Usually without pants.

Next to the typewriter is a framed photograph of the two of us. It's at least a decade old, from back before Bex was born. I was so beautiful then. Supermodel tall. Neck like a swan, smile like a sunbeam, eyes as blue as springtime. My blonde mane is cut in a dreadful early-'90s style, all bangs and crimps. Matty is almost unrecognizable, with his Led Zeppelin T-shirt pulled tight over his muscled chest. Dense, rusty hair. Just the single chin.

Seeing him like this gives me a feeling of lovesick nostalgia, and I catch myself pining for my own husband. For the Matty that was. The one who didn't take me for granted. The one I could love and trust unconditionally. I sigh and try to convince myself that man is still inside my Matty somewhere. Buried under a sea-lion-thick layer of insulating blubber.

In the corner next to the desk are a few low bookcases packed with toys. On the top shelf, a train of linked wooden letters spells REBECCA. An unloved gift from Matty's mother, the only person in the world who calls our daughter by her full name. All the toys here are second-string losers Bex has cut from our house in Venice Beach. Most are things I gave her. Beautiful things. Pink and elegant and abandoned. A life-sized Barbie styling head smiles vacantly into the darkness, her mangled hair pulled tight into a single ponytail at the top of her scalp. Stitches of coarse twine sew her eyes and mouth shut. A chicken bone pierces her nose. She should have been Bex's gateway into the world of personal cosmetology. Instead she ended up looking like a shaman's shrunken head.

A book leans against Barbie's ear. A slim, leather-bound volume. Another gift from me. I pick it up and run my fingers over the embossing of delicate Art-Nouveau swirls around the title. *A Tündér Könyv.*

I don't know what it means. It's Hungarian. I picked it up for Bex a few years ago when I was overseas filming *Blood Blitz 4: Crypt of Anarchy.* All the text inside is the same foreign nonsense, but I thought she'd like the pictures. What normal little girl wouldn't?

I set down my flashlight and open the book, slowly turning its stiff, illustrated pages. Each one holds a hauntingly beautiful scene of nature populated with fairies. Perfectly proportioned miniature women with lovely faces and finely detailed wings and gowns. I'd hoped it would inspire her. I'd hoped she'd behold these gorgeous creatures and want to be more like them. More like me. But that summer the book was exiled to the cabin, never to return home.

I turn a page and it sticks to its neighbors in a clump. They're bound at the top and bottom with two yellowed pieces of Scotch tape. Heat prickles up my neck. I buy her such nice things and she ruins them. Taking everything I do for granted, just like her father. Sometimes I don't know why I bother.

My finger slides between the taped-together pages and breaks the strips with a pair of brittle *snaps.* I turn the page and catch a glimpse of black wings and sinister eyes, glowing orange like hot embers.

"Mom! Don't!"

A hand snatches the book and I shriek and recoil. My heart is already exploding before the words make it from my ears to my brain. *Mom.* Bex has somehow snuck up beside me, stealthy as a shadow. I plant a palm on my chest and suck a breath. "My gosh, Bex! Are you trying to scare me to death?"

My daughter fidgets and holds the book to her pudgy belly, wrapping it tightly in both arms. "I'm sorry. It's just . . . don't open the taped pages, okay?"

"Why not? Why did you tape them together in the first place?"

On the other side of the room her father bangs through the door, loaded down with a cardboard box of supplies, six plastic grocery bags hanging from his forearms like saddlebags. Bex flinches and casts a subtle glance at him. "We taped . . . I taped it because . . . uh . . . Because those pages have the ugly fairies. You know, the ones for *boys*. I only want to look at the fairies for girls."

Matty shifts the weight of the box on his gut and chuckles. "Gee, that's not how I remember it. I seem to recall a certain little lady who was *afraid*—"

"Dad, stop! Nobody wants to hear your dumb stories!"

Bex's harsh tone slaps the color from her father's face.

"Wow, tough room," he mutters.

I brush my fingers through the satin-smooth auburn wave of Bex's hair. "Be nice, please. Ladies don't shout."

Her cheeks droop. "Sorry, Mom."

She sets down the book with a twitchy apprehension. A second later she puts Barbie on top of it and takes a quick step back as if she's afraid it'll leap off the shelf and bite her. God only knows what's going through her little head. She has her father's deranged imagination.

I grab my flashlight and follow Matty into the kitchen. The rustic theme continues here, but with a more contemporary design. Cabinets with frosted glass doors framed in rough-hewn wood. Artisanal, mosaic tile countertops. Faux-antique appliances that marry classic style with modern performance. I open the electrical panel hidden in the cabinet by the door and flip the main breaker with a crisp snap. Lights crackle to life all around the shuttered house and I click off the flashlight and breathe a sigh of relief.

"Looks like we won't have to break out the candelabras tonight."

Matty lowers his voice and speaks in cartoon French. "Ah, but mon chéri, pairhaps we will use zee candles aftair zee wee one is asleep. In zee boudoir. For *l'amour*."

He wags his eyebrows at me. I force a smile. "We'll see."

I avoid eye contact and pick up a grocery bag. It's full of two kinds of Doritos and three kinds of Cap'n Crunch. I check the next. Hot dogs, chicken nuggets, and a six pack of beer. The garish colors peeping from every sack tell me it's all the same over-processed imitation food garbage. Matty digs into the box and pulls out a fat plastic barrel.

"Hey Beeeeex," he croons. "Look what the snack fairy brought for you."

Bex bounces into the room and her eyes light up.

"Yeah! Cheese balls!"

Matty grins. "That's right! Who loves ya, kiddo?"

"Thanks, Dad!"

He tosses her the barrel and she greedily rips open the lid. A fistful of puffed orange crap is halfway to her mouth before I can put a steadying hand on her arm. "Don't eat that."

"But Mom, they're good."

"They're empty calories. They're not good for you. Here, you can have some of my . . ." I check another bag for something healthier but come up with nothing. "Matty, where are the rest of the groceries?"

"This is pretty much it, except for the drinks in the cooler. We got OJ, purple stuff, soda, Sunny-D . . ."

"This is not it. This is all junk food." I wave a sack of marshmallows at him. "Where's the stuff I bought for my detox cleanse? The kale and jicama and everything?"

"Ugh. Barf me out. Right, Bex?" He sticks his finger down his throat and pretends to gag. Bex doesn't respond. She just gazes wistfully at the cheese balls. "Come on, Kim. We're on vacation! Forget that Hollywood diet voodoo and enjoy some actual human food with us." He grabs a blue box of crackers and tears it open. "Check it out! I got Chicken in a Biskit! Just like the old days!"

I turn up my nose. "That is not food. That is greasy wheat flour soaked in MSG."

"That's what makes it so good! Remember when we first started dating?" He turns to Bex. "Back before you were born, your mom and I would stay up late talking and laughing and eating whole boxes of these things." He grabs a handful of chicken-flavored crackers and stuffs them in his mouth. "Mmm. That's the stuff. Come on, Kim. You know you want it. Here comes the airplane!"

He makes a *zoooom* noise and pilots a cracker toward my face. Heat rips through me and I slap it out of his fingers. "Stop it! God, you are so selfish."

"Selfish?" he says, blowing crumbs from his lips. "What did I do?"

"What did you . . . ?" My jaw aches with the chore of holding back a scream. I can't even look at him. "Bex, go outside and play."

"By myself?"

"Yes." A few dirty outdoor toys fill a bin next to the back door. I grab the first thing off the stack and thrust it toward her. "Here, go play with this."

"That's Velcro catch. You need two people for—"

"I'll be out in five minutes."

She takes the toy and gives me an uncertain look. "You're gonna play this with me?"

"Yes."

"But . . . this is a boy game."

My throat tenses, but I keep my voice steady. "Bex, just go. Please. Your father and I need to have an adult talk."

The severity of the situation registers on her little face. She glances at Matty, then back at me, then nods and goes out through the living room. I wait until I hear the front door close before I turn on him.

"Damn it, Matty! What were you thinking? You know I can't eat this crap!"

He flinches, but grins. "Aww, I'll bet you can if you really put your mind to it. Here, I'll coach you." He offers me a Twinkie and points to my mouth. "It goes in this end."

10

Redness burns over my cheeks. "This isn't funny."

"Come on, it kinda is." My glare wipes the mirth off his face. "Okay, it isn't. I'm sorry. I'll drive into town and pick up all of your health food stuff tomorrow."

"You'll go right now."

He rolls his eyes. "Jeez, Kim. It's just one night. We're at the cabin. Nobody is looking. Why don't you cut loose a little? Just let yourself go."

"Let myself go? Oh, like *you* did?" My temperature spikes and I poke him in the gut, forcing him to take a defensive step backwards.

"Whoa, hey now. Low blow."

I poke him again. "Do you think I don't want to eat junk food? Do you think I choke down kelp and amaranth salads because I *like* them? I don't, Matty! I'd love to sit around like you, eating this junk all day, but . . . I'm almost forty years old! My metabolism is ruined. Do you have any idea how hard I have to work to stay looking this good?"

"Is that what this is about? Oh, man." He chuckles and wraps my long hands with his stubby fingers. "Kim, I don't care what you look like. I love you for who you are on the inside."

I yank my hands away and ball them into fists. "This isn't about you! I start shooting *Blood Blitz 6* in a month and my ass is already five pounds too fat to fit into my costume. And my ass needs to pay the bills because yours can't."

"What bills?" Matty whines. "We've got enough money to last until Bex is collecting social security. We're loaded!"

I jab a finger in his face. "No. *We* are not loaded. *I* am loaded. I am loaded because I've been busting my butt for the past decade. I've been making sacrifices for this family while you've been loafing around the house gaining weight and losing hair."

"Hey, come on," Matty says, rubbing his receding hairline. "I've been working hard too. I've written four screenplays."

"And how many of them have you gotten produced? How many of them have you even gotten optioned? Zero."

"That's not fair!" His eyebrows lower. "My scripts are hilarious. Any of them could have been greenlit in a second if I could get a big star attached. Someone like—gee, I don't know—the one I'm married to."

My breath is hot in my throat. "Oh, that is so you. Blaming me for your failure. Blaming anyone but yourself." I shake my head. "I can't just do this for you, Matty. I need you to stand on your own two feet. I need you to make an effort."

Matty stares at me, simmering. "Fine. I'll try harder. All I'm saying is, maybe you could throw me a bone here instead of just letting me flounder and struggle while you parade around in front of me with everything you've ever dreamed of."

The heat of my anger runs ice cold. "Is that what you think? Honestly? That my dream was to make a fortune in glorified vampire porn? It isn't. I don't want to make their action movies. I don't want to make your comedies. I want to be an *actress*. I want to make films that *matter*." My vision goes moist and hazy. "All this time I thought you didn't care what I want. But it's worse than that, isn't it? You don't even *know*."

"Hey, that's not true. I know you're unhappy. I know you want to do more artsy stuff. I know. I get it." The tone of his voice subtly tips from defensive to offensive. "And I'm sorry I've been in a slump lately, but I've had other things taking up my time, okay? I mean, maybe I'd have more time to do pitch meetings if I wasn't pretty much single-handedly raising our daughter."

My voice goes cold. "Don't. You. Dare."

"Don't I dare *what?*"

"Don't you even try to act like taking care of Bex is some big burden on you! You're lucky you get to see her at all after what you did to me!"

12

Matty looks away and puffs his cheeks, as if he can't decide whether to yell or break down crying.

"I'm sorry. I don't know how many times I can say I'm sorry!" It starts as a whisper and ends as a scream. "I'm sorry for what I did! I'm sorry I hurt you! I am! A thousand times over I am! But I have no regrets, because—"

"Oh! You have no regrets!" I shriek. "Well, that's just great! You betrayed me, wrecked my body, and gave me a second mouth to feed, but I'm so glad *you* have no regrets!"

Matty's shoulders slump and his gaze tips to the floor for a long time. When he finally looks up his eyes are wet and shimmering.

"I know you've been trying to turn her against me."

Pressure builds in my chest. "Listen to yourself. Blaming someone else for your problems. Again. Like always." My voice goes low and cold. "I didn't turn Bex against you. *You* turned Bex against you. Do you think she's proud of you? Do you think she brags to her little friends at school about her unemployed dad, loafing around the house pretending to be a writer? No, she's proud of *me*. I'm the one bringing home the bacon. I'm the one with the legions of fans. I'm the one with the star on the Hollywood Walk of Fame. I'm Kimberly *fucking* Savage!"

I'm so angry my vision goes fuzzy, darkening the shadows lurking in the corners. Matty wrings his hands. "And I'm nothing. I'm a big fat freeloading piece of shit. Is that what you want me to say? I'm trying, Kim. I swear to you, I'm trying to be a better father. A better husband. I'm trying to be a better man." He gives a weak smile and reaches for me. "I know things have been difficult between us the past few years, but I'm really trying—"

Rage blazes through me and I pound my fists on his meaty chest. "Stop trying! You *try* all the time but you never actually *do* anything! Over and over again, you screw up, you promise to try harder, and you don't change! I'm done with it. And I'm done with you."

The words come out of my mouth before I can stop them. Everything goes quiet. Matty's jaw hangs open, like he wants to promise to try harder but doesn't dare. It's out. I said it. I know I should take it back, but I can't. Because it feels too right. I look him straight in the eyes and speak with a perfect sense of calm.

"Matty, I want a divorce."

His eyebrows work up and down, as if his brain can't process what it's hearing. He just stands there for an awkward eternity. Eventually he shrugs and simply says, "No."

I straighten up, towering over him. "You don't get a say in this. I've made up my mind. Honestly, I think I made it up a long time ago."

His mouth tries to speak, but nothing comes out. "A ... a long time ago? But ... *what?* No. Everything is okay. We're at the cabin for the summer. As a family. Same as always."

"I came here because I thought I could fix us. I thought if we came out to the cabin we would ..." Buried emotions kick a crack in my frustration, spilling a tear down my cheek. "We were so happy here once and I thought ... I thought if we came back we could find it again. Like our happiness was a thing we forgot in the gazebo, and I could pick it up and dust it off and hold it and own it again, but ..." My lips tremble. "But it's not here, Matty. It's not anywhere. It's just gone."

Saying it out loud somehow makes it true. My whole body trembles as it acknowledges a love lost forever. Matty shakes his head. "It's not gone. It's still here." He pats his chest. "And it's right here."

He reaches out and taps my sternum. It's personal and intimate. A long time ago it would have felt romantic. But now his touch only makes me feel violated. I cross my arms against it. "Matty, please. I just want to go home."

"No."

14

His petulance cuts through my sorrow. "This isn't a discussion. We're going back to LA."

"No. We're not." Matty's eyebrows lower as his voice hardens. "We're going to stay here and fix this. Away from the city, away from the noise, away from all the Hollywood bullshit. Just us, alone in the peaceful woods. We can work through this. The two of us, and Bex too. Nobody is leaving until we're all cool again."

My breath quickens. "So, what? You think you can hold us hostage until we're happy?"

"If that's what it takes." Passive aggression stains his voice. "You know I don't have a job to rush back to. You've made that point very clear."

There's a sudden darkness in his face. I calmly extend my hand. "All right, that's enough. Just give me the car keys."

"No. I am not giving you the keys, and you are not leaving. You can't leave." He bristles, slipping into desperation. "You can't leave this cabin, and you can't leave me. You can't. Please."

My skin tingles. All light and heat seem to leech from the room. "Don't make this harder than it already is." I flex my fingers. "Give me the keys."

"No! I can change. Let me prove it to you." He shifts his weight on his feet, clenching his hands into fists and releasing them. "Please! I'm sorry. I can be the man you want me to be! I'll do anything!"

His voice is shrill. His desperation frightens me. My heart jackhammers and I feel lightheaded. Shadows swim through my vision like eels, slithering over the walls. Around our bodies. Choking me. I have to go. I have to leave.

"God damn it, Matty! Give me the keys!" I lurch forward and shove him with both hands. He stumbles backwards and his skull hammers the log wall with an audible crack. Darkness grips Matty and a dazed fury burns his eyes. He lunges and shoves me back, driving his full weight into my chest. I smash into the tall glass door of the linen cupboard, shards of frosted glass biting me as I plunge through.

15

Shock and pain paralyze my mind. I'm on the floor now, my head and shoulders crammed inside the narrow cabinet. Broken shelves jab my back. Blood drips from my arms. I try to scream but can only groan.

Matty just stands there in the shadows, staring at me, flexing his fingers. His eyes are wide and vacant. A face flashes in my mind's eye. A stranger I've only seen in photographs. Dr. Laurie Cheung, the family therapist.

I know, somewhere deep in my subconscious, that Matty is about to kill me.

"Get away from her!"

The voice is a screech. Bex is in the kitchen, pounding her tiny fists into her father. Matty raises his hands defensively and steps back. He shakes his head and blinks as his anger cools and his face loosens. "Stop. Bex, stop it!" He nudges her aside, locking his attention on me. "Kim, are you all right?"

"You hit her," Bex wails. "You hit Mom!"

"I didn't!"

"Don't lie! I was hiding in the other room! I saw you!"

She saved me. My baby hid and saved me. Adrenalin overpowers my pain and I wrestle myself out of the cabinet. Broken glass rains off my body and tinkles to the floor. The darkness has vanished from Matty's face, leaving only contortions of guilt. "I didn't mean to! Oh, God! I didn't mean it! I'm sorry!"

I try to stand and Matty reaches to help me. Bex throws herself between us. "Don't you touch her!"

Her fist smashes Matty's nose. "Aagh! Damn it, Bex!" He stumbles as blood dribbles down his lip and onto his shirt. He doesn't fight back. He just sobs and bellows pitiful apologies. "I'm sorry! I'm so sorry! I didn't mean it, Kim! You know I would never! I hit my head and freaked out. It was an accident! I swear it was an accident!"

Bex stares him down. "It's always an accident with you! Just like all the times you hurt me!"

16

Matty's expression shifts to pure mortification. "*What?* I never hurt you! Kim, I swear, I never hurt her!"

Bex's chubby little body goes taut. "Don't lie! Every time Mom went away you'd hurt me and say it was an accident! I ended up in the emergency room! You told me not to tell her!"

"They *were* accidents!" Matty's voice chokes with panic. "Kim, you have to believe me! I never meant to hurt either of you! Please. Please say you believe me!"

I push myself to my feet. Bex remains between me and her father, ready to defend me. I put a hand on her shoulder and pull her close, extending the other, slick with my own blood. "Matthew, give me the car keys."

Matty pulls the keys from his pocket and puts them in my palm. There's no fight left in him.

"Please don't go. Not like this. Please." He looks at me and Bex with tortured eyes. "We can fix this. We have to. I can't live without you. I need you. I need both of you."

"I know you do," I whisper. "But we don't need you."

I back Bex away from her father and toward the front door.

He doesn't follow us.

CHAPTER TWO

Matty

Rosebud is mopping. That's it. Just dunking the filthy mop into the filthy water and pushing it across the filthy floor of the Rex Mex. But there's something hypnotic about it. The flap of her ill-fitting uniform polo against her lean arms. The way her unflattering Cintas uniform pants hug her butt with every thrust. I can't stop looking.

Stop looking, Matty! What's wrong with you?

I throw my eyes to the cash register on the counter in front of me. The oily touch screen shows a grid of buttons with labels like "Raptor Quesadillas" and "Carnosaur Asada Tacos."

I squeeze my eyes shut. God, what am I doing here? How is this my life? I should quit. I should quit and get serious about my writing. Without this job distracting me I could fully dedicate my time to finishing—

"Uh, hey man. Can you get me a . . . uh . . ."

I open my eyes to see a scraggly guy on the other side of the counter. His bloodshot gaze drifts to the menu above my head and hangs there, paralyzed by the number of options. His hair and beard are one continuous, wild mane of salt and pepper. By that I mean the hair is black and gray, and also that it's dusted with old condiments. The mangy board shorts and T-shirt hanging off his skeleton reek of, let's say, "outdoor living." His bony hips make me so self-conscious about my own ballooning gut that I have to look away.

My eyes want to drift back to Rosebud, but I force them up to the TV mounted in the corner of the dining room. A crack from some long-forgotten rowdiness divides the screen over an ambulance-chasing lawyer shouting his commercial to the empty dining area. My eyes wander again, desperate for some form of distraction, but there's none to be found. The place is exactly like every other Rex Mex in Southern California. A bizarre clash of Mexican and Mesozoic design elements homogenized into a fast food cliché then covered with grime and etched with decades of gang tags. A shitty, worn-down old workplace for a shitty, worn-down old man.

"Uh ... Can I get the Seven-layer Burritosaurus with Volcano Fries?"

My attention blinks back to the customer. "Do you want to Extinction-Size it for ninety-nine cents?"

"Um ... naw. Naw, man. Jus' that."

I grab his food from under the heat lamps and shovel it into a bag that blossoms with grease stains. "That'll be four sixty."

The guy digs into the pockets of his shorts and pulls out a single wrinkled dollar, thirteen cents, a guitar pick, and a roach clip. He drops it all in front of me and feels around his other pockets. "Four sixty? Uh ... has this always been that much? I was in the Rex over on Pico the other day and it was like, a buck fifty. So ... "

His voice drifts off and he stares at me with his hollow, hungry eyes. All I see is the face of what could have been. I could have been him. I *should* have been him. My useless ass deserves to be the one standing there with a gnawing hunger and a putrid stench and a sob story nobody gives a shit about.

I push the bag across the counter, using it to snowplow his pocket junk back to him. "It's fine. Just take it."

He gives me a skeptical squint. "Really?"

"Yeah, don't worry about it." I toss a quick glance over my shoulder into the kitchen. Brody is distracted, shooting the breeze with a line cook. "Take it and go. Before my assbag manager sees."

19

Condiment Beard smiles and snatches the bag. "Right on! Stick it to the Man! Up top."

He raises a fist, scarred and caked with dirt. I reluctantly give him a bump and wave him toward the door. "I know, I'm Robin Hood of the deep fryer. Now seriously, get out."

I wipe my knuckles on my uniform as the guy takes off for the exit, leaving an almost visible haze of stench behind him like Pepé Le Pew. Rosebud watches him leave, then pushes her mop bucket to the counter. I stand up straighter and suck in my gut.

"Hey, Matty. Did you just give that guy free food?"

She cocks her head and looks at me with her big, dark eyes. All shiny and full of spirit. Rosebud Lopez is working here to pay her way through veterinary college. Twenty-three years old, smart, funny, and with the best days of her life still yet to come. I envy her.

"Eh." I shrug. "He looked like he needed it more than we did."

Her thin eyebrows rise. "Aww! You are the sweetest guy, you know that?"

I wave her off. "It's nothing. It was easier than fighting with him about it."

"Fighting? What you fightin' about, bro?"

The sound of his voice instantly puts me on edge.

Brody. Mother fucking Brody.

"Nothing." I look down at the till and pretend to be engrossed in something. "Hey, I think you need to place an order for hot sauce packets."

Rosebud stares vacantly at a garbage can. "Yeah, we're almost out."

Refusal to engage. No eye contact. Diversion. This strategy has a ninety percent success rate in getting our jackass manager to move along before he settles in for a chat. We call it the "Brody Bounce."

"Nah, we good. I hit up my guy this morning. Wassup inventory control? Boom. Brody's on it, bitches." He thrusts his pelvis. "Ugh! You like that?"

I grind my teeth. Rosebud rolls her eyes. We have an entire conversation in a single shared glance.

"Nobody likes that, you prick," she implies.

"He's such a douche," I silently agree.

"Can you believe this idiot is our boss?" She looks away.

"This job would be unbearable without you here," I don't say.

"So for realz," Brody says. "What are y'all fighting about? Did that bum try to pull some shit? 'Cause if they give you trouble, you call me and I'll bust some heads, ya know?"

I sigh. "He wasn't causing any trouble. He was just hungry. I gave him a burrito."

Brody narrows his eyes at me. "I'm sorry, what? You just *gave* him a burrito."

"No. I gave him fries too."

Brody shakes his head. "Oh, Matty. Matty Matty Boom-ba-latty. Come on, bro. This is a business. Somebody's gotta pay for that food."

"Fine. Take four bucks out of my paycheck. I'll keep the other half."

Rosebud snorts a laugh through her adorable button nose. "Ooh, Matty's salty today." She leans over the counter in front of me, giving me an inadvertent glimpse down the wide-open neck of her shirt. I slam my eyes shut, but my brain locks in the image. A voyeur snapshot of smooth mocha breast nestled in hot pink brassiere.

For God's sake, Matty. You're more than twice her age. Behave yourself, you dirty old creep!

I guiltily turn my attention to the floor as she fishes the TV remote from under the counter. "Please don't get yourself fired," she says. "I need somebody to bitch about *Red Carpet Riot* with."

"Or you could try doing some actual work," Brody says.

Rosebud shrugs. "Meh."

She flips the channel to a vapid celebrity gossip show. It's a bunch of sleazy "reporters" squawking about who slept with whom and what drugs they were on at the time. A relentless audio-visual assault of tasteless innuendo and fake scandal. Grade-A, top-shelf garbage television. It's our guilty pleasure. Today's lead story is about some gold-grilled rapper in a legal battle with his neighbors.

One of the gossip hounds leans on the news desk. "Okay, so the dude just wants to build an addition on his garage. NBD, right? But when he tries to get a construction permit his neighbor fully cock blocks him."

The picture cuts to the rapper, lost behind a pair of oversized sunglasses and a baseball cap with stickers on the flat brim. He talks to the camera as he limps through a four-car garage, filled to capacity.

"It's crazy, y'all. Sick-ass respirator bitch next door got some kinda beef about construction noise, so now I gotta park my Bugatti and Maserati outside? That ain't right. It just makes me sad, ya know? Like, my belly hurt, 'cause I got depression."

I shake my head. "Worst episode of *Fresh Prince* ever."

Rosebud slouches and speaks in a dull slur. "I got more riches than three popes, but I got the blues so bad 'causa insufficient parking." She shakes her head. "If I had his money I'd never be sad another second in my life."

I chuckle under my breath. "Being rich doesn't make you happy. Trust me on that one."

Brody snorts. "The hell you talking about, *'Trust me on that one'*? You're a million miles from knowing jack shit about being rich, bro. I should know. I sign your paychecks."

Humiliation prickles through my cheeks. Goddamn Brody. Goddamn twenty-shit-year-old asshole. I don't need his shit. I don't need this job. I'm gonna rip him a new asshole then tear my greasy nametag off my greasy shirt and mic-drop it before I kick open the door and never come back. I'm out, bitches. Peace!

I glance at Rosebud and sigh. "I'm goin' on break."

Brody nods. "Don't forget to clock out, po boy."

My shoulders tense, but I don't say a word. The gossip reporters on the TV continue braying through their next news item.

"...the bandits got away with two of Clooney's three Grecian urns, leaving the fung shui of his bathroom totally funged up. And speaking of ancient relics gone missing: Has anyone seen Kimberly Savage lately?"

They pass around a fake "MISSING" poster with one of Kim's headshots from twenty years ago. One of them whistles and laughs.

"*Daaamn.* That's a flash to back in the day. This chick was the piece you and all of your friends wanted to do bad things to before you even knew what the bad things were. I mean, come on. Look at this!"

The TV cuts to a clip from the original *Blood Blitz*. The infamous scene where the vampires crash Scarlett Bedlam's wedding night. Kim in thigh-high white stockings and satin panties, using a katana to hack apart the undead with one hand while barely holding her lace corset closed with the other. Her long, pale body absolutely sizzles with sex appeal. God, she was so fit. I must have seen this clip fifty thousand times over the past twenty-five years and it still quickens my pulse.

Brody clasps my shoulder and shakes me, pointing at the screen. "Hey! It's your girl, bro!"

I push him away. "Yeah, yeah. I see her."

He prods me with an elbow, mugging like a chimpanzee. "She was so hot. I can't believe you used to hit that."

I sigh and mutter, "You and me both, pal."

Rosebud turns and raises a quizzical eyebrow. "Wait, you actually *know* Kimberly Savage?"

"In the Biblical sense," Brody says. In case his meaning isn't clear, he punctuates it with a lewd hand gesture. "Matty-boy liked it and put a ring on it. And threw a D in it."

I scowl at him. "Jesus, Brody. Could you at least pretend like puberty isn't still new and exciting to you?"

Before he can reply, Rosebud turns and gives me her full, incredulous attention. "No way. You're married to Kimberly Savage? *The* Kimberly Savage?"

I shrug. "I used to be. She wasn't *the* Kimberly Savage when we got married, but yeah."

Rosebud squeals. "What the hell, Matty? How did I not know this about you?" She hops up on the counter and swings her long legs over to my side. "How did you two meet? I want to hear everything!"

She's absolutely beaming with excitement. I can't remember the last time anyone was so interested in anything I had to say. Her incandescent anticipation warms some long-dormant part of me, forcing a smile of false modesty to my lips.

"Well, it's not really that exciting. We met backstage when I was working on *SoCalites*."

"*What?* You worked on *SoCalites*? I love that show!"

Shame tickles my belly. Of course she does. I knew she would. That's why I name dropped it. Back in the '90s, everyone loved that show—a sitcom about six absurdly attractive yet hilarious young Southern Californians sharing a Malibu beach house. It ended almost twenty years ago, but it's taken on a life of its own in syndication. The reruns are the only reason Rosebud even knows what *SoCalites* is. We aired our series finale when she was a toddler.

She swings her legs and grins. "So, what did you do on the show? What was your job?"

"Oh. I worked in the writers' room."

"Shut up! Oh my God, Matty! You are seriously, like, the coolest guy!"

I blush, despite myself. Up on the TV, one of the entertainment jerks pulls up Kim's IMDb page on a tablet. "Okay, so that was then. This is now." He hovers his finger over a link and slouches back in his chair. "No. I can't even do it. I can't disrespect the memory of that smokin' hot vampire slayer by showing this."

"Come on, man. You gotta," another chuckles. "You gotta do it! Tear off the Band-Aid!" They all laugh.

"All right! Brace yourselves. Here's Kimberly Savage in her latest movie, three years ago."

He taps his tablet and the screen changes to a clip of Kim from *The Last Seaside*. About a decade ago the vampire films finally dried up and she flipped one-eighty and went through a family-friendly phase. After that her work transitioned into serious, heartrending dramas adored by critics and ignored by actual humans. She's a master of reinvention, constantly evolving to survive.

In *The Last Seaside* she played an aging environmental activist trying to save her childhood beach from the same industrial polluters who caused her cancer. A real tear-jerker. At the time she was forty-eight years old, but still stunning, with her tiny smile lines and streaks of gray running through her golden hair like—

"Aaagh! My eyes!" a TV douche screams. "I can't unsee that!"

"Oh man! Now every time I watch a *Blood Blitz* I'm gonna think of Grandma Boner Killer!" another groans. "You ruined it! I'll never spank it to Scarlett Bedlam again!"

I scowl. "Okay, can we turn this off, please? These guys are assholes."

"That's what makes them funny," Brody says.

Rosebud ignores him. "So, oh my God! Did you two like, go to big movie premieres and parties and stuff?" She hops off the counter and wrings her long, elegant fingers. "Did you get to visit the set when she was filming movies? Tell me everything!"

Sweat beads on my scalp. Rosebud and I have always palled around at work. We mock the TV and kvetch about Brody together. Nothing too deep. This is different.

She gazes at me as if she really sees me for the first time. And her looking at me lets me look back. Not furtive, guilty glances across the dining room, but a genuine face-to-face. She's long and willowy, at least five inches taller than me. Her hair is short spray of jet-black tufts falling in bouncy little scoops off the sides of her head. Her lips—coated in glittery pink lipstick—slightly part in eager anticipation of my reply. God, she's so beautiful.

Quit bragging, Matty. You're being gross. Change the subject.

25

My heart thumps and I feign boredom. "Eh, the schmoozing stuff wasn't really my scene. I mostly stayed home with our daughter."

"I didn't know you had a kid! Oh my God, you must be the coolest dad ever. How old is she?"

"Gosh, she's probably about . . ." The words turn to bile in my mouth. "She's about your age now."

Rosebud's flawless, pouty face suddenly nauseates me.

This girl is literally the same age as your daughter, you sicko. What is wrong with you?

I look back to the TV, pretending to be interested. The gossip asses are talking to someone on a grainy internet video call. I recognize the goateed little weasel as Kim's publicist, Carl.

"So according to the buzz on social media, Kimberly Savage has been missing for over a week now," a reporter says.

Carl shakes his head, annoyed. "I assure you, Ms. Savage is perfectly fine. She's just taking some personal time, and we ask her fans to respect that."

"Really? Because our source at the LAPD tells us as of this morning they're officially treating her as a missing person."

The publicist squirms. "Well, I can't speculate on that. I can only emphasize that Ms. Savage is perfectly fine."

This guy's acting chops are weak. This has to be some publicity stunt the two of them cooked up to get Kim's name back in the headlines. The prologue to her next great reimagining.

Brody nudges me with his elbow. "Spill it, bro. Where's she hiding?"

"How should I know?"

"Come on, you know," Rosebud says conspiratorially. "She wouldn't take off and not tell you where she is. You're her baby daddy."

Half a laugh clucks out of my throat. "I haven't been a part of her life in a very long time. Or our daughter's. Seriously, if I was still married to a movie star do you think I'd be working in this dump?" I try to laugh it off, but my eyes sink to the floor and lose focus. "Our divorce was a debacle. I've been on my own since then."

Rosebud's eyebrows arch. "Oh, Matty. You poor thing. That sucks ass."

She takes one of my hands in both of hers. The sensation is almost unbearable. Warm and soft. It's the first time a woman has touched me with tenderness in at least a decade. Half of me wants to put my other hand on top of hers and own the moment. The other half wants to recoil in self-disgust. The two sides cancel each other out, leaving me paralyzed in guilt-ridden balance.

"I never stopped loving her," I say. "And I never will."

It sounds sappy, but it's the truth.

Then why are you standing here holding hands with a stunning co-ed and playing the sympathy card?

Brody claps me on the back. "You need to quit being such a sad sack and man up. Get yourself back on the pussy wagon, bro! You can't sit around forever dreaming about your ex-wife's cobwebby old cooch!"

Rosebud lets go of my hand and gives Brody an angry slap on the arm. "God! Shut up! You are disgusting!"

He laughs and backs away, palms raised. "Just sayin', man. Just sayin'."

His shit-eating grin disappears through the kitchen doors. Rosebud's face softens as she turns back to me. "Okay, he's disgusting, but he's not wrong. Maybe it's time to move on. There are other fish in the sea, you know."

She gives me a flutter of eyelashes and an enigmatic smile that make my heart lurch in my chest. I look away and kick at the worn rubber floor mat. "Well, I think my fishing days ended a long time ago."

"Aww!" Rosebud claps her hands on my forearms and squeezes. "Matty, listen. You're a great guy, but you need to have some self-confidence. You think you're never gonna find another girl, but who knows? Maybe the one you've been looking for has been right in front of you all along and you didn't even notice."

Our eyes meet. My heart races.

I did notice.

Caught up in her gravity, my body moves forward and my arms rise to embrace her. My head is on her shoulder, my cheek nestled against her long neck. Her hands are on my back and mine on hers, holding each other tight. Her warmth seeps into me and spreads through my body, rekindling a flame I never thought would burn for anyone again. I close my eyes and breathe her in. I don't want this to end. I don't want to let go. I want to just stand here in her arms until the health department finally shows up and demolishes the building around us.

"You should keep an eye out for a silver fox at your retirement home," Rosebud says. I blink. I blink again. Rosebud is standing in front of me, her hands still squeezing my flabby forearms, as if the tape of reality had rewound fifteen seconds.

"What?"

She releases me and shrugs. "Or at bingo. Or at the early-bird buffet. You know what they say about those gals." She grins and elbows me in the ribs. "Always in bed by six PM, right? Wink wink."

Old man jokes. She's messing with me. A cold wave of reality extinguishes the flame in my fevered imagination and I force a laugh.

"You're assuming someone my age can still get it up."

"Well, of course you can, silly." She taps my chest with the back of her hand and smiles. "There's pills for that."

She winks, hops back over the counter, and goes back to work as if nothing happened.

Nothing did happen, Matty. Nothing will ever happen.

I pretend to look at the TV as I watch Rosebud mop.

CHAPTER THREE

Rebecca

"If you look at the bar graph on page three of my proposal, you can see how the projected income will cover the startup costs of Strong Fitness within eighteen months. Keep in mind that's a conservative estimate. Based on the performance of other fitness centers in the area, I could make back the loan in as little as six to eight months."

I point to the glossy page, but the loan officer barely looks at it. He can't stop looking at my face. He thinks I can't tell, but I can. Cautious peeks. Pretending not to notice. Polite. Like an adult. Kids don't bother with the charade. They openly gawk. Sometimes they ask if I'm a pirate.

Kids have so much imagination.

The scar starts in a fork under my left eye, swings up over the bridge of my nose, then skates away across my right cheek. A pale pink memorial to the late Bex Savage. A lesser Rebecca would try to cover it with makeup. I don't. I'm not proud of my scar, but I refuse to be ashamed of it. It's a bump on the road of life that helped make me who I am now. The past is nothing but road in my rearview mirror. I can't change it. I can only keep looking forward and take the best path that's still ahead of me.

That's what they used to say in group.

The loan officer flips the page of my proposal, then another. He's not reading it. The guy is probably about twenty years older than me. Mustached. Intimidating in a beat-cop kind of way. He's been sitting behind a desk at First Inland Empire Bank so long the smell of it permeates him—the musky stench of wrinkled dollar bills and obsolete dot-matrix printouts slow roasted under energy-efficient LED track lighting.

He leans back in his chair with a creak. "I'm sorry, but I'm just not convinced, Miss . . . Strong?" He blinks at my paperwork and looks up with an idiot grin. "Strong. Is that your real name?"

"It is."

Now. Legally.

He chuckles. "Funny. A girl named 'Strong' wants to open a gym. Too bad you weren't born 'Rebecca Baker.' Maybe you could have opened one of those cupcake boutiques." He leans in and points at me with his pen. "Now *that's* the kind of business someone like you should get into. You been to Girlie-Q's Bake Shop downtown? Those young ladies are making some really cute stuff. Fattening, but cute."

He barks out a laugh that makes heat prickle under my collar. My cheap business suit is too tight in the shoulders and biceps. The seams of my pants threaten to pop down the length of my thighs if I shift too much in my chair. The tag in my shirt digs into the back of my neck like a burrowing insect.

"Well, I'm interested in opening a fitness center, so a cupcake bakery would be the exact opposite of what I'm trying to accomplish." My tone adds an unspoken "*. . . you stupid fuck!*" The scowl sliding onto his face tells me he heard it anyway. I'm losing control. I smile as broadly as I can. "Not that I wouldn't love to be able to bake those adorable things. It's just that physical fitness is my area of expertise."

The banker idly flips through my business plan, still not reading a word of it. He pauses on an image of me coaching a client. There are thirty glowing endorsements of my skills on that page, but he doesn't see them. All he sees is five foot, two inches of tight feminine muscle filling out a form-fitting Under Armour shirt and yoga pants.

"I don't doubt that, Miss Strong. But being good at running a 5K doesn't make you good at running a business. And every time I turn

ONE MUST KILL ANOTHER

around there's a new workout this or CrossFit that popping up in this area. The market seems pretty saturated. What makes you think you'd be able to bring in customers?"

That's a great question. One you'll see I gave an in-depth answer to if you'd read my motherfucking proposal!

"Well, I am very involved with the local fitness scene. I've been working as a personal trainer here in Pomona for three years, specializing in therapeutic strength training. I have a long list of existing clients already committed to enrolling in my program. If you look at my endorsements here . . . "

I reach for the paper and my sleeve pulls away from my wrist, revealing an elegant calligraphic tattoo reading *Fuck the World*. He sees it before I can pull it away, but I do anyway. His eyes linger on my cuff.

"I think I've seen enough." He closes my copy-shop presentation and pushes it across his desk. "Clearly you've put some thought into this, and I commend you for that, but . . . let's be honest. You're not really the 'business type,' are you?"

Muscles tense up my back and through my shoulders. I could leap over this desk and snap him in half without even breaking a sweat. And he knows it. But I won't. And he knows that, too. His blasé rejection of my loan isn't because my proposal is weak. It's because he wants to feel strong. Stronger than me.

I take a shallow breath. In through the nose, out through the mouth, aligning myself with the Energy of the Universe.

"I've made mistakes in the past. I admit that. But I refuse to be defined by those mistakes for the rest of my life." I pull up my sleeve and raise my wrist. *Fuck the World*. "I'm not that person anymore. I'm turning my life around, and I'm asking for your help to take the next step." He's trying not to make eye contact, but I lean forward to push the issue. "I promise you, I am *very* driven to succeed."

He catches my glare and goes quiet, lost in my sky-blue eyes. The rest of my face I inherited from my father, but my eyes are all Mom's.

Bright and piercing and seductive. I scowl and blink away, breaking their spell.

"Obviously you are." The banker's gaze ticks to the empty cubicle beside us, then to the security cameras above. "Look, I'm not trying to be the bad guy. It's just that you're asking for a very sizeable loan. I'm going to need more proof your business is viable." He leans forward and speaks in a low tone. "Maybe you could give me a few one-on-one workout sessions. You know, show me the goods. Convince me you're comfortable getting physical. If I like what I see, I can talk to the guys upstairs about getting this loan pushed through."

He smiles like he's doing me a favor. Is he serious? Is this happening? Has word of the "Time's Up" movement not yet reached the San Gabriel Valley? Anger corkscrews around my body, burning into my muscles. But even through my fury, some part of me, buried in my deepest subconscious, is considering it. For a five-figure loan I could give this jerk-off his "one-on-one" sessions. Lord knows I'd given plenty of them for less.

The idea ignites a fire in my chest. No! Bex Savage had given them. Rebecca Strong had not. And will not. Ever. This is another fork in the road. Another chance to continue forward on the right path.

Not that any of it matters. There's no way he's giving you a loan once he does a background check and learns where your scar came from.

The banker's grin fades as I stand up and lean over the desk. Even with him seated I'm barely taller than he is, but my muscle mass sends the threat that my height can't.

"I find your offer unacceptable," I say coldly. "And I'd like to speak to those 'guys upstairs' about the disgusting way you're treating their customers."

He looks me straight in the eye. Emboldened. "Be my guest, Miss Strong. You claim to be a personal trainer. I asked for proof of your skills to establish your qualification for a loan. I'm sure when you report this to my colleagues they'll commend me for my due diligence." A smug smile ticks at the corners of his lips. "In fact, I wouldn't be surprised if some of them make the same request of you."

His grotesque power play stokes my fury. Fuck this prick. I will not be treated this way. I'm going to stand up and speak out. I'm going to take this asshole down.

Why now? What do you think will happen? In a best-case scenario the bank fires him purely for the P.R. damage control. It doesn't get you your loan. It just ties you up. Saps your energy. Slows you down.

Rise above. Stay focused. Move forward.

I extend my palm for a shake. "Then I'll have to take my business elsewhere. Thank you for your time."

"It was my pleasure." He stands and takes my hand, pulling me closer. His voice creeps through his mustache. "And if you change your mind, the offer is still on the table."

I squeeze his hand until I feel it pop.

CHAPTER FOUR

Matty

Delete. Delete. Delete.

Undo delete.

Redo delete.

Fuck!

I plant my elbows on my desk and bury my face in my hands. My beard bristles through my fingers, basting them with skin oil. The heels of my palms come to rest in my eye sockets and I groan. Since I got home from work I've started writing this scene a half-dozen times. I know how it's supposed to go. I can picture it so vividly in my mind. But every time I actually write it down it goes off the rails and comes out shitty. And I delete it and start over. And every time it's no less shitty.

I pull my hands away from my eyes and focus on the screen. Party girl Juliana Cruz says, "If you *really* want to have fun, come with me."

Aging rocker Angus Blackwood replies, "Where are we going?"

Juliana gives him a mischievous grin, then . . .

CUT TO:

The cursor just sits there in a field of white. Blinking. Mocking.

Cut to *what?*

A yawn starts deep in my belly and howls out of my mouth. I worked the opening shift at the Rex Mex, which I hate because I have to get up ass early in the morning, but like because it gives me more time to write when I get home. Of course, I'm exhausted from getting up ass early, so my brain is useless.

I lean back in my Aeron chair and squint through the huge picture window behind my desk. It's barely three in the afternoon and the winter sun has already dropped low over the ocean. I've been meaning to move my desk to the other wall so it's not facing the glare, but in the morning I'm always running late. By the time I get home I'm too tired. So it stays where it is.

When I stand to lower the blinds the eaves shade my eyes, letting them focus on the view of Venice Beach. My office is on the second story of the house, overlooking the front deck which butts right up against the public bike path. Some tourist or vagrant has left a collection of empty Bud Light cans on the low cement wall that separates them. Beyond the bike path is the beach. In the summertime this strip of sand is alive with people. In February, not so much. It's a frosty sixty degrees out there. The dead of Los Angeles winter. Still, the view is breathtaking. A postcard-perfect spectacle of Mother Nature painting her seaside canvas with vibrant pink and orange light.

I drop the blinds and the room plunges into darkness, lit only by the blue-white pallor of my computer screen. I vow, once more, to never open this shade again. I don't deserve this view. An epic screw-up like me shouldn't be living in a three-million-dollar beach house. I should be sleeping in the park in Santa Monica, begging for change and shouting at pigeons. That's what I deserve.

Suck it up! Focus! Write! Do you want to work at Rex Mex for the rest of your life?

I plant my palms on the desk and lean in front of the screen.

"If you really want to have fun, come with me."

"Where are we going?"

The cursor blinks. I blink back at it. Where are they going? Just figure that out and you can go grab a beer. Come on, Matty. Earn your reward. Where do foxy young things go for fun? Some kind of house party? Like, a wild kegger at a rich kid's place when his parents leave town for the weekend? Oh hell no. That's such a cliché it's practically its own genre. Think harder. Where do they go? What do they do?

The cursor blinks. I blink back at it.

Screw it.

I head for the fridge.

The kitchen is light and airy, done up in white subway tile with black granite countertops. Stainless steel appliances that were best-in-class twenty years ago glint dully in the sunset. I grab a beer. I don't know what it is. Some microbrew from Trader Joe's I heard was good. I pluck the magnetic bottle opener from the fridge door and wrench it open. With a flick of my arm I pitch the cap across the room and into the sink with the dirty dishes. The opener goes back on the door next to the grocery list.

Orange juice. Toothpaste. Windex. Celery.

The list is written in faded purple ink in Kim's loopy cursive script. I sometimes wonder if she ever bought these things when she moved to her new place in the Hollywood Hills. I take a swig of the beer and wince at its bitter, hoppy taste. Uch. IPA. Why is everything IPA these days? Goddamn hipsters, ruining beer for everyone.

I lean back on the counter and choke down another gulp, hoping the taste will grow on me, and my vacant gaze settles again on the fridge. Several pieces of sun-faded construction paper art cling to its waist like an apron. Bex's old crayon and tempera masterpieces depicting tribal masks and tiki gods—artifacts from deep within the Forbidden Jungle. Of course, the "Forbidden Jungle" was actually the woods around our cabin near Lake Arrowhead, overlaid with the old-fashioned kind of augmented reality: childhood imagination.

In the center of the fridge door is a drawing of two misshapen stick figures, limbs growing straight out of their big smiling faces. A tall one and a short one. Me and Bex, explorers on an ongoing expedition to find the Lost Temple of Zamrycki and recover the legendary Mystic Stones. They're depicted on an adjacent paper. Three blobs set in a triangle, each with its own magical powers. The brown "Life Stone," the white "Death Stone," and the black "Wish Stone." Why Bex chose those bland colors out of the rainbow in her sixty-four pack of Crayolas I'll never know. I never asked. It didn't matter. That's what colors she said they were, so that's what colors they were.

But as Bex got older her interest in our pretend quest waned. I tried to keep her involved, but her interest in me had waned as well. Eventually, these pictures were all that remained of the Savage Expedition. After the divorce, I couldn't bear to take them down. A decade and change later they've become a permanent exhibition.

I suck a long pull of bitter beer, letting it mix with my bitter memories. My eyes drift from the ancient drawings to a glossy paper stuck to the freezer door with a magnetic Chip Clip. It's the only thing hanging on the fridge that I actually put there. A page torn out of *People* magazine with a picture of Kim and Bex together on the red carpet at some awards show. Even as the newest item on display, the clipping is still getting long in the tooth.

Kim is in a dazzling crimson sequined dress, her hair cascading in luminous blonde curls down the slope of her neck and across her bare shoulders. Her short hemline and stiletto heels accentuate the perfect musculature of her legs. She's striking a pose for the camera. Confident. Statuesque. Flashing that glowing, ear-to-ear Julia Roberts smile of hers.

Bex is behind her. She's in mid stride as the picture is taken, giving her a weird, off-balance posture. She looks pencil-thin in her black velvet dress, her long auburn hair piled on top of her head. Her lips are painted a subtle shade of mahogany and her pale blue eyes are striking in dark eyeliner. The whole thing is clearly the work of a professional stylist, but even so, Bex still looks like a kid playing dress-up with her mommy's things. She must be about fifteen or sixteen, her awkward and gawky adolescence about to give way to young womanhood.

This is the most recent photo I have of Bex. A fake memory from a phase of her life I wasn't invited to. Kim got full custody in the divorce after her tearful testimony about how I was "abusive" and "chronically unemployed." The former I denied. The latter I could not. It didn't matter. Bex didn't want to stay with me anyway.

Then they were gone, leaving me alone in our hollowed-out home while they went on to new adventures. I can't fault them for leaving. Cutting me out of Bex's life was the best thing her mother could have done for her. By now my little girl is out making a life of her own. Probably at an Ivy League college or something. Every once in a while I Google her name, but nothing ever comes up. Wherever she is, Bex Savage is leading a private life.

I raise my beer to the photo. "Here's to your happiness, kiddo."

The bottle tilts to my lips and I drink deeply. Ugh, this shit is terrible. I dump the rest of it around the dishes in the sink and give my hands a sharp clap.

"All right! Stop procrastinating! Time to write!"

I march down the hall and stride into the darkened office, energized, ready to let my creative juices flow. On my way in I touch my lucky script, pausing long enough to let its good juju flow into me. I've succeeded before. I can do it again. I'm so close.

My chair glides across the hardwood as I push it aside and tap the "up" button on my ergonomic desk. With a motorized whirr the desktop rises, its surface automatically coming to rest at the programmed height of my elbows. Medical studies have shown that alternating between sitting and standing while working is good for focus and creativity. I grab the chrome arm that holds my 4K UHD screen and raise it to the optimum viewing angle, one inch below my eye line.

"If you really want to have fun, come with me."
"Where are we going?"

Where are they going? The screen is slightly askew, so I adjust the arm. Too far left. I adjust it back. Too far right. Gently this time. Perfect. I shift my weight from foot to foot and rest my hand on the mouse. When we first moved in I had a clunky old tower PC with its big CRT monitor set up on a folding table in here. When Kim and Bex left, I started splurging on new gear. A serious writer needs serious tools. It was worth dipping into her money.

Legally, it's my money. In my heart, it's still hers.

I didn't even want to sign the pre-nup. I thought it went against the spirit of our marriage. Why plan for a heartbreak that could never happen? But Kim had been dragged through the shit when her parents divorced, so she insisted. She didn't want to get screwed if things went sideways. When our marriage dissolved each of us was entitled to half of our combined wealth. Which was considerable, thanks to her. Irony's a bitch, I guess.

It was bad enough being dependent on Kim's money when we were married. I'm sure as hell not going to be dependent on it now. I'm a grown man, and I can earn my keep. That's why I'm working at the Rex Mex until my writing career takes off. I intentionally picked something shitty so it wouldn't be too much of a distraction. I mean, if I was like, a production manager or producer or something it would involve a lot of overtime I don't want to do. I'm not qualified for any of those jobs anyway. Rex Mex was the only gig I applied for that actually called back, so I took it.

It doesn't matter. It's temporary. Writing is my road to financial freedom, and I'm getting so close to making it work. In the meantime, Kim's money is strictly for the upkeep of the house. And the property taxes, and utilities, and part of the groceries. But for everything else I use my paycheck. Unless there's an emergency or something I absolutely need. Or want.

"If you really want to have fun, come with me."

"Where are we going?"

39

Where are they going? I've been gnawing on that question so long I've forgotten where they even came from. I roll my finger on the mouse's wheel, scrolling back five pages. It helps to read in. To get a running start and then just bust through that wall and start writing.

I review the pages, focusing on each word. The script has changed so much in rewrites that it's hard to keep track of what's on the page and what's not. Sometimes I get muddled up and make references to things that happened in defunct drafts, then I have to do another round of edits to fix it. The mouse wheel clicks as I slowly scan through the lines of dialogue.

Originally the story was about a struggling musician. No matter what he did, he couldn't catch his big break in the music business. This caused him to become estranged from his wife and daughter. Finally he stops bullshitting and writes the song that's in his heart. When his family hears it, there's this huge emotional reunion, because they realize the song is about them, and he used his art to express his love for them in a way he never could in person.

Yeah, it was pretty sappy. Not really my jam. I'm a comedy writer.

I chuckle as I read one of the new scenes. The story is still the same at its core, but the details have all changed. Now the musician is Angus Blackwood, a single, aging rock star who can't write hits anymore. I combined the wife and daughter characters into one— Juliana Cruz, a twenty-something groupie who falls for him and reignites his creativity. It's a metaphor for how true love transcends all. I'm hoping to get Bill Murray and Selena Gomez attached.

The mouse wheel clicks and a field of white emerges at the bottom of the screen. Blackwood has taken Juliana to the club where he was first discovered and launched to stardom back in the '80s. He promises her it's the coolest venue where all the coolest people hang out. In fact, tonight's headliner is a punk band he idolized back in the day. But when they show up the place is a sad, broken-down relic, representing how he himself is a sad, broken-down relic. The band is all these old dudes who look sick and frail. Their hearing aids keep making feedback, and one of them is in an iron lung. Blackwood is depressed and defeated and apologizes to Juliana. He's sorry he brought her to this lame club full of old farts. It was supposed to be fun.

"If you really want to have fun, come with me."

"Where are we going?"

Where are they going?

God damn it, where the fuck are they going?

My pulse quickens and my face gets warm as I pace the floor, grabbing at my thin hair. How is this so hard? What the hell is wrong with me? I can do this! I used to work in the writers' room of *SoCalites*, for God's sake!

Wow, Matty. You've told that lie for so long you don't remember it's not true.

I stop pacing and gaze at a frame on the wall. The glass is smudged with years of oily fingerprints. Behind them, two three-hole-punched pages hang side-by-side in a double matting. One of them is the cover of a teleplay, the other is the first page of the shooting draft. *SoCalites* episode #118, "Son of a Beach." Written by Matthew Savage. My lucky script. The best thing I ever wrote.

I did work in the writers' room of *SoCalites*. That is a fact. A carefully worded fact. When I tell people I worked in the writers' room they always assume that I worked there as a writer. And I let them make their assumptions. The truth is I was a writers' assistant. Basically a glorified production assistant, typing and scheduling and getting coffee for the actual writers. The showrunner was kind enough to let me write two scripts in my eight years behind the copy machine, giving my half-truth just enough of an IMDb paper trail to make it credible. To this day I still receive the occasional laughably small residual check from the ubiquitous reruns. Every time I get a payment from the WGA for "Son of a Beach" I wonder if Kim is also getting one from SAG-AFTRA.

I wonder a lot about Kim.

My knees start to hurt so I slump into my chair, but my attention hangs on that framed shooting script. My mind's eye looks through it, back in time. Back to the first moment I ever saw her. Youthful and aglow. Fresh-faced and tight-bodied. The beauty of the beach. On a soundstage. In Burbank. But even as the image forms it ripens in my mind. Crow's feet dig subtly into the corners of her eyes. Faint wrinkles crease the edges of her million-watt smile. Her long, luxurious blonde hair flutters away, leaving behind a short bob streaked with highlights of gray.

It's not the Kim I remember. It's Today Kim. The one from the gossip show at the Rex Mex. The one who is allegedly "missing." Brody asked me where she ran off to and I told him I don't know, but I do. She's at the cabin near Lake Arrowhead. She has to be. The whole reason she bought the place was so she'd have somewhere private to hide and regroup. As soon as she's had a chance to get her head together she'll return from her "disappearance," ready for her next reinvention. Nothing to worry about.

I punch the "down" button on my desk and it lowers into my lap, shoving my writer's block in my face.

"If you really want to have fun, come with me."

"Where are we going?"

Where are they going? Where would Juliana Cruz go for fun? What would Juliana Cruz *do* for fun? I clearly have no idea.

I have to do some research.

With a click, my screenplay disappears behind my browser window. As soon as I start typing the URL it autofills into the search bar. A whirl of a loading wheel and I'm looking at a gallery of pictures uploaded by user "RosieMeowMeow."

Portrait and landscape images of different sizes intermingle in an algorithmically designed crazy quilt of Rosebud's life. Bored selfies wearing blue scrubs in one of her vet-school classes. A Throwback Thursday of her as a teenager wearing flowery shorts and a T-shirt shouting *¿Qué pasa?* from its chest. A bunch of photos tagged

"#clubbin" with sweaty lineups of Rosebud and her friends, their bodies wrapped in inches of fabric.

A sizzle of dopamine cooks in my brain.

You shouldn't be looking at this. This is creepy.

It's not creepy. It's research. Maybe "#clubbin" is the answer. Maybe that's where Juliana takes Blackwood. I click an image to pull it full screen, then keep clicking to tab through the photos one by one. *Click.* Rosebud with a snowboard, bundled up in winter gear. *Click.* Rosebud at a music festival, covered in mud, her mouth wide in laughter. *Click.* Rosebud at a formal event, looking sharp in a blue gown.

My heart flutters, beating hard and weird. She's so active. So full of life. I wish I could capture her essence and put it into words. She's exactly what I want Juliana Cruz to be.

Click. Rosebud with a group of friends in front of the Eiffel Tower in Vegas. *Click.* Rosebud at Halloween, dressed as Hermione Granger. *Click.* A #nofilter of Rosebud in bed, her hair rumpled, an oversized sweatshirt hanging *Flashdance* style off one bare shoulder.

My right hand keeps clicking the mouse and my mind goes comfortably numb, drinking in the images. I know I'm wasting time, but I just want to see one more. Just one more. Just one more.

Click. Rosebud looking into camera. It's a close-up. The background is indistinct. But the picture is very high resolution. I can see the individual hairs on her head. The smooth, creamy texture of her tanned skin. I can see her pores. The lines in her full lips. The reflection of the light in the thin sheen of saliva on her perfect teeth. I look into her dark eyes and absorb each brush stroke of brown and gold glittering in her irises. There's something perversely intimate about it, as if our faces are inches apart. Close enough to feel her breath on my skin.

My own breath comes in shallow pants and I realize my left hand is kneading my crotch through my jeans. Its action is unconscious. A muscle-memory conditioned by years of sexual partners delivered exclusively via broadband. The stimulus-response reflex of a man in a disgraceful but committed relationship with digital smut.

Rosebud glares at me from the screen, silently judging. A wave of icy shame crashes through my body and I shove the monitor away in disgust, smashing it against the wall.

I lean forward, elbows on my knees, palms over my eyes.

I sob.

I sob long and I sob hard.

I'm an old, fat, perverted sack of pig shit. I had my chance at life and I blew it.

If I wasn't such a shitty writer I could have made something of myself.

If I wasn't such a selfish asshole Kim wouldn't have left me.

If I wasn't such a terrible father Bex would have kept in touch.

But I am all those things. And Kim and Bex are gone.

Forever.

And I'm going to die alone.

So maybe I should just get it over with.

There's a bottle of sleeping pills in the medicine cabinet. It would be so peaceful.

Clear your browser cache first.

The phone rings.

CHAPTER FIVE

Rebecca

The door to my apartment sticks and scrapes through an arc carved into the laminate floor as I push my way inside. Rage pours through me, stinging my upper lip and the backs of my eyes. I grab the sagging old door and the muscles in my fingers tense. I want to slam it so hard it shatters into splinters.

Don't. Don't do it. Anger solves nothing, Rebecca. Breathe.

Just breathe.

Just fucking breathe!

My teeth grind and a roar rattles my throat as a wave of muscle fires all the way from my hips to my fingertips. The door flies shut and its corners bang against the misshapen jamb, bouncing it open again. My jaw unhinges and I scream, launching myself forward, pounding my fists and feet into the warped wood, smashing flakes of blue paint off its distressed face. The door bucks and bounces against its frame, refusing to find its way home. I raise my foot to my hip and give it a sharp side kick just below the knob. The click of the latch finally falling into place is lost behind the sound of my cheap slacks splitting their seams from ass to crotch.

"God damn it!"

I throw my messenger bag into the corner and stomp down the short hallway to the kitchen. My roommate Emily is there, perched on a stool at her easel. Paintbrush in hand. Frozen. Eyes wide like she's stuck in the path of a runaway truck.

"Are you okay?" she asks. "What's wrong? What happened?"

Her carob complexion is flushed, her leg muscles tight and ready to flee. She's never seen this side of me. I can't let her see it. This side cost me too many roommates before I got it under control. I breathe into my anger, collecting it and pushing it out like a toxic cloud.

"Sorry, I freaked out. I'm okay. It just . . . it was a rough day."

I smile, and the spark of panic dims in Emily's eyes. I feel terrible for scaring her. She's so frail, like a bird. With her little bird legs, wrapped in stretch pants, sticking out of an oversized men's shirt smeared with paint.

"Uh, yeah. I can tell," she says. Her glance ticks to my arm and she nods. "Want me to fix that?"

I look down. The seam holding the sleeve to my jacket has ripped almost all the way around my shoulder during my tantrum, revealing the white blouse beneath.

This is what happens when you let your anger control you. It tears things apart. It's a metaphor. Remember this. Use this.

"Yes, if you wouldn't mind. Thank you." Another patch of stitches pops as I try to shrug the jacket off my shoulders. Emily sweeps behind me and pulls the sleeves from the wrists, dragging them over my arms. My biceps feel a tingling release as they come out of their cotton-poly sausage casings.

Emily evaluates the damage. "It's a clean tear along the seam. It should be an easy fix."

"Thanks, Em. I appreciate it. I appreciate you." She rolls her eyes. I don't care if she thinks I'm corny. It's true and it's important to show my gratitude. "Oh, and if it isn't too much trouble . . . " I turn and shift my weight so my ass pushes a crescent moon of lime green underwear through the tear in my slacks. "Could you fix the pants too?"

Emily shrugs. "I don't know. Maybe you should just save 'em for your next date night."

I snort out a laugh. Em leans on the stool in front of her painting. It's a brain in a stainless-steel hospital tray, cut open to reveal a Victorian library full of gears and sparking electric books, like a clockwork memory factory. I wish I had her creativity. But that's just another of our Odd Couple quirks. She's creative, I'm not. She's scrawny, I'm ripped. She has an awesome boyfriend, I'm incapable of swiping right.

Emily picks up a chipped mug and takes a swig. Fingerprints of old paint obscure the name of the coffee shop she stole it from. I can smell from here that it's not full of coffee. Another of our differences.

"So," she says. "I take it things didn't go well at the bank?"

"I got turned down," I say. *Because the banker was an aging rapist prick looking for collateral in my vagina,* I don't add. "It's all right. I've made peace with it."

Emily snorts and red wine dribbles down her chin. She wipes it away with the back of her oversized sleeve. "Yeah, I can tell you're totally over it by the way you just Hulked out."

"I didn't Hulk out."

"You got so angry you ripped through your clothes. That's like, the literal definition of Hulking out." She swishes a paintbrush in a Mason jar of cloudy water. "Come on. What put the bug up your butt?"

I pull my phone from my pocket. A backup battery hangs by a short USB cable from its bottom. The main battery won't hold a charge anymore and I'm too broke to get it fixed. I stare at the phone, as if its very existence is proof of something I can't believe.

"My mother called."

As soon as I say the words out loud the anger starts bubbling back. I pivot out the door and down the narrow hallway to my bedroom. My sanctuary. Its water-stained walls are hidden behind faded, second-hand tapestries woven with various mandalas, dimly lit by a string of white Christmas lights. An old IKEA bookcase is loaded with softball trophies and dog-eared books ranging from health and nutrition, to meditation and spirituality, to really far-out stuff like lucid dreaming and astral projection. It's a mini-timeline of the phases of my life since the last time I spoke to my mother one million years ago.

I wake up my clunky CD changer, filling the room with an ambient drone laced with singing bowls. Emily bounces in behind me, manic energy bubbling through her thin skin.

"She actually called you? You're kidding! When?"

I cringe. "Just before I got home. In the Uber. I don't even know how she got my number. I shouldn't have answered."

I fish my keys out of my pocket and toss them on the bed with my phone before stripping off my ruined pants.

"No, it's good," Emily says. "I'm proud of you for being the bigger person and hearing what she had to say instead of blowing her off. You did the right thing." She crosses her arms. "So what did the gorgeous old bitch want?"

I half smile. Emily knows who my mother is. She's the only one I trust with my secrets. Some of my secrets.

I slide into a pair of track pants and unbutton my shirt.

"She wants to see me."

Emily's kinky hair bounces around her head as she does an overdramatized double take. "Are you shitting me?"

"I shit you not."

My shirt slides off, revealing a tank top and a gallery of unfortunate ink etched into my flesh. Pink cherry blossoms bloom over my right shoulder. A barbed-wire heart with a banner reading "Nobody" twitches on my left bicep as I grab my keys and stuff them in my pocket. Emily is practically foaming at the mouth. "Come on! Details!"

I already regret telling her the truth. I could have told her I was upset about the bank and left it at that. But there's no putting the cat back in the bag now.

"I don't know. She says she misses me. She wants to make things right."

On the phone I had shown restraint. I'd kept my cool. But in my mind I had screamed at her. In my mind I am still screaming at her.

I don't need you to make things right! I make things right for myself. Without you! Bex Savage is dead! You killed her! Stay the fuck out of my life!

My knuckles go white squeezing my phone. I cram it into my pocket before the glass can crack. Emily slouches against the defunct cast-iron radiator, cupping her wine mug to her chest. I smell its acrid bouquet and feel its phantom burn on my tongue.

"So, you gonna go see her?"

"No. I have nothing to say to her."

She needs to drop it. I'm done talking about my mother. I want to forget she even called. I want to blot out the whole day. I return to the kitchen and the open bottle of Two-buck Chuck sitting next to the sink. One hand grabs a mug and the other reaches for the bottle but stops before it gets there. I press my palm flat against the worn countertop and count to ten. I fill the mug with lukewarm water from the tap.

Emily leans against the kitchen doorway. "I think you should go."

"I'm not going to go."

"Oh, come on, Becky. You're into all that mystical positive energy hippy shit, right?" She wiggles her fingertips in the air. "This can't be a coincidence. It's fate."

I squint at her. "The hell are you talking about?"

"Do I have to spell it out? Do you need pictures?"

She darts to her art supplies, grabs a sketchbook, and slaps it down on the table. Her fingers find a pencil in a mug of brushes as she sits down and starts sketching. I watch over her shoulder, spellbound by how easy she makes it look. Jealous, honestly. I used to be able to draw a little, but nothing like what she does. Her sketches are fast and simple, but really good. The first one is a bank. A muscular figure stands outside, flexing her biceps and crying.

49

"That's you, obviously," she says, slashing a scar into the figure's face. "You didn't get your loan. Boo hoo. So sad."

Her hand whips across the page, drawing a horizontal line. Below it she draws the same muscle girl in the back seat of a car, flexing and talking on the phone.

"I'm not always flexing," I grumble.

"Hi Mom!" Emily does a squeaking impression that sounds nothing like me. "So weird you called. I need money and the bank won't give it to me."

"Oh, my sweet baby." Her voice becomes a breathy drawl as she draws jagged lines coming out of the phone. "I miss you evah so much! Come and see your long-lost sugar mama!"

"That is not how my mother talks."

"Whatever. I've seen *Peach Blossom Blues* like, six dozen times."

I roll my eyes. Of all my mother's films, my roommate is obsessed with the one where she played an unconvincing southern belle. Emily's pencil slashes another line across the page, creating the third panel of her comic. This time the flexing girl is digging into a pig trough of cash, filling her pockets. Next to her is a mile-high beanstalk of a woman. Her smile is a ridiculously large unhinged hippopotamus jaw, yet somehow it looks exactly like my mother.

"Take all the money you need, honey child," Emily groans sensually. "Your dear mama shall provide!"

I lean back on the counter. "Are you serious? I am not crawling to my mother for money."

"You're not crawling. *She's* crawling. She called *you*, remember? Something's got her feeling all warm and squishy. Cash it in. Exploit her affection."

"It'll never work. My mother is incapable of affection."

Even as I say the words my mind is contradicting them. It could work. My mother has more money than she can spend in ten lifetimes. The amount I need to open my fitness center is pocket change to her. I could swallow my bile and buddy up long enough for her to cut a check. My father got paid when she threw him away. Why shouldn't I?

I squeeze my eyes shut, trying to crush the vile idea before it can take root. Emily wags her pencil at me. "You know, you can act all 'my chi is balanced and my shit don't stink' for the rest of the world, but I see through you. You're so into this. This is your chance to finally make peace with Mom. You can slay your inner demons and get *paid* for it. Don't even pretend like this isn't the best idea ever."

I swish the water around in my mug, bluffing my disapproval, but I know she's not wrong. Things happen for a reason.

The Universe wants me to achieve my dreams. It wants me to open my fitness center, but it's making me prove I'm worthy. The pervert loan officer was a test to see if I would stay strong in my convictions or throw it all away for an easy solution. I passed that test and it gave me another.

My hand finds its way into my pocket and pulls out my car key. I absently rub the serrated edge as my brain races. The Universe has given me the ultimate test: Can I forgive my mother? Can I find peace with her? Can I take hold of her extended olive branch and reap the benefits—spiritual, psychological, and financial?

Just thinking about the question flicks on my high beams. Suddenly the dark and muddled road ahead of me becomes perfectly clear. It's not a matter of whether or not I can forgive my mother. I *must* forgive her. The only path to finding true harmony and achieving my goals is by reopening my old wounds and healing them with love instead of cauterizing them with hate.

"You're right," I say. "You're deranged, but you're right. I'll go see her."

"Damn straight, you will." Emily eyes my shabby workout wear and waves me off. "Go get dressed for success and I'll drive you to LA to visit Mommie Dearest."

I shake my head. "She's not at her house. She said she's at the cabin."

"What cabin?"

"It's this other property she has. Kinda near Lake Arrowhead."

Emily's eyes roll back in disgust. "Ugh. Rich people having houses all over the damn place." Her voice goes low with fake annoyance. "Fine. I'll drive you all the way up there, but your beefy ass is paying for gas *and* taking me skiing or some shit."

She pounds the rest of her wine in an epic four-second chug and gets up to put the empty mug in the sink. The bottle is almost spent, but she clumsily mashes the cork back into place with her palm, leaving tiny reddish-purple rings on her skin. I bite my lip and rub my thumb over the Mustang embossed in my car key.

"Don't worry about it. I'll just call an Uber."

CHAPTER SIX

Kimberly
Fifteen Years Ago

Bex squirms in the chair as I pull the brush through her knotty mane.

"Aagh! Mom! You're pulling my hair!"

She scowls at me in the lighted vanity mirror in front of us. I have a full hair-and-makeup station in my master bedroom. The same setup they have at the studio, chair and all. Professional gear for professional results.

"I'm sorry, sweetie. I'm just trying to make you pretty like a princess."

"Ugh! I don't want to be a princess!"

I frown and hit her with another spritz of detangler. What eight-year-old girl doesn't want to be a princess? I'm just trying to help her become her best self. Why can't she see that?

"You know, when I was your age my mother would take me with her when she ran errands. People used to say, 'My goodness, what a beautiful little girl you have.' Mom would always say 'If you like her so much, why don't *you* take her home.' Har har. Still, it made me happy." It was the only thing that made me happy. Scraps of affection thrown off by strangers. An old anger flares and I tamp it down. "You're a beautiful little girl too, Bex. And I want everyone to see it. I want you to see how nice it feels to be noticed." I brush her nappy bangs away from her eyes. "Do you want Mommy to put makeup on you?"

Bex twists her tiny lips. "Can you do tiger?"

"What do you mean?"

"You know, tiger. Dad took me to the pier and a guy painted my face like a tiger. One time he did a butterfly too. And one time he did me like SpongeBob. It was super fun, but you missed it all 'cause you were gone."

Frustration prickles the back of my neck. "I didn't go away because I wanted to. I had to go away for work."

Bex's lips jut out in a pout. "You always go away for work. You're never home anymore."

Her clumsy guilt trip raises my hackles. "Sweetheart, you know I had to be in New Orleans for shooting. That's where my new movie takes place. It's very far away from here." And it's not like *Blood Blitz 5: Cities of the Undead* was a pleasure cruise. I spent two months battling vampires while wearing a ribbed leather catsuit in ninety percent humidity. Phoning in another insipid sequel to keep a roof over your head. A little appreciation would be nice. I smile as warmly as I can. "But that's all finished now. I'm back with my baby and we're having girl fun together."

"Aww. Girl fun isn't real fun!" Bex whines and twitches in her seat, tugging her tresses through my hands. "Oow! Mom, you're pulling my hair!"

"You're pulling it! Sit still!" My jaw and fist clench, and I exhale and force them to relax. "Look, I'm going to give you a nice pretty French braid, then we can—"

"*Huurrraaaaagh!*"

My heart stops as Matty bounds into the bedroom wearing a hideous rubber gorilla mask with matted black fur. He crouches and thumps his fists together, both lost inside ridiculous, inflatable boxing gloves. Bex squeals and leaps out of the chair.

"Watch out, it's a sasquatch!"

Matty bellows back at her. "Where dat stinky little human? Me rip her tiny face off and eat it for din din!"

ONE MUST KILL ANOTHER

He hustles toward us, swinging his giant red mitts. Bex shrieks and scurries away. My blood boils.

"Matty, please. Not now. We're having mother-daughter time, okay?"

If he hears me he doesn't acknowledge it. He's too busy chasing Bex, growling and punching at the furniture.

"Don't worry, Mom! I'll protect you!" Bex grabs my hairdryer and brandishes it at her father. "This is a tank-ill-izer gun! I'll make you go to sleep!" She pumps her finger on the trigger. "Pew pew pew!"

I snatch the dryer away from her. "Bex, no! That's not a toy!"

Matty clutches at his chest and falls to his knees. "Aagh! I've been hit. But ... wait ... sasquatch blood is immune to tranquilizer! *Huurrraaaaagh!*"

Bex grabs my hand, screeching and giggling. "Come on! Before he gets up!"

She tries to tug me toward the door, but I don't budge. "Bex, stop it! Sit down. We're going to play beauty salon, remember?"

"But he'll get us!" Her eyes are wild and pleading. "Come with me! Please!"

"No!" I snap. "I don't want to play this stupid game!"

Matty scrambles to his feet, roaring and growling inside his mask. Bex lets go of my hand as she screams in fake terror and bolts out of the room. Matty chases her, and their manic horseplay thunders away through the house, leaving me in cold silence.

I'm alone.

I sigh and pull a clump of Bex's auburn hair out of the brush. It's the exact same shade as Matty's. She truly is her father's daughter.

The front door bangs open downstairs. I lean on the broad windowsill and watch them tumble out onto the deck below, sandwiched between the house and the beach. Now Bex is wearing the gorilla mask and the boxing gloves, roaring and pummeling Matty's belly. He writhes and shouts as if she's clawing out his entrails before collapsing to the ground, flat on his back. Carried away in a manic frenzy, Bex drops to her knees on top of him, straddling his chest and pounding her inflatable fists into his face. He winces and holds his palms to her, fingers in a triangle, shouting through his cackling laughter.

"Rafiki! Rafiki!"

Without a word, Bex rolls off of him and strips off the mask and gloves. Matty picks them up and the chaos begins anew.

Anger and sorrow form a noxious cocktail in my belly as I watch them play from afar, like a third wheel in my own family. Of course she loves Matty more. He's always home. He hasn't had a job since *SoCalites* wrapped almost ten years ago. After Bex was born we were strapped for cash, so I caved to a *Blood Blitz* sequel. Just one, strictly for the paycheck. Just to get us out of that stinking condo in Studio City. My daughter deserved better than to rot in squalor. I dropped a down payment on a palace on the beach. A home befitting the family of an A-list celebrity.

And the A-list was within my grasp. After *Blood Blitz 2* I managed to get the lead in *Peach Blossom Blues*, an allegory on racism in the guise of an antebellum period drama. I should have been nominated for that picture, but when the first trailer came out there was so much backlash from the vampire fans—my "real fans"—that the studio got cold feet and sent the film direct to video.

After that I made another *Blood Blitz* just to pay off the beach house. Then another to pay for private school. Before I knew it the franchise was a box-office perennial, each new release pulling the typecasting noose tighter and tighter around my neck.

I've sacrificed everything for Bex while Matty's done nothing, yet she still loves him more.

I take a deep lungful of sea air and watch the two of them spar and tussle in the summer sun below. Matty's hands are the size and shape of overripe watermelons in those idiotic gloves, and Bex bounces and giggles as he jabs her with them. Her sneakers squeak on the deck as she hops up onto the wooden bench of the picnic table, then onto the table itself. She's taller than her father as they bounce and jockey and whack each other, having the time of their lives. Matty flicks his wrist and bops her with the back of his hand. She stumbles backward and laughs and he does it again. And again. Obliviously pushing her toward the edge of the table.

I bang my palm on the window glass. "Matty! Be careful!" Lost inside his mask, he blindly rolls his hands in a goofy twirl like a cartoon punching a speed bag, pummeling our daughter's face. I stick my head out the window and scream. "Pay attention! Stop!"

Bex's laughter is a piercing squeal by the time her foot slips off the edge of the table. It happens so fast she's still smiling as her knees hit the ground and her chin smashes the tabletop. Her whole skinny little body jerks in a spasm of pain as she bounces back and collapses. A scream looses a dribble of blood from her mouth.

I'm halfway down the stairs before I even realize I've moved. I explode through the front door to find Matty kneeling over her, jabbering like a fool. He tries to pull off his mask, but the clumsy swipes of his inflatable mitts can't get a grip.

"Oh my God! Oh, Bex!" he blathers. "Oh God! I'm so sorry!"

I shove him aside. "Move!" I drop to my knees and gently cradle her head. "Oh my poor baby. Shhh. It's okay."

Bloody spittle flies from her hysterical lips as she shrieks. "I'm bleeding! Mommy, I'm *blee-eee-eeeeding!*"

Her piercing wail attracts the attention of beachgoers on the other side of the bike path. People are staring. I already hear my name floating on the air. *That's Kimberly Savage! From the vampire movies! Oh my gosh! Look! Kimberly Savage!*

This is not a moment to be shared with the public. The paparazzi will not feed on my daughter's misery. I stand and gently help Bex up. "Come on, baby. Let's go inside."

Matty manages to yank off one of his gloves. "Yeah, we'll go get you all fixed up."

He reaches for Bex and she recoils and whines into my hip. I slap a hand on the top of his head and rip the gorilla mask off his idiot head. He squints and blinks into the sun, flushed and sweaty. I shake the mask in his face. "Back off. She needs a minute, okay?"

His lips quiver and he nods. "I'm sorry, Bex. Okay? It was an accident. I'm so sorry."

She doesn't look at him. I wrap my arm around her and take her back into the house, closing the door behind me. Her hysterics have subsided by the time we reach the bathroom, but her mouth is still gushing blood. I fling the mask onto the counter next to the sink.

"It's okay. Mommy is here. Mommy will take care of you." I sit her down on the edge of the bathtub and soak a washcloth in warm water. "Open up, honey." She opens her mouth and I tenderly wipe away the blood. The wound is superficial. Just a couple of pricks in her tongue in the shape of her little Chicklet front teeth. Her knees are barely scraped. She'll be fine. Thank God.

Tears blaze down her face. "Ow, Mommy, it hurts! Daddy hurt me!"

"Oh, no sweetie. He didn't mean to. It was an accident."

She sniffles and shakes her head. "I know. That's what he always says too."

The surrender in her voice chills me. "What do you mean 'always'?" I squat down in front of her. "Has he hurt you before? While I was away?"

Bex wrinkles her nose and shrugs. "I dunno."

I slide my fingers under her chin and turn her face to look into my eyes. "Bex, you can tell me."

Her lips pull into a defensive scowl. "It's just, like, one time we were doing sock skating races in the kitchen and I slipped and hit my elbow on the 'frigerator. We put ice on it and it was okay."

She tries to look away but I hold her gaze. "Anything else?"

"I dunno." She looks at the floor and unconsciously rubs her jaw.

"What happened to your jaw?"

Her eyes go wide, as if I had read her mind. "Nothing."

"Bex."

"He told me not to tell you."

My heartbeat races, forcing a tremble into my voice. "Bex, what did he do to you?"

"Nothing! I was . . ." She swallows a mouthful of blood and dread. "I was riding his shoulders 'cause he was my horse and he ran my face into the ceiling fan. Two teeth fell out."

"Oh my God."

Bex shakes her head violently. "It was okay, though! I was bleeding but we went to the 'mergency room and they said I was okay and they were just baby teeth. He told me not to tell you 'cause he knew you'd get mad." She fidgets and looks at the floor. "Are you mad at me?"

"No. No, sweetie. I'm not mad at you." I take her hand. "But I am upset at how your father has been treating you."

"But it was just accidents!"

I know they were accidents, but that does nothing to stifle my rage. He hurt our daughter. Not out of malice, but out of incompetence. I trusted him alone with our child and he hurt her, God knows how many times. An idiot manchild making the same mistake over and over again, never learning his lesson. And then he hid it from me. Worse, he made Bex hide it from me. He made her a silent accomplice in her own abuse.

I want to go find him and scream at him and slap him around, but I know there's no point. He'll whine and he'll apologize and nothing will change. He's incapable of change. The fact that this has apparently become a routine is proof enough of that.

I can't change him. But I can change her.

"It seems like you two have a lot of accidents playing your games, don't you?"

Bex bites her lip. "I guess."

I meet her eyes. "Can I tell you a secret? Just between you and Mommy?" She hesitantly nods. I take a dramatic breath. "Before you were born, your father wanted you to be a boy."

Dismay clouds her little face. "Really?"

I nod. "I'm sorry. I knew it would hurt your feelings if you found out, but it's time you knew. He always talked about how he wanted a son to do boy things with."

Her face goes pale. "But it doesn't matter if I'm a girl. Me and him do boy things all the time."

"I know. You see? He wishes you were a boy so much he's trying to turn you into one. But you're not a boy. That's why you keep getting hurt when he forces you to do boy things."

"He doesn't force me. I like boy things."

I tenderly dab the blood from her skinned knee. "You don't like getting hurt, do you?"

"No. I hate it."

"I hate it too. I don't want you to break your legs. Or poke your eyes out. Or bite your tongue off. Those things happen when little girls play boy games, and I don't want them to ever happen to you. Okay? Promise me you'll be careful when your father makes you play his games."

She swallows hard. "I promise."

"Good. Because I love you." I brush aside her hair. "Just the way you are. As a girl. As my sweet, precious, perfect little girl. It would break my heart if something bad ever happened to you. Do you know that?"

Her little jaw quivers as she looks into my eyes. "I know, Mom. I'll be careful, I promise." She throws herself against me and squeezes as tightly as she can. I hold her close, feeling the fear pounding on her heartbeat. After a long moment I release our embrace and wipe away her tears.

"Okay, I think you're all better now." I pick up the gorilla mask and offer it to her. "Do you want to go play with your dad some more?"

Bex shrinks away. "No. I want to stay with you." She picks at her thumbnail. "Will you play with me instead?"

"I'd love to, sweetie." I caress her knotted hair. "We can play anything you like. Something fun for mothers and daughters."

The words hang in the air like a baited fishhook. An idea brightens Bex's eyes.

"Can we play beauty salon?"

"Of course, darling. Meet me upstairs. We'll make each other so pretty."

Bex smiles and bounces away, eager for the safety of a "girl game."

I fold the gorilla mask in half and stuff it in the trash can.

CHAPTER SEVEN

Matty

My old Sport Wagon's tires carve a path through the fresh snow. It's not deep, barely half an inch, but it's still falling. Big puffy flakes, streak through my high beams like stars past a movie spaceship's windows. There's a kind of serene beauty to it all, but it's a pain in the ass to drive in. The rear end has fishtailed so many times the car is basically swimming up the mountain.

I'm reminded why we only ever went to the cabin in the summer.

The private dirt road leading up to the property is completely invisible under the blanket of snow. I drive past it twice in the pitch dark before I finally find it, barely more than two tire ruts in the dirt cutting between the trees. I ease my car off the pavement and slowly work my way toward the cabin, navigating the half-mile of curves by means of faded memories, experimentation, and blind luck. As I pull around the final bend my headlights sweep the house, highlighting the sharp, unnatural angles of a man-made thing wedged into the overgrown organic discord of the pines. The tires slip and I tap the gas.

"Whoa, come on, old girl. Come on." My body is heavy against the back of my seat as the aging BMW's nose tips upward, mounting the last incline of the road. I feel like an astronaut in launch position. "You can do it. Come on."

I ease onto the accelerator and the tires scream a ghostly howl as they spin freely in the snow. The whole vehicle lurches to one side. It bucks forward as I turn into the skid, then slips again. I let off the gas and drift backwards then pound it to the floor. Speedometer and tachometer needles fling themselves to the right but the tires refuse to grip. My heart spasms with adrenaline, raising my awareness while clouding my vision. The car is working as hard as it can but it's not getting anywhere.

Story of my life.

I lay off the gas and the wagon immediately slides backwards. The wheel pulls through my grip and the whole vehicle pivots, its front tires plowing arcs of snow as they slide sideways. My instinct is to pound the accelerator, but the headlights are now pointing into the trees. Instead I stand on the brake. The wheels lock, but it doesn't matter. This car is going where it wants to go.

The wagon comes to rest at the bottom of the incline, nearly perpendicular to the driveway and half off it. I continue to clamp the wheel, breathing heavily. I swear I can see my heart beating through my jacket—the fabric pulsing like the head of a drum. I close my eyes and take deep breaths.

"Okay." The word tastes metallic in my mouth. "Okay. So. Close enough."

I cut the engine. The door opens with a squeal and I step out. As soon as I leave the heated vehicle my breath becomes a heavy mist. Frigid air pricks at my ears and the tip of my nose. Patches of dirt peek through the scars left in the tire-ravaged snow, and I gingerly place my feet in them as I work my way up the last impassible chunk of driveway.

By the time I reach the top my eyes have adjusted to the pale moonlight. The woods are silent. The snowfall seems to make them more so, as if the flakes are soundproofing the world. I gaze at the house as I've never seen it before. It's a Christmas card. A rustic log cabin covered in a perfect winter-wonderland blanket of sparkling snow. There's a black Lexus SUV parked next to the front steps.

It has to be Kim's car.

Kim is here.

My heart lurches in my chest as shit suddenly gets real.

I step into the clearing at the top of the road, my canvas sneakers crunching in the virgin snowfall. There are no footprints. No tire tracks. It's a totally unblemished blanket of white cotton down. But the closer I get to the cabin, the more the Currier-and-Ives illusion fades. Streaks of rust dribble from the steel window shutters. Patches of rot and weather damage are evident on the heavy log exterior. A long stretch of rain gutter lies on the ground by the side of the house, its wrenched brackets pointing down at it from the eaves.

It doesn't look like anyone's been here in years. Which I suppose makes sense, considering what went down the last time we were all here together. I wouldn't want to come back either. Or maybe she just didn't need her secret hideaway anymore once she finally started making art films. There's no need to get away from it all when you're perfectly happy.

I actually don't know if Kim is happy, or anything else about her anymore. Sure, I read the gossip, but I don't know anything real. I don't know where she spends her summers. I don't know her favorite TV show or restaurant or song. I don't know her hobbies. I don't know how she really dresses when she's not in front of the cameras. I don't know what she finds interesting. Or attractive. Or revolting.

Oh God. The minute she sees my fat ass she's going to regret inviting me here. She's going to realize she made a mistake. My clothes smell brand new. They *are* brand new. I bought them on the way here. These rugged-looking, faux-distressed jeans. The too-crisp shirt, still creased with packaging folds. The black leather jacket.

Leather jacket. Who do you think you are, the Fonz?

I stop and my breath hangs heavily in the air. I should have worn my own clothes. These clothes are . . . they're cringeworthy. I look like I'm trying too hard. I am trying too hard. Why did she even call me?

She said she misses me and wants to make things right.

I want to make things right.

64

I keep walking. The living room storm shutters are open but there are no lights visible inside. Wet groans creak from the front stairs as I make my way up them to the door. I raise my fist, but I can't bring myself to knock. It feels weird standing here empty handed. I should have brought something. Flowers. Oh God, not flowers. But something. Sweat beads at my temples despite the cold. I shift my weight from foot to foot.

Just do it. Stop being such a pansy and do it!

I knock on the door. The thick planks deaden the sound, absorbing rather than projecting it. The living room is dark. She's somewhere else in the house. Somewhere she couldn't have possibly heard me.

I knock again. Harder. Swinging my arm in sharp arcs from the elbow.

Knock! Knock! Knock!

Pain shoots through my chilled knuckles. I wince and clasp them in my other palm. And I wait. My crisp new canvas sneakers are like sponges, soaking up the cold snow and saturating my socks. I check the clock on my phone. I wait. I knock. I repeat. I check my phone again. My fingers are numbed to the point unlocking it is a challenge. Seven minutes have passed. My instincts tell me to leave. Clearly there has been a misunderstanding. But I try the doorknob, just in case.

It's not locked. I push it open a crack and stick my head inside.

"Hello? Hey, it's Matty. Matty Savage."

She knows who you are, dumbass.

I enter and close the door behind me to keep the heat in, but it's no warmer inside than it is outside. I grope in the darkness and flick the light switch. Nothing. The power must not be on. I fumble my phone out of my pocket and turn on the flashlight. Dust swims in the bright LED beam.

A few tarnished old candelabras are set up around the room. I remember them from the summer the electricity kept crapping out

65

on us. We went into town and hit every garage sale we could find, collecting candlesticks so we'd be prepared for the next blackout. There were a lot of ghost stories that summer. And candlelit dinners. And candlelit bedsides.

On the coffee table a gaudy menorah holds nine candle nubs burned down to their holders. Next to it is a folded paper bag and a neat stack of boxed emergency candles.

"Hello?" I call out. "Kim?"

I sweep my light around the room. Two bundles of grocery-store firewood—wrapped in plastic with a rough handle of rope stapled on—lay beside the giant stone hearth. There are fresh ashes in the grate but the chimney is dead cold.

Something thumps above me. My heart seizes and I flick my beam upward. There's nothing there but planked ceiling. Obviously. I don't know what I was expecting to see. Another thump. Footsteps upstairs.

"Kim? Hello? Hey, it's Matty!"

She knows who you are!

I shine my phone on the broad staircase and climb up. From the landing I can see the doors to all the upstairs rooms. Three bedrooms. Bathroom. Every one is hanging open. None lit. It doesn't make any sense.

Another thump. A creak. In the master bedroom.

Something is wrong. It's not Kim. My heart beats so hard I smell blood. A tall candlestick sits on a small table in the hall with half of an emergency candle sticking out of it. I grab it by the neck and heft the heavy base like a hammer.

"All right, quit screwing around or I'ma fuck you up!" I try to bark it like a badass, but my voice cracks like a terrified prepubescent. The darkness closes in and swallows me. My own rasping breath is a scream in my ears.

Every single rational thought in my brain tells me to run. This is the stuff horror movies are made of. The dumb fat clod who walks

66

into the weird dark place, shining his flashlight and saying, "Derp! Is anybody there?" until he gets a pair of hedge trimmers shoved through his Adam's apple. But I raise my candlestick and peek into the bedroom anyway.

The dusty linens are stripped off the bed and there's a sleeping bag on the mattress. It looks expensive. Thick with specialized fabric layers and shaped like an Egyptian sarcophagus. I don't see anyone in the room, but my hand trembles, making every shadow created by my flashlight a lurking threat. The bathroom door hangs half open. Beyond it, darkness. Something inside creaks.

Shitting hell!

I'm too scared to run. And what's the point? Whoever is in there knows I'm here. He's heard me yell. He's seen my light. The second I make a break for it he's going to pounce on me and stab me to death and make a ball gown out of my skin.

My mind and muscles burn with adrenalin. A decision is made without consulting logic. I scream and charge toward the bathroom. Element of surprise, motherfucker!

My shoulder sends the door smashing against the wall. My candlestick is raised and I'm in a half crouch, pivoting at the waist to shine my outstretched light around the room. It's like a scene from the world's stupidest cop drama.

A claw-foot bathtub hogs the far side of the bathroom. Between us is a slate countertop with two sinks with individual medicine-cabinet mirrors. A toilet with a wooden seat lurks in the corner. I sweep the area three full times. There's nobody here.

My brain sends the signal to stand down red alert, but my body lacks the agility to follow through. I'm still breathing heavily as I flick the light switch. The lights don't come on. My knees wobble as the panic drains from my muscles, and I lurch into the room and sit on the toilet. From here I notice four 2.5-gallon plastic tap jugs of drinking water stacked by the counter. Two of them are empty, another is most of the way there. My mouth is paper dry. I get up to grab the open jug and my flashlight glints on something on the countertop.

It's a clean drinking glass. In it is a purple toothbrush. Next to it, in neat rows, are tubes and pots of various toiletries. The sight of it almost makes me tear up with sentimentality. The arrangement is so Kim. So intimately, meticulously Kim.

But something is off here. It's all moisturizers and cleansers. Toothpaste and deodorant. There's no makeup. Our bedroom in Venice used to look like a cosmetics store, dozens of tiny plastic cases and tubes organized with obsessive-compulsive perfectionism.

The medicine cabinet is ajar. Curious, I squeak it open on its rusted hinges.

Before I can see inside, something lurches from the shadows and cracks against my forehead like a whip. I yelp and jerk backwards, slipping on the bathmat. My phone flies from my hand as I hit the ground. Pain shoots from my smashed hip and elbow as I roll myself over on the tile floor.

"Aagh. God damn it."

I reach out in the darkness and grab for the countertop to pull myself up, but only manage to catch the under-sink cabinet door. It swings open and a screech cuts my ears. A weight hits my chest and tears at my shirt. I scream and flop over on my back as claws dig in and muscles twitch, throwing the heaving mass into the air.

I roll over and grab my phone, slinging the light toward the bedroom just in time to see a terrified squirrel thump the floor, springing across the room and out into the hallway.

"Shit. Holy . . . hell. God . . . God damn it." My brain is trying to push expletives out of my mouth but my lungs are gasping for breath too hard to let it. I shine my light into the open cabinet, revealing a squirrel nest and a harmless cache of acorns.

I had it all wrong. I'm not the dumb fat clod who gets murdered. I'm the jump scare when the killer isn't even there. I'm a horror-movie cliché.

Your life is as hacky as your screenplay.

I freeze and my breath catches in my throat as a feminine shout echoes up the stairs. "Hello? Is somebody there?"

It's Kim. I haven't heard her actual voice from her actual mouth in so many years. It sounds as youthful and bright as I remember, but undercut with a rasp of worldliness.

She's here.

Anticipation sizzles through me, pumping cold sweat from my palms and upper lip. All I can smell is the department-store musk of my new clothes. I shouldn't have bought them. I look like a douche.

Not now, Matty! Pull yourself together!

I hustle to my feet and give myself a quick glance in the mirror. Claw pricks of red seep through the white of my shirt. The slice on my forehead oozes inky blood. *Shit! You do not need this right now!*

I grab a wad of toilet paper and quickly blot my scratches. It's okay. It's dark. Maybe she won't even notice. *Maybe she won't notice your beard is full of double chin. Maybe she won't notice your hairline is receding like the Antarctic ice shelf.*

"Hello?" Kim calls again.

"Hello! Hi!" I call out. My voice wavers with panic. "I'm up here! I'll be right down!"

I cram the bloody clump of toilet paper in my pocket. It's go time. Let's do this.

My flashlight rakes the rustic balusters on the staircase, throwing long vertical shadows into the living room below me as I head downstairs. As my eye line clears the upstairs landing the room is revealed in a bottom-to-top sweep. And so is she. The whole thing takes fewer than two steps, but my mind is racing so hard it seems like a slow-motion eternity.

I see her feet. Athletic trainers. Black with green highlights. Soaked through. The wetness continues up the ankles of her tight jeans but stops before reaching her muscular calves. More than muscular, her legs have become outright beefy. And short. Short? A

69

ratty gym bag hangs against her hips. Then a red track jacket heavy with snowfall. Powdery flakes clinging to long, auburn hair.

The eyes that flash in my phone's light are Kim's, but the rest of the face is not. It's a young, feminine version of my own face, cracked across the center like a broken plate. She stuffs her hands in her pockets and looks at the floor.

"Hi, Dad."

My heart stops. My jaw goes slack. The word takes forever to come out because my brain refuses to believe what my eyes are seeing.

"Bex?"

She winces. "Rebecca, please."

"What?"

"I go by Rebecca now." There's an unnecessary sternness in her voice.

"Oh. Okay. Sorry."

I can't believe it. It's my daughter. She's here. With me. She tips her head back, gesturing at me with her chin. "What happened to your face?"

My *face? What the hell happened to* your *face?* The thought screams through my mind so vividly I swear I said it out loud. But I didn't. The scratch on my forehead stings as I dab it with my fingers. "It was . . ." *Don't say killer squirrel.* "I banged my head in the dark."

She nods discreetly. "Oh."

I've daydreamed of this moment for years. It was supposed to happen after my screenplay is produced. I'm a household name with millions of fans. Bex realizes I'm not the screw up she always believed I was and gets in touch. We arrange to meet at some Hollywood eatery, nice, but not too posh. With my success, I've had the time and money to hire a personal trainer. So I'm leaning against the bar, looking lean and cool in a slim-cut suit. She comes in and looks around, searching for a saggy old fatass. She doesn't recognize the new me, but I recognize her instantly. Time has made her taller and more elegant, but she's just a mature variation on the gawky teen

ONE MUST KILL ANOTHER

from the *People* magazine photo. She's still my Bex, all grown up. I smile at her and she smiles back, and it's like no time has passed. We talk and laugh and her pale blue eyes are as innocent as they were when she was ten years old.

Bex squints into my flashlight, raising a hand to shield her face. Part of a tattoo peeks from her sleeve. All I can see is the word *fuck* written in neat calligraphy. I'm too paralyzed by shock to lower the beam. After all these years, seeing Bex for the first time isn't ... it isn't what I expected. Her muscles looked normal from the stairs. Ordinary. But now they repulse me. She looks overstuffed. Like some beefy changeling has squeezed into the skin of that skinny girl from the magazine photo. And what happened to her face? Was she in a knife fight? My brain can't reconcile my expectations of childhood innocence with this tattooed, scarred Lady Schwarzenegger.

But it wants to.

"It's good to see you," I say. "Welcome back to Outpost 132."

She squints. "Excuse me?"

"Uh ... Outpost 132?" I gesture at the walls. "Home base to the Savage Expedition to the Lost Temple of Zamrycki?"

She just stares, as if dredging up the ghost of a past life. "Wow. I can't believe you still remember that crap."

We fall into a deep, awkward pause. I try to kill it. "So ... your mom didn't tell me you'd be here."

"She didn't say you'd be here, either." Bex's glare ticks over my body. Sizing me up. Trying to figure this out. She has a million questions to ask and doesn't know where to start. Maybe I'm just projecting. "I see you're still driving that old station wagon."

Her tone is flat. I can't tell if it's an observation or a judgment. I force a chuckle. "Yeah. It's a classic. The drive got kinda hairy on the way up. Sorry if I blocked the road."

She waves her hand. "It's fine. I walked. Followed your tire tracks, actually."

My eyes fall on her soaked feet and pant legs. "You walked?" Incredulity cracks my voice. "From *where*?"

"The end of the driveway. My Uber driver was afraid his Prius would get stuck in the snow if he went off the pavement."

"Oh. Dang." It's all I have to say, but it seems inadequate. I add, "That sucks."

"It's fine."

Another pause. This is all so cold. Like we're former work acquaintances who ran into each other in line at the movies and are reluctantly forced to acknowledge each other for the duration. This isn't how our reunion was supposed to be. I need to get it back on track.

"I missed you," I blurt. She is visibly caught off guard. Her eyes flick to mine, skeptical. She doesn't believe me. She needs more. "I missed you so much. Every day."

Almost imperceptible muscle twitches tug at her face. Words aren't enough. She needs proof. I smile and spread my arms for a hug, but when I step forward she steps back. A quick, bristling step. My face goes slack and I lower my arms. She turns away, sniffling and wiping her reddened nose on the cuff of her jacket.

"So, where's Mom?"

"I don't know. I don't think she's here."

Bex looks up sharply. "What?"

"It looks like she's been here, but ... " I raise my hands, gesturing vaguely to the dark emptiness. "She's not here."

Bex crosses her wet arms. "So what are you doing here?"

"Your mother called and asked me to come up here for the weekend."

She gives me a skeptical squint. "So are you two, like ... cool now?"

I shrug at the carpet. "I don't know. Maybe. I hope so. I really do." I meet her eyes with optimism. "Does she ever ... talk about me?"

Bex snorts derisively. "I wouldn't know." She sees the question on my face and adds, "We're not close."

The bitterness in her voice stops me from pressing the issue. "Oh. Okay."

She crosses her arms and looks around the room. Dwelling on some things and breezing past others, as if picking old memories out of the shadows of my phone's meager light. It's so serene. So different from the manic, high-energy Bex I remember. She's changed, but she's still my daughter. And this weekend I get to meet her all over again. I'll learn her hopes and dreams for the future. Maybe even become a part of them. Finally her eyes drift back to me. She speaks.

"Well, I'm gonna head home."

"What?" I splutter. "No! You just got here. Your mom isn't even here yet. Don't you want to, you know, hang out?" I gesture to her wet jacket. "At least get dried off?"

She picks at her thumbnail, looking at nothing. "I can't. It was good to see you again but I shouldn't be here."

"Why do you say that?"

"Because I came for the wrong reasons." She rolls her hands in the air, searching for the right words. "I tried to convince myself it was for the right reasons, but I was being selfish. I see that now." I can tell she's not talking to me. She's talking to herself, trying to satisfy her own doubts. She pulls out her phone. A backup battery on a short cord dangles from its base like a plumb bob. "I'm just gonna call an Uber."

"No. Come on. Don't." I want to reach out and snatch her phone away, but I resist. "It doesn't matter why you came. The only thing that matters is that you're here. And I'm here. And I'm sure any minute your mother will be here. I think she wants to put things back how they were. She wants us to be a family again, Bex."

Her eyes flash. "Rebecca."

I raise my palms. "Sorry! I'm sorry. Jeez, you used to think that name was cool."

She frowns and starts to speak, but stops herself. Instead she taps at her phone and mumbles. "A lot has changed since then."

"I'm sure it has. But that's why you should stay. We've got a lot of catching up to do. Are you still into *Kim Possible?*"

She groans and drops her arms, rolling her head back on her shoulders. "Ugh. I've got no signal here."

I can't help but smile. "Well, that's got to be a sign, right? The Universe wants you to stay and wait for your mother. It's meant to be."

She glances up at me, skeptical but contemplative. As if my crapped-out cliché had been incredibly profound. I can tell she's considering it.

"Can you please drive me into town? I'll call a ride home from there."

My heart cracks, but my voice stays steady. "No. I don't want to leave the cabin. What if your mother shows up?"

Her nose wrinkles, dragging that horrible scar up her cheeks. "*My mother* is probably already in town," she says bitterly. "She probably bailed as soon as the snow started falling. We're going to get snowed in here and freeze to death because she was too selfish to warn us not to come." Her voice is acid, her acrimony palpable. For a moment I'm almost afraid.

"She didn't leave," I say calmly. "Her car is still here."

"Maybe she left with somebody else. Whatever. It doesn't matter. I just need a ride. You can drop me off and be back here in two hours if you want to wait for her."

Frustration ripples through me. Why is she so desperate to leave? Kim reached out to us and she's not even willing to give it a chance? My jaw is almost too tight to force out the words. "No. We are not leaving. Your mother wanted us to come up here and work things out."

"There's nothing to work out. All this family does is wreck each other's lives. We're all better off steering clear of each other."

"You're wrong!" It comes out harsher than it was supposed to. "You're wrong. I've been nothing since I lost the two of you. I won't let you just walk out without giving this a chance."

"Let me?" Her eyes harden. "I'm not a child. I don't need your permission."

"I'm sorry, I didn't mean it like that." She turns toward the door and I grab her by the arms. "Stay. Please."

Her biceps turn to steel in my hands. "Let go of me."

"No. I can't." Panic tightens my grip. "Please! I let you go once and it was the worst mistake of my life! I won't let you go again, Bex."

"Don't call me Bex!"

Her hands thump against my chest like cannonballs and I hit the ground hard. My lungs can't take breath and my eyes bug out like a goldfish that jumped its bowl.

Bex's petite bulk towers above me. Her cracked face is tight and red. I'm afraid she's going to hit me again, but her brawny arms lower. Her eyes close. She breathes deeply. As she finds her breath, so do I. She opens her eyes and the rage is gone.

"You can bring me to town in the morning."

CHAPTER EIGHT

Rebecca

The fire crackles and spits sparks up the chimney as I nudge it with the cast-iron poker. It's not enough to warm the whole house, but the living room is sleepy with heat. My jacket and jeans hang over kitchen chairs, drying in front of the huge stone hearth. My shoes are off, their tongues pulled out to expose themselves to the flames. Emily ordered me to dress like a "grown-up human" to impress my mother, which was her way of saying "no workout clothes," which is basically everything I own. She begrudgingly let me bring a pair of yoga pants and a pullover hoodie on the condition they were for pajama use only. Not for my mother's eyes.

I'm wearing them now. It's not a violation of her rules. My mother isn't here to see me.

Cabinets bang in the kitchen. My father is trying to scrape together a meal from whatever my mother left when she took off. He insists on "cooking" for me, desperate to be a good parent. To take care of his precious little *Bex*, as if I've spent half my life just floundering hungrily, waiting for him to show up. As if I need nutritional guidance from a man who looks like he eats deep-fried hippo butter for breakfast.

I wrinkle my nose. *Seriously, Rebecca? Are you seriously body shaming someone who is trying to reach out to you?*

Heat prickles across my face and I can't tell if it's from the fire or shame. I hit him. I let my anger get the better of me and I hit my father. Here. In the same goddamn cabin where he hit my mother. It's like our family demons have put down roots in the Navajo carpet.

I hate this place. I shouldn't have come.

I can see now that this is a test that I have failed. I'm not ready to forgive my mother. I'd convinced myself I was because I had something to gain from it, but if I was truly ready to forgive her I would do it with no expectations of anything in return. The act itself would be its own reward.

I tried to fool the Universe and the Universe didn't fall for my bullshit.

With every minute that passes I feel farther away from forgiveness. I thought I was getting better. The anger was under control. The wounds were closed with blistered scars, but they were closed. And then, out of the blue, she rips them wide open with one careless phone call then leaves me here to bleed out.

Where the hell is she? Why did she call me here and then not show up? And my father too? What the hell is she up to?

I breathe deeply and try to see this as an opportunity for personal growth. Maybe I'm not ready to forgive my mother, but maybe I'm here because I *am* ready to forgive my father.

The father who abused you?

I push the thought away. By this point the memories of him hurting me have been replaced with memories of memories. I remember the pain, but the details all come from my mother. Whenever I asked about Dad after the divorce she always changed the subject. I understand why. I can almost still hear her tortured words echoing in this awful house.

"You're lucky you get to see her at all after what you did to me!" my mother shrieked. *"You betrayed me, wrecked my body, and gave me a second mouth to feed!"*

Mom was never so cruel as to say it to my face, but she dropped enough hints over the years to paint the picture. Dad did something horrible to her that she could never forgive. He abused me and she saved me from him, but I know she didn't want me either. How could she?

Nobody loves a rape baby.

I open my eyes and a hideous face comes into focus, glaring at me. My heart thuds and I jolt, even as rational thought erases the threat. On the top of my old toy shelf an abused Barbie fashion head smiles vacantly into the room. I stand and pluck her from the bookcase, running my thumb across the twine stitching her pouty pink lips together.

My mother gave her to me in a desperate attempt to get me to embrace the concept of makeup. I ended up turning her into a shrunken-head talisman to protect me and Dad on one of our quests through the "Forbidden Jungle." The memory twitches the corners of my lips into a tiny grin. Mom was so pissed. I straighten the chicken bone rammed through Barbie's plastic nose and move to set her down, but before I do, something else catches my attention. A book she had been sitting on.

A Tündér Könyv.

I haven't thought of this thing in years. It was a gift my mother got me overseas. I pick it up, admiring the beautiful spirals of stitches in its dusty leather cover. The pages feel heavy in my hands as I turn through them.

Each cheerful illustration digs up a unique treasure chest of childhood memories. Since I couldn't read any of the Hungarian text, I made up my own stories to go with the pictures. There are blue-green fairies with wings like gauzy fins and hair like seaweed who swim down clogged drains to push hairballs away. And the purple ones with the little saws who spend all night ruining pencil erasers. And the orange ones with the orange flowers who make dust for Cheetos.

The top and bottom of a page is marred with two ancient strips of Scotch tape. I remember them. They were there to bind the group of pages with illustrations so terrifying little six-year-old Bex Savage couldn't bear to look at them. My father gave me a line of bullshit about how if we taped the pages together it would trap the bad fairies inside so they couldn't hurt me. The story calmed me down, but I still quarantined the book to the cabin the first chance I got.

Of course my mother didn't know any of that. I remember freaking out when she broke the tape, as if the monsters would instantly burst out of the pages and kill us all. I chuckle. It's funny to think there was a time when I was so frail I could be scared by drawings in a storybook.

I turn the page and my smile fades. The images prick some old, dormant terror in my soul. I used to call these creatures "smoke fairies," but that barely begins to describe them. These things are cold-blooded demon beasts straight out of Satan's nightmares.

The dark fairies are like hunched bird skeletons wrapped in shrouds of ragged, smoky evil. Their broad faces are split with gaping frog mouths jammed tight with spiny, uneven teeth. But the worst part is their eyes. They don't have the dull, stylized beauty of the other fairies in the book. They've got human eyes, drawn with disturbing realism and filled with the fury of Hell. Their photorealistic orange irises aren't just looking at me, they're threatening me. They *hate* me.

My heart is beating like I'm halfway through a marathon when I hear scratching on the bookcase. I look up just in time to see a shadow launch from the darkness and strike me in the forehead like a whip crack. I shriek and stumble back, grabbing the wound. Heavy steps pound the floor and my father is beside me, pale faced and clutching a bag of seaweed crisps.

"Shit!" I hiss. "What the hell?"

"What happened?"

My brain throbs in my skull. I pull a blood-streaked hand away from my scalp. In the dim light of the fire it looks black as oil. "Something jumped off the shelf and hit me in the head!"

My father's cheeks prickle red and he grunts. "Squirrel."

"What?"

He grabs the fireplace poker and tramps around the room, glaring into the shadows. "The crazy little bastard attacked me upstairs. It's cuckoo for Cocoa Puffs. Probably got rabies or something." He tries to soften his scowl as he looks at me. "Are you okay?"

The gash across my forehead burns. *Rabies.* I can feel the filthy infection already sizzling along the wound. "No, I'm not okay! I can't get rabies! I don't have health insurance!"

My father's lips part as his eyes meet mine, then look away. "It's okay. I can ... I'll take care of you. I'll pay to get you shots or whatever. For now there's some old stuff upstairs. I can patch you up."

He reaches for me and I reflexively slap his hand away. His eyes bulge as he takes a half step back. He's scared I'm going to hit him again. I exhale.

"Forget it. Get your car keys. We're leaving."

Dad's bearded jowls quiver. "But ... what if your mother—"

"No. Don't even. If she's going to invite us here and then not show up, then fuck her. Seriously. Come on, we're leaving."

I grab my clothes off the chairs by the fire and crush them into a ball. My father follows me as I head for the front door. "Rebecca, be reasonable. Her car is here! She'll be back!"

I snatch my gym bag off the floor and something shifts inside it. Heavy and alive, it grips the nylon and vaults onto my arm. My eyes haven't seen it, but a primeval part of my subconscious is already screaming, *"Squirrel!"*

My fingers release the bag and my other arm swings out, ready to clamp down on the back of its furry, diseased little neck. But before it can, my conscious mind catches up to my reflexes and seizes my hand in midair.

Time slows and a chill explodes from my belly. The thing on my forearm isn't a squirrel. It isn't alive. It isn't *real*.

It's a winged skeleton, webbed with mottled, paper-thin flesh and plumed with black smoke. Glowing orange eyes drill into me with pure, directed hate. Its head splits across the center, baring gnarled teeth and screeching like a teapot. My father joins its screaming, but I do not.

With an adrenalin-fueled burst of muscles I smash my forearm into the wall. Brittle bones shatter against the heavy logs, and the monster goes silent. I jerk my arm back to my chest, leaving the thing stuck to the wall like a squashed bug.

I blink. It's a dream. It's a fast-acting hallucination brought on by the rabies. I blink again, expecting the carcass to vanish. It doesn't. Its squash-ball skull drops to the floor with an audible *clunk*, as if to prove how real it is.

My father clutches his heart and gasps for breath. "What . . . what the hell is that?"

Shock overrides all emotion and logic. "It's a smoke fairy."

"A *what*?"

"A smoke fairy." My tone is numb, despite my pulse being spiked through the roof. "They're not real."

"It looks pretty goddamn real to me!"

It does look pretty goddamn real. Too real. It is real. But it can't be. How could it be? It isn't. It's impossible. My father lifts the fireplace poker and cautiously prods the mangled body. We both jump back as the creature goes up in a flash of fire, licking flames up the wall.

"Oh shit!" I yelp.

"Put it out! Put it out!"

I grab a pillow off the nearest chair and beat the blaze into submission. As I do, a teapot screech sounds behind me. My father screams, "Shit! Another one!"

I turn to see a second smoke fairy on the coffee table. A third on the fireplace mantel. Pairs of glowing orange eyes blink out of the darkness all around the room like demonic Christmas lights. Terror vibrates cold and blue through my body.

The smoke fairies are definitely real. And they're *everywhere*.

My father swings his poker. The fairy on the table becomes a sticky black stain before going up like a burner on a gas stovetop. He doesn't even have a chance to lift his weapon before three more creatures pounce on him, digging their claws into his ridiculous leather jacket.

"Look out!" I vault over the chair and grab a smoke fairy off his back. It squeals and bites my hand, carving a ring of puncture wounds in my skin. I scream and fling the little asshole away, but it spreads its tattered wings midflight and joins the rest of the flock.

The air is alive with monsters, screeching and circling in the dim firelight like a murmuration of starlings. Claws and wing tips nip at my bare hands and face as the flock sweeps past my body. A sharp thud hits my leg, accompanied by the pinch and weight of talons anchoring in my flesh.

A smoke fairy clamps its jaws closed on my thigh, and with a surge of horror I grab it and rip it out of me like a barbed fish hook. Spandex and skin tear as one, spilling blood down my knee. The monster squeals and squirms in my fingers and I panic and crush it like a juice can. The smoky plumage turns to grease and bursts into flames in my hand. I scream and drop to the floor, slapping my palm on the carpet until the fire snuffs out.

The room gets brighter and hotter as the slaughtered fairies catch the furniture ablaze. I rake my hair out of my eyes and see my father near the front door, clutching his chest with one hand. He's basted in sweat, gasping for air and swinging his fireplace poker at the swarm. The shaft connects with an airborne fairy and it erupts and sprays the curtains like napalm. In seconds, flames encircle the whole window.

"Stop! Stop killing them!" I shout. "We're going to burn the house down!"

My father can't hear me over his own hoarse screams. He swings at a fairy on the windowsill, smashing the head of the poker through the window. Shards of glass flash in the moonlight as they tumble through the icy air outside.

The energy in the room instantly changes. The smoke fairies are no longer screeching. They're chirping and chattering excitedly. As if thinking with one mind, the whole churning swarm alters course and funnels through the open window like black water down a storm drain. A moment later they're gone. My father falls to his knees, crying and sobbing, surrounded by flames. I scream at him.

"Close the shutter!" If he heard me he doesn't acknowledge it. He just continues to bawl. The flaming curtain burns through its rod and drops to the floor beside him. "Oh, for fuck's sake!"

I scramble to my feet and run to the kitchen. I look. I remember. Under the sink. I jerk the cabinet open and see the old red fire extinguisher, sitting in a ring of rust. Expired May 2007. It feels almost weightless in my hands as I grab it and race back to the blaze.

I rip out the safety pin and blast the extinguisher at the fire, belching a clotted, dusty white cloud from its hose. There's not much pressure, but there's plenty of volume. I sweep it around the room, suffocating the flames all the way to the window. I push my weeping father aside with my hip and lean through the broken pane. My hands slam the shutters and twist the latch, and I slump to the floor in the heap of smoldering draperies.

My father is curled on the carpet in front of me, pale and saturated with sweat. His sobs are a crazed chatter. "Oh my God. Oh my God. What the hell? Jesus, what the hell? Jesus! Jesus hell!"

"Dad!" His head snaps to the side, glaring at me in wide-eyed panic. I try to keep my voice level. "Dad. Listen. We have to go."

"Go?" He says the word as if he's never heard it before. "We can't go! They're out there!" He grunts himself upright, pointing at the shuttered window. "They're out there! It's not safe out there!"

"Well it's sure as hell not safe in here! Pull your shit together! We have to get to town!"

"No! We can't go! It's not safe!" Terror has blocked his ability to think.

"Fine! Stay here! I'm getting the fuck out!" I cross the scorched ruins and sit on the hearth to yank on my shoes. My father follows and plops down beside me.

"Don't go! You can't go, Bex—" He catches himself. "—becca! Bebecca!" He trips over his tongue but plows on. "You can't walk, it's too far!"

I stand and pull on my track jacket over my hoodie. "I've run marathons. I can get to town in four hours. Less if I catch a ride along the way."

"But the monsters! They'll kill you! You'll die if you try to run!"

I zip up and scowl. He's not wrong. Even if the smoke fairies don't kill me, the weather might. Running the LA Marathon through the streets of downtown is not the same as running unfamiliar, snow-covered mountain roads in the middle of the night. My father might have lost his dignity, but apparently I've lost my mind.

"Then drive me."

"No."

"Dad, I'm leaving! Am I doing it on foot or in your car?"

My father sniffles and swallows. He digs in his pocket and pulls out a set of keys.

"Take it."

"What?"

"If you won't stay then take my car." He grabs my hand, turns the palm up, and slaps his keys into it. "Go to town. Get help. I have to stay and find your mother."

The keys glisten in the firelight. My throat closes up.

"You have to drive. Come on. Let's go."

"No! Not without your mother!"

God damn it, forget that bitch! I crush the key ring in my fist and fight the urge to throw it in his face. *Just go, Rebecca. Stop being such a pussy and do it. Go!*

"I can't go without you!" I scream. "Fucking asshole!"

84

The keys jangle as I pitch them as hard as I can into the rock face of the chimney. They drop to the floor and everything is silent except the crackle of the dying fire.

Something rattles.

My ears prick up. Dad stiffens with wild-eyed alertness. It rattles again. He points a trembling finger and whispers.

"The door."

I turn around. Something thumps against the front door. Thumps hard. High and then low. I take a step toward it and my father grabs my wrist. I scowl and rip my arm from his grip without looking at him.

I spring across the room and retrieve the fireplace poker. The doorknob rattles. I can't peek out the window without opening the shutter. It's impossible to tell what's outside. I position myself next to the door and raise my weapon above my head. My heart is beating fast with terror, but I welcome it. My breath is quick. My blood is racing. I am a machine in high gear, ready to destroy whatever is coming through that door.

The knob turns and the door swings open. From my vantage point I see the outside knob slowly arc into view. It's covered in blood.

Another thump against it and a foot crosses the threshold. In an Ugg boot.

A scrape and another thump. A second boot attached to a long, bloody leg, crutched up with a bent aluminum shaft knotted with badminton netting. My eyes follow the pole up to a blood-stained pink pea coat to a slender neck and a tangle of short blonde hair.

The tension in my arms goes slack. My father launches to his feet and hustles over, his face mangled between horror and joy.

"Kim! Oh my God!"

My mother takes another thumping step, pushing herself inside on her makeshift crutch, dragging her wounded leg. She's ghostly pale, her face and neck pitted with dozens of tiny claw marks. Her feral eyes look right past me, focusing instead on my father as he races toward her. Her cheeks twitch and her mouth dribbles words in a breathy croak.

"Matty. Thank God you're here."

Her legs give out and she pitches forward into my father's arms. He catches her against his chest and holds her tight. She buries her face in his shoulder and sobs.

My father puts a hand on the back of her head and speaks gently. "It's okay. Everything is going to be okay."

I close the door behind her and throw the deadbolts.

CHAPTER NINE

Matty

"What is *happening*?" Spittle flies from Bex's mouth. "What is going on? Explain!"

She plants her palms on the kitchen table and leans over it like she's the "bad cop" interrogating a scumbag in a movie. Kim sits on the opposite side, nursing an old *Great Muppet Caper* glass full of whisky. Her cloudy, haunted eyes roll to her daughter.

"I don't know."

"What do you mean you don't know?"

The open hostility in Bex's voice is too much. "She means she doesn't know! Jeez, is it so hard to believe she's not an expert on undead fire sparrows? She's not a member of the Occult Audubon Society!"

Bex turns her glare to me, kneeling on the floor next to Kim. My hands are red with blood, oozing through the saturated bath towel I gingerly hold on Kim's leg. It grips with a sickening adhesion as I pull it back to take a look. The gash in her thigh starts near the knee as barely more than a scratch, but balloons up the side of her thigh to a gaping hole pooled with gore. The sight of it makes me light headed.

"Stop looking at it," Bex snaps.

All I want to do is stop looking at it. Stop smelling its coppery stench. Stop feeling its hot, sticky burn oozing through my fingers. I'm seconds away from vomiting.

"I have to stop the bleeding!"

"Then stop looking at it!" Bex says. "Stop lifting the towel. You have to keep constant pressure on it."

I lower the soaked cloth back onto the puddle of Kim's leg and press it gently. She sucks a hiss and her muscle goes tight in my hand. "Aagh! Damn it, Matty!"

"I'm sorry! I'm so sorry!" I release my grip and her thigh goes slack. She pounds a palm on the table and shoots a long pull of whisky, dribbling it down her chin.

"Oh, for fucks sake," Bex says, grabbing a clean towel. "Let me do it." She kneels down and nudges me out of the way. Relief spills through me as I let her. I stand and lean back against the counter, breathing through my nausea. Bex speaks without remorse. "Take a deep breath. This is going to hurt."

She carefully positions the towel over the wound and clamps her whole palm over the most gruesome part. Kim wails in agony. "Agh! Damn it!" She bangs her glass on the table, sloshing booze over its rim. Bex adjusts her weight and holds steady. Her crouch makes her pants ride low, revealing a lower-back tattoo of a biohazard symbol with the word TOXIC. The sight of it turns my stomach almost as much as the bloody carnage. It's just so . . . *skanky*. Why would she do that to herself? Why would *anyone* do that to themselves? Who is this "toxic" person and what has she done with my sweet daughter?

"I know it hurts," Bex says calmly. "Breathe through it."

"Stop it!" Kim cries. "Stop! Aagh!"

Her face boils red with agony. I can't stand to see her in pain. I can't stand to see Bex be so hard and cruel. I can't stand the fact that the old cabin is apparently infested with flying skeleton demons. It's all so jacked up. This isn't how our reunion was supposed to be.

Bex's face hardens. "Sit still. We need to keep pressure on the wound for at least fifteen minutes."

"Then let me do it," Kim seethes.

"It's better if someone else—"

"Let me do it!"

Kim's other leg lifts and kicks forward, planting a heel in Bex's chest. The impact barely rocks her solid frame, but she lets go and raises her bloodied palms. "Fine. At least holding the towel will keep your hands too busy for this." She stands, plucks the half-empty glass of whisky off the table and moves it to the counter, out of reach.

"Give that back!" Kim says. "I've earned a drink!"

"A drink is not a reward." Bex's voice is dead cold. Her crystal blue eyes catch her mother's. Some wordless aggression is launched and received. Kim blinks away.

"I'm sorry."

My attention darts from Kim to Bex and back again. The stifled argument is too taut to be about whisky. Kim refuses to look Bex in the face. There's history here.

"It's okay," Bex mumbles. "You shouldn't be drinking. You've lost a lot of blood."

My focus turns back to Kim's injury. "She's right. You need to take it easy." I slide into a chair by her side. "What happened? To your leg, I mean?"

Kim winces and adjusts her grip on her wound. "Those things trapped me in the shed and, they . . . they stuck me with a pair of pruning shears. Two of them, working together." She holds up a hand and spreads two trembling fingers like scissors angling upward. "They dug in at the knee and pushed up until they were in good and deep and then . . ." She snips her fingers together.

The memory of it sends a visible quake down her back. She reaches for the whisky that isn't there, then drops her hand on the table in limp defeat. My own hand grasps my outer thigh, clutching at a stab of sympathetic pain. "Dang."

Kim stares glassy-eyed at the floor, her voice reduced to a mumble. "I couldn't walk. I couldn't even stand up. I just pushed myself into a corner and they . . . they tortured me." Her watery eyes flash, catching mine with a piercing intensity. "Why didn't you come for me? Didn't you hear me? Didn't you hear me *screaming*?"

Her trembling lip tears a hole through my heart. The red claw marks in the porcelain white of her face flare accusingly, each one a grisly souvenir of her ordeal.

Why didn't you go look for her, you lazy shit? You half-assed your search just like you half-ass everything. You were just sitting on your fat ass eating her groceries while she was down there fighting for her life against those . . . things.

Guilt strains my voice. "I couldn't hear you." I glance at Bex for support. "*We* couldn't hear you."

Bex shakes her head. "We couldn't. We didn't think you were here."

Kim's jaw quivers open. "Didn't think I was here? I invited you here! My car is in the driveway! Where the hell did you think I was?"

"I'm so sorry. So, so sorry." Remorse is thick like phlegm in my throat. "I knew you were here somewhere, I just . . . I'm sorry."

"We're both sorry, okay? We should have looked harder." The sincerity in Bex's voice is present, but strained. "But you can stop trying to throw a guilt trip on us. I'm not having it."

I gasp. "Rebecca!"

Bex raises a palm. "No! Come on! Like we were supposed to know she was being attacked by impossible storybook monsters? Don't act like any of this makes sense! Don't act like we should have known!"

Kim looks at her bloody leg and mutters. "I'm sorry I called you. I should have just died here alone."

The idea cocks Bex's head to the side, raising an eyebrow. My own face tightens in uneasy dread.

"Wait," I say. "Are you saying you called us here to . . . die *with* you?"

Kim gives me a repugnant glare. "What? No. Don't put words in my mouth. I just meant . . . " She waves her hand dismissively. "I was being dramatic. I'm an actress. It's what we do."

Skepticism flares in Bex's face. "So you *didn't* know those things were here when you called us?"

Kim's eyes narrow. "No! Oh my God. What kind of monster do you think I am?" Her voice grates with quiet resentment. "Look, I came up here about a week ago. I needed to get out of the city. I needed to get away from the . . . from all the *noise*."

Even through her frustration I can feel a deep helplessness in her. I know what she means by "noise." I remember the douche clowns on the TV gossip show mocking her. Praising her twenty-year-old ass while shitting on her fifty-year-old face. The ache in her voice tells me this is not an isolated incident. It's the new status quo of her life. Kimberly Savage: the tragic old lady who used to be hot.

She rakes a clump of hair behind her ear, painting red over strands of gold and silver. "I haven't been up here in years. I just wanted to let the place rot into the ground after . . . "

My stomach plunges in icy guilt as her eyes tick to the glassless door of the linen cabinet. A plastic bucket still sits next to it, still full of broken shards soiled with her dried blood and time's dust. Right where I left it thirteen years ago, when I tried to clean up before I left the cabin for what I didn't realize would be the last time.

Kim looks away from it and shudders. "I had to be alone for a while to sort things out. Away from the TV and the internet. I knew the power and water wouldn't work anymore, so I came prepared. I thought it would be fun. All 'back to nature.' Like a camping trip."

I remember my exploration of the house. The stash of emergency candles. The water jugs. The single sleeping bag. The bathroom bereft of makeup. The artifacts of a woman self-sequestered from society in the abandoned husk of her secret luxury home.

Kim's head shakes, as if engaged in an argument only she can hear. "I feel so alone all the time. But to be here. To be actually, physically alone with all of our old stuff, right where we left it. It brought back memories. Bad ones, sure. But so many good ones, too." She looks deep into my eyes and bites her lower lip. "Despite everything, being here made me miss you."

My heart thrums. She misses me. After all these years, all it took was a break from the noise to realize it. The second she turned her eyes and ears away from the Hollywood machine it lost its power over her. I can see it all unfolding in my head. Kim here in her sanctuary, letting her mind clear, letting her priorities shift. The woman before me isn't the closed-off celebrity preoccupied with success over all else. She's the undiscovered, struggling actress, still able to laugh and love without fear of judgment. She's the old Kim. The Kim whose love can pull us all back together.

Bex crosses her arms. "So you got mopey and spontaneously called us up here for a big fat family reunion?"

Dang, Bex. What's wrong with you? Give her a chance!

Kim nods. "I wanted to have a blazing fire going when you got here. I wanted the place to seem welcoming and not all ..." She frowns at the darkened room, blackness clinging to every surface the candlelight can't reach. "The firewood I brought was almost out, so I went down to the shed to see if there was still any left down there."

Her voice goes quiet and her eyes cloud as her attention drifts back to her bloody leg. I imagine what happened next and my stomach knots with dread. Bex's arms remain crossed, but her tone softens. "So that was the first time you saw them?"

The word sends a chill down my back. *Them.* Kim looks up and blinks, as if roused from a dream. "Yes. No. I don't know." She shakes her head, clearing it. "I could feel something in the house. Like I wasn't alone. Like there was some ... presence scuttling in the shadows. Watching me." Her shoulders curl in, as if she's trying to hide inside herself. "I thought I was imagining things. The shed was the first time I actually saw them."

Them. The unknown horror of *them.*

"But where did they come from?" I ask. "What the hell *are* they?"

Bex tensely shifts her weight. "I told you. They're smoke fairies."

Her words are nonsense, but her tenor is absolute confidence. I think back to when the first one attacked us in the living room. The way Bex spoke about the smashed corpse was like a parent dismissing an imaginary monster under her child's bed.

"*It's a smoke fairy,*" she had said. "*They're not real.*"

"But what is a 'smoke fairy'?" I ask. "How do you know about them?"

"They're in the fairy book. The one Mom got for me." Bex turns to Kim. "Remember? When you were making a vampire movie overseas?"

Kim shrugs. "I'm sorry. It was a long time ago."

"How can you not remember? That thing traumatized me as a child! Ugh!"

Bex stomps out of the room, and her exasperation digs into my mind like a trowel. I do remember. She must have been five or six years old. Kim brought the book home as a gift after she finished shooting *Blood Blitz 4*. The whole thing was cutesy-girly, Art-Nouveau fairies except for the pages that looked like the cover of a goddamn Megadeth album. Bex was too terrified to sleep in her own room for days after she saw them.

She storms back into the kitchen, opens the fairy book, and stuffs it under her mother's nose. "See? Smoke fairies. Is that what attacked you?"

Kim recoils from the picture and raises her palms as if the book were a snarling dog. "Oh God, that's them! What are they? Why are they here?"

"I don't know," Bex huffs.

"Well what does the book say?"

"I don't know!"

"Well, read it!"

"I can't read it! It's written in Hungarian!"

"Give it to me." Kim reaches out impatiently. Bex looks doubtful. "You know Hungarian?"

"I picked some up when I was over there." Kim takes the book and looks at the gibberish inside. "Ez ... ezek a tun-der-ek ... That's, 'ezek' like ... I don't know. But 'a' is 'the' and ... Okay, something 'the' something and ..." Irritation trembles her thin frame and she slams the book. "Damn it!"

Bex sneers. "Yeah. That's what I thought."

I feel so helpless. I need to do something. Kim needs my help. She's hurt and scared and Bex's attitude is just making things worse. Everything is falling apart. I wrap my arms around my chest and squeeze, trying to hold myself together. Something jabs into the soft flesh of my man boob, tucked in my leather jacket's inside pocket.

I can fix this.

"Let me see that." I pull my phone from my breast pocket and unlock the screen. "I've got a translator app."

"It won't work." Kim said. "There's no signal up here. I had to drive into town to call you."

"No, it's cool. I've got all the language packs downloaded on my phone. I think Hungarian is on there."

I know Spanish is, at least. I bought the app in an effort to communicate better with the kitchen staff at the Rex Mex. All I ended up doing was learning to say swear words in seven different languages.

Kim lays the book on the table and I focus my camera on the text. It's a short block, printed in a storybook's huge, sixteen-point font. Progress wheels spin over the foreign words on the screen as a soothing but stilted female voice translates them aloud.

"THESE FAIRIES ARE CAPTURE TRAVELERS ON ROAD. TO LET THEM GO THEY REQUIRE SACRIFICE OF BLOOD."

Holy shit! Putain de merde! ¡Santa Mierda!

Bex leans in. "What else does it say?"

I move the lens past the last word. "Nothing. That's it. It ends after 'sacrifice of blood.'"

"They capture travelers," Kim says, her voice inching toward hysteria. She rests a hand on her bloody thigh. "They're going to drain our blood!"

Bex nods slowly, pulling a steady breath through her nose. Finally she speaks in clear, cold syllables. "Fuck. That." She crouches next to her mother. "Can you move? We're getting out of here."

All eyes turn to Kim's thigh, still oozing with blood.

Sacrifice of blood.

"No!" I gasp. "The fairies want our blood! That's why they cut your mother. If we go outside they'll massacre us. We're safe in here."

Bex launches to her feet. "They already attacked us in the living room! This house can't keep them out. This house can't even keep out the goddamn squirrels!"

"Well it's still safer than being out in the open!" I argue. "In the dark. In the snow!"

"Stop it!" Kim shouts. "Rebecca's right. We have to go." She shifts in her chair. "My car is built like a tank. The snow won't slow it down. Neither will the monsters."

"Great. Perfect," Bex says. She turns to me. "I'll carry her out. You drive."

My throat swells shut. This is a terrible idea. Are we really going to do this? Are we really going to just make a break for it against bloodthirsty Molotov-cocktail demons? This is batshit insane!

Kim slides her hand into the pocket of her tattered pink pea coat. "Here, Matty. Take my keys." Her stained fingers push through a scar in the fabric, coming out at her hip. "No. No no no!"

"What?" Bex says.

"They're gone! The fairies ripped my pocket! The keys are gone!"

Bex pounds a fist on the countertop. "Shit!"

They're both freaking out, but I feel only sweet relief. *Thank God. We're saved from this deranged escape plan. We'll stay put until we figure this out. Right here. Where it's safe.*

My thoughts are interrupted by a sharp whimper. A teardrop rolls down Kim's scraped cheek, and she wipes it away, replacing it with a smear of blood. She blinks at the sight of her wet, red fingers and breaks down into full-on sobbing. My heart shatters.

95

"It's okay, Kim. It's going to be okay." I step to her side and put a hand on her shoulder. "We're going to be all right, okay? We'll figure this out. We're safe."

She looks up at me, her eyes glistening with tears. Her cheek glistening with blood. "We're not safe. We're going to die here." Her lower lip wrestles against itself, trying to force back a sob. She takes my hand. "We have to get out, Matty. We have to leave."

Her fingers squeeze mine. They're so frail and cold. I feel the fear pulsing through them and all I want to do is make it stop.

I take a deep breath. To hell with it.

"It's okay. We can take my car."

CHAPTER TEN

Rebecca

My mother is by my side, on her feet. She's a full head taller than me, which makes it easy to drape her arm over my shoulders and support the weight her wounded leg can't. Her bleeding seems to be under control and I've dressed her wound with a clean hand towel and a snug wrap of old duct tape. Hopefully it'll hold until we get into town. My own dressings aren't much better. All the ointments in the bathroom first-aid kit were long past their use-by dates. I still squeezed a bead of antibiotic goop into the fresh gash running down the center of my forehead and wrapped it with gauze. The last thing I need is another facial scar.

My father stands between us and the front door, gripping his car keys in one hand and the narrow, flat shovel from the fireplace poker set in the other. Despite the chill he's already sweating. "Are you . . ." His voice cracks. He swallows and clears his throat. "Are you two ready to go?"

My mother nods. "I'm ready."

He looks to me. His face is pale and sickly. It does not inspire confidence.

I blow out a breath. "Okay. Let's run through it one more time. Just to be clear." I point at my father. "You run to the car. Open the back door and keep moving. I'll get Mom into the back seat while you get to the driver's door. The second the doors are closed we roll. Got it?"

Dad nods and mops his forehead. "I got it. I got it."

"All right. I want to see hustle out there. We gotta move like we mean it." I look up at my mother. "Ready? On three."

We gently bob our knees for a steady three count before I sweep my hand under her ass and she hops into my arms. I barely feel the strain. She's six feet tall and can't weigh more than a buck forty. For once my mother's psychotic dieting works in my favor.

My father throws the musty comforter from their old bed over us. From underneath, Mom holds it closed at my neck, draping my face like a hijab. It's not much, but should give us some protection if the fairies swarm us again.

We position ourselves near the front door and I shift my weight from foot to foot. Band-Aids tug gently at the wounds on my fairy-bitten hand and thigh. My father grips the knob, opening and closing his fingers, steeling himself to open it. "All right. Here we go. Here we go. Ready, set . . . go!"

He throws the door open and bounds onto the porch. I swing my mother sideways through the doorway and follow him. He's only two steps from the bottom of the staircase when he slips on the ice and takes a screaming nosedive into the yard. The snow is powdery but barely an inch deep, not enough to break his fall. He hits the ground with a sickening *whumph* and the shovel flies from his hand and skitters across the clearing.

Oh for the love of . . . You had one job!

He rolls onto his side and grabs his smashed knees, sucking air through his teeth. "Aagh! Goddamn it!"

I give him a gentle but firm kick in the ass as I rush past. "Get up! Move it!"

"What is it?" Mom asks, huddled under the blanket at my chest. "What's happening?"

"Nothing. We're fine. Hold on."

I pass the black Lexus. If we had the damn keys we'd be inside it by now.

My eyes blink hard as they adjust to the moonlight. The snow is undisturbed except for two sets of footprints heading toward the cabin—mine and my father's—which are already filling up with fresh snowfall. Fresher, uneven tracks lead down from the shed, stained with drops of my mother's blood. My father fumbles upright on the ground behind me. "Dad! Get up! Come on, move it!"

The station wagon is just at the other side of the clearing—a lump in the moonlight under the sparkling snow cover. I pull my mother's weight tight to my body and break into a full run toward it. Something thumps dully against my elbow. Against my back. My hip. The blanket gets heavier.

The screeching begins.

My mother tenses and kicks her legs at the knee. "Agh! They're on me! They're on my legs!" From inside the blanket she can feel the clawing weight landing on her body but can't see what I can see.

The smoke fairies are swarming. It's impossible to tell how many there are in the darkness. They're just a massive, angular cloud of flagging mist and glowing eyes. Stragglers drop from formation and crash into us, digging their claws into the blanket. Our shrouded mother-daughter lump must look like a beehive as they land and crawl over each other, scrambling to find a grip. I want to swat them away but my arms are full.

"Get off!" I shout. "Get off, you little shits!"

I stop running and jerk back and forth, trying to fling them away. A few fall off and hover in angry zigzags, screeching bloody murder. Something smashes the bridge of my nose and my vision goes black. Tiny claws tear at my chin as smoky wings beat against my cheeks, dusting my eyes with a sooty sting. I want to scream, but the stench of sulfur gags me.

The blanket falls open and my mother's pale hand slaps me hard across the face, flashing hot in my vision.

My frail body pitches sideways. Hits the wall. Collapses to the tile floor.

"Get out of my house. Get out and don't ever come back!"

The memory explodes from the long handprint of pain sizzling on my cheek. I blink it away as the broken fairy tumbles off my face and over the blanket, going down in flames in the snow in front of me. My mother's eyes go wide in mortified horror.

"I'm sorry! I didn't mean to hit you!"

"It's okay!"

"It was on your face and—"

"I said it's okay!"

My father screams. "No! No! Augh!"

I spin to face him. He's on his feet, swinging the tiny shovel like a cast-iron flyswatter at the fairies circling him, biting and scratching. His leather jacket may look douchey, but at least it's protecting him from their claws. A fairy dives out of the air and smashes into the side of his head, dropping him to his knees with a scream.

"Dad!"

I take a lurching step toward him to help. Dozens of claws and teeth rake my back and arms through the tattered blanket. Mom screams and kicks, gripping my shoulders with one arm and slapping away fairies with the other. It's too much. Too much chaos. Too much pain. Too much weight.

"Mom! Stop moving! I'm putting you down!"

"Don't! I can't—"

I drop her legs and set her on her feet. Her wounded leg immediately buckles and she pitches over. The fairy-covered blanket hangs heavy as a lead X-ray apron over my head. I grab the corners, thrust my fists out to my sides, and fall backwards onto the ground like I'm making a snow angel.

The crackle of shattering fairies runs all the way down my back as their frail bodies bend and snap under my weight. I roll over and tumble off the blanket as the whole thing bursts into a bonfire of greasy orange flame.

My father thrashes on the ground, screaming in agony. "Get off! Get off me!"

I scramble over and fall on my knees beside him. A half-dozen monsters scratch and bite at his body. I grab the shovel and knock them away, but his clothes are already streaked with oil and fire. My father's screams pitch upward as the flames grow. The air reeks like a hair barbecue.

"Shit! Dad! Hold on!"

He thrashes and jerks in uncontrolled spasms of pain, and I drop a knee on his chest, pinning him down on his back. Both my hands scoop loads of snow and clap them into his flaming jacket. There are screams. There is steam. The fire is out. Dad coughs and shoves at my leg, and I lift my weight off his chest and stand up. He rolls over and violently pukes on my shoes.

"Agh! Damn it, Dad!"

Behind me, Mom kicks and howls on the ground, swatting at the fairies that scratch and nip at her. Panic and rage collide in my chest. All we had to do was run to the car. Just one simple task and we screwed it up in the most spectacular way possible. It's the Savage family in a nutshell.

I grab my father by his lapels and pull him upright. "Dad! Come on! Get up!" His whole body shudders in my grip. He's crippled with shock and fear. It's more than justified, but this is no time for weakness. "Get your ass up!"

I hoist him to his feet. He stumbles and coughs, wiping the vomit off his chin. "I'm good. I'm good!" He swats my hands away. "Get off me! Help your mother!"

He grabs the shovel and staggers toward Mom and the station wagon. I bolt forward, reaching her first. She thrashes in blind panic against the monsters, but I squat beside her and throw out my arms. "Mom! Grab my hands! On your feet! Let's go."

She is bawling. Hysterical. "I can't! I can't!"

There's no time to be polite. I shove her heels to her ass, grab her arm, and haul her body over my shoulders in a fireman's carry. She screeches in pain. She'll thank me later. Dad teeters past me and I move to follow him, but my barf-slicked shoe slips in the snow. I drop to one knee and my mother's weight crashes down on my spine. She shrieks. Every muscle in my body screams as my vertebrae pop in protest. I try to push myself back to my feet but my knee refuses to leave the ground. It's too much. I'm too tired. I can't. I just can't.

Yes, you can! "Can't" is not in your vocabulary!

"Bex!" The word cuts my ear and I look up. My father has made it to the car. The back door is open. He's waving me in. "Come on! Come on!"

I focus. I pull the Energy of the Universe from the ground. From the air. From my mother's quivering terror. A grunt blisters my throat and I push myself to my feet.

The car isn't more than ten steps away but each one is agony. Pain races up my calves and across my back as my heels pound the frozen ground. I drop my shoulder, lunge forward, and stuff my mother into the back seat before my muscles completely give out. Her head and elbow clip the doorframe on the way in, but she's in. I pile on top of her and slam the door behind me. Mom pushes and kicks at me, grabbing the back of her smashed skull. Blood seeps from the torn dressings on her leg.

"Aagh! Damn it, Rebecca! Get off me!"

The car rocks and creaks on its suspension as the front door opens and Dad drops into the driver's seat like a wet sack of cement. The engine roars to life and tires skid in the snow. My mother and I lurch as the wagon swings its nose down the mountain and rockets away. We untangle ourselves and I peer out the back window to see an infinite cloud of fairies rippling through the air in pursuit.

"They're chasing us! Go faster!"

"I'm going as fast as I can!" Dad barks.

He pounds the gas and pumps the brake, whipping the car through the hidden bends. The wheels slide and fishtail, but he keeps the wagon on the road, weaving between the dense trees.

"I think we're losing them!" Mom cheers.

The headlights rake thick stands of pine and oak as my father pushes the car around the last curve before the main road. But instead of bumping up onto pavement, the tires lose traction as the front bumper tips toward the sky. Dad is pale and sweaty behind the wheel.

"What the . . . what the hell?"

The fairies catch up, pounding into the rear of the car with metallic thuds. The wagon is stopped, headlights pointed up at the cabin, unable to climb the last bit of incline into the front-yard clearing. Frustration throbs in my skull. "You looped us back to the house!"

"I did not!" Dad screeches. "The driveway doesn't loop! It only goes down!"

Tiny black bodies dive-bomb the car in a kamikaze frenzy, shattering into smears of flame across the paint. Their screeching is overwhelming. Mom clutches her ears and howls. "Don't argue! Drive!"

Dad doesn't even bother turning around. He just stands on the pedal and guns it back down the mountain in reverse. I strap on my seat belt and brace myself for the first curve, but the first curve somehow doesn't come. Dad cranes around with his arm over the seat, his eyes wild in disbelief. "What the hell?"

Smoky black wings obscure the view as the cloud of fairies swarms around us on all sides. Dad hasn't turned the wheel an inch by the time they clear away and the car slows to a skidding stop on a muddy incline.

With its rear end facing the cabin.

"God damn it, Matty!" Mom shouts. "We're back where we started again!"

I turn and look out the windshield. The dirt road lies in front of us, full of its usual twists and curves. Dad pounds the wheel. "What the shit was that? What is happening?"

Panic closes a fist over my heart. "It's the fairies! They're messing with the road!"

"How?" Mom cries. "How could they do that?"

"Fairy magic? I don't know! How the hell should I know?" Fairy bombs explode against the doors, sending flame and smoke pouring over the windows. The heat is unbearable. "This isn't gonna work! Get out of the car!"

Mom's face flushes. "No! They'll get us!"

"We're going to burn to death! Get out!"

I reach over her, unlatch her door, and throw it open. Before she can protest I shove her skinny ass out of the car. She hits the ground and scrambles away from the flaming wreck in a frantic, clawing crawl. I vault out behind her as Dad knocks his door open and fumbles out into the snow.

I spring to Mom's side and squint into the blaze. Flames have engulfed the wagon, pushing off enough heat to singe my exposed face and hands. "Shit. Shit!" Adrenalin kicks on an emergency reserve of power and I grab Mom's arm. "Dad, help me!"

My father grabs Mom's other arm and we throw them over our shoulders and haul her to her feet. We move. Clumsily and deliriously, but we move. Fairies swirl and screech around us, but they don't attack as we put ground between ourselves and the blazing car. Orange flames fringed with black smoke light the clearing as we drag ourselves up the front steps and push through the still-open door. We slam it behind us and tumble to the carpet.

The cabin jolts as a concussive explosion pounds through the earth, the floorboards, and our bodies. And then all is silent except for our gasping breath and the piercing honk of the Lexus's car alarm outside.

My father glares at me. His voice is a hoarse croak. "I told you we were safer inside."

CHAPTER ELEVEN

Matty

It's way past midnight. I'm too exhausted to be awake and too wired to fall asleep.

The roaring flame in the hearth mocks us. After nearly being burned alive by the fairies, the last thing any of us want is more goddamn fire. Or rather, it's the second to last thing. The actual last thing we want is to freeze to death. Though really I guess the actual last thing we want is to let those little monsters tear us open and drink our blood. Still, freezing to death is definitely in the top three, so I throw another grocery-store log on the blaze.

At least we're back inside. Safe. For now. Kim slouches languidly in an easy chair. Its upholstery is scarred with burns from the living room fire earlier, but she doesn't seem to care. She doesn't seem to care that the new dressings on her elevated leg are already spotting with blood. Or that we're under siege by a hoard of arsonist micro demons. She doesn't seem to care about anything except draining the glass of whisky in her hand.

I can't say that I blame her.

Thankfully she brought a big bottle and is willing to share. I press a washcloth soaked in Jameson to a burn on my shoulder and wince through a pain like sizzling bacon. The cistern water from the taps runs green with sludge, and everything in the cabin's first-aid kit expired when George W. Bush was in office. So cowboy antiseptic it is.

I'm also using a tumbler of it applied orally to sanitize my bloodstream. Because fuck it.

With the remains of my car still smoldering at the edge of the clearing, we've come to an agreement. We're staying the night. If we're lucky those flying nightmare creeps might go dormant during the day. At any rate, when the sun is up, Bex and I will armor up as best we can and trek up to the shed. We'll find Kim's car keys and get the hell out of here while it's too bright for those magical little shits to play tricks on our eyes.

The booze burns down my throat as I ease into my own sooty armchair. Bex sits cross legged in front of the fire, pressing a towel into something in her lap. I can't see what it is; her knees are in the way. I tip the tumbler to my lips for another sip and she sneaks a scowl at me. She thinks I don't see her, but I do—distorted through the bottom of the glass, but obviously judging me. For what?

Right. The alcohol thing. That drama I noticed when Bex took Kim's drink away from her in the kitchen. *"Alcohol is not a reward,"* she'd said.

What happened between them after the divorce? Did Kim develop a drinking problem? Did she hurt Bex? Did she give our daughter that horrible scar in some drunken rage? A scenario half forms in my befuddled mind. Kim, gripping a bottle of Grey Goose by the neck. Smashing it into a blade on the kitchen counter and slashing it across Bex's little face.

I blink and shake the image away. It's too stupid.

Bex puts the towel aside and raises the object in her lap to the firelight to get a better look at it. It's her shoe. Splattered stains dapple its athletic mesh. My stomach plunges guiltily as I realize why she's cleaning it.

"Oh, hey. Sorry I, uh . . . went to Disneyland on your shoes."

Bex snorts through her nose. "Don't tell me you still say that."

I smile and shrug. "It's a good euphemism."

"It is not."

Kim's head wobbles unsteadily on her shoulders. "You know, to this day whenever I see the Mad Hatter I still smell it."

Bex grumbles with indignity. "Let it go. It was twenty years ago. I can't even remember it."

"You're lucky." The booze is heavy in Kim's voice. She looks over her glass at me. "'Let's get Bex some cotton candy,' he said. 'Let's get her ice cream. Let's get her a churro. You don't go to Disneyland every day!'"

I raise a finger, addressing the court. "Your honor, I would like the record to show that it was the plaintiff, Kimberly Savage, who suggested we ride the teacups."

Bex covers her ears. "Stop. Right now. I am not hearing this story again."

It's too late. I see the spark of memory in Kim's eyes. I know the scene is exploding, clear and vivid in her mind, as it is in mine. The first time we took Baby Bex to Disneyland. She must have been, what? Three? Four years old? Of course this was when Kim's stardom was blazing in the stratosphere, so we had to be subtle about it. I wore a nondescript polo and cargo shorts. Ray-Bans. Dodgers cap. Just another dad in the crowd. As if I had some delusion *I* would be the one people would recognize.

Kim, on the other hand, is physically incapable of subtle. She sported a white blouse, hourglass-cut to her figure, unbuttoned just far enough to let your imagination see what your eyes couldn't. Painted-on jeans. Her hair was badly hidden, tucked into this wide-brimmed, Audrey Hepburn hat. Except for the single coy lock of blonde curl bouncing over the temple of her oversized sunglasses. This was her idea of going incognito. It was ridiculous. Even if you didn't already know her name, one look at her made you desperate to learn it.

Kim rests her elbow on the arm of her burned chair and swirls her whisky at me. "If I recall correctly, *you* were the one spinning the teacup until she turned green. I thought she was going to lose it right there on the ride. But no. She held it."

I grin. "She gets her perfect comic timing from her father."

Bex concentrates on cleaning her shoe, pretending to ignore us. I can't see her face, but I think her air of offense is a put on. It's difficult to tell. I don't think she's smiled once since we got here.

Kim adjusts her weight and holds one arm cupped at her side. "I've got her right here. On my hip. I'm taking her to a bench in the shade so she can settle down and get some air. Then that redneck shows up . . . "

I pull out my *Hee Haw* voice. "Hey! Ain't you th' girl from them vam-pyre movies?"

Kim shudders. "Suddenly everyone is looking at me."

"Everyone was already looking at you," I note.

"Suddenly everyone is looking at me with their *cameras*."

"We're surrounded by the *klak* of shutters," I say dramatically. "The grind of thumb-wheels advancing film. The tourist paparazzi!"

"I try to smile," Kim says. "Have some poise. Give them their thrill. Then the fountain show starts."

Bex rolls her head back on her shoulders and groans. "Enough."

"*Bwlllaaaagh!*" I gurgle and slash a finger through the air across Kim's body. "A fire hose of pea soup right across your chest."

"All down the front of me. Into my shirt." She puts a hand on her bosom. "Into my *bra*."

"I . . . I try to . . . " I'm laughing, trying to force words through it. "I try to take her away from you, and as soon as you let go . . . "

"*Bwllaaggghh!*" We both do it, mimicking the violent spray with our hands. We're both laughing now. She continues. "It's like catching a hot, chunky water balloon in the face." Her voice pitches upward on her giggles. "It's up my nose. It's in my mouth. I can taste the baby bile." She wheezes. "I can taste the *churro*."

I'm doubled over, guffawing. "You . . . you take off your sunglasses and it's like . . . It's like . . ." I circle my fingers around my eyes. *"Baby puke raccoon face!"*

Kim and I both cackle and gasp for breath. Bex flings up her hands. "For fucks sake."

My gut aches from laughing so hard. I suddenly realize we're laughing together. Really laughing. Kim and I. Just like we used to before . . . everything. We settle into residual spasms of chuckles and I catch her eye and smile.

"I told you someday we'd look back on this and laugh."

Kim wipes her eyes. "Thank God it was back when something like that could happen and nobody ever knew except some tourists and whoever developed their photos at Walgreens. Nowadays everyone has a smartphone. Everyone knows everything." The thought sobers her. She takes a drink and sighs. "It was a different time."

Bex props her shoes by the fire and stands. Her voice is utterly without humor. "Well, if we're done rehashing our greatest hits, we should probably take turns getting some rest. We need to be sharp tomorrow. Not *hung over.*"

The passive aggression is palpable. Kim waves her hand at the floor, her words loose with liquor. "No. Sit. Sit. I'm sorry. You're right. I didn't call you here to talk about baby barf."

Bex's eyes narrow. "Then what *did* you call us here for?"

Kim smiles. It's warm, but tainted with regret. "To talk about now. We've all become strangers. I don't know anything about you anymore. Either of you." Her gaze turns to Bex and her voice drips with sweet sincerity. "How *are* you?"

"I'm fine."

Kim waits a beat, using the silence to coax an elaboration that doesn't come. "I'm glad to hear it. Do you still live in LA?"

Bex shakes her head. "Pomona."

"Oh. Well. That's nice. I hear it's nice."

Kim sounds genuine, but the undercut of Hollywood snobbery is unmistakable. Bex seems to notice it too but her tone stays civil. "I like it there. I've got a cool, funky little place."

"That's wonderful. So it's a house? Or like a bungalow? Do you own it?"

Bex's nose wrinkles. She's done being interrogated, but her mother is too drunk to see. Or care. I expect Bex to snap, but a placid expression loosens her face. "I'm not really home that much. I'm too busy with work."

Kim purses her lips. "Oh! What is it that you do?"

There's a spark in Bex's eyes. "For the past few years I've been working as a personal trainer. I'm very active on the local fitness scene."

I think, *No shit, She-Hulk*. Kim puts it more diplomatically. "Obviously. You're in very good shape. I'm glad you're finally taking care of yourself."

Bex's voice stays light even as she forces her words through a clenched jaw. "I'm also taking care of tons of clients. Keeping them active. Advising on their nutrition. It's a whole package. I love helping people reach their fitness goals."

She smiles. Actually smiles. For the first time since we got here Bex seems genuinely engaged with us. I did not see this coming. I thought Kim's incessant needling would drive her farther away, but now I understand. Kim wasn't nagging. She was throwing out bait. Trying to find the topic that would sink a hook. Her radiant smile spreads across her face. She feels the tug on the line.

"It's so wonderful you found something you enjoy that also helps others. Not everybody is so lucky. So do you work at a big gym? Or do you have a place of your own?"

Bex's tongue darts over her lips. She smiles tightly. "I'm in a kind of transitional phase now, actually. I have my own personal training business, which is doing fine, but I don't have my own space at the moment. I'm working on it, though. I'm only a few thousand dollars short of my launch goal." She makes eye contact with her mother, then breaks it. "One more investor will put Strong Fitness over the top."

"I wish I had your confidence," I say with a chuckle.

Bex's head snaps to me as if she forgot I was here. Her eyes narrow. "What's that supposed to mean?"

"Uh, I mean you're over there talking about your long-term business plans while I'm sitting here just praying we survive the night."

Bex's face goes pale. She looks at nothing and fidgets with her thumbnail. I still recognize my daughter's discomfort tic. And I feel like a jerk for shitting on her hopes and dreams just when she was opening up.

"You're right," she mumbles. "You're right. It was inappropriate. I'm sorry."

"Don't be sorry! I'm sorry. You should be excited." I give her a self-deprecating smile. "I wish I was half as fit as you. I mean, seriously, if we have one more tangle with those little shit grenades I'm gonna have a heart attack. Then you won't need an investor. You'll have an inheritance!"

I chuckle at my own joke, but Bex looks away and crosses her arms. She seems disgusted with me. Maybe this isn't the right time for gallows humor. Or maybe she's upset by the possibility of losing me. Yeah, I'm gonna go with that. I regret souring her mood, but I can't help but relish the idea that my daughter cares if I live or die.

"Don't talk like that," Bex says. "We're all going to survive."

"To survival," Kim slurs, raising her glass. "Rebecca's going to open her gym. I'm going to win my Oscar. You're going to . . ." She looks at me and smiles. "What *are* you going to do, Matty?"

It's a setup line. A perfect setup line. She lobbed a comedy writer a high, slow one. My brain burns with possible zingers.

I dunno. Celebrate with a round of hair plugs and liposuction?

No! Be confident! Women love confidence!

I dunno. Clean up the house so it'll be ready for you to move back in?

Be confident without being a dickhead. Be honest.

I dunno. Call you and hope you'll actually answer when you see it's my number?

You know it's possible to be too honest, right?

"I dunno," I say. "See if my car insurance policy covers 'Acts of Satan'?"

Kim snorts a laugh.

Nailed it.

"No, I mean, what are you going back to? What's your life? Are you still writing?"

"Oh yeah, for sure. Still writing."

"Any big projects I should be watching for?"

I nod noncommittally. "Yeah. I've got a bunch of stuff cooking. Incubating. Lots of irons in the fire. The whole thing is such a process. So many moving pieces. There's everything with the studios and—" *Shut up, Matty! Shut the fuck up!* "—You know how it is."

Kim smiles. "I do. I'm glad you're still in it, though. Do you ever hang out with any of the old gang from *SoCalites?*"

"Kinda. We're all tight online, and we still meet up from time to time. We did a big reunion dinner at the Islands in Burbank a while back."

Seven years ago. I haven't heard from a single one since. And half of those pricks didn't even remember me. The other half cracked jokes about how I'd let myself go since I stopped getting them coffee. Har-de-har-har, jackass hacks.

My fingers fidget with my empty tumbler. Sweat beads on the back of my neck. This was more fun when Kim was grilling Bex. Now that I'm in the hot seat I feel like I'm gonna go to Disneyland all over myself. But I remember what she's doing. She's throwing bait. Trying to sink a hook. Trying to figure out what I'm passionate about.

Kim brushes the arm of her chair. "That sounds fun. You still in Venice?"

"Yeah. Yeah, still on the beach. Still in the old place."

Her crystal eyes roll to me, slow and sultry under heavy lids. She bites her lip.

"All alone?"

My heart hammers. The question is so loaded. So flirty. I'm speechless. She can tell. She smiles. The hook is set. She found what I'm passionate about. It's her. Can I tell her that? She's already reeling me in and I don't know what to say when I land in the boat.

Just tell her the truth!

Well, yes. I'm alone. Because I never stopped hoping you'd come back. And now you have. And I'm the happiest man on Earth.

Too soon! You'll spook her! You have to make her want you. Make her jealous!

Well, no. I'm not alone. I've kinda got a girlfriend.

Like that's even plausible. Who would be your girlfriend?

Why am I picturing Rosebud? Do not say Rosebud!

My throat is so dry. I open my mouth.

"Well . . ."

I jump as something thumps against the window. We all turn to look, even knowing the shutter is closed tight. Another thump. Another. Scratching. Clawing. Screeching.

Bex is already on her feet. "The smoke fairies are back!"

The noise is muffled but all-encompassing. The house echoes with the sound of their claws scraping the steel shutters. They're swarming, looking for a way in.

They're going to kill us.

Kim turns her attention away from me and I exhale in relief.

113

CHAPTER TWELVE

Rebecca

"For the past few years I've been working as a personal trainer," I say. "I'm very active on the local fitness scene."

My mother's hazy, booze-lidded eyes roll up and down my body. "Obviously. You're in very good shape. I'm glad you're finally taking care of yourself."

Finally taking care of yourself, she says so goddamn smugly. *Finally.* At long last, her fuck-up daughter has managed to pull herself out of her spiral of self-destruction and put herself on the right road.

No thanks to you!

I force a smile onto my face and into my words. "I'm also taking care of tons of clients. Keeping them active. Advising on their nutrition. It's a whole package. I love helping people reach their fitness goals."

"It's so wonderful you found something you enjoy that also helps others. Not everybody is so lucky." My mother speaks her platitudes with actress sincerity. "So do you work at a big gym? Or do you have a place of your own?"

My tongue darts over my lips. I smile tightly. I've steered her liquored-up line of questioning right where I want it to go. You want to talk? Fine. Let's cut the played-out "Disneyland" crap and talk about why I'm really here. *Let's get down to business, Mom.*

"I'm in a kind of transitional phase now, actually. I have my own personal training business, which is doing fine, but I don't have my own space at the moment. I'm working on it, though. I'm only a few thousand dollars short of my launch goal." I throw her a pointed glance. "One more investor will put Strong Fitness over the top."

Her head gently tips, giving the slightest nod. It's a sign of the idea flipping a switch in the Machiavellian workings of her mind. I can almost see the gears turning—*Rebecca needs money. I have money. For some reason I want her affection now. Maybe I can buy it.*

She opens her mouth and draws a breath to speak.

"I wish I had your confidence," my father snorts.

Mom's mouth closes. She looks at him and takes a drink. The thought dies in her head.

Goddamn it, Dad!

"What's that supposed to mean?" I snap.

"Uh, I mean you're over there talking about your long-term business plans while I'm sitting here just praying we survive the night."

The words hit me in the gut like a medicine ball. Oh my God. What am I doing? What the hell am I doing?

"You're right." I mutter. "You're right. It was inappropriate. I'm sorry."

Dad waves his hand and screws up his face. "Don't be sorry! I'm sorry. You should be excited. I wish I was half as fit as you. I mean, seriously, if we have one more tangle with those little shit grenades I'm gonna have a heart attack. Then you won't need an investor. You'll have an inheritance!"

He laughs like it was a joke, but his words cut deep. He could die. Mom could die. *I* could die. We're stuck in life-and-death peril against impossible monsters from Hell and I'm trying to get into my mother's wallet?

Am I really so damaged that I prioritize money over human life?

No wonder nobody loves you. You're fucked up!

My internal monologue is shrieking. I cross my arms and force it to be still. Judging myself solves nothing. I have to acknowledge I have strayed into self-destructive thoughts. Accept it. Put it away.

Resolve to do better. To *be* better. To let it slip into the rearview mirror and keep moving forward in the best way I can.

"Don't talk like that." I look my dad in the eye. "We're all going to survive."

I flinch as my mother thrusts her glass upward and shouts. "To survival! Rebecca's going to open her gym. I'm going to win my Oscar. You're going to . . ." She looks at my father. "What *are* you going to do, Matty?"

She shifts her weight in her seat and fixes her focus on him. My skin practically tingles cool, as if a hot spotlight has been turned away from me. I settle back against the wall as my mother lobs drunken questions and my father fumbles his answers, like two high-schoolers playing Truth or Dare. They're both slurring their words in a way that grinds my gears. This is not the time to be impaired.

I should have taken the whisky bottle and dumped it out before they'd gotten this far into it. I had a hard enough time defending their dumb asses when they were sharp and alert. Now they can barely think, let alone fight. If the fairies come at us now I can't save them. We're dead. Simple as that. Dead.

I should have taken the bottle.

As I think it a bottle is in my hand. But it's not Mom's magnum of Jameson. It's Malibu rum. Open and half empty. It doesn't make sense. I blink and the sleeve of my hoodie vanishes. My arm is skin and bones. Something is in my lap, hot and wet, probing my crotch.

I jolt and snort and my hand is empty. My sleeve is back. I yank it up over the elbow to reveal my broad forearm. I squeeze my thighs together against the phantom dampness in my underwear. It was a dream. I've been awake too long and been through too much. My brain is having blackouts of mandatory downtime. Microsleeps, they call them.

But it wasn't a dream. It was a *memory*.

I push it away, focusing on my mother as she paws at her chair.

"That sounds fun. You still in Venice?"

My father nods. "Yeah. Yeah, still on the beach. Still in the old place."

Mom barely looks awake. "All alone?"

Dad opens his mouth but doesn't speak. He closes it again. He takes a breath. "Well . . ."

Something thuds against the window shutter outside. We all jolt at the sound. It happens again. Another thud. Another jolt. Scuttling and screeching.

I jump to my feet. "The smoke fairies are back!"

My heart and lungs and brain light up as adrenaline sharpens my body for a fight. My mother sits bolt upright but her eyes are cloudy. She tries to set her tumbler on the end table but completely misses. It hits the floor and shatters. My father pushes himself out of his chair, staggers, and falls heavily back into it. Shit! They're useless. This is exactly what I was afraid would happen. I grab the fireplace shovel.

"Don't move! Sit still. Be quiet."

Fortunately my parents do as they're told because I don't have a plan. The walls are alive with scratching and otherworldly chatter. With the shutters closed we're completely blind to the outside, but it's not hard to imagine the whole house swarmed with them, clawing over each other, trying to find a way in.

I close my eyes and focus on the sound. I tell myself it's just harmless noise. The walls are thick. The windows are covered. We're safe.

A piercing scream drives a dagger into my ear. My mother is pressed into her armchair, arm outstretched, pointing behind me. "The fireplace!"

I whirl around. Two fairies creep out of the roaring fire onto the hearth. The flames lick harmlessly over their smoky plumage as they screech at us. I bring the shovel down on the first fairy. *Whak!* Then the second. *Crak!* Their corpses ignite on the stonework.

"The chimney!" my father howls. "Close the damper!"

I grab the lever and jam it to the left. A squeal rumbles in the fireplace's stone throat, followed by a low metallic clang. Then a thump. Another. A screech and scratching of claws on steel. The fairies pile up in the chimney, but they can't get in.

With the damper closed, smoke from the fire starts to pour over the mantel, blackening the wall. My father lumbers to his feet. "Shit! Put it out! Put it out!"

I rush into the kitchen, grab the old extinguisher, and hurry back. The black cloud pools at the ceiling, and my parents fumble out of their chairs and onto the carpet to escape it. I crouch next to the fireplace and blast chunky white vapor at the flaming logs, choking out the fire and plunging us into darkness.

I drop to the floor, coughing and wheezing for breath. A shard of Mom's broken tumbler jabs into my arm and I curse and pick it out. A single point of light cuts through the smoke like a lighthouse on a foggy night. It's in my father's hand—the flashlight on his phone. I scramble over to where he and my mother are huddled. The cloud swirls above us. A menacing black void hiding unknown terrors. The fairies scratch at the shutters, their claws screeching against the steel.

"Are you all right?" I ask.

My mother coughs and pulls the neckline of her sweater over her nose. Dad scans the room with his light. "I think so. I think we're okay." He eyes the cloud uneasily and holds Mom tighter. "I think we're okay."

"We're not okay!" my mother cries. "They're going to kill us!"

I shake my head. "No. We're safe. They can't get in now." I know it's a lie. They will get in. They'll find a way. Or make one. It's just a matter of time.

The scratching seems to get louder and my mother presses her palms to her ears. "Make it stop! Make them stop! Make the noise stop!"

Dad gasps. "The book! We can trap them in the book!"

ONE MUST KILL ANOTHER

"What?" I ask. "How?"

"We just have to tape the pages! Like before! Remember?"

I do remember. When I was a kid, terrified of the illustrations of the smoke fairies, Dad said binding the pages would trap the fairies between them where they couldn't hurt me. And it did. Until I got here and opened the book.

I squeeze my eyes shut. "That's the stupidest thing I've ever heard!"

My mother is hysterical. "What do we do? What do they want from us?"

A clear feminine voice speaks over the clawing chaos. "TO LET THEM GO THEY REQUIRE SACRIFICE OF BLOOD." My father flinches away from the sound coming out of his own hand. His phone screen blinks on, showing the translator app and its image of the text from the fairy book. The voice repeats. "THEY REQUIRE SACRIFICE OF BLOOD."

Dad tries to close the app. "Shut up! Not now, you buggy piece of shit!"

My stomach plunges into ice water. "They're doing this. The fairies are sending us a message."

"By possessing my phone?" Dad shrieks. "How? Do they have wifi coming out of their asses?"

"TO LET THEM GO THEY REQUIRE SACRIFICE OF BLOOD," the phone repeats. "SACRIFICE OF BLOOD. SACRIFICE OF BLOOD."

"What does that even mean?" Mom shouts, clutching her leg. "How much do I have to bleed before you bastards are happy?"

Dad snaps his fingers. "Maybe it's not just blood! Maybe there's a ritual or something. Draw a pentagram. Burn some sage. That kind of shit!"

The chaotic noise of the fairies is unbearable. I scream at the window. "Stop it! Stop screeching and tell us what you want!"

"ONE."

We look at each other, then at the phone. The screen has glitched out, but translation wheels still spin under the distortion. It speaks again.

"ONE."

My breath catches, waiting for an elaboration that doesn't come. "One *what?*"

Something smashes in the kitchen. Mom's face turns white. "One broken window!"

"Shit!" I launch to my feet and scuttle toward the sound, ducking low under the smoke. I've got the fireplace shovel, but I don't have a plan. I'm flying purely on instinct.

The kitchen is pitch black. I wrestle my own janky phone out of my pocket and light it up. Eerie shadows dance in the bright beam. A phantom fairy in every corner and crack. The window shutters are closed. Something glints on the floor and I swing my arm downward.

The tile is covered in a spray of nuts and broken glass. At its center a monocled Mr. Peanut doffs his top hat at me. Label. Glass. Crash. Something knocked a peanut jar off the counter.

A flutter of motion catches my eye. I slash the light toward it and a squirrel drops into a startled crouch. Its cheeks are fat with unsalted, dry-roasted peanuts. It darts by as my parents fumble into the room behind me. Dad wields the poker, Mom hides behind him. I raise my hand to calm them.

"It's okay! It's a squirrel! It's just a squirrel."

The squirrel keeps its black eyes locked on us. Apparently more hungry than threatened, it creeps back to the edge of the spill and continues nibbling. Dad coughs and plants a palm on his chest. Mom hobbles sideways on her ripped leg and slumps against the doorframe. "Oh, thank God."

"ONE MUST."

The words come from Dad's pocket. He pulls out his phone. The screen is more distorted with garbage but the voice is the same emotionless feminine velvet. Dad raises an eyebrow. "What did it say?"

"One must," I reply.

Mom frowns. "One must what?"

"ONE MUST KILL."

The digital words creep ice up my spine. "They don't just want blood," I say. "They want us to kill something."

Tiny nails scrape the floor. The squirrel skitters to the side and stuffs another nut in its mouth. I have a grisly thought. My mother has it too.

"Then let's do it! Matty, get that little bastard!"

She claps a hand on Dad's back and shoves him forward.

"Oh God. Oh shit. Okay. Yeah. Okay!"

He lifts the poker and the squirrel is gone—a flash of fur darting behind the refrigerator. Dad hustles over, stuffs his weapon in the gap between the fridge and the counter, and bangs it back and forth. "Hey! Get out of there! Get out!"

Mom pounces into the room, hopping on her good leg and gripping the countertop. "Stop! It's going to get away! Crush it! Push the fridge and crush it against the wall!"

Dad drops his poker and plants his palms on the freezer door. His feet grind peanuts into the tile as he grunts and shoves.

The refrigerator scrapes the floor and inches backwards.

The squirrel screeches in terror.

The fairies clawing the window shutter reach a fever pitch.

A streak of fur shoots through the crack next to the refrigerator and clears half the room in a single, sailing bound. Mom squeals and fumbles out of its way.

It all happens in a fraction of a second, but my heart is beating so hard it slows down time. The squirrel's legs pound the floor, launching it in a smooth arc of muscle and tail. I'm the only thing between it and the door. My softball instincts kick in. Years spent fielding grounders as a shortstop have turned complex physics into tightly wound reflex. I unconsciously calculate trajectory and velocity. My knees bend, my arm scoops upward. Rough fur brushes my palm and my fingers close.

My muscle memory is already winding up to throw the squirrel to first base before I even realize I've caught it. Its wiry body wriggles in my grip and I stumble forward and slam it down on the kitchen table. The little furball screeches and thrashes, but I hold it down on its back, my palm pressing its belly. It glares at me from between my thumb and forefinger, its black, empty eyes brimming with terror.

My stomach knots, but I know what I must do to survive.

Swing up. Swing down. Connect with the table. Repeat until the blood sacrifice is complete.

I squeeze and the squirrel's rear legs kick out. Its claws dig into my forearm, squirming and scratching. Over and over in frantic, hummingbird-quick strokes.

Scratch scratch scratch.

My arm is bare and skinny. It pulls a door closed, blotting out chirping birds and bright morning sun. I'm in a three-car garage. I drop a mesh bag of soccer balls in the corner next to a battered leather case covered in signatures. It's full of wooden stakes and holy water and stuff. Mom used it in all six of her *Blood Blitz* movies. The whole crew signed it and gave it to her as a goodbye present after they killed off Scarlett Bedlam and replaced her with that new girl in *Blood Blitz: Rebirth*. It's been sitting here gathering dust ever since.

I creep toward the door to the house. The one in the Hollywood Hills where me and Mom moved after the divorce. I slip silently into the enormous kitchen. I am a twelve-year-old ghost ninja. I kick off my muddy sneakers on the gleaming black-and-white checkered floor. Why did this have to be Corazón's day off? My nanny wouldn't even notice what those girls did to me. Or care. But my mother . . .

A cold shock of panic jolts through me. Calm down. It'll be okay. It's early. Mom is probably still in bed. I'll hit the shower. Soap. Hot water. If that doesn't work, long sleeves. She won't see. You've got this, Bex.

I'm creeping down the hall when I hear her voice.

"Are you even listening to me? I said no. No! I don't care what it pays, I'm not doing the goddamn werewolf movie! This is a chance to finally put that kind of garbage behind us and you're trying to drag me back into it? What's the matter with you, Joel?"

Oh God. Mom's awake. She's on the phone with her agent. And she's *pissed*.

Mom's argument echoes out of the living room. I need to sneak past its big entry arch to get to the grand staircase and upstairs. It's okay. She's distracted. She won't see me.

I shift my backpack on my shoulders and press my right arm tight against my chest. I move. Mom sighs. "What about the biopic? The feminist computer thing. Any word on that?" I peek at her as I scurry past. She's still in her sexy pajamas—short silk shorts and a camisole wrapped in a tiny, dove-white bathrobe. Even her bedhead looks sexy, like she's ready to pose for early-morning paparazzi shots if one could actually make it past the security fence and up to the window. There's a glass of red wine in her hand. "They said *what*? How am I too old to play Ada Lovelace? I'm only forty." Her face reddens. "I'm an actress! I can *act* thirty-six!"

She knocks back her drink and happens to glance my way. We make eye contact and I know I'm doomed. She pins the cordless phone to her ear with her shoulder, jabs a finger at me, then at the floor in front of her. *You! Here! Now!*

Crap. There's no sense disobeying. That'll only make it worse. I press my arm harder against my chest and reluctantly step into the room. She's only half paying attention to me, distracted by the voice buzzing in her ear. "Don't tell me I'm typecast! I have range nobody's ever had a chance to see because you can't do your job! Find me a better part!" She screams into the receiver. "Do your fucking job, Joel!"

123

She beeps the "off" button and hurls the phone at the couch. The rest of her drink goes down her throat and she coughs then turns to me. "Why are you wearing that?"

I shuffle my feet and look down at my clothes. "It's my soccer uniform. My team had a sleepover last night. Remember?"

Mom pinches her eyes closed. "Soccer team. My God. I *am* too old. Kimberly Savage has literally become a soccer mom."

No, to be a "soccer mom" you'd have to participate. Or come to games. Or even know I play soccer.

"Corazón said you said it was okay. It was over at Adilynn's house. Her mother just dropped me off."

Mom nods and pours herself another glass of wine. "Right. Right. I remember." She sighs. "I don't know why you insist on running around in the dirt like that. Soccer is a boy's game."

My cheeks feel hot. "It's girls' soccer. My whole team is girls. It's a girl game."

"Ugh. You know what I mean. It's not feminine. You're such a pretty girl, I don't know why you insist on . . ." Her eyes narrow. "What's wrong with your arm?"

My arm involuntarily presses tighter to my body. It's crossed over my chest, gripping the opposite backpack strap at the shoulder. So obviously weird.

"Nothing."

Mom frowns. "Don't lie to me, Bex. Did you get injured playing sports again? See? This is what I mean. Boy game. I wish you'd give it up. You know I can't stand to see you hurt." She sets down her glass and perches on the edge of a spotless white armchair. "Let me see."

"It's nothing. I'm just gonna go take a—"

She extends a hand. "Let me *see*."

Her glare is piercing. I release my death grip on my bag strap and slowly uncurl my arm. The inside of my forearm is inked with a scrawl in black Sharpie marker from wrist to elbow.

Yo mama has a fat ass.

Mom blinks several times, but her eyes never leave the words. Her breath quickens. "Who wrote that?"

I pull my arm away. "Mom, don't freak out, okay? It's not about you."

"How is it not about me? I'm your mother!"

"It's just a lame 'yo mama' joke. I swear. Last night these two older girls wrote dumb stuff on everybody after they fell asleep. They thought it was funny."

"It's not funny," Mom says gravely. "It's disrespectful. To me and to you. I don't want you hanging out with those girls anymore."

"I have to. Carlee and Hilary are jerks, but they're on my team."

Mom's eyes go sharp. "I mean I don't want you hanging out with *any* of those girls anymore. The whole team."

My breath catches. "But they're my only friends!"

They aren't my only friends, but they are my only *real* friends. The only people at school who don't care that my mother is the famous action-movie star Kimberly Savage. Mom's hand catches my wrist. She twists my arm to my face and forces me to look at the words.

"Do friends do this? Tattoo each other while they're asleep and helpless? Do you want to look like you're in a gang? This is not how respectable young ladies present themselves!"

She squeezes my arm and shakes it hard, like she's so mad she can't remember it's attached to me. My whole body rocks and thrashes against her.

"Stop! It's just marker! It'll wash off!"

"You're damn right it will. Let's go."

Mom drags me toward the kitchen. Her furious stride is so long my short legs can barely keep up, banging and bumping me against her hip. She pulls me to the sink and flicks on the hot water tap, then grabs the dish liquid and squeezes out a zig-zag up my narrow forearm like she's putting mustard on a hot dog.

"Mom, I can wash it off myself." She ignores me. She grabs a sponge, runs it under the steaming water, and slaps it on my arm. Scalding pain shoots through my skin. "Ow! Stop! It's too hot!"

"It has to be hot or it won't come off." Mom scrubs like a maniac. I pull against her grip but she leans against me, pinning me to the counter. "Stand still!"

The soap foams and flies in splatters but the ink doesn't fade. With a frustrated grunt Mom flips the sponge over. The abrasive, pot-scrubbing pad lands on my already raw forearm, and she keeps scrubbing.

"Ow! Mom, stop! Please!"

"It's just a sponge! Stop being such a baby!"

I keep struggling as my mother rakes the rough pad up and down the inside of my arm like she's sanding a two-by-four.

Scratch scratch scratch.

A squirrel flashes in my subconscious. I don't see it. I sense it. I'm holding it. It wriggles in my grip, scraping gouges into my forearm. My arm is huge and tattooed. Real tattoos. I blink and it's just Sharpie. My mother holds my skinny arm over the sink, scrubbing it like she's trying to draw blood.

"Mom, stop it!" I wail. "Stop it! Stop!" I ram her with my hip and yank my wrist from her grasp. It slides free with almost no resistance. We're both too soaked in soapy water for her to grip me anymore. I back away, wide eyed, clutching my scraped arm to my belly. "Stop it! You're hurting me!"

Mom's teeth bare. "I'm doing what's best for—"

"Shut up! You don't care about me! You're just mad because you think someone thinks you have a fat ass!"

"Bex! You apologize right—"

"No! You're crazy! You don't care about anyone but yourself! I hate you!"

Tears well in my eyes as I hold my stinging arm. My mother just stares at me. She's a mess. A ragged, psycho mess. Her bathrobe hangs off one shoulder, streaked with green dish soap. The wet fabric of her camisole clings to her skin. A tremble runs through her whole body as her hands close into fists. I'm terrified she's going to hit me, but instead of throwing a punch she lets out a single, heavy sob.

"Oh, God. I'm sorry. I'm so sorry, Bex." She steps forward and reaches out to hug me. I flinch away. "I didn't mean to hurt you. I just ..." A tear streaks down her cheek. "I just want you to be perfect. I want to protect you and care for you, but I ... I don't know what to do. I try so hard and you still don't love me."

She breaks down and cries. Really cries. Hot, wet, ugly sobbing. She covers her face in shame and turns away from me and the bottom drops out of my stomach. I did this to her. She hurt my arm, but I hurt her heart.

"That's not true," I mumble. "I do love you."

"You just said you hate me!" Mom howls. "And I don't blame you. I'm a terrible mother. I know I am. I'm so sorry. I'm doing the best I can."

Her whole body convulses with her crying. I can't stand to see her so sad.

"I'm sorry I said that. I don't hate you. I really don't. It's just ..." I pick at my thumbnail. "I wish you cared about me as much as you care about work."

Mom takes a shuddering breath. "I do! I care about you more! How can you think that I don't?"

Guilt twists my stomach. "I'm sorry! It's just ... It seems like since you stopped making movies you haven't done anything but try to get into another one. You're never home. I miss having someone around all the time like ..." I bite my lip. "Like Dad was."

Mom's face looks sick. She sits on a kitchen chair and takes my hands in hers. We're nearly face to face, her eyes just below mine, looking up at me.

"Sweetheart, you know the reason I work so hard is to provide the best things in life for my precious little girl. To buy you the best house and the best school and the best ... everything. Your father was always around because he didn't work. I had to work for all of us, because he refused to contribute."

I nod. "I know Dad was lazy and he never had a real job. But ... sometimes I still miss him. Can't we go to the old house and visit? Just one time?"

The corners of Mom's lips twitch but fail to make a smile. "You're sweet. And I'm proud of you for being so forgiving. But your father ..." She looks at the floor. "He isn't a good person. He hurt me."

Images of blood and screaming and broken glass flash in my head. "I know. I remember what happened at the cabin."

"It wasn't just that." Mom crosses her arms and squeezes her bare thighs together. "You don't need to know the details. Just please understand that he did something I can never forgive." Her eyes shimmer. "I should have left him then. He should have never been a part of your life." She shakes her head. "Now that it's over I can't let him back into our lives. I just can't."

My blood is cold in my heart. I remember all the times Dad had "accidents" that hurt me and I still miss him. I can't imagine what he did to Mom that was so bad she never wants to see him again. It had to be super bad. I feel mean for bringing him up. I'll never do it again.

"I'm sorry. I didn't mean to upset you."

Mom's lips pull tight. "No. I'm sorry. I'm sorry I lost my temper and yelled at you, and hurt you. I'm sorry for everything. It's not your fault. I'm just going through a tough time."

I frown. "Is this about the phone call?"

"I'm sorry you had to hear that. But I guess it's best you know." She looks at me, her eyes heavy with sadness. "My career is falling apart. My whole life they wouldn't cast me as anything but a sexy action star. Now I'm too old for that and they won't cast me in anything at all. The only work I've had in the past year was in a shampoo commercial. I just ... I don't know what to do."

I shuffle my feet. "Maybe you could do something else. Like maybe . . . " I put my hand on hers. "Maybe you could just take a break and be my mom for a while. Would that be okay?"

She's quiet for a long, thoughtful moment. "Yes." She sniffles and nods. "Yes. I can do that. I can take a break."

"Really?"

"Yes, really. I'll take a break on my terms, not theirs. I'll stop letting them control me and pour my heart into the role I was born to play. Bex Savage's mom." She nods, like she's trying to convince herself. She nods again, then smiles. "Yes. Okay. So, my lovely daughter. What would you like to do first?"

Warmth spreads inside my chest. She's doing it. I can't believe she's doing it! She's going to quit acting and be my mom!

"You can come to my soccer game this afternoon!"

"Soccer! Oh." She peeks at the smudged ink on my arm and her smile goes flat at the edges. "Yes! That sounds fun. I can't wait to finally see you play. I'll cheer louder than any other . . . Oh, wait. Oh no."

"What?"

"I'm sorry. I just remembered I've got a spa session today." Her expression sinks. "It's been scheduled for months and it's impossible to cancel so late. Oh, sweetie. I'm so sorry to do this to you."

I sigh. "I understand. Maybe another time."

"Oh, I feel so terrible. I just promised you we'd spend more time together and now I'm forced to run off again. This is so unfair. I wish there was some way I could go to the spa and still spend the day with you."

Her eyes are so sad they make me want to cry. She really wants to spend time with me, and I want to spend time with her. So much. My heart pulls in two directions at once. I've been doing extra drills to prepare for this game all week. I'm so psyched for it. But I play soccer all the time. I never hang out with Mom. I guess a chance to be with her is worth skipping one match.

"How about, um . . . If you can't come to my game, maybe I could go with you to the spa instead?"

Mom's miserable face brightens. "Oh, Bex! That's a fantastic idea! We can make it a whole mother/daughter day. We'll do deep cleansing facials, and hair treatments, massages . . . the works! Oh, they'll make us so beautiful."

Every part of that sounds awful, but Mom is so happy her happiness sticks to me and makes me happy too. "Sounds like fun. I can't wait."

"That's my girl. Come here, sweetie." She spreads her arms wide for a hug. I lean into her and squeeze her tight. She squeezes back. The dampness of her clothes soaks my uniform, but that's okay. I guess I won't need it today. And I don't even care. My mother is holding me. That's all that matters. She whispers in my ear. "I love you, Bex."

Hearing those words from her mouth makes it all worthwhile. I close my eyes and nuzzle against her long neck. "I love you too, Mom."

"Hold on!" Mom shouts. "Don't let go!"

"I won't if you don't!" My voice is too deep and too raspy.

My eyes pop open and I'm looking at a squirrel pinned down on a tabletop by my own hand. Its hind legs and tail are spattered with my blood. Its screeching pierces my ears. I'm back in the cabin like somebody flipped the channel from a memory to reality.

But it wasn't a memory. I didn't remember it. I was there.

A scream.

A flash of steel.

A spray of hot blood.

The squirrel goes limp in my hand as my mother pounds a meat cleaver into the center of its face. A fault line opens in the wood as the heavy blade sinks a quarter-inch deep in the tabletop. The top of the squirrel's head rolls away like half a walnut shell as its blood pools on the table. I yank back my arm and clutch my fingers, realizing how close the cleaver came to removing them at the knuckles.

My eyes go wide in disbelief. "Mom!"

She ignores me. Her hand and face are speckled with squirrel blood. She lets go of the cleaver's handle and wipes her cheeks, then raises her red palms and shouts at the wall. "There! There's your blood sacrifice! Are you happy?"

The insane scratching doesn't let up. If anything, it intensifies. My father is still standing by the fridge, staring at the scene, agape and dumbfounded. He had been trying to crush the squirrel behind it only seconds ago in his reality.

I clench my eyes. In *the* reality. There's only one. But even as I think it, I can smell the citrus tang of dish soap on my skin.

My father's phone speaks in his pocket.

"SACRIFICE OF BLOOD."

He pulls it out.

"ONE."

As it says the word its LED flashes in his eyes. Dad winces and turns it over to look at the screen. It speaks again.

"MUST."

The flash blinds me.

"KILL."

Another flash, throwing a hard shadow of my mother against the wall.

"ANOTHER."

I look at Mom. She looks at me. Dad looks at us both.

"Another squirrel?" he asks.

"ONE. MUST. KILL. ANOTHER. ONE. MUST. KILL. ANOTHER. ONE. MUST. KILL. ANOTHER."

My father puts his hand over his mouth, staring at the screen, wide eyed.

"What?" Mom says, staggering to his side. "What is it?"

I move closer and peer over his shoulder. The screen cycles through three images, one with each spoken word. Unflattering photographs caught in a harsh flash. A low angle on Dad. Me, standing by the bloody table. Mom, leaning against the counter.

Dad. Me. Mom. Dad. Me. Mom. Dad. Me. Mom.

"ONE. MUST. KILL. ANOTHER. ONE. MUST. KILL. ANOTHER. ONE. MUST. KILL. ANOTHER."

Dad's mouth chews the air as a whimper flutters from his throat. "No." His eyes narrow. His teeth bare. "No!" He raises the possessed phone over his head and brings it down on the corner of the kitchen counter again and again, pulverizing the glass.

The voice goes silent.

The fairies scratch and screech outside, ravenous for a human sacrifice.

CHAPTER THIRTEEN

Matty

Candlelight makes the master bedroom seem inviting and cozy. Three candelabras holding ten emergency candles create the illusion of warmth, but I can practically see my breath in the cold.

I shove through the door, my arms loaded with the blankets and pillows from the two other bedrooms. Kim sits on the enormous bed, tucked into her expensive Techno-therm, Cyber-warm, Arctic-expedition-special sleeping bag. She's upright, but dozing. Pretty soon I will be too. Adrenalin can only do so much.

No! Keep it together, Matty. Don't fall asleep.

The bedding in my arms feels heavier than it is. My hands tremble. My knees wobble. Even with my pulse still racing, my consciousness is giving up. It has to be two or three in the morning by now. I drop the blankets and reflexively pull out my phone to check the time. All I get is a dark, smashed screen.

Right. I wrecked my phone because it was telling me to kill my family. I'm betting demonic possession is not covered by the extended service plan.

I toss it on the nightstand on top of the fairy book. The book is wrapped side to side and top to bottom in duct tape. It didn't make any difference. The monsters still scratch the walls, clawing and shrieking. It's so consistent that I don't notice it until I think about it. A minute later I've shut it out again. It's the crinkle of a cigarette pack. The sound of something that will inevitably kill you, just not at the moment, so fuck it.

Those little assholes can't have what they want. No discussion required. None of us will murder another. We're sticking to the plan. We rest. We get our strength back. Get our wits back. In the morning, when the sun is up and everything isn't so goddamn *Evil Dead* around here, we'll find Kim's car keys and get the hell out of Dodge.

Kim's head lolls. She snorts and jolts upright. "Matty!"

"I'm here. It's okay. It's okay."

"Where's Rebecca?" Her voice tenses as her eyes widen. "What happened to Rebecca?"

"Shh. Shh. It's okay. She's fine."

Heavy sock feet thump in the hallway and Bex enters, arms loaded with her gym bag, food from the kitchen, extra candles, and the fireplace set (aka the fairy extermination kit). I help her set it all down. We've decided to gather our resources and hole up in the master bedroom for the night. With the fire out of commission there's no heat, but at least there's a California King bed.

"All right. That's everything useful." Bex rubs her arms. "God, it's freezing in here."

I pull a few blankets from the heap on the floor and hand them to her. "Here, bundle yourself up and take a snooze. I'm gonna stay up and keep an eye on things."

She shakes her head. "Yeah, no. You're exhausted and drunk. I'll take first watch." She lays out the blankets on the bare mattress next to Kim and gestures to it. "Get some sleep. I'll wake you up in two hours to relieve me."

Goddamn it, Bex. Throw me a bone here. I'm trying to be a good father to you. I'm trying to cowboy up and be the man this family needs me to be. A protector to my daughter and my wife.

Your estranged daughter and ex-wife. They don't need you, Matty.

I smile at her. "I got this, kiddo. You get some rest."

Bex glares at me. "Dad. Lay down."

It's like she's talking to a misbehaving dog. My Bex would never talk to me like that. But this isn't my Bex. This is *Rebecca*, the grown-up, 'roid-raging version of Bex. She has no respect for me or for anybody. Not even herself. I'm trying to be kind, but she's working so hard to shut me out. And it's seriously pissing me off.

"Ladies first. I insist."

Kim moans. "Ugh. Enough with the dick measuring contest. I'm too tired." She slaps a palm on the mattress beside her. "Matty, shut up and get your ass in bed."

I blink. Oh. Well. Those are words I never thought I'd hear again. An anxious sort of warmth spreads in my cheeks and suddenly my beef with Bex is ridiculous. It's so important to her to have first watch? Fine. Whatever. She can have it. I don't care. I'm going to bed with my wife!

Ex-wife!

I kick off my shoes and heave myself under the blankets next to Kim for the first time in over a decade. I try to savor the moment, but my eyelids are lead. I'm sinking into sleep. Drowning in it. I expect Bex to settle into the armchair in the corner, but she moves toward the door.

"Wait," Kim says. "Where are you going?"

"I'll be right back."

I force myself upright on my elbow. "You said you'd keep watch!" *You practically arm wrestled me for it!*

"I will! I just need a minute."

"A minute for what?" I ask.

Bex huffs. Her hands work the air. "I have to go to the bathroom, okay?"

Kim points to the en suite. "Use the one in here."

"Uh, no. I think you two can look after yourselves long enough for me to take a shit in private."

I push myself up and wave my hand dismissively. "Go. I'll keep watch."

Bex rolls her eyes. "Okay. Whatever. Thank you."

She grabs a candelabra and closes the door behind her. Her footsteps thump down the hall. Kim slouches down and works her head against the pillow. Her ass pushes against my hip.

"Spoon me."

A jolt of electricity sparks from my heart and hits the lightning rod in my crotch. My mouth works before my brain.

"Really?"

The word sounds so surprised. So disbelieving. So eager. *Too* eager. I'm embarrassed as soon as I hear it. Kim thrusts her hips without looking at me, tagging me again with her butt. "Yes, really. Come on. I'm freezing."

Oh. I see. She just wants my body heat.

Whatever. I'll take it.

I lay down and snuggle up to her. She pushes her back against me and grinds her ass into my groin. There's an immediate response. If she can feel it through the three-inch thickness of her turbo-fleece sleeping bag she's gracious enough not to mention it. I bend my knees under hers and put my arm around her waist. Her hair tickles my nose. It hasn't been washed in days. Camping hair. It doesn't smell like strawberries and cream. It smells like her. Her oil and her sweat. Genuine Kim stink.

Consciousness ebbs away and I forget where I am. When I am. The intoxicating odor of her transports me to our house in Venice and our four-poster bed there. The same bed I sleep in now. Alone. Still huddled to my caved-in side of the mattress as if she's there. I drift toward slumber with the actual Kim in my actual arms. Living my dream.

A voice hauls me back from the brink of sleep.

"You never answered my question."

"*Wghut?*" I snort.

Kim turns and cocks her ear. "Downstairs. By the fire. You never told me. Do you live alone?"

"Yeah."

The word falls out of my mouth like a brick. My brain is too weary to play games. It can only spew out facts in the smallest possible chunks.

"Oh." There's a pause. Kim adjusts her head on the pillow. She swallows, and I'm close enough to hear it all the way down her long, slender neck. "So . . . is there anyone special in your life?"

A face flashes in the darkness of my half consciousness. Big dark eyes. Adorable button nose. A sound pushes from my throat and a jolt of alertness snuffs it out in my mouth.

DON'T SAY ROSEBUD! WHAT THE FUCK, MATTY?

I squeeze her. "There is now."

My eyes flip open and my breath catches. What did I just say? My fatigue is truth serum. The corniest, sappiest truth serum in the goddamn world, apparently. Kim is motionless. Quiet. I made it weird. Shit. *Shit!* I made it weird!

She chuckles. "Ah, Matty. Still a charmer." Relief oozes from my every pore. Her shoulders roll and she snuggles in against me. "Do you remember the first time we met?"

"How could I forget?"

"Tell the story."

It's impossible. My entire body flashes a critical battery alert. I can't words.

"Let's just sleep."

She nestles tighter against my warmth. "Come on. Tell me a bedtime story."

I can't.

My eyes slide closed.

I'm gone.

I'm there.

Soundstage Four at Starlight Central Studios.

All the *SoCalites* sets are lined up in a long row in front of audience bleachers. The beach house interior. The beach house "exterior" on the other side. Burger Shack. Boardwalk. The bleachers are empty.

It's a pre-shoot day. We'll get most of the scenes in the can today and do the rest for the live audience tomorrow.

I'm behind the cameras, watching their four feeds simultaneously on a huge, quad-split television mounted on a cart. I get to sit in the cluster of tall director's chairs with the writers, because this week I am one of them.

We're taping episode #118 "Son of a Beach." The first episode of *SoCalites* I've written. The first episode of anything I've written. I got my foot in the entertainment industry's door when the showrunner here hired me as a writers' assistant. Now, after just three months of picking up lunches, he let me write a freelance script. Every unemployed writer in Hollywood has a *SoCalites* spec ready to throw over his transom, and he chose to give the slot to me. Johnny Nobody. I know I should be thrilled, and I am. I totally am. Yes. The sweat pouring out of my palms is definitely a side effect of being thrilled.

We're almost done shooting this B-story scene in the Burger Shack. In real life the set is way smaller than it looks on TV. Just a counter and a half-dozen small tables of extras gathered around the big one at front center where the principals always sit. Three of them are in this scene. The girls. Mandy, the nerdy brunette. Sharon, the sarcastic redhead. Nicolette, the ditzy blonde.

"Then it's settled. We're going to stand up to that jerk. Together." Mandy extends a hand over the center of the table. "All for one and one for all!"

Sharon puts her hand on top of Mandy's. "When the going gets tough, the tough get going!"

Nicolette claps a palm on top of the stack. "Be kind, rewind!"

Sharon rolls her eyes. "You're lucky you're pretty."

The showrunner laughs. The writers all laugh. At my joke.

Nailed it. Oh, thank God.

The director shouts, "Cut! We got it. Moving on."

A bell rings twice. The red warning lights by the doors blink out and the crew bustles into action. The first assistant director adjusts his headset and makes an announcement. "Stop tape. That's a cut. Moving on to act one, scene C. In the beach house."

My pulse slows, but the bile still rolls in my belly. Everything is going so well. Too well. It's just a matter of time before something goes wrong and they realize they've made a mistake. They're all going to see that I'm a hack and they'll never let me write again. I'll be lucky if I can keep my assistant job.

I wipe my hands on my jeans for the eight-millionth time as the crew starts moving the whole operation fifty feet to the left so we can shoot the next scene in the next set. Beside me, the showrunner pushes himself out of his chair with a groan.

"All right. Here we go. One scene closer to the grave." Norman is the big boss. Silver hair. Saggy jowls. He's been working in sitcoms since they were black-and-white. "Matty, could you get me a cup of . . ." He shakes his head. "What am I saying? You're a *writer* this week." His voice goes high in a bad impersonation of youth. "I wrote this episode! Get your own damn coffee, old man!"

I laugh too hard. "It's fine. I don't mind. I don't want to get rusty. After all, I'll be just an assistant again on Monday."

Norman smiles. "Someday we're all gonna be working for you, kid."

He claps me on the shoulder and hobbles off toward the beach house set. An embarrassing blush warms my cheeks as I head to craft services. Maybe he's right. Maybe someday it will be me, sitting in the big chair, calling the shots. Or maybe it's beginners luck. Maybe I'm a one-hit wonder and this script will be my only professional success ever.

Maybe I should just get Norman's coffee before I give myself an ulcer.

Crafty is behind the audience bleachers. A few long folding tables of junk food and junk beverages to keep the crew's blood sugar up. The background extras from the restaurant scene have already been herded over here—a bunch of wannabe actors who earn a living by sitting around ten feet behind the real actors. A career forever out of focus. I grab a Styrofoam cup and head for the stainless-steel coffee urn.

Her back is to me when I first see her.

A golden goddess, towering over the rest of the misfits. Flawless and creamy-smooth as a marble statue. She wears board shorts and a ringer-T with no logos. The same dumpy, generic, wardrobe-approved attire all the Burger Shop extras wear. But pulled tight around her curves they're haute couture.

She turns, and seeing her face is like looking into the sun. Full lips. Turned-up nose. Eyes like sapphire flame. Short, jet black hair falling in uneven, flirty scoops.

It's wrong. Something in my gut tells me it's wrong. My head throbs and I feel like I'm going to pass out. I blink and refocus.

She turns, and seeing her face is like looking into the sun. Full lips. Turned-up nose. Eyes like sapphire flame. Wild waves of dense blonde hair cascade from her scalp in high, arching curls. She notices me staring and I pretend I wasn't.

"Hey," I mutter.

She gives a terse nod. "Hey yourself."

Her eyes scan me and I unconsciously stand straighter and tighten my abs. Normally, as an assistant, I'd just be wearing a hoodie and whatever else I picked up off the floor that morning. Today, as a writer, I had actually made an effort to class it up. Snug-fitting jeans, ripped ragged at the knee. A blazer with patches on the elbows hanging rakishly over a Night Ranger concert T. My thick hair gelled into a spectacular John Stamos mullet. I actually don't look too bad. For me.

I don't know what to do with my hands. I put them on my hips, then in my pockets, then take them out again. She's still looking at me. I have to make words.

"So, uh, were you just in the Burger Shack scene? I didn't see you."

She scowls. "No. The second A.D. hasn't actually placed me all day. He says I'll distract from the principals if he puts me in a scene." She draws finger quotes in the air. "He says I'm 'too hot' for background work."

He's not wrong, I think.

"He's not wrong," she says.

I chuckle. "Well, at least you still get paid, right?"

She shakes her head and sighs. "Honey, nobody does extra work for the money. I'm here to be seen." She tips her chin to me. "So what's your deal? You on the crew?"

"Staff, actually." My lips pull into an involuntary grin. "I, uh . . . I wrote this week's episode."

Her eyebrows arch. "Oh. You're a writer."

No, I'm just pretending to be until I get called out as an imposter.

"Yes. I mean, kinda. Technically I'm an assistant here. But I am working on a screenplay in my spare time. You know, like every other wannabe writer in LA." I wrinkle my nose and extend a hand for a shake. "Hello, my name is Matty Savage and I will be your cliché for the evening."

She laughs. "Well, I'll see your writer cliché and raise you one struggling actress doing background work while she tries to break into the movies." Her palm glides into mine. "Future Academy Award winner, Kimberly Wrzesniewski."

Her name hits my ears like a six car pileup. *Werzsheschnevskee.* I can't even place the vowels. If there are any. It's what's left on the tray after a losing game of Scrabble.

My eyebrows lower. "I'm sorry. Say again? Wer . . . werza . . . "

Her beaming smile fades as she releases my hand. "I know. I know. I need a professional name. Something simple and striking. Like yours. Savage. Kimberly Savage." She considers it in her ear like a fine wine. "Not bad."

I give her a wry smile. "Well, I don't want to jump the gun here, but . . . Yes, Kimberly. I will marry you."

The way she rolls her eyes wipes the stupid grin off my face.

Shit. Too much. Too flirty. You should have quit while you were ahead. Idiot! A girl like her probably has assholes making passes at her all day long. Assholes like you. Did you really think she could be interested in—

"Well, before we pick out rings you should at least take me out for a drink."

She smiles. I blink. Was that a joke? No, it was an invitation. This dazzling woman wants me to ask her out. On a date. And suddenly I can't think. I can barely see. My whole world is ringed in a dreamy, Vaseline-lens haze of hearts and flowers. Drink? Sure, we can have a drink. How about coffee? There's already an empty cup in my hand.

Cup? Norman. Taping! My sphincter clenches hard enough to knock Cupid's arrow out of my ass. I peer through the vacant bleachers to see the beach house scene on the other side, already in progress. Without me. Shit!

"Drink. Yeah! For sure." I stuff the coffee cup under the urn's spigot and grab a handful of creamers and sugar packets. "Sorry, I have to get back to work. Are you here all day?"

She nods. "They're holding us for the boardwalk scene later. Maybe I'll actually be in it."

"Awesome. I'll meet you back here when we wrap, then we can go for that drink. Yeah?"

Her long fingers rake her hair behind her ear. Her mouth and eyes smile as one. "Yeah."

Yeah. Never has one word meant so much. Yeah, the most spectacularly beautiful woman I've ever seen wants to go on a date. With me. Yeah. Fuck yeah.

I return to work on cloud nine. Twenty minutes later I'm in Hell.

The beach-house scene is part of the A story. The meat of the episode. Reggie the musclehead and Serge the aloof talent agent are pacing the floor with a baby. Actually a realistic baby doll. We'll have the real baby on set later and do some insert shots. It's a production thing.

The guys are swapping jokes and laying narrative pipe. Reggie found a baby on the beach. He brought it home, because that's what Nicolette did when she found that lost puppy. Serge is freaking out. *A baby is not a puppy! This is kidnapping!* And hilarity ensues. In theory.

The writers are dead silent, scribbling in the margins of their scripts.

My scene is tanking.

But at least I can save face on the blow. The last joke of the scene. It's one of my favorites in the whole script.

The "baby" is crying. Reggie holds it at arm's length. "I think the little guy is hungry. Where's Jayce with the food?"

"I don't know," Serge says, looking at his watch. "He should be back by now."

Jayce, the lovable stoner, bursts through the door with Chinese take-out containers. "Hey! I got some chow for the rugrat!"

Serge grabs a white box and pops it open. "Are you crazy? We can't feed this to a baby!"

"Dude. If you can't feed it to a baby . . . " Jayce plucks a meaty curl from the container and looks puzzled. "Why is it called *baby shrimp?*"

I guffaw. I'm alone.

The director calls, "Cut!"

Norman frowns and leans back in his chair. "Oy vey. Who farted?" He turns to the writers. "Who's got some punch-ups?"

The staff huddles, each pitching replacement jokes and gags, completely trashing and rewriting my scene on the fly. Norman just nods and chuckles. "Yes." "Good." "We'll give that a try."

I try to laugh at the new jokes, but my laughter is hollow. Each cut to my script carves a gash in my self-worth. I knew this would happen. I don't have any business writing for a prime-time hit. I screwed it all up. Oh God, I am in so far over my head. I'm on the verge of projectile vomiting by the time they slash and burn their way to the end of the scene. Norman draws a furious circle around it in his script. "Okay, who's got something for the blow? Matty? Come on, kid. Make us proud."

I flip through the wrinkled pages of my script as if I have some uncut comedy gem waiting in reserve to dazzle them. I don't. I'm stalling. I'm obviously stalling. *Think, Matty! Think, God damn you, be funny!*

"Uh, sure. How about this? Instead of baby shrimp, Jayce brings home ... baby carrots." Norman raises a bushy eyebrow as if to say, *Are you shitting me?* I laugh. "I'm kidding, obviously." I swipe the sweat off my upper lip with the back of my hand. "But seriously, he could bring baby back ribs. And Reggie could be like, 'We wouldn't be in this mess if we could give the *baby back.*'"

I cackle like an inmate at Arkham Asylum. Norman gives a long slow nod. "Uh huh. Listen, Matty. Could you be a pal and get me some more coffee?"

He doesn't look at me. Blatantly doesn't look at me.

"Oh, yeah but ... I have a few other ..." I glance to the other writers for support. Each of them finds something else they urgently need to be looking at. "I mean, yeah. Of course. I'll be right back."

Norman hands me his empty cup. "No rush."

I know I'm a dead man walking as I shuffle back to crafty, head down. That's it. It's over. I had my shot and I blew it. An entire career begun and ended over twenty-two minutes of Betacam tape.

"You all finished already?"

The melodic voice cuts the gloom. I look up to see the golden goddess, Kimberly Unpronounceable. Her dark, smoky eyes are eager and inviting.

They punch me in the gut like food poisoning. The dark eyes are wrong in a way that pollutes my senses and makes me sick. I look away and breathe through the nausea as pain sizzles across my forehead. I grope a scalding gash in my skin that doesn't exist. The burn dissipates.

I look up to see the golden goddess, Kimberly Unpronounceable. Her crystal blue eyes are eager and inviting. I swallow hard and get my bearings.

"No. No, not finished yet. I'm just taking a little break." I hold up Norman's cup. "Coffee break. To clear my head so I can think up a new gag to end the scene. The showrunner isn't a fan of the shrimp thing."

"Aww, really? I thought it was good. Cute pun. Goofy visual." She shrugs. "I laughed."

She laughed. Part of me feels like that's all that matters. My career is over, but at least I made this sweet girl laugh.

I smile at the floor. "Thanks. I'm glad."

"No, you're not. You're miserable."

I glance up. Our eyes meet, and I feel a spark of connection. I want to say I'm fine, but I can tell there's no point in lying to her. She's too smart for my bullshit.

"I am miserable. That whole scene was a catastrophe top to bottom. The writers just banished me to crafty so they can find a new blow without me standing there barfing up joke cancer."

Kimberly puts a soft hand on my shoulder. "Aww. I'm sure you'll think of something."

"I won't. I'm out of ideas. Like, what other 'baby' food is there? Baby spinach? Baby corn?" I blink. "Wait, baby bok choy. Is that funny?"

She shakes her head. "Maybe you should try a whole different direction. Like, I don't know. What do babies actually eat?"

"Baby food, I guess. Like, mashed up stuff that comes in little jars. Or milk." I snap my fingers. "Oh! What if Jayce brings back a whole cow? Or, wait, I guess little babies get their milk from ... uh ..."

I blush and gesture around my chest. Kimberly laughs. "From where? The lungs? The heart? I'm sorry, Matty, I have no idea what you're trying to say. Could you please explain in detail where little babies get milk?"

Her giggling is contagious. This is funny. This is a funny area. "What if Jayce brings a girl home from the beach?" I say. "She's wearing a bikini and he points at her chest and is like, 'If the baby wants milk, here's a couple of big jugs!'"

Kimberly gives me the stink eye. "Really? Big jugs?"

I regret opening my mouth. "Ugh, no. I don't know." I bury the heels of my palms in my eyes and rub. "It doesn't matter. We can't do it anyway."

"Why not?"

"It's too production heavy. We'd have to do a rush casting call for girls, then pick one and get her through wardrobe and hair and makeup. We'd have to shoot around it and come back for a pick-up shot, and by then the whole crew would be going into overtime, and—"

My ramble goes silent as Kimberly grips the bottom of her T-shirt and whips it off over her head. She shakes her bouncing mane over her bare shoulders and pink brassiere. My eyes go wide taking it all in. Two perfect scoops of pale vanilla breast. Toned abs at the peak of ripeness. I don't look away. I can't look away.

"What the hell are you doing?" I sputter.

"I'm saving you a casting call, obviously."

She gives me an impish grin as she pops the snap on her boardshorts. They slide without friction down the ivory of her legs and hit the floor. She steps out of them and straightens the waistband on a pair of panties that perfectly match her fancy bra. Through the lens of a TV camera they could totally pass for a bikini.

Nearby crew members start to elbow each other and point. Someone wolf whistles. My heartbeat accelerates and I grab her clothes off the floor.

"Um, okay. I get it. Thank you, but no. No. Get dressed."

I stuff her clothes into her hands. She pouts.

"But you need a bikini girl."

146

"It was just an idea! Half an idea! I can't just go over there and be like, 'Hey Norman, I think I have an area for the blow. Oh, and also a mostly naked extra.' It's insane! They'd fire my ass in a heartbeat."

Kimberly shakes her head. "Stop focusing on what could go wrong and focus on what could go right. You need a bikini girl. I need to get on camera. It was meant to be. So what do you say?"

"I say no. No, no, absolutely not, and also hell no."

Her lips curl in a roguish smile. "Fantastic. Let's do it."

With a playful flick of her arm she tosses her clothes in my face. The scent of them is intoxicating—a springtime-fresh blend of perfume and pheromones. They warm my flushed skin like the brush of a lover's cheek. I reflexively catch them and throw them down to see Kimberly in a full supermodel catwalk stride across the soundstage. Her insanely long legs devour the distance faster than my mind can comprehend what's happening.

"No. No, shit! Wait!"

I break into a run but she's already strutting up to Norman's side by the time I reach his chair. His weary eyes flick up and down her body.

"Well. There's something you don't see every day." He droops. "Unfortunately."

Kimberly laughs a musical little laugh. "Hi. Norman, right? I'm a friend of Matty's."

My palms go slick with sweat. At first I thought this girl was just insanely attractive. Now I realize she's actually, literally insane. She's going down in flames and trying to take me with her. I have to find a parachute.

"Uh, yeah. Well, actually . . . Norman, this is . . ."

I gesture to her standing there. A thing of glimmering beauty totally out of place among the hunched, pudgy lumps of the writers. Her pink underwear is gone. She's completely nude. Long, dark, and elegant. She sticks out her hip and draws my eyes up her smooth legs to a thin landing strip of fuzz above her crotch. The sight of her mocha-colored skin drills agony into my brain, like a piercing siren I see instead of hear. I drag my gaze upward, past the perfect willowy curve of her hips. Past her bare, nubile breasts and petite Hershey's Kiss nipples. Up to her face. Her adorable button nose. Big dark eyes. Shaggy black hair.

Rosebud. The name claws its way out of my burning forehead. I don't understand. Who is Rosebud? What is Rosebud?

She smiles at me, and the smile is mischievous as fuck. She's not supposed to be here. She *knows* she's not supposed to be here. I feel like I'm going to throw up, but the vomit comes out as words.

"Uh, yeah. Well, actually . . . Norman, this is Kimberly."

And it is Kimberly. The other girl sizzles out of my mind like spit on a hot radiator. Kimberly tosses her blonde curls and smiles. It's breathtaking. An ear-to-ear contradiction of sweet innocence and raw sexuality.

"Matty was just telling me the hilarious joke he came up with for the end of the scene." She giggles. "Oh my God, it's so funny. Tell 'em, Matty."

The whole stage seems to go silent as every eye turns to me. My head feels too heavy. My legs go weak and prickly. My mind is a complete blank.

"Okay, yeah. Okay. So. How about this? Jayce comes in with a hot bikini girl from the beach. Serge is like, 'What is this? You were supposed to get food for the baby.' Jayce is like, 'Dude, I did! Don't you know what babies eat?'" I gesture at Kimberly's buxom chest. She pulls back her shoulders and gives me a perfect sitcom "Oh *you!*" smile. "Then Reggie is like, 'If the baby can't finish, I'll take the leftovers!'"

Norman's eyebrows lower as his sunken eyes drift from Kimberly's breasts to me. The moment lasts a suffocating eternity before he barks out a laugh and claps his hands. "Gangbusters. Let's do it."

I suck a breath, feeding oxygen to my strangled brain. My own words echo in my mind, and I chuckle despite myself. I was born several decades too late to use the word, but I can't disagree. That joke was fucking gangbusters.

Norman turns on the other writers, shaking his pencil in a caricature of condemnation. "My God. The lot of you were sitting here for five minutes spewing mouth diarrhea while the golden boy was out snaring gals to cast his own goddamn gags." He smiles at me. "All right, hot shot. Get your friend to casting and get the paperwork filled out, then get your ass back over here. Apparently the rest of us dinosaurs can't do this without you."

I try to nod but I'm numb with shock. I was number one on Norman's shit list, and now I'm back in his good graces. All because of her.

Kimberly takes Norman's hand and gives it a graceful shake. "Thank you, sir. I really appreciate the opportunity. I'll get back here as quick as I can." She turns her spotlight smile on me. "All right, lead the way."

She lifts her hand like a princess needing an escort out of her enchanted pumpkin coach. I take her delicate fingers and her bubbly energy vibrates up my arm and into my chest as I guide her away.

"I can't actually believe that just happened," I say breathlessly. "You really saved my ass."

She squeezes my hand. "All I did was stand there. You wrote the joke."

"But I didn't write it. I mean, I had a vague idea, but I didn't know what I was going to say until you forced me to say it. Then it all just came out in one perfectly formed blurt. That doesn't happen. Ever."

Kimberly shrugs. "Maybe you're more talented than you think you are."

"Or maybe I just needed a muse." Confidence bubbles through my belly, pushing a giddy smile to my face. "And by the way, it's S. A. V. A. G. E."

149

Her eyebrow lifts. "Excuse me?"

"The proper spelling of 'Savage.' You know, in case you want to use it on your casting paperwork."

She gasps with mock offense. "Too forward! I thought you were taking me out for a drink before I took your name."

"Uh uh. You just went from extra to day player. That's a huge pay bump. You're taking *me* out for a drink now."

She laughs, but my own joke pulls a grim haze over me. The surging excitement of new love chokes under a dark shadow. Kim paying for me was funny then. On the first day. Even for that first year, when I was the one with the steady gig and she was still living check-to-check on bit parts.

It stopped being funny when Kim was paying for all the drinks. And every bill. And a house in Venice and one near Lake Arrowhead.

The black cloud of inadequacy and self-hatred pours over me until everything is dark. I feel a warm, stale breath on my lips and open my heavy eyelids.

I'm lying in bed with Kim. At the cabin. We're old. Lit only by a few sputtering candles. She's rolled over and the top of her forehead is pressed against mine. Our faces are inches apart. She smiles and whispers.

"I like that story." She takes my hands and her eyes drift closed. "I wish we could be like we were in the old days. Back before Bex was born. When it was just you and me."

My heart skips a beat. I debate. I say it. "Maybe we could give us another try. If . . . if we survive this."

Her voice is a dreamy breath. "We'll survive, Matty. One way or another."

The words wash over me as I lose consciousness.

We'll survive, Matty. Just you and me.

CHAPTER FOURTEEN

Rebecca

"Uh, no. I think you two can look after yourselves long enough for me to take a shit in private."

My father struggles to push his drunk ass upright and gives me a smug wave. "Go. I'll keep watch."

He cuts a glance at my mother, lying beside him. It's an "A man's gotta do what a man's gotta do" look. A marked acknowledgement that I'm leaving Mom in harm's way while he's staying to protect her. A display of his incredible compassion for her in the face of danger.

I let him have his moment. They'll both be dead asleep by the time I get back.

"Okay. Whatever. Thank you."

I grab a candelabra and leave, closing the door behind me. My sock feet thump down the hall. Past the extra bedroom. Past the bathroom. To my old room.

Frigid air tingles against my skin as I step inside. The blankets are missing from the little twin bed, taken to my parents' room for tonight's slumber party, but the rest is just as I left it thirteen years ago. Dusty toys and games. Magazines with pictures of cute celebrity boys I secretly hoped my mother would introduce me to. An overstuffed spiral notebook on the nightstand. I push it aside to make space for the candelabra and the flickering light plays across its cover.

Savage Expadishon Log Book.

The battered old thing smothers me under a wave of nostalgia. When I was a kid, my father and I made up a whole fantasy world in the woods around this cabin. This notebook was its bible.

I set down the candles and flop open the cover. The second I touch the pages I'm nine years old again, yanked back in time by the stiff, clumpy texture of construction paper mounted with non-toxic white school paste. The faded pages crack and stick as I turn through drawings of African tribal masks and Aztec temples and Polynesian tiki gods. Looking at it now, I realize the "Forbidden Jungle" was an impossible cultural mix-up of clichés stolen from adventure movies and NatGeo specials. But when I was a kid, it didn't matter. These were all things that existed in "the jungle," so they were all things that existed in *my* jungle.

I turn another page to find a drawing of the treasure at the end of our imaginary quest. Three blobs set in a triangle. The Mystic Stones, each with its own magical power. I run my finger over the raised wax of the crayon lines and the memories rush back to me. The Wish Stone, black and flecked with pinpricks of glittering white. It looked like the night sky, because, as the cartoon bug says, when you wish upon a star your dreams come true. The Death Stone was a fist-sized white diamond that glowed, because I'd seen one too many "near death experience" talk shows with people talking about dying and heading into the light. The Life Stone was brown, because that's what color Life cereal is.

Taped under the picture of the stones is a tracing of two tiny hands. The thumbs and index fingers are tip-to-tip, forming a triangle between the palms. Unsteady letters spell "RAFIKI" in blue ink. It was the name of the mandrill in *The Lion King*, which I learned meant "friend" in Swahili. In our world, it was a safe word that every creature in the jungle would respect. Something for Dad and I to shout if our play fighting got too intense so nobody got hurt.

The thought of it makes my heart heavy. Despite having a safe word, I know I got hurt all the time. Just like my father hurt my mother when he shoved her through the cabinet downstairs. I know he was abusive, but all these years later I barely remember the injuries. All I remember is how much fun we used to have.

The relentless screeching and scraping of the fairies behind the walls drags me back to the here and now and reminds me what I'm here for. I close the scrapbook and sit cross-legged on the floor. The cold of the hardwood pushes through my yoga pants and underwear all the way to my butt cheeks, but it's all right. The cold is bracing. It keeps me alert and renews my focus.

My hands dig into my hoodie's pockets, pulling out my phone and a set of earbuds. I plug them into the jack and my ears. I straighten my back and wake up the screen. There's still no signal, but I don't need it.

I need to clear my head.

I set the phone and its battery on the floor and run my hand over my forearm. The chill of my skin soothes the sting of the squirrel's scratches, but those aren't the wounds that bother me. I'm haunted by the old ones. The psychological scars from a time I've tried to lock away. A time I *have* locked away.

But downstairs in the kitchen it all came rushing back to my sleep-deprived mind. Memories of an adolescence spent coping with my mother's erratic behavior and emotional manipulation. The dream had been too vivid. Too real. Seeing my parents again is freeing my mental demons, and there's only one way to seal them back up. I have to clear my mind and realign my consciousness to the Energy of the Universe.

I tap the icon for my guided meditation app and my ears fill with the sound of gently falling rain. I close my eyes and try to focus on it and let my thoughts become one with the white noise. A bright, soothing voice emerges from the downpour to guide me on my journey. She asks me to relax my body, part by part, starting at the top and working downward.

"Concentrate on your forehead and brow. Without judging, observe any sensations you feel. Is your forehead warm or cool? Is there discomfort or tingling? Acknowledge anything you feel, and let it be."

I become hyperaware of the gauze wrapped around the gash on my forehead. My hands reach up to peel it away and toss it aside, letting refreshing cold air embrace the wound. I remember the shadow that lurched out of the bookcase and hit me like a whip crack. It must have been a smoke fairy. But where did it come from? Where did any of them come from? None of it makes sense. And those little freaks sure as hell aren't getting a human sacrifice. I'll grow old personally smashing every last one of them with a shovel before that happens.

"Feel the sensation in your legs and bottom. Feel your weight contacting the ground. Observe the hardness or softness of your seat."

Seat? Shit. Goddamn it. Focus, Rebecca! You've missed everything between your forehead and your ass. Your mind is wandering. Rein it in. Be present. *Concentrate.*

"Now we're going to focus on the breath. Don't force it to be anything it's not. Just let the breath flow naturally. In and owt. In . . . and owt."

The word pricks my ears. It always does when she says it. The meditation leader is Canadian. I can tell by the way she sometimes pronounces "about" as "aboot." Somebody must have told her to sound more American, because in the breathing exercises she doesn't say to breathe "oot." Or "out." She says *"owt."* Like she's consciously struggling to form the word in a way her brain and mouth are rejecting.

Fuck you, Rebecca! Stop critiquing her pronunciation and concentrate! Let your mind go blank and find some inner fucking peace! Jesus fucking Christ!

I roll my head. Roll my shoulders. Sit up straight. Breathe. In and out.

This was so much easier when I first started. Back then I wasn't listening to an app, but a real person actually in the room with me. With us. All of us in the group trying to calm our inner turmoil. The rehab counselor's voice didn't have the Canadian woman's polish. She had a tobacco rasp and the slur of cracked, damaged lips. It was the voice of someone who had been through the shit, emerged on the other side, then come back to help others find their way out.

The sound of her voice still echoes deep in my memory. I follow it, drifting farther into calm. The digital rain in my ears gets softer, and my thoughts and worries peel and fall away, returning me to that windowless basement room at the rehab center. The place where Bex Savage died and Rebecca Strong was born.

Warmth sizzles through my body, starting at the base of my spine and expanding to my solar plexus and heart. It flares in my throat and across the top of my head. It's an odd sensation I've never felt before. I can tell that this strange energy surging through my chakras is hot enough to burn my physical body to a cinder, but I feel no pain.

Its white light spirals in explosive arcs around me like slashes forming in ice under a twirling figure skater. In the center of my forehead my ajna chakra awakens. The spinning, burning light goes still, leaving me in perfect silence. Perfect calm. My consciousness sets down on a glowing plane of white light shrouded in an endless sea of luminous golden mist.

This is not meditation. This is something different. An unfamiliar place I've never been. But I'm not afraid of it. I just experience it.

A shadow creeps in at the periphery of the hazy light. I don't see it with my eyes. I see it with my mind. I sense it with my awakened third eye. I feel the shadow and know it's there.

As my awareness grows, the shape gathers detail. It's a dark cloud, swirling with heavy particles. I don't focus on it. I just remain aware of its presence and take a step closer. The clumps flutter. They flock. They are smoke fairies. We are all that exists here. Me and them inside this infinite golden void. Alone. Nothing else.

The monsters swirl and dart in a great sweeping mass. Agitated. They don't want me to know they're here. They want to escape the gaze of my mind's eye, but there's nowhere to go. There's nowhere to hide.

They change.

It's a shift of impossible subtlety. A slide from three dimensions to a geometry beyond human understanding. I am aware of the entire flock, and at the same time I am aware of only one consciousness. The fairies are not many. They are an illusion of many.

They are one thing.

It is a swarm. And it isn't. It doesn't want me to know. It doesn't want me to see. It took this form to scare me, but I am not afraid here. The consciousness becomes a single shape etched black against the yellow light, simultaneously a flock of fairies and a girl. The silhouette of a long, lean girl. Her hair thrashes in short, jet-black tufts of shadow as she rushes toward me at speed. I do not flinch. I know she cannot hurt me inside my own mind.

The shadow girl pulls back an arm and jabs four stiffened fingers into the gash in my forehead. Pain shoots through my frontal lobe like a shotgun slug.

Flash.

My eyes fly open and I tumble backwards, sucking a gasp of air. I'm back in my bedroom at the cabin. The sharp sound of rainfall is injected into my head. Dull fairy scratching pours in somewhere behind it. I yank the buds from my ears, and my body tingles like I've been rubbing on shag carpet. What the hell was that? I've been meditating for more than five years and I've never seen anything like it. I stuff my phone in my pocket and scramble to my feet. I don't know what it was, but I know it's important. I have to tell my parents what I saw, the shadow thing and—

Flash.

Dazzling pain so intense I can see it. A hot white beam of torment. I falter. I take another step.

Flash.

The agony is beyond physical. Something stabs the pain receptors deep inside my brain. A sledgehammer lands on the gash in my forehead.

Flash.

Photographers circulate, taking candid pictures. I'm in the ballroom of a club in downtown Los Angeles. Dim lighting soaks into dark wood and red velvet curtains all around me. Chatter and light music fills my ears. I'm surrounded by formalwear. It's an awards afterparty. I can tell by the giant reproduction of the golden statuette at the front of the hall. My hair is piled on top of my head, and I'm wearing the same tight black pencil dress I wore last month at my fifteenth birthday party. Mom says the camera loves me in it. She says it makes me look sophisticated.

A waiter sweeps up to me with a tray of crab cakes.

"Would the lady care for an hors d'oeuvre?"

Oh God, the lady would devour that whole tray if she could. I got rail thin after I stopped playing sports. My mother loves it. She says "classic waif" is a perfect style for me, and I know she's right. Sometimes it makes me upset that I can't eat what I want, but I just want to be perfect for her.

"No, thank you. But they look lovely."

The waiter nods and moves on. I spot Mom standing at a tall cocktail table, swirling a tumbler of whisky, gorgeous in her red sequined dress. She's trying to appear upbeat and gracious, but I know her too well. She's devastated.

Mom was up for Best Supporting Actress for her performance as a stoic single mother in *The Cupcake Club*. She didn't win. People say it was a fluke she even got nominated, since the movie was a romantic comedy. The award ended up going to the lady who played the drug-addicted Army sergeant in *Blood and Duty*. I glide up beside her and she gives me a sideways look and sighs.

"How are you feeling, Mom?"

"I'm enduring," she says quietly.

I can tell. There are three empty tumblers hiding on the chair under her table. I fidget with my silver charm bracelet. "You should have won, you know. Your performance was the best."

She sips her drink. "I know. But my movie was garbage."

"It wasn't. It was awesome. People loved it."

"People loved it. Not critics. It was a sappy romcom masquerading as poignant cinema." Mom looks out over the sea of Hollywood hot shots. "*Blood and Duty* was dark and gritty. It had gravitas. It meant something. That's the kind of film that wins awards. Not the cutesy drivel I do."

Shame twists my belly. Mom never did "cutesy drivel" movies before I made her start spending time with me. But once the paparazzi got shots of the two of us in public her whole image instantly changed from "badass action star" to "vivacious mom." She got offered the role of the fashion-model mother in *Day Care Divas*, because the director said candid photos of us together showed she had "a mom vibe without a mom bod." After that movie was a hit, she played the moms in *Princess of Huntington High* and *Parent Teacher Disassociation* before *The Cupcake Club*.

She hasn't been home much since Hollywood discovered what a great mother she is.

"Your movies aren't cutesy. They have heart." I smile. "Everyone says you're America's favorite mom."

"Don't remind me." She shoots the rest of her drink.

Worry shivers up the back of my neck. "But . . . I thought you liked being a mother."

"I like being *your* mother. That doesn't mean I want to be the mother of every snot-nosed tween who can pass a screen test." Her eyes are dull and dilated as she runs her finger around the rim of her empty glass. "I want to do a film that means something. I want to be *fierce*. But I've gotten sucked into an endless whirlpool of warm, soft mother roles and I'm drowning in it."

Her face is radiant in her full awards-show makeup, but I can see the deep sadness beneath it. Guilt creeps through me like frost.

"It's my fault. Nobody ever would have cast you as a mother before I made you start hanging out with me. I ruined your whole image."

She puts her hand on my arm. "It's not your fault, sweetie. It's theirs. They refuse to believe I can act, so they stick me in roles that mirror what I really am." She smiles sadly. "They'll never see me as anything but a loving mother."

A brick drops in my belly. She's too nice to say it, but I know she blames me. And she should. She's not *a* loving mother. She's *my* loving mother. She's typecast as a mother because of *me*. Because *I* made her stop looking for meaningful roles so I could have her all to myself. I'm such an asshole!

Rage seeps through my muscles and hardens like ice. I hate myself so much. I wish I could go back in time and stop myself from destroying her career, but I can't. I can't unbreak what I broke. I just have to hope Mom can forgive me someday.

None of this shows on my face. I remain a cool slate of calm. Mom taught me to never look upset when there are cameras around. Those are the pictures they'll use when they run some negative gossip about you and make you look like a monster.

I feel like a monster.

"Kimberly Savage. The biggest tragedy of the evening." It's a man's voice. I blink and see him easing up to our table. He's stocky with a wild shock of gray-streaked black hair and round, wire-rimmed glasses. "You were robbed. Absolutely robbed. I thought you were magnificent in your film."

His accent is indistinctly foreign, European or Baltic or something. Mom straightens up and gives him a beaming smile—equal parts modest and flirty. "Thank you. That means a lot coming from you. I have tremendous respect for your work, Mr. VanDuzer."

He waves his hand. "Please. Mr. VanDuzer was my papa's name. I'm just Robert." He smiles and gestures at me. "And who is this lovely creature?"

I blush. "I'm Bex. Bex Savage."

"Oh. Savage." His eyes flick to Mom, then back to me. "Yes, I see the family resemblance. Sisters?"

"She's my mother."

"We're like sisters." Mom quickly adds. She tips her head and gives him a coy grin. "We're both very impressed with your haul tonight. How many awards did you pick up? All of them?"

VanDuzer chuckles. He's talking to Mom, but still looking at me. "Well, just the ones I was nominated for. Best Picture, Best Director, Best Original Screenplay."

The swagger in his tone is justified. Robert VanDuzer is a real Hollywood big-shot. People *and* critics loved his latest movie. *The Last Fifteen Minutes* is a dystopian nightmare about a terrorist cult that uses reality TV to recruit followers and start World War III.

Mom moves closer. "You must be so proud. That's such a huge accomplishment." She flutters her eyelashes. "So, what's next for tonight's big winner? Do you already have another project in the works?"

VanDuzer nods distractedly. "Yes, of course. My next script is about a woman who becomes a vigilante killer while seeking justice for her murdered daughter. It's a gritty exploration of trauma and loss and their effects on mental health, but I think ultimately a story of female empowerment."

Mom bites her lower lip. "It sounds delicious. Do you have anyone attached?"

VanDuzer shakes his head. "Not yet. There's a lot of new talent interested, but I'm looking for someone a little more worldly. It's a meaty role. I need someone with a track record."

My mother is practically drooling, but VanDuzer is oblivious. He's preoccupied with me. Her daughter. With me standing here he can't see her as a gritty vigilante killer. He's too blinded by my cutsey drivel. I have to do something.

"It sounds like a perfect Kimberly Savage role," I say, putting a hand on my mother's back. "She's very worldly. And experienced. She's traveled all over the place shooting movies."

VanDuzer purses his lips. "Is that so?"

Mom smiles. "Well, yes. And as a mother, your idea really strikes a chord with me. I know the bond between a mother and child on a visceral level, so I understand how a woman could be driven to extreme measures in the name of justice for her daughter."

"Uh huh." VanDuzer nods and tips a hand to me. "Are you a footie fan?"

I blink. "A what?"

He shakes his head sharply. "I'm sorry. *Soccer* you call it here. Are you a fan?"

My eyebrow raises. "Um, yeah. But how did—"

"Your bracelet," he says, pointing to my arm.

I unconsciously put my hand over my charm bracelet. It's so subtle. Just three tiny soccer balls on a sterling silver chain. They just look like big silver beads unless you look really close.

He must have been looking really close.

"So, who's your favorite for World Cup?" he asks. "I'm thinking USA doesn't have a chance."

I shrug. "Maybe in men's. Our women's team just won the CONCACAF U-20 Championship. They're rocking it this year."

A chuckle escapes VanDuzer's throat. "That is true. If Leroux keeps it up she'll be taking home the Golden Boot for sure."

"Well, I think she's a *shoe* in," Mom says. Her voice is playful, but I can tell she's acting. A musky tension pulses off her, like she knows she's losing her audience and doesn't know how to get him back. She puts her hand on VanDuzer's upper arm and catches him in the high beams of her smile. "I love soccer. We should go catch a game together some time."

VanDuzer politely pulls himself free of her grasp. Her smile fades.

"Of course. We could all go. I have season tickets for the Galaxy." VanDuzer grins at me. "I also have a signed Beckham jersey upstairs."

I cock my head toward the open mezzanine. "Upstairs?"

VanDuzer rolls his eyes. "Right. Sorry. I live in this building." He points up. "Thirty-seventh floor. Penthouse. My den is like an unofficial FIFA hall of fame." He meets my gaze. "Maybe you'd be interested in coming up for a little show and tell?"

The hair on the back of my neck bristles. Something about this feels wrong. Greasy. I catch my reflection in his tiny round glasses and imagine myself as he sees me. My black velvet dress making my narrow body appear curvier than it really is. Bold mascara making my pale blue eyes more striking than they really are. Mahogany lipstick plumping my lips. Artfully applied blush raked against my cheekbones to throw them into high relief.

I'm fraudulently beautiful.

I suddenly feel sick. He's not staring at me because I'm throwing Mom's motherhood vibe in his face. He's staring because he's *crushing* on me.

Mom puts her hand on my back and tosses her hair. "Oh, that would be wonderful! That's so generous of you to offer."

"Nonsense. I'm proud to show off my collection." VanDuzer claps his hands. "Tell you what. Let me go grab my statuettes from my manager and we can go up right now."

"Fantastic," Mom says.

VanDuzer smiles and hustles away. Mom grips my hand and speaks in an excited whisper. "Bex, that role is perfect for me."

"I know! It totally is."

"I need you to do me a favor." She cuts a quick glance at VanDuzer trotting across the room, then turns back to me. "Go look at his sports stuff and change the subject back to the movie. Turn on the charm and convince him how great I'd be for the part."

"Yeah, okay, but . . . We're both going to do that, right?"

Mom shakes her head. "I'll just come off as a desperate egomaniac if I do it. It's more sincere if you say it without me looming over you like a coach. Plus I don't know jack about soccer. I'd only embarrass myself in front of him." Her smile beams. "This is all you. It's your moment to shine, sweetheart. Make me proud."

A lump forms in my throat. "I don't think I should go up with him alone. I . . . I mean . . ." I lean in closer and whisper confidentially. "Mom, I think . . . I think he like, *likes* me."

Mom wrinkles her nose. "Don't be ridiculous. He's just looking for someone to show off to. That's how men are. You have to learn to take advantage of these moments if you want to get ahead in the world."

I pick at my thumbnail. "I know, but I just . . . I don't want to go alone, okay? You come up too."

My mother gently shushes me. She puts her hands on my shoulders and leans in. "Bex, you know I'd do anything for you. Because I love you more than anything. Do you know that?"

I nod. "I know you do, Mom."

"I've worked so hard to give you everything you've ever wanted and I've never asked for anything in return. Now I'm just asking you for a favor. One simple little favor. You have VanDuzer's attention. Make him see things your way. Please. It would mean so much to me."

Her eyes are inches from mine. Intense. She wants this so bad I can feel it pulsing off her. I'm stupid to resist. VanDuzer just wants to show me his sports stuff. That's all. I could easily turn the conversation to the movie. I can get her that role. I owe her.

VanDuzer prances back over to us. He's got two statuettes in one hand, one in the other. He glances at Mom before focusing on me. "Are you ladies ready to go upstairs?"

Bile and adrenalin slosh in my guts. Sweat beads on my scalp and under my arms. I look up at Mom. She looks at me, her eyes soft and pleading. I turn to VanDuzer.

"Oh, uh. Some reporter guy just came over and said he wants to do a post-show interview in a few minutes. So she's gonna have to stay here for that." My throat closes. "Do you mind if I come up by myself?"

"Oh, well, that's fine, I just . . . " He blinks and turns to Mom. "We can wait. Are you sure you don't want to join us?"

Mom looks from him to me. My longing for her to stop this burns in my eyes. I can feel it. She can see it. She looks away.

"No, you two go have fun. I'll catch up with you later."

Her face is blank as she turns and walks away, taking long, purposeful strides toward an interview that doesn't exist. VanDuzer watches her go, then grins and sticks out an elbow.

"All right, then. Shall we, m'lady?"

I don't want to touch him, but I don't want to be rude. I thread my arm through his, feeling the warm humidity of his body. He leads me toward the elevator and my entire soul goes heavy with dread. My feet are like ice, frozen to the ground. Anxiety burns through my veins like lava but my skin is icy cold.

It's not right.

The cold isn't right.

I grab it with my whole awareness and pull myself toward it. The nightmare drags against my consciousness like a cheese grater and I scream as I scrape through it. Hazy yellow light burns through me and I open my eyes to the frosty air of reality.

I reel with disorientation. My forehead throbs. My stomach burns with bile, sizzling all the way up my throat. I taste it on my tongue and feel it dribbling down my chin. The flavor is a long-forgotten memory.

It's not bile. It's whisky.

My fist is clenched around the neck of Mom's bottle of Jameson. I gag and fling it away like a poisonous snake.

"What the—"

My sock feet are freezing and wet. I'm not in my bedroom. I'm standing in snow. The sound of the clawing, screeching fairies is close and clear and sharp.

I'm outside the cabin.

Outside! Fairies! Fuck! I'm fucking dead!

I spin around and drop into a fighting crouch. The cabin looms in front of me, alive with smoke fairies. Hundreds of thousands of them swarming like black ants on a gigantic gingerbread house. My snowy footprints lead backwards up the stairs to the front door, which hangs wide open into the living room entryway. A solid rectangle of fairies still gnaw at its wooden face, as if they don't even realize they're already inside the house.

They're not trying to get in.

Then what the hell are they doing?

Figure it out later!

I break into a run toward the porch. My body feels wrong, heavy and off-balanced. I push through it. I have to get to my parents. Nothing else matters. The world drifts in a lazy spiral as I mount the front stairs. I pitch forward and slam against the frozen wood. My vision flashes but I don't feel any pain.

I'm too drunk to feel anything.

The night is illuminated by strings of tasteful paper lanterns and the wriggling blue web of light reflected off water. My hair is wet. There's a mostly empty bottle of Malibu rum in my right hand. I'm slouched in a stained white armchair next to a pool. My mother's pool. This chair belongs in her living room. My meager weight barely makes a dent in its plush cushion. I'm a seventeen-year-old skeleton etched with tattoos.

Something slides up my numb thigh and into my crotch. It's warm and wet against me. Inside me. My head bobbles loose on my shoulders as I look down at myself. I'm wearing nothing but a soaking-wet black tank top and a pair of pink Hello Kitty panties pushed aside to expose the goods. My left hand grips the hair of a boy with his face buried in my lap.

The boy groans and comes up for air. He's cute, whoever he is. Like a low-rent James Franco. I squint at him. "Did I tell you to stop?"

He flashes a charming smile. "Come on, girl. It's my turn. How about something for me?"

"Quit being a little bitch and eat my pussy."

I take a hard pull of rum and push his face back into my snatch. He doesn't resist, he just goes to work. Lapping and grunting. He's fucking loving this. All I feel is the sandpaper of his stubble against my thighs.

My eyes drift and try to catch focus. Images fade in and out like they're painted on layers of cellophane. We're not alone. Mom's backyard is full of people—teenagers mostly. Some could be in college. Somehow a bunch of furniture has made its way outside. Mom's king-size mattress lies in the grass under a gang of hornballs gearing up for an orgy. The living room couch is by the edge of the pool with three soggy dudes sitting on it, dangling their feet in the water while they pass a bong. Everything is noise in my ears and eyes. Splashing. Laughter. Music. Red Solo cups.

It's a party.

My party, apparently.

Mom's out of town again, shooting another of her gritty, socially relevant, piece-of-shit shaky-cam dramas. Her streak of uplifting family-friendly films ended after she played the psycho vigilante mom in *Justified Killing*. The movie and that shitlick VanDuzer won Best Picture and Best Screenplay. Mom was nominated for Best Actress, but didn't win. It didn't matter. After that, people finally wanted her for their "serious" movies. She was happy as a pig in shit, and that selfish fucking bitch forgot all about me.

My teeth grind. My anger is a constant, white-hot flame in my soul. Keeping the fire wet is the only thing that prevents it from burning me alive.

The Malibu sloshes in my throat as I take the rest of the bottle in a single long, hard pull.

Budget Franco lifts himself out of my lap and wipes his glistening chin on the back of his hand. "Mmm. Good and juicy." He leans back, butt on his heels, and grins. "Now you gotta give me something. I've earned it."

My eyes narrow. "You haven't earned shit. Fuck off."

He chuckles and unzips his pants. "Don't even play like you're not DTF. You've banged half the guys at this party. You're a dick dumpster."

Fury scalds through my numbness. I'm furious at him for saying that. I'm furious at myself because it's true.

"I said fuck off!"

I lurch forward and pound a bony fist into his face. He laughs. He rubs his cheek and fucking laughs. "Dang, you're a wild child, aren't you?"

My arm throbs all the way to the shoulder. This asshole thinks I'm playing. I hit him as hard as I could and he thinks I'm playing. I scoot back in the deep chair and pull my knees to my chest. The knobs of them are cartoonishly large against the sticks of my legs. I wish I wasn't so goddamn skinny.

You have to be skinny. You're a classic waif. Nobody will love you if you're not skinny.

Budget Franco wrestles his throbbing cock out of his boxers and waves it at me. He thinks he's going to fuck me. He thinks he deserves it.

I've earned it, he said.

Fuck that. My pussy is hard currency. This guy doesn't have anything I want. He's lucky I let him go down on me at all. I'm not a fucking charity.

He plants his hands on the arms of the chair and pulls himself up off the ground. A grin spreads on his face as he moves to slide on top of me. I lean back and kick a heel into his Adam's apple. He drops to his knees on the concrete pool deck, gasping to pull a breath through his swelling windpipe. I push myself over the arm of the chair and wobble to my feet, calmly strutting past a few gawking strangers and through the open sliding-glass doors into the house.

Fucking asshole.

All the doors are hanging open, but there's barely anybody inside. Mostly just people too fucked-up on drugs to cope with the noise and commotion in the backyard. A college guy with no sleeves and a backwards baseball cap comes through the front door hugging a box of mismatched liquor bottles. Just the sight of him cools the fire raging through me.

"Davis, my darling!"

I sweep over to him and reach for a bottle. He turns away from me. "Ah ah. Not so fast." He eyes me with fake skepticism. "You're twenty-one, right?"

A smirk cracks my lips. "Yes, officer. Let me show you my ID."

I lift my shirt, flashing him my tits. Two perky teardrops of premium jailbait perched on visible ribcage. Davis smiles. "Yes, ma'am. Everything appears in order."

"Thanks, doll." I slide a bottle of Cuervo out of the box with one hand and caress his bristly face with the other. I plant a kiss on his lips. He kisses back, wet and sloppy, contaminated with flakes of chewing tobacco. We both understand this is just a down payment. He'll want to party for a while before I pay the balance. Davis and I have an arrangement.

He reaches for his pocket. "There's some beer in the trunk if you want to grab it."

I realize something is flying toward my face. Time seems to slow down as it lazily tumbles toward me. A couple of car keys on a ring looped through a ragged hemp bracelet. Somehow my hand moves in front of it and it slaps into my palm.

I blink and smile. "You're too good to me, babe."

But he's already gone. Off to find his friends. I slip the bracelet around my bony wrist and its weight seems to pull me off balance. The room spins around me. I need to sit down, but there are only indentations in the white carpet where the furniture should be. I laugh. Right. It's in the backyard. My hands instinctually crack open the fresh bottle and tip it to my lips. I know the tequila is burning in my throat but I can't feel it. I'm so numb. So wonderfully numb.

My feet move. I'm walking. Staggering down the hallway toward the kitchen. There's someone in front of me. Someone tall. Too tall. A red scowl peers out of a yellow wreath.

"What the hell, Bex? What the *hell*?" The voice is quiet but hot with rage. I blink. I focus.

It's my mother.

She's pulling a roller bag. Back from shooting on-location in East Whereverthefuck. I smile. "Hi, Mom. I threw you a welcome home party."

Her face is tight with fury. "Rebecca Lynn Savage, you get these people out of my house this minute!"

"Oooh. Or what? You gonna call the cops on me? Or are you gonna throw down some of your famous *vigilante justice*?" I wobble and catch my balance. "Go ahead. Call 'em. Be a drama queen about it. Maybe you'll finally win your precious gold statue."

Mom's cheeks boil. "God damn it, Bex! What is *wrong* with you?"

"Aww, you seem tense." I grin and raise my tequila. "Can I get you a drink?"

Mom snatches the bottle in my hand and tries to yank it away, but freezes when she notices the flaky ink on my wrist.

"Oh God! Another one?" I wince as she cranes my arm around to get a look at it. Fancy script scrolling across my wrist screams *Fuck the World*. She throws my arm away in disgust, sloshing booze on the wall. Tears pool in her eyes. "You are seventeen years old. Why are you doing this to yourself?"

"Don't act like you care."

Mom's hands tighten into fists. "I do care! How can you think I don't care?" Her horror cycles back to anger. "Who did this to you? Who? His ass is going to prison! You can't tattoo an underage girl. It's against the law!"

I shrug. "I know a guy who likes blow jobs better than paperwork."

My mother just stares. "So is that what you do now? Is that who you are? Someone who exchanges sex for favors?" A storm of emotion crackles behind her eyes. "My God. What happened to my perfect little girl?"

"Don't act like you don't know," I growl.

"I don't!" she cries. "Why don't you tell me?"

Anger scorches my throat, lowering my voice. "Your perfect little girl died when she fucked Robert VanDuzer. Because *you* asked her to."

Mom's face flushes white. Her voice is a ghost. "I did no such thing."

"Don't even try to play innocent! You wanted to be in his movie so bad you practically stripped me down and threw me in his bed with a fucking bow on my crotch! And then you didn't even care what happened!"

My mother's eyes go wide. "*What?* I never ... I didn't know *anything* happened!" Her tone is pure surprise. Too pure. Actress pure. "You just went to look at sports things, didn't you?"

"Really? Fucking really, Mom?" My blood is hot in my ears. "I came back to the party twenty minutes later with my hair all fucked up and my makeup smeared, walking like I got kicked in the crotch, and it never occurred to you that maybe we didn't just look at some old FIFA jerseys? Really?"

Mom blinks away. "I was upset that night. I was drinking. My senses were dulled." She clears her throat and looks at the floor. "I only asked you to talk to him. Nothing more. If anything else happened, it was your own choice. And I'm sorry if you have regrets, but I am not responsible for your actions. You are."

Her words are so carefully chosen they feel rehearsed. She knows what happened. She's always known. The boiler in my chest belches flame.

"*Regrets?* I let him fuck me to get you that role and you took it and abandoned me like garbage! Now you're in all these fancy-ass movies acting like you're hot shit, but you know the truth! You're an aging, no-talent has-been who couldn't score a decent part without pimping her daughter's pussy!"

My mother's hand cuts the air, slapping me across the face hard enough to throw me off balance. I hit the wall. Drop the bottle. Crumple to the tile floor. She towers over me, seething. "Get out of my house. Get out and don't ever come back!"

She grabs her roller bag and storms down the hall, her boot heels pounding like hammers. She's up the stairs. She's gone.

The furnace in my soul explodes. Searing rivets puncture my skin and flames rip through my brain. There is no more thought. No more reason. Nothing is left but white-hot rage. I grab the spilled bottle and pour half of it down my throat, then climb shakily to my feet and fumble toward the front door.

I hate her. I hate her with a blinding intensity. For the very last time I'm going to do what my mother told me to.

I'm going to leave and never come back.

I fall through the open door and fumble onto the porch. Down the steps. Into the driveway. It's a parking lot of shitty cars owned by the shitty people at my party. I pinball off scraped fenders and dinged doors as I make my way to the street. My legs give out and I hit the pavement in front of a rusty old Mustang.

I know this car. This is Davis's car.

The keys jangle on my wrist.

I pull myself up and grab the handle of the driver's side door.

No!

No! No! Hell no!

171

I'm screaming inside my mind, clawing at the walls of my psyche. I don't want to relive this memory. I don't want to *have* this memory. Every part of my subconscious pushes against it. I feel like I'm underwater, scratching through a crust of ice, desperate for breath. Shit. Shit! These flashbacks aren't random. They're the worst days of my life. That dark shadow is in my head, digging through my brain, trying to break my—

I gasp a frozen lungful of air. I'm out. My hand isn't gripping the door handle of the Mustang. It's gripping the door handle of a snow-covered Lexus. The image comes into perfect focus for a blip of a second before the mental ice crashes down on me and pushes me back under the surface of my own mind.

I'm behind the wheel of Davis's car. I'm driving. Fast. So fast the whole world is a blur. The car swings heavily through the narrow curves of the Hollywood Hills. Tears stream down my face. I punch the clutch. Grind the gears. Go faster.

I pound my bare foot onto the gas, turning my rage into horsepower. The engine and I roar as one. I want to drive fast enough to get away from my mother. Away from myself. Away from this whole fucked-up world.

My skinny arms don't have the strength to drag the wheel through a sharp turn. Metal scrapes and glass shatters as the Mustang sideswipes parked cars. Through the mud in my senses I overcompensate. Swing wide. Cross the center line.

Headlights blind me. Two or ten or a hundred. It's impossible to tell. My eyes are clouded with booze and tears. Tires scream. A horn blares. I want to turn away but I don't even know which direction away is.

For the briefest instant a tree flashes in the headlights.

The hood crumples.

The steering wheel goes through my face like an axe splitting a log.

CHAPTER FIFTEEN

Kimberly
Twenty-Three Years Ago

Something is beeping. Uneven beeps. More than one beeping thing. I don't know. I can't move. The doctors cranked my epidural so high my body is a vague dream. Flesh and bones have melted away into dull sensations. A wall of blue curtain stands on my chest, blocking my view of my dismemberment. I feel no pain, but I feel pressure. Heavy pressure on my ribcage. Pulling. Ripping. It's a nightmare inside my own skin.

Panic tries to grip me but slides off my numbed muscles like Teflon. They're tearing me apart and there's nothing I can do. Nineteen agonizing hours of labor only to be forced into an emergency C-section. As if pregnancy hasn't done enough to destroy my body, now they're carving me like a Jack-O'-lantern. I'll be hideous.

I can bounce back from hideous. Just please, please let there be complications. Let there be some unforeseeable "tragedy" that ends this thing right now before it can end me. Before I end up like my mother, dragged down by an anchor at the end of an umbilical cord.

Tears stream down my cheeks and I can't even move my hands to wipe them away. Matty's rubber-gloved fingers do it for me as he coos supportive gibberish.

"It's okay, honey. You're doing great. Just keep breathing. You're doing really great."

He looms over me, draped in a hospital gown and hair cover. That asshole. He did this to me. I want to stab him in the belly and rip the wound wide and deep. I want him to feel what I feel. I want him to know what it is to be violated. A sob chokes my throat and Matty's eyes go wet with compassion.

"I know it hurts. Be strong. You're so strong. You can do this."

Shut up! As much as I yearn to punish him I know it's not what I really want. I want to wrap myself around him and pull him back in time. I close my eyes and think of the gazebo. I want to be there. I want to be then. I want to go back to when I believed I could trust him. Before he hurt me. But that time is gone forever.

The pulling stops. The doctors' chatter intensifies.

A baby cries.

My baby. It's here. It's alive and it's real.

Matty's eyes smile. "It's over. You did it, honey. You did it."

The room fills with gasping screams, high pitched from an undersized throat. Matty's surgical mask kisses me on the forehead and he's gone. I'm alone. I'm a disembodied head abandoned behind a curtain. I don't know how long I stare into the lights before I decide I want to go into them. I don't want feeling to ever come back to my wrecked body. I don't want them to stitch me back together. I just want to be free of all this.

I want to die.

As the darkness closes in, a nurse comes from behind the curtain with Matty in tow. Even with his mask on I can see the smile pulling the skin of his cheeks to their breaking point. His palm caresses the top of my head. "Congratulations, Mom. It's a girl."

The nurse carefully rests a screaming blanket on my chest, just below my face. It's too loud and too close. I crane my neck to look at it. A wrinkled, misshapen purple lump slathered in my blood.

My daughter.

She's so tiny. A human on an absurdly miniature scale. So frail and vulnerable. An overwhelming sense of wonder mixes with terror as maternal instinct attempts to bind my soul to this new life I have created.

I brought this person into the world. She came out of me. I made her.

I will try to love her.

CHAPTER SIXTEEN

Matty

I drift on the vaporous edge of consciousness. One arm is wrapped around something soft and warm. The other tingles with pain. My eyelids peel open, drawing me fully out of slumber.

The candles have burned out, but the bedroom is still bathed in a dim glow. The source of it stings my eyes in the darkness—a narrow, sideways H of scalding white light pushing from the edges of the closed window shutters.

Sunlight.

Hope rises in my chest. It's morning. We survived the night.

My left arm is curled around Kim's waist. She's still in her sleeping bag on the bed beside me. I can feel her breathe, the gentle rise and fall of her solid core swaddled inside the fluffy thermal layers. My right arm is under her pillow, crackling with pins-and-needles. The blood flow has been choked off by the weight of her head, but I don't even care.

I'm so close to her. My lips are inches from the back of her long neck. I could nuzzle in and kiss her behind the ear. Gently coax her awake like I did so many sleepy Sunday mornings in the house in Venice. It's a muscle memory of my heart. It feels so natural. So right. I pucker up and move in.

Kim's eyes jolt open with a snort. "Whazza? Whuh?" Her weight bucks and shimmies in my grip as she blinks her eyes into focus. "Ugh. Whaz happening?"

I retreat to my side of the bed, guilt jabbing at my guts. *Oh, nothing. You just happened to wake up before your creepy-ass ex started making out with your unconscious body Bill Cosby style. For God's sake, Matty! What were you thinking?*

"It's okay. It's morning." I rub my numb arm and get up, like it had been my plan all along. "The sun's up. We can find your keys and get out of here."

Kim sits bolt upright. "Where's Rebecca?"

I sweep a glance over the room. There's no sign she ever came back from the bathroom last night. "I don't know. She was supposed to wake me up after—"

"Shhh!" Kim's eyes are huge. "Listen!"

I do. I hear nothing but the faint chirp of birds outside the barricaded window. "What?"

"The fairies. They're gone!" She grabs my arm and squeezes. "Oh my God, Matty. They got her blood. They killed her!"

The thought chills me to the bone.

They killed Bex. Those little monsters killed your only daughter because you fell asleep instead of protecting her. She's dead because you're a useless, irresponsible sack of shit.

I hurl myself off the bed and my socks slide on the dusty floor. "No! She's fine!" I yank open the bedroom door, fumbling the knob in my numb fingers. The air in the hall is frigid. "Rebecca!" Kim wriggles out of her sleeping bag and springs to her feet beside me. In an instant we're both darting in and out of darkened rooms, screaming her name. She doesn't answer.

A shaft of sunlight is beaming up from the stairway. It doesn't make sense. My feet pound the steps down to the living room. It's a wreck from last night's fighting and fires, and the ceiling is black with soot. I see it all clearly for the first time, illuminated in broad daylight blazing through the front door.

The front door is open.

Snowflakes stick to the far edge of the carpet, swirling in on the chill breeze. Kim throws a hand to her mouth and gasps. "She went outside!" She hobbles past me at speed, clutching her wrecked leg, the pain eclipsed by her need to move. Her bare feet stamp petite prints in the wet snow as she hops down the front steps. I follow her.

I sense something is wrong before I see it.

The Lexus is gone.

Kim's scream echoes through the naked winter forest. Her black SUV is on the other side of the clearing, off kilter. Its front end is wrapped around an ancient white oak.

"No! Oh God, no!" Kim shrieks. "Rebecca!"

She blasts across the field toward the car. I trot along behind her. The morning sun is making short work of the thin snowfall, but it's still no picnic to be running in without shoes. My soles burn and my socks grow heavy with slush. I spit an expletive as my frozen toe cracks against something, sending it skittering away.

It's the huge bottle of whisky, completely drained.

Kim reaches the car and throws the door open. Bex's body slouches lifelessly in the driver's seat, the spent airbag hanging flaccid in her lap. Her lips are blue as a glacier. Kim takes her daughter's pale face in her palms and rubs it with her thumbs. "Oh God. Please be okay. Please be okay."

My heart is beating so hard it pulls pain through my left arm. I'm going to have a heart attack and I don't even care. I'm too shocked to care about anything. Bex is gone. My sweet, funny little girl is dead. Because of me. I didn't protect her and now she—

Kim laughs. A single, sharp gag of wet, snotty joy. Bex's eyes are open. Just a crack. A whisper croaks from her throat. "Mom?"

My pounding heart stumbles with a surge of relief. "Oh thank God."

Bex blinks and hisses as she tries to pull her head upright. Kim releases her and backs off. "Go slow. Take it easy. You're going to be okay." She turns to me. "Matty! Pop the trunk. There's a space blanket in the emergency kit."

I do as I'm told. Packed with some jumper cables and a reflective triangle is a pouch labeled *Emergency Blanket—90% heat retention!* I tear open the packet and shake out a large sheet of thin, crinkly Mylar. When I turn to bring it to Bex, I glimpse the cabin and stop dead.

It's a standing ruin. The whole thing looks like it got put through a dull belt sander. Hundreds of thousands of tiny claw and teeth marks have eroded the husky logs of the walls to a ragged fraction of their former thickness. The shingles of the roof lie in shredded scraps over bare wood. The blanket of slush around the foundation is brown and bristled with sawdust.

But the fairies are nowhere to be seen.

A tiny seed of relief takes root as I hustle back to the driver's seat. Bex sits sideways with her feet on the running board, hunched over and shivering. Kim takes the foil blanket and wraps it gingerly around Bex's shoulders, and she gathers it closed in her trembling hands. "Thank you."

Kim looks into her daughter's face. "Rebecca, what happened?"

Bex shakes her head and sucks a hiss through the whiplash. "I don't know."

"What are you doing out here?"

"I don't know!" Bex snaps. Her eyes wobble blearily between us. "Something happened to me last night. It was like a nightmare, but it was real. It made me drive the car."

"So you were like, sleepwalking?" I ask.

"I wasn't asleep. The fairies made me do it." She crushes her face. "I mean, the thing that wants us to think it's fairies did."

Nothing she's saying makes any sense. Kim sniffs the air and horror overtakes her face. "You've been drinking."

"No, I haven't," Bex says.

"Don't lie to me. I can smell the whisky on your breath."

Bex's blue lips tremble. "I didn't drink it."

Kim closes her eyes and her face droops. "I can't believe it. The same mistake after all this time." She shakes her head. "I honestly thought you were better."

"I *am* better!" Bex shrieks. She stands and takes two shaky, belligerent steps toward her mother. "I didn't drink! I've been sober for five years!"

Sober for five years. Images and concepts click together in my mind like magnets. Bex's disapproval of me and Kim drinking. Her refusal to drive my car last night. The scar running across her face. The empty whisky bottle . . .

The same mistake after all this time.

My God, Bex got that scar in a drunk driving accident. I'm so dumbfounded I can't speak. I can't even think. Kim fills the silence with a tremble of words. "Wait, you drove my car . . ." Her bare feet are hot pink with cold as she backs away from Bex. "You . . . you found my keys. Or you stole them!"

"I did not!"

"Then how did you start my car?"

"I didn't!"

I lean into the Lexus and push the airbag aside. A set of keys are in the ignition—a car key with a few others hanging from a plain ring. But the car key is halfway out and askew. It doesn't fit in the tumbler.

I pull it out and get a better look at it. One side is imprinted "Product of Ford Motor Company." The other has the embossed silhouette of a running horse. Kim snatches the ring out of my hand. Her forehead wrinkles.

"These aren't my keys."

Bex's eyes widen. "They're mine."

Kim freezes and turns to Bex. "Is this . . ."

Bex nods. "Yes. Probably." Kim's brow forms a question. Bex answers it. "My counselor gave it to me when I left rehab. She said she had a friend at the insurance company pull it from the wreck. I don't know if it's true."

My brain spins out, desperate to ask questions too sensitive to broach. "So that's the key to . . . uh . . . "

Bex gently takes her keys from her mother. "To the car I almost killed myself in while driving drunk. Symbolically, at least." She rubs her thumb over the pony. "I keep it as a reminder. Something physical to hold on to. To keep me strong." She gives Kim a biting look. "To keep me from making the same mistakes again."

I don't know what to say to this. It's too much history to process at once. My brain rejects the challenge and focuses instead on the present. "But . . . How did you start this car with the keys to a different one?"

The foil blanket rustles as Bex pulls it tighter. "I don't know. I think it has something to do with the thing pretending to be fairies."

Kim purses her lips, annoyed. "Maybe we should go inside and wait to have this conversation when you've sobered up."

"I am sober!" Bex barks. "Last night I saw the truth. The fairies aren't real."

"Okay, uh . . . " I gesture at the mangled house. "I'm gonna go out on a limb here and say they are."

"Ugh. Yes! They are a real thing, but they're not really fairies! They're some kind of . . . I don't know!" Bex pinches her eyes and takes a deep breath. "Something weird happened to me last night. I was meditating, and I felt this crazy disturbance in my energy. I felt like I wasn't in my body anymore. Like I astral projected to some weird mental plane."

I roll my eyes. I can't help it. Meditation? Astral projection? Mental plane? Jeez, how new-age crystal cult can you get? She's talking crazy, but I know it's just the booze and the trauma of it all. Last night fully kicked her ass.

"Uh, okay. It sounds like you had a pretty bad dream, but everything will be okay now." I rub my chilled arms. "Let's just get you inside, okay?"

"It wasn't a dream," Bex says defensively. "I saw the fairies in a whole new way. In a non-physical way, like I was looking at them through my third eye." She taps her forehead, right on the scabby scrape. A wince tightens her face. "I saw them for what they really are. They're just one thing. It's one dark, shadowy thing, pretending to be a swarm of fairies because it knows I used to be afraid of them. It's trying to scare us."

"That doesn't make any sense," Kim says.

"I know it sounds crazy, but it's true." She turns to me, desperate for support. "Dad, it's true."

The idea seems absurd, but the fairies are unquestionably real. They are *something*. And given the options, "A 'dark shadowy thing' mining Bex's brain for nightmare fuel" seems slightly less insane than "A local infestation of the exact, specific Hungarian fairies that we just happen to have a storybook about and are also real."

Still, I'm skeptical. "But how would this thing know what you're afraid of?"

"Because it got into my head. Literally got inside. Here."

Bex points to the scrape on her forehead. I raise an eyebrow. "Uh, no. That's just a scratch from when the squirrel—"

"It wasn't a squirrel! Listen to me! It was the shadow thing!" Her shriek is loud enough to incite a panic in my heartbeat. "I was in the living room looking at the fairy book and remembering how much it used to scare me and something stung me in the forehead. The first fairies appeared seconds later. It's connected! It saw my fear and made it real."

"That's ludicrous," Kim says. She rests a hand on the bloody dressings on her leg. "The fairies attacked me before you even got here. They didn't come from inside your head!"

She makes a good point. Bex just scowls. "Well, are you sure it was fairies that attacked you? It must have been dark up in the shed. Could it have been something else? Maybe it took the form of something *you're* afraid of? Spiders or lizards or something?" She blinks, as if struck by a thought. "Could it have been a girl?"

"What?" Kim's question comes out suspiciously sharp. Her mouth seems to notice and drops more words to dull its impact. "I can tell the difference between fairies and a girl. What are you even talking about?"

Bex rubs her temples, as if drawing the memory out. "When the shadow first appeared to me it looked like fairies, but as I became more aware of it, it turned into a girl." She taps her chest. "It wasn't my fear. I'm not afraid of girls. Wait—" Her eyes tick to mine. "Are you afraid of girls?"

The question catches me so off guard I stutter. "What is *that* supposed to mean?"

"I just mean, maybe they're . . . a source of anxiety for you." She contemplates my sagging jowls and thin hair and her meaning becomes crystal clear. "It's nothing to be ashamed of. Be honest. I won't judge."

Oh, I feel pretty fucking judged! *Hey, I'm Rebecca the Steroid Hippie Psychologist. I think Fat Matty hasn't boned a girl in so long he's afraid of them now!*

"No! I'm not afraid of girls! I'm not nine years old! Why would you even say that?"

"Because the girl isn't my fear! And I thought . . ." Bex's glance drifts to the cut on my forehead. "I thought maybe mine wasn't the only brain the shadow has infected."

I reflexively reach for the scrape on my scalp. "What? No. I got scratched by a squirrel."

Bex's eyes narrow. "You said you bumped your head in the dark."

"I bumped it after the squirrel startled me! Jeez!"

"Are you sure that's what happened? Are you sure you're not having any like, weird mental stuff going on?" Bex's voice takes an interrogative edge. "Have you seen any visions of a girl? A long, dark girl?"

Before I can even deny it I'm seeing visions of a long, dark girl. Rosebud. Shame rumbles in my colon like diarrhea. I did see her last night. Willowy and seductive and stark naked. I knock the thought away. I didn't see her. It was a dream. I was asleep. Wasn't I? No, I was awake. I was telling a story to Kim. But I saw Rosebud in my story. The sight of her made me nauseous, like my brain was trying to puke out the poison of her. Like she was a shadowy foreign invader in my mind.

Oh shit. My pulse quickens. Keep it together. I didn't get stung by some kind of brain shadow. It was the squirrel. It jumped out of the medicine cabinet in the bathroom and hit my forehead. I fell down and pulled open the under-sink cabinet door, then it jumped on my chest. I scared it. Its nest was under the sink.

Its nest was under the sink.

Realization throbs my heart against my ribs. Something shot out of the darkness and hit me in the head *before* I scared the squirrel out of its home. It was two separate attacks. Blackness sliced my skull and then flesh and blood clawed my chest. Panic squeezes adrenalin into my veins.

Holy shit! The shadow thing is in your head! It made you see Rosebud.

But Bex said the shadow looked like fairies because she was afraid of them. I'm not afraid of Rosebud.

Oh you so are! You're batshit terrified someone will find out about your crush on her, you sick pedo creep!

Shut up! That's crazy! Every last bit of it is crazy. Bex didn't somehow pull a vision of Rosebud out of my dream into hers. This isn't *A Nightmare on Elm Street*. It's insane. It's impossible.

I have to be sure.

My words are a noncommittal half-question. "Long and dark, you say ..."

Bex latches on to my non-denial. "Yes! She appeared to me as a black silhouette. Tall and thin with short hair. Did you see her too? Do you know who she was?"

My panic runs cold. *Oh sweet holy hell, Matty. You know* exactly *who she was.*

Kim's hand flies to her mouth. "Oh my God." She steps back and grabs my arm. "Oh my God, Matty! She's going to kill us!"

"What?" Bex cries. "I am not!"

"Yes, you are!" Kim's fingers are claws in my flesh. "You've been possessed by the evil spirit!"

The phrasing pricks my ear. She means possessed by *an* evil spirit. Not possessed by *the* evil spirit. Using the definite article implies a subtext of familiarity.

Ooh, look at Matty with the big writer brain. Now is not the time to be a Grammar Nazi, jackass!

I put my hand on Kim's and squeeze. "Calm down. Let's just go inside and figure this out."

"Figure it out? It all seems pretty clear to me!" Kim yanks away from me and takes two cautious steps back from Bex. "She got drunk and stole my car! She crashed it so we couldn't escape! She trapped us here so she could kill us!"

"I did not!" Bex shrieks. "I didn't do any of that! It was the shadow! It gave me hallucinations of my worst memories and took control of my body somehow. *It* drank the whisky. *It* crashed your car. Not me."

"Don't give me that!" Hysteria chokes Kim's words. "Whose foot pushed the gas pedal? Whose hands steered the car into the tree? It was *you*, Rebecca! You trapped us here! You did this!"

"But I wasn't in control!"

Kim scoffs. "And what happens the next time you're 'not in control'? Are you going to slash my throat and then tell my corpse it wasn't your fault? Are you going to blame that on this 'shadow' too?"

185

Bex's breath puffs white in the frigid air. "It's not like that. I had some kind of out-of-body experience. I'm not psychotic." She reaches for her mother. "Mom, please. Just—"

"Get back!" Kim shouts, her eyes ablaze with panic. "You're possessed! Dr. Cheung is in your head!"

Bex and I blink at each other. The name is a complete non sequitur. "Who in the hell is Dr. Cheung?" I ask.

"The girl. The tall girl she saw!" Kim's whole body trembles, and I can't tell if it's from the chill or her ratcheting paranoia. I extend a cautious hand.

"Kim, please. Calm down. Let's all just go inside and talk this out."

Her bare feet pedal backwards in the slush. "Are you kidding? I'm not going to be trapped inside with her! She'll murder me!"

"Oh please," Bex grumbles. "If I wanted you dead you'd be dead by now."

"You see?" Kim shrieks.

"I was kidding. Calm the hell down," Bex says, rolling her eyes. "I know you think I sound crazy, but—"

"Stay away from me! Stay away from both of us!" Kim turns to me, her expression wild with panic. "Run, Matty!" She turns and breaks into a loping sprint toward the woods. Her wounded thigh throws her gait off kilter, but her legs are long and lean enough to compensate.

Bex groans. "Ugh! Mom, stop! You're going to freeze to death, you lunatic!"

She drops the Mylar blanket and takes off after her mother. Her own stocky gallop is stiffened from the crash, but her powerful legs pound the earth like a race horse, pushing her forward at speed. I chase after them both, but my fatass waddle puts me in a distant third.

My fragile feet seethe with agony as they squish in the cold mud. I don't even like to walk around the house without shoes on, let alone run through a pine forest. My heart is a stick of dynamite exploding six times per second, but I push through the pain. I have to. I have to catch Kim. I have to get her back to the cabin. I have to convince her nobody is going to hurt her.

At least I'm not.

Kim dashes through the trees in front of me with Bex on her heels. With every passing step they're more distant until I can't see them at all. I force my burning lungs to share a breath with my mouth.

"Kim! Stop! Rebecca! Kim!"

They're too far away. I can't even hear them anymore. All I hear is my own echo and the rush of blood in my ears. Sweat pumps down my back as I follow their footprints through the trees, zigzagging deeper and deeper into the woods. The overexertion pushes clouds into my vision, and my whole brain throbs from my eyes to my spine. I see a break in the tree line ahead and push myself toward it with all the energy left in me.

My tortured feet emerge in a clearing next to a wrecked black Lexus. The half-devoured cabin looms before me. Kim and Bex aren't here. The footprints I followed here point the other direction. Into the woods. I'm back where I started.

The scar on my forehead burns like it's laughing at me.

CHAPTER SEVENTEEN

Rebecca

Dull pain from the crash throbs through my limbs as I chase my mother through the trees. Sharper pain leeches along my chest and face from the airbag impact and whiplash tightens my neck. The morning sun has nearly melted the thin snow cover, but the air is still frigid enough to sting my lungs with each visible puff.

Despite all this, I'm gaining on her.

The trees start to taper off, and all I can see ahead of us is sky. We break through the foliage to a small clearing at the top of a cliff overlooking a wide, forested ravine.

My mother stumbles to a frantic stop. I stop behind her, thankful that nature finally threw a roadblock in her way. She turns to face me and raises her hands in surrender.

"Stay back. Please. Please don't kill me."

I roll my eyes. "For fucks sake, Mom. I'm not going to kill you."

"Don't call me 'Mom,' you demon! I know what you are!"

"Enough with the theatrics, all right? I'm not possessed by a demon." I stretch my stiff neck. "My middle name is Lynn. My birthday is April sixth. I grew up with you and Dad in the house on Speedway in Venice Beach until the divorce when we moved to the Hills. You used to hide your vibrator in a tampon box in your bathroom."

Mom gasps indignantly. "Rebecca!"

I point at her. "Exactly. I'm Rebecca. You see?"

She stares me down for a long moment. The fear dissolves and her shoulders slump. "Oh God, I'm sorry." She looks at her bare feet, wet mud splattered up to her knees. "I don't know what came over me. I was acting crazy." She looks at me. "I feel so ashamed."

I wave a hand toward the woods. "It's fine. Let's just get back to the cabin."

"It's not fine. I was acting like a lunatic and treating you like garbage. You deserve better. You've always deserved better." Her voice lowers. "I can't believe you care enough to chase after me, even after your accident."

I shrug. "Well, I wrecked your fifty-thousand-dollar car, so I guess let's call it even."

She shakes her head. "Not that accident. The old one. The one you got into because you were running away from your terrible mother." Her lips tremble. "I know it was all my fault you got in that wreck. I've lived with the guilt of it every day since."

My eyes narrow. *Oh, it must have been so hard for you, coping with that horrible guilt while you abandoned me in the hospital to make your artsy-fartsy movies.*

"Don't even start, okay? Let's just go back."

She reaches for my hand. "You have to believe me, not a day goes by that I'm not haunted by—"

My hand darts and slaps hers away. "I don't want to hear about your guilt! Stop making this about you!"

My mother recoils. "I'm sorry. I didn't mean for it to come out that way. I'm just trying to say . . . I love you, Rebecca. I always have, more than you know."

Her sappy insincerity grates my nerves. "Are we really doing this? Here? Now?" My sock feet squash in the cold mud. "Okay. Fine. If you loved me so much, why did you throw me out of your house when I needed you most? Why did you abandon me?"

She shakes her head. "I didn't."

"You did! You never even came to visit me after the accident!" My shout makes Mom take a defensive step back. I force cool into my voice. "I woke up in the hospital with a fractured pelvis, two broken legs, a broken arm, three shattered ribs, and a collapsed lung. My face was crushed." I dot my finger across my facial scar. "There are six screws and two metal plates in my skull. My jaw was wired shut for a month. It took an army of doctors and physical therapists to put me back together. Not that you would know."

"I know. Of course I know!" Mom takes a trembling breath. "Who do you think paid for all that? Who do you think paid for your rehab? Who kept you out of jail? Who spent half her fortune burying the whole thing so deep that even the gossip rags never saw a blip on their radar?"

My mind dredges an echo from the past. *"Sweetheart, you know the reason I work so hard is to provide the best things in life for my precious little girl. To buy you the best house and the best school and the best … everything."*

"Don't act like you did that for me. You did that for *you*. You always do what's best for you."

"How can you say that? I did it because—"

"Because what would happen to the great movie star Kimberly Savage's career if the press found out she raised a slutty drunk with an eating disorder? It would ruin her image. She'd never be nominated again. They'd chisel her star out of the Walk of Fame and shit in the hole. So you threw money at the problem until it went away."

"That's not true. I did it for you. To protect you. From me." Mom's shimmering eyes roll to the sky. "I never knew how to be a mother. I was terrible at it. We both knew it. That's why I cut you loose. It wasn't because I didn't love you."

I scowl. "So, what? You just gave up?"

"I didn't give up. I just … stepped aside." She takes a breath and tries to blink away the tears. "I did come to the hospital to visit, you know. I was there as soon as you were stable enough to be seen. You were still unconscious, covered in white casts and bandages. Your face wrapped tight in white gauze. You just looked so . . . blank. Like you'd been wiped clean of everything." She fights to push words through the twitching of her lip. "I knew I had to let this blank girl develop into a woman without her dreadful mother ruining her again. I had to step aside and let you be a phoenix, free to rise from your ashes in your own image." She meets my eyes. "It was the hardest thing I ever did, but I don't regret my choice. Look at how you turned out. I did the right thing."

My mother gives me a self-satisfied smile that slaps a handprint of fire across my cheek.

"Get out of my house. Get out and don't ever come back!"

"Don't. You. *Dare* try to take credit for how I turned out!" My roar drives my mother back another step. She throws a half glance at the cliff edge behind her, but doesn't break her focus away from me. I pound a fist on my bruised chest. "How I turned out is because of *me*. *I* was the one who suffered through alcohol withdrawal while I was too wrecked to even sit up. *I* was the one who had to relearn how to walk. *I* was the one who had to go through years of therapy to learn to function like a normal adult human being. *I* was the one who fixed everything *you* broke." I thrust a finger at her. "You don't get to take credit for anything I've achieved. At all. Do you understand?"

"I do! I really do." Mom raises her hands in a calming gesture. "I didn't mean it like it sounded. I just meant . . . I'm proud of you. I'm proud of all you've accomplished. You grew into such a strong woman on your own. And then . . . I messed it up again." She casts her eyes to her reddened feet. "I'm sorry I invited you to the cabin. I'm sorry I got you stuck in . . . whatever this is."

I smirk. "It's not your fault. You didn't know any of this would happen." Suspicion pricks at the back of my mind. "Right?"

Mom looks wounded. "What? Know that I was calling you into a hive of bloodthirsty skeleton fairies? Of course I didn't know."

"Then why *did* you call us here? Honestly."

She sighs. "I called you because I'm getting old." I roll my eyes but she persists. "I'm old and I'm lonely. I know you feel like I singled you out for neglect, but that's not the case. I've made a lot of mistakes in my life and pushed a lot of people away. I wanted to spend the time I have left fixing the things I still can." She shrugs. "I wanted to make things right between us. I still do. And I hope you can find it in your heart to forgive me."

There's a sincerity in her voice that I'm not used to. I take a deep breath. "I don't want to carry this baggage anymore either. I want to put it behind me. Not just locked away, but really put to rest." I catch her eyes. "But you need to understand you can't just ask for forgiveness. We both have to put in the effort to actually heal our relationship. Are you willing to do that?"

Mom nods. "I am. I really am. If you and I get out of this alive, I promise I'll do whatever it takes to make things right." She smiles. "Starting with cutting you a check."

I blink. "What?"

"To open your fitness center."

Disappointment grumbles in my belly. "Goddamn it, Mom. This isn't about money."

"Of course it isn't. It's about me helping my daughter. I want to make it easy for you to forgive me."

I shake my head. "Look, you can't buy my forgiveness."

"I'm not trying to. I just want to be the best mother I can be for you. And I promise to do everything I can to make your dreams come true if the two of us manage to escape." She lifts an eyebrow and looks away, pretending she didn't just drop that seed. All my dreams will come true if *the two of us* manage to escape a monster demanding a human sacrifice. My gut goes cold as her smile goes warm. "I'd do anything for you. Because I love you more than anything. Do you know that?"

I've seen this performance before. My breath quickens as images of red velvet curtains and awards-show formalwear prickle at the back of my mind.

"I know you do, Mom."

"I've worked so hard to give you everything you've ever wanted and I've never asked for anything in return. Now I'm just asking you for a favor. One simple little favor. You have VanDuzer's attention. Make him see things your way. Please. It would mean so much to me."

My temperature rises. Her compassion is all an act. A lie. Another bullshit trick to manipulate me into doing what she wants. And this time she doesn't want me to be a whore, she wants me to be a cold-blooded murderer. She steps toward me and reaches out for a hug and a crucible of rage overturns in my soul.

Fuck off, you sociopath bitch!

The insincere smile is knocked from my mother's face as both my palms shoot out and pound her in the chest. She reels over, throwing out her arms to catch herself, but there's nothing to catch but empty air. She falls backwards, sailing toward the valley as her heels pivot off the cliff's edge.

The sight of it cracks a peephole of clarity in my rage blindness, and my hand lashes out to grab her wrist. My legs bend, and in a massive, jerking twist of my body I yank her back and heave her onto the ground behind me. She rolls in the frosty mud, a bony clump of flailing knees and elbows.

My tunnel vision clears as the fire in my blood turns to ice. Mom stoked my anger until I lost control, and I pushed her off a fucking cliff. Oh God. It's too much. My head spins. My pulse surges with remorse. Mom scrambles to her feet, clutching her chest.

"You tried to kill me! You *are* possessed! I knew it!"

"I'm sorry! I'm so sorry!" I fall to my knees. It's partially an act of prostration. It's mostly because they've gone too weak to hold me up. "I didn't mean to. I swear I didn't mean to!"

My mother leaps back toward the trees. "I know who you are! Stay away from me, Cheung! You murderer!"

She bolts into the woods. I slump back on my ass, feeling numb and feeling too much all at once. I got so angry I almost killed my mother.

I can't blame her for this.

I can't blame the shadow.

It was all me.

CHAPTER EIGHTEEN

Kimberly
Twenty-Five Years Ago

People are staring. I'm just an average tourist, walking with my husband through Lake Arrowhead Village. The shape of my body is blunted under big denim overalls and one of Matty's rock-and-roll shirts. I'm unrecognizable. I don't look like me. I barely look like a girl. So why are people staring?

It's the wig. Why did I get the red wig? If you don't want to be noticed you get the brunette wig. Brunettes disappear in a crowd. As a redhead I'm a beacon for attention. I may as well not be in disguise at all.

My mind is sluggish and addled and my body aches all the way to the bone. I've been running both full throttle since before *Blood Blitz* even hit theaters. As a B-movie the marketing budget wasn't huge, so the studio sent me to do the rounds on the late-night talk shows. First looks at Hollywood's newest star. I worked my butt off, charming audiences with my lovable demeanor and easy laughter, then sucker-punching them with a clip of me in white lingerie hacking vampires apart with a sword. Fun-loving, approachable, sexual, kick-ass. Kimberly Savage is the whole package. When I started that promo tour nobody had ever heard of me. By the end of it, everyone in America either wanted to be me or screw me.

Blood Blitz opened number one at the box office and stayed there for eight consecutive weeks. It's not exactly high art, but people can't get enough of it. I'm just happy the attention will open the doors to better projects. Holly Hunter's first film was a low-budget summer-camp slasher. This year she won a Golden Globe, BAFTA, and Oscar. If she can do it, I certainly can.

But for now I'm just America's Number-One Action Star. Adored and worshiped to the point of being hunted down in my own home. The paparazzi are entrenched around our condo, aiming their long lenses at the windows like sniper rifles. Every picture they manage to snap becomes a potential tabloid sensation.

Me, straight out of bed, wearing sweats and drinking coffee in the kitchen—*Booze blitz! Kimberly Savage a wreck after all-night bender!*

Me, running on my treadmill—*Kimberly Savage exercise binge! Sexy starlet not afraid of vampires, terrified of cellulite!*

Me, accepting a package from the mailman—*Exclusive photos of mystery man! Kimberly Savage's secret lover?*

The constant invasion of privacy is suffocating. I can't breathe. I need to step away from it all and clear my head. Rest. Reset. But there's nowhere to go. My star is suddenly shining too brightly to hide away.

I tip my fake copper tresses in front of my sunglasses and snuggle closer to Matty's side. He puts his strong arm around my hip and squeezes. For the briefest moment, nothing else matters. It's just me and him. My rock. My sweet Matty. He doesn't care about Scarlett Bedlam. He only cares about me. The real me. The me the cameras don't get to see.

It was his idea to come up to Lake Arrowhead for the weekend. He thought it would help me relax if I got out of the city for a while. Just me and him, young lovers enjoying a quiet getaway in the quaint little village like normal people. But I'm too on edge to enjoy it. My throat aches. I'm getting sick. I've pushed my body too hard for too long and it's shutting down in self-preservation.

Matty spots a little pink shop and his eyes light up. "Ooh! Ice cream! Let's get ice cream!"

I peer over my sunglasses into the store windows. The place is packed. I shake my head. "I can't. Too many people. They'll recognize me. I'll be trapped."

Matty frowns and nods. "Yeah, you're probably right."

He looks so disappointed. I squeeze his hand. "You go pick up something for us. I'll wait here."

"Yeah?"

"Yeah. Get me a small, non-fat vanilla froyo. In a cup, not a cone."

He smiles. "Wow, does this girl know how to cut loose or what? Would you like a glass of decaf water with that?"

"Just go, funny man. Before I change my mind." I slap his butt and he does a silly little Three Stooges bit as he hustles away. I can't help but giggle. My sweet, goofy husband. While I've been away filming and promoting, he's been grinding out his own long hours, working days on *SoCalites* then staying up all night working on his comedy screenplays. The man is a machine. There's no limit to how far he'll go.

As Matty disappears into the shop, a teenage boy catches my eye. I notice him because he's noticing me. He's just standing there on the other side of the street, openly gawking. Damn this red wig.

I turn and pretend to be interested in the storefront window in front of me. It's filled with a grid of gold frames containing photos and descriptions of luxury real estate properties nearby. Mansions on the lake and lodges in the woods, each absurdly unaffordable. Summer homes for a class far above mine. I just pulled a six-figure paycheck and looking at them makes me feel like I'm still living in my parents' double-wide.

In my peripheral vision I see someone approach and stop beside me. I cast a subtle glance that direction and the gawking boy grins eagerly.

"You're her, aren't you? You're Kimberly Savage." He fidgets with nervous energy. "Can I have your autograph?"

Warmth spreads in my chest. It happens every time someone asks for my autograph. I've been practicing my signature since my first high-school play. Nobody wanted it then, but I promised myself someday someone would. And ten grueling years later, everyone does. People care. I matter. But anxiety frosts the edges of my bliss. I want to give the kid his autograph, but it's never one autograph. The second I admit who I am, fans will overrun this street, lining up for their brush with fame. I'll be standing here signing napkins and candy wrappers until the sun sets. The very thought of it leaches my strength. I just want to lie down. I just want to sleep.

"Nah. I get that all the time," I say gruffly. "Could be worse people to look like, right?"

The boy shakes his head. "Okay, whatever. You're so her. I've seen *Blood Blitz* four times." He frowns. "You're so hot in that. Why do you look so dumpy in real life?"

My stomach knots. I dressed dumpy so nobody would recognize me. But they do recognize me. They recognize me as dumpy. I can see the tabloid headlines now. *Kimberly Savage lets herself go! Starlet hides her plus-size shame!*

I scowl. "I can't really talk now, okay? I'm busy."

My eyes lock on the real estate listings as if they're the most interesting thing in the world. I study the specs on a rustic manor with an oversized cobblestone chimney. Three bedrooms, two-and-a-half bathrooms. Private mountain hideaway. Its price is two full digits shorter than any other property in the window.

A stringy-haired woman hustles over and grabs the boy by his shoulder. "Nathan! Stop bothering this nice lady." She turns to me. "I'm sorry if my son was . . . holy shit, you're Scarlett Bedlam. Oh my God, it's Scarlett Bedlam!"

She's shrieking like a schoolgirl. Everyone in the street is now looking at me, elbowing each other and gasping. Mentally peeling away my wig and clothes and matching my body with the scantly-clad vampire hunter in their collective subconscious. They move in like zombies, excitedly pulling out their Instamatics.

"Shhh!" I hiss. I pull a fake smile and whisper. "Okay, you got me. I was trying to keep a low profile, but I can't hide from big fans like you. I'll be happy to sign an autograph, but then I have to—"

The flash of a battered point-and-shoot fires in my eyes like a shotgun. I blink through the haze as the lady cranks the film advance wheel. "Nathan! Get closer! Cozy up so I can get a picture!"

The teen weasel shoves himself under my arm and squeezes me around the waist. "I touched her! I touched Kimberly Savage! I can now die a happy man!"

His wiry fingers grope my flesh. One hand on the side of my hip, the other on my ribcage, not-accidentally too close to my left breast. Random strangers take pictures of the little molester and laugh at his moxie. I want to sock him in the jaw, but I force a giggle and edge myself away. "Oh stop. You're too cute. Look, I've got to get going, so thank you for—"

Another flash fires in my eyes. And another. A crush of people jockey for position, each of them shouting orders at their bumbling photographers. A pear-shaped mom grabs my arm and turns me toward an old guy in a fishing hat.

"Kimberly, over here! Wave to Rodney!" Before I can react a blinding flash pops off in my face. My head swims and my knees go weak. I feel like my whole body is going to give up. The woman crows again. "Now one without the wig!"

Bobby pins tear my scalp as her meaty hand rips the red wig from my head. A scream tries to form but I swallow it. Kimberly Savage does not scream at her fans. My mangled blonde hair twists from my skull in frizzy, matted clumps, captured by a dozen more flashes. Hands are on my arms. On my back. Someone squeezes my ass. Everyone screams my name and brays and laughs. They're chimps at the zoo and it's feeding time. I try to push through them but I have no strength.

I'm so tired.

"Okay! Okay, thank you everybody! I love you, but I have to go!"

They've completely blockaded the sidewalk. There's only one direction to move. I smile and wave and step back. Away from the hoard, toward the shop window. I slide sideways and push through the door. A bell jingles as it swings shut and cool air conditioning washes over my flushed skin. Nobody follows me.

I slump with exhausted relief into a chair in the lobby and try not to break into a full sob. They love me, but they don't respect me. I'm not an actress. I'm an autonomous sex doll with eighty hours of martial-arts training. I'm a thing to be stalked and groped and bragged about. My eyes go misty as my mother's words ring in my ear. *Take advantage of what God put in your sweater, 'cause he sure didn't put anything in your head."*

I crush my eyes shut. I wish Matty were here. I need him to hold me and tell me that everything is going to be okay. I need him to remind me this is just a stepping stone. I need him to tell me that someday I'll be like Holly Hunter and *Blood Blitz* will be nothing but a forgotten VHS tape gathering dust on a bottom shelf at Blockbuster.

I need a goddamn minute of peace and quiet to pull myself together.

"Good gracious, that's quite a commotion out there, isn't it?" An old man in a new suit comes out of a cubicle and peers out the window. He looks at me. "Did you see what got them all wound up?"

I look away and shake my head. "I have no idea."

"Well they're making me nervous." He lowers the blind, blotting out the crowd and the sun. A salesman smile bends his lips as he turns to me in the dimmed light. "Sorry to keep you waiting. Is there something I can help you with, miss?"

He speaks to me as if I'm a complete stranger. I relish it.

"Oh, I don't . . . I was just window shopping."

"Well, what kind of property are you interested in? Near the lake, or something a little more woodsy? We have some superb cottages up in the mountains. Beautiful views. Very secluded. Totally private."

"Honestly, I wasn't looking for . . ." My sluggish mind catches up to his words. "How private are we talking?"

"Well, we have a lot of different options. Why don't you come back to my desk and I'll show you some of our—"

"What about that one in the window? The cheap one?"

"The cheap . . . oh." His face blanches. "That one is priced to sell for sure, but I don't think you'd be interested in that particular property."

"Is it private?"

He adjusts his tie. "Well, yes. It's miles from the nearest neighbor, off a hidden dirt road. It doesn't even have a proper address. But we have much nicer—"

"I'll take it."

"W . . . what?"

I stand up and pluck the remaining pins out of my ruined hair. "I said I'll take it. Give me the keys and I'll write you a check right now."

"You . . . uh . . ." The realtor stammers and pinches his fingers. "Well, we can, uh . . . we can definitely start that process for you, but . . . before we do I'm legally required to make a disclosure about the property."

My heart sinks. "Ah. And now we find out why it's so cheap. What is it? Toxic mold or something?"

"Oh no. No. Nothing like that. It's just . . ." He sighs. "Come on in, I'll grab the file." I follow him to his desk, and he sits behind it and pulls a manila folder. His voice tightens as he flips through it. "The previous owner of the property was a local. Dr. Laurie Cheung. Used to have an office not far from here." He adjusts his glasses and hands me a glossy junk-mail flyer for her practice. The blurb next to her photo says she's a family therapist. Cute, too. Short hair. Tall for a Chinese girl. The realtor continues. "She, uh . . . well, two summers ago she had a . . . I guess they call it an 'episode,' and she . . . she killed her husband."

I blink. "In the cabin?"

He nods. "No history of mental illness, then one day she just . . ." He shakes his head. "Right in front of their two-year-old son. The police report says she claims an 'evil spirit' made her do it. The whole thing is so sad."

"So that's it then? It's a murder house in the middle of nowhere?"

The realtor squirms. "In a word . . . yes. But we have many other comparable properties that—"

"Where do I sign?"

***

The pink light of the summer sunset stoops under the roof of the gazebo and nuzzles warmly against my skin. My hair is down. My real hair. Blowing in the breeze. The chains of the bench swing creak as I move in a tiny, gentle arc, listening to the glorious sounds of nothing at all. A week ago I dropped out of the Hollywood rat race and retired to my new cabin in the woods. Temporarily, of course. Every day here strengthens me. Makes me feel more ready to face the world. To chase my dreams. To rise above and become the true artist I am meant to be.

But until then. I sit. And I breathe. And I smile.

The wooden step creaks as Matty comes up from the yard, holding a bottle of wine and two glasses. "Good evening, madam. Might I interest you in a glass of the finest vintage the local general-slash-hardware store has to offer?"

I grin. "I would be delighted, good sir."

Matty sits next to me and pours. "To our new secret hideout."

I raise a toast. "Mum's the word."

We clink our glasses and take a sip. Matty smacks his lips. "Wow. That's really . . . I think the word I'm looking for is *repugnant*."

I laugh. "No. It's perfect. It's all perfect."

He rests his arm on the bench swing's back and I cuddle in beside him. My husband is warm. The sun is warm. The wine in my belly is warm. It's all so soft and warm and peaceful. It's an afternoon nap in an overstuffed feather bed, seeping through my body and soul. Across the yard the cabin is aglow with the orange and pinks of the sunset, subtle and elegant like an impressionist painting. Our cabin. Our sanctuary from the world. Just me and the man I love, alone in tranquility.

A tear runs down my cheek and drops onto Matty's shirt. His voice goes soft with concern. "What's wrong, honey?"

I shake my head and smile. "Nothing's wrong. Nothing at all."

He grins, and his grin wraps me like a cozy sweater. "Okay."

And it is okay.

I nuzzle into him, and for the first time in my life I understand what it is to be truly, unconditionally happy.

CHAPTER NINETEEN

Matty

I throw another log on the blaze in the fireplace and try to keep warm. I don't know what else to do. Kim and Bex have been gone for at least an hour, maybe more. It's impossible to say without a working phone or clock. They'll come back soon. They have to. Bex will calm Kim down and bring her back to the cabin and we'll all get out of here. Somehow.

My wet socks are laid out to dry on the warm stones of the hearth. I pull up a slightly burnt chair and sit by the fire, propping my bare feet up to thaw. My body is still sluggish with cold, but my mind feverishly plans our escape. The fairies destroyed my car. Bex destroyed Kim's. The nearest neighbor is about five miles away. I know because I had to hike there the last time I was here, when Kim abandoned me without a car or phone to call for help. The trek through the woods isn't easy, but it's possible.

Assuming the fairies let us leave.

I absently brush the stinging gash in my forehead with my fingertips. As much as I want to deny it, I know Bex is right. Something is inside our heads, messing with us. When I chased after the girls I followed their footprints through the woods like a bloodhound. The tracks didn't break. They didn't cross themselves. I didn't double back. Yet somehow the trail led me right back where I started. It's exactly what happened when we tried to drive out. The road just twisted toward the cabin. All roads lead back to the fairy freakout shitstorm.

I realize any attempt at physical escape is futile. We're not getting out of here until we defeat this shadow thing. Until we kill it.

Or you could just give it what it wants.

Fuck you, brain! I'm disgusted with myself for even letting the thought creep in. I will not kill Kim. I will not kill Bex. Not under any circumstances. Familicide is not an option a decent, rational person would even dream of considering.

But am I considering it? Or is it the shadow monster inside my head? What if I lose control like Bex did? What if Kim is right, but about the wrong person? What if I suddenly wake up with a bloody knife in my hand, standing over her corpse? Or Bex's? Or both?

A shiver rolls down my spine and throbs in my frostbitten feet. Thankfully they're cold enough to distract me from the horrible thoughts I desperately need to be distracted from. I wish I had a dry pair of socks. Technically I brought some. I'd be wearing them now if I'd had the foresight to bring my luggage inside before my car exploded. Of course, Kim and Bex's clothes are all here. I'll bet I could squeeze into a pair of Bex's socks if I tried.

The floor grows ever colder against my feet as I leave the fireside and plod upstairs to check. Everything useful in the house is still in the master bedroom where we left it. My stomach growls as I cross its threshold, and I grab a box of kale crisps off the dresser and stuff some in my mouth, trying to trick my taste buds into believing they're food. Some candelabras still hold untouched candles. I light a few and spot Bex's bag in the shadows—on the floor with the blankets she never got to use last night.

I pick up her bag, but my hand hesitates on the zipper. Is this okay? Can I just paw through her things? This isn't like when she was eight and I was checking her backpack for stolen Thin Mints. She deserves her privacy. She's not a kid anymore.

She's not *a* kid, but she's still *my* kid.

My aching feet invoke parental privilege and the zipper zings open. Nothing inside is folded. Besides the one pair of jeans it's all wads of stretch cotton and nylon and spandex. I carefully prod the heap with one finger, trying to uncover two socks and zero drugstore lady products I don't want to imagine my daughter needing.

"Ooh, somebody is being a naughty boy."

The unexpected voice tweaks my adrenalin so hard I leap into the air like a startled cat. I whirl around to see a shadowy figure leaning in the bathroom doorway. A perfect silhouette of long, slim femininity.

I drop the bag and step back. "Kim?"

It's not Kim. I know it's not Kim, but my brain can't think of any other solution to this puzzle so it says it anyway. The shadow girl glides into the room and candlelight embraces her, wrapping warmly around the satiny-smooth sheen of her mocha skin. Her glittery pink lips twist into a smile. "No, Matty. Not Kim. I'm what you really want."

It's Rosebud. Flawless, nubile Rosebud.

She's a brick pitched through the plate-glass window of my sanity. She can't be here. Yet there she is, her pert nipples poking through a form-hugging Rex Mex polo cut short to reveal a mile of taut, girlie midsection flowing into a little black thong.

"What . . . What the hell?"

I take a step back as a thousand conflicting emotions and reactions collide. My brain tells me this is impossible. My eyes say it's not. My dick wants to get a closer look at the problem.

Shut up, dick! Stay out of this!

Rosebud groans seductively. "Aww. Don't be shy. We both know you want me. Remember? 'The one you've been looking for has been right in front of you all along.'" She leans in close and whispers. "You can keep your secret from your family, but you can't keep it from me."

She rests her hands on my arms and my heartbeat surges, jackhammering in my skull and crotch. My mind tells me to run but my body doesn't listen. I can't move my legs. I can't move anything. I'm bound in a numb, dreamy paralysis.

Rosebud's lips glide over my own. The glitter in her lip gloss is lightly abrasive, like sugar crystals. Her tongue slips into my mouth. She tastes like dulce de leche. Our lips smack apart as she leans back and smiles. "Mmm. Was that everything you've always dreamed of?"

My cheeks burn with humiliation. "Get away from me! I know what you are. You're that shadow thing Bex saw!"

"*Pfft*. Dude, I'm so much more than that." Her dark eyes glitter with mischief. "I can be anything. One thing. A bunch of things. I can take any shape your heart desires." She grins. "I can even be the girl of your dreams."

"You're not even a real girl!"

She smooths my collar. "*Derr*. Obviously. I tried to be all theatrical, with the fairies and the haunted phone and all that junk, but apparently you need it spelled out for you. So I picked out a form I knew you'd actually listen to. Someone you're *desperately* in love with."

"I am not! Shut up!" I shriek. "You don't know anything about me!"

I tell my legs to move but they don't. Rosebud presses against me and rests a soft finger on my lips. "Shh. Matty, you don't have to lie to me. You *can't* lie to me." She moves her hand to the scar on my forehead, and each gentle tap of her finger along its length scalds like the burn of a cigarette cherry. "I'm inside your mind. I know all your secrets. I know your deepest, darkest fantasies. You can't hide what you want from me."

She rests a hand on my chest and gently pushes. My feet involuntarily step back until she's backed me up to the armchair in the corner. She gives the tiniest push and I fall into it like a lovesick sailor being seduced by a showgirl in a musical. It's a gag. The action is so playful it sends pure liquid horror surging through me. Because it is playful. Despite my terror, I'm being complicit in the playfulness.

I'm flirting with her against my will.

She struts around the chair, giving me an erotic eyeful of her long legs and tight ass. "I want to make a deal. It's a total win-win. You give me what I want, I give you want you want." Her hips swivel as she runs her hands over them. "You can have this, Matty. This body, doing every single dirty little thing you've ever dreamed it could do. All I want in return is one stupid little human life." She cocks her head and smiles. "I don't care which. The old one or the young one. I'm not picky."

I want to make a run for the door but I can't stand up. I can't even lift my arms off the arms of the chair. "Let me go!"

She rolls her eyes. "Oh my God, I'm not even touching you. Just get up and leave if you really want to."

"I can't and you know it! You paralyzed me!"

"No, Matty. *You* paralyzed you." Rosebud perches her firm ass on my lap and runs a smooth hand over my scalp. "You poor thing. You want to get with me so bad but you act like you don't. Your conscious mind is all jacked up on guilt and shame, but your unconscious mind doesn't give a shit. It only knows what it wants. What *you* want. And it's in control now."

The warmth of her smile makes my heart happy. My hands rise and my fingers slide up her soft jaw line and into the flirty swoops of her hair. Her eyes close and her lips part as I pull her in and kiss her. I kiss her long, and hard, and deep. Lusty groans vibrate in her throat as she returns my passion. Her body is so tight and warm, grinding against my lap. The pure carnal joy of it sends electric prickles racing through my entire being. It's perfect. It's everything I ever fantasized kissing Rosebud would be.

Because she's in your head, jackass! She's reading your mind! She's reproducing your own wet dreams! Wake the hell up!

I pull out of the kiss, but my hands still caress the sides of her head, her warm, rosy cheeks resting softly in my palms. I want to scream. To my eyes she's an angel, but to my gut she's a bucket of spiders. I feel it so deeply that I somehow see it. Not with my eyes, but with my brain. It's like I'm looking through the gash in my forehead at a mass of bony spurs clumped in black tar sitting in my hands. I shriek and it's Rosebud again, luminous and smiling.

She sucks a gasp as I clamp a grip on her head and twist sharply. There's a sickening pop that I feel as much as hear as her neck snaps. Her eyes go dim and the full weight of her body slumps against me.

My hands drop to my sides and my heart races in my chest. Oh my God. Holy shit! I did it! I've seen that trick a thousand times in movies, but I never thought it would actually work. I never thought I would actually do it!

Relief sizzles through me as my body numbs with endorphins. The Rosebud thing lies heavily across my body, her head turned sideways and limp on my shoulder. I killed her. I killed *it*. I need to find Kim and Bex and get out of here.

My legs flex, but I can't stand up. Panic grips me as I realize I'm tied to the chair. But I'm not. I'm part of it. The fibers of its weave are stitched through my clothes and my flesh. There's no blood. No pain. I have somehow become one with the chair.

Rosebud's weight shifts on my lap. She leans back and her head slides off my shoulder and falls heavily to her chest, bent at an impossible angle on her flaccid neck. The gruesome vision pulls a hysterical scream from my throat. I'm desperate to get away but all I can do is twitch and spasm against my upholstery bindings. Rosebud grabs two fistfuls of her black hair and twists her head back into place with a sickening crunch. She rolls it on the bruised stalk of her neck and turns her waxy, dead eyes to me with a coy smile.

"See how easy that was? I knew you had the killer instinct, Matty. Now all you have to do is get 'er done. One little human sacrifice and you're good to go."

"No!" I scream. "I won't kill for you! I won't!"

Rosebud's face twists into a shadowy scowl. "All right, no more screwing around. I tried to do this the fun way but you had to be an asshole about it. So here's my new offer: Either you kill one of those bitches or I kill them both."

"You keep your hands off of them! I won't let you *near* them!"

"You can't stop me." She leans in closer and whispers with stinking breath. "But if I kill them, you don't get to leave. You'll stay here with me forever, staring at their corpses, knowing you let them die for no reason." She grins. "Or you could save one of them. And yourself."

Impotence and anger crash through rapids in my chest. "I don't believe you!"

Rosebud smiles. "That's fair. I'm gonna be straight with you. I would let you feed me both of them if I could, but I can't. One sacrifice puts me in a total food coma. Fill my belly and it's lights out." She snaps her fingers. "I snooze and the rest of you walk. For real. Just ask Dr. Cheung."

Who the hell is Dr. Cheung?

"Okay, fine. You want a human sacrifice? Fine! You can have me."

"Ugh. You're not even listening."

"I am! I'll kill myself if you let them go! I swear I will!"

Rosebud shakes her head. "I don't want another bland suicide. I need the feast of a true human sacrifice."

"It is a true sacrifice! I sacrifice myself! I sacrifice my human life to you!"

She rolls her eyes and groans. "Oh my God. *One. Must. Kill. Another.* I don't know how I can make it any more clear. None of you can die on purpose. You can't kill yourself. And if you try to pull some 'suicide by surrender' bullshit I will keep you alive, no matter how bad they mess you up. You will never be allowed to die, because you'll want it. You'll want it *so badly*. And a willing sacrifice isn't a sacrifice at all, so you'll live in agony forever. For nothing. It would be so stupid." She smiles and chucks my chin. "Or you could just kill one of them now and go home. Whaddya say?"

"I say 'Fuck you!'" My arms launch upward. A hand is around her throat before I even realize I'm no longer a part of the chair. I never really was part of the chair.

My other hand balls into a fist and hammers the Rosebud thing's disgusting, beautiful face. Pain shatters my knuckles but I draw back my arm and throw it again. The monster cries and wriggles in my grip, pulling us both to the ground. My lungs release a primal scream as I straddle her body and pin her to the floor, pounding her face bloody. My eyes see my fists mashing flesh and bone but I know it's not really there. It's a trick, just like the chair. Fireworks of light and agony explode from the gash in my forehead, blinding me. "Die you monster! Die!"

My knuckles ram into wooden planks over and over again. I yelp and blink yellow haze out of my vision. I'm kneeling on the floor. Alone. Cold shadows flicker in every corner untouched by the candlelight. I scramble to my feet and clutch at my chest, gasping for air.

She's gone.

If she was ever here at all.

I plant a palm on the scar sizzling across my forehead. Shit. Shit hell. I'm losing it. I'm losing my mind. I need to find Kim and Bex and get out of here before—

There's clunk downstairs and a squeal of hinges. The front door opens and closes.

They're back. Oh, thank God.

But how can I be sure it's them?

I hustle to the stairs and down to the living room. A line of wet footprints glistens across the floorboards in the dim light. Blood and grime. I look up to see a feminine form silhouetted against the blazing fire in the hearth and my heart jumps in panic. Before I can act on it, the shadow speaks.

"M—Matty . . ."

The voice isn't Rosebud's.

"Kim!" My eyes adjust to the light, revealing her crouched by the hearth, shivering and pale. She's covered in mud, and a vicious redness licks the skin of her bare feet all the way up over her ankles.

The soles are raw and bloodied, each of them a glue trap of pine needles and dirt. I rush over and plop down next to her on the hearth. "Kim, oh my God. Are you all right?"

"Oh, Matty, I . . . I . . ."

She sputters out a sob before collapsing against me. I throw my arms around her trembling bones and squeeze, trying to force my heat into her. She returns my embrace, and despite her chill, her touch warms my heart. There's something infinitely comforting in Kim holding me. Like she used to.

Choke on that, Shadow Rosebud! Screw you and your bullshit! This is what I want! Kim is the girl of my dreams! Not you!

I tenderly rub her filthy sweater. "I'm so happy you're back. I was so worried about you." Realization strikes me. "Where's Bex?"

"I left her in the woods. She . . ." Kim shudders in my arms. "She tried to kill me."

A spasm of cold knots my stomach. "What?"

Kim pulls away and sits up, her lip quivering with terror. "She's gone crazy, just like Dr. Cheung did."

That name again! I have so many questions my tongue feels too big for my mouth. "Uh, remind me, who is Dr. Cheung?"

Crying breaks Kim's response into fitful jags. "She murdered her husband here. She said an evil spirit made her do it."

Her words kick me in the head. "*What?* Are you serious? When?"

"A long time ago. Before I bought the place." Kim sniffles and shrugs. "I never told you because I know you're superstitious. I didn't want you to think the house was haunted or something. She murdered her husband right in front of her son. I thought she just went crazy, but now . . ." She squirms against the stones. "It's real, Matty. Whatever it was that possessed Dr. Cheung is real, and it's gotten to Bex."

Kim falls against me, wracked with sobs. I put one arm around her shoulders and squeeze, letting it all sink in. This has happened before, just like the shadow said.

I snooze and the rest of you walk. For real. Just ask Dr. Cheung.

I imagine this Dr. Cheung, here in this cabin, relaxing and enjoying the great outdoors with her family until the shadow got in her head and convinced her to slaughter in cold blood. The same shadow that's in Bex's head now.

And in mine.

My jaw clenches. No. The shadow may be in my head, but it doesn't control me. I refuse to accept it's controlling Bex. "I believe you. I know Bex isn't herself right now, but are you sure she tried to kill you? Is it possible it was an accident? Or maybe—"

"It wasn't an accident, Matty!" Kim yanks away from me, firelight reflecting brightly in her eyes. "She cornered me at the top of a cliff and tried to calm me down. She tried to make me think she was still my daughter, but I knew she was going to kill me." She crosses her arms and grips herself. "I tried to reason with her, but the second I tried to make amends she ... She shoved me over the edge." A tremble rocks her body so hard it transfers into my own, shivering cold up my spine.

"Dang," I whisper.

"I just remember her hitting me and then falling over the edge. I must have ... I don't know, blacked out or something, because the next thing I knew I was lying in the mud with her standing over me. She's so strong and so angry. All I could do was run for my life." Kim's eyes snare mine, glistening and vulnerable. "I got away, but she's still out there, Matty. She's possessed and she's going to kill us."

I droop against the warm stone of the chimney. "I can't ... I'm sorry but I just can't believe that. I mean ..." A steadying breath rattles in my lungs. "Kim, she's our daughter. She's family. She ... she loves us."

"No, she doesn't," Kim says mournfully. "Not anymore."

"She does. I know she does, and—"

"She doesn't, Matty! She's not the sweet little girl you remember." Sorrow tightens her lips. "After the divorce she changed. She got mixed up with the wrong crowd and I lost her. My perfect daughter became a . . ." She clenches her eyes. "I don't even know. She was underage, screwing older men for favors. For drugs and alcohol and who knows what else."

My mind instantly conjures the worst possible image. My precious little Bex with pigtails and blinky LED sneakers, bent over her plastic racecar bed, sucking on a bottle of Jim Beam while Ron Jeremy pounds her from behind. I shake it off.

"That's . . . no. I can't believe that."

"It doesn't matter what you believe! It's true. You weren't there. I was." Kim rubs her wrist. "You've seen her tattoos. Fuck the World." Her fingers tap her bicep. "'I love nobody.'" Her lower back. "Toxic. She got a biohazard symbol inked on her flesh. Like she's proud of her toxic behavior." Kim shakes her head. "She's not the little girl we raised. She's got so much anger. And she hates me more than anything. The demon is exploiting that."

Kim buries her face in my shoulder and threads her arms under my jacket. I hug her and hold her close. Her chilled tears drip on my neck, each one a liquid call to action. When I married Kim I promised to love and protect her, till death do us part. Now here I am, so committed to do the former and impotent to do the latter. There has to be some way out of this. I can find it. I have to.

Or you could just kill one of them now and go home.

Shadow Rosebud's words drill through my mind. The rules of engagement really are too simple for a loophole. One. Must. Kill. Another. I know the shadow is in Bex's head as well. She's seen the girl. Is it Rosebud to her? Or Dr. Cheung? It doesn't matter. That monster is poisoning her mind the same way it tried to poison mine. I was able to resist it, but Bex isn't as stable as I am. She's a lapsed alcoholic with anger issues. But even so, how could my sweet daughter Bex try to murder her own mother? There's only one answer I can see.

This isn't my sweet daughter Bex.

This inked-up monster "Rebecca" killed my sweet daughter Bex a long time ago. Part of me still wants to find the old Bex and save her, but I know I can't. She's too far gone. Rebecca's figurative demons are working hand-in-hand with the literal demon infecting her mind.

And even if I could somehow talk her down, the shadow will kill her anyway. Or Kim. Her threat was as clear as it was ruthless: *Either you kill one of those bitches or I'll kill them both.*

One of us has to die.

I can't sacrifice myself.

I can't save them both.

Kim's nose cuts a chill path across my cheek as she drags her lips to my ear and whispers. "Matty, I'm so scared." The air transmits the butterfly quiver of her mouth so close to my skin. "We can't escape. Bex is going to murder me."

I squeeze the fragile icicle of her body to the protective warmth of mine.

"Not if I can help it."

CHAPTER TWENTY

Rebecca

The afternoon sun hangs low and dim over the woods. Wet clumps of mud stick in the wool of my socks as I trudge back from the cliff to the cabin. I know it must be above freezing, but my body can no longer gauge temperature. I am thick with numbness, racked with piercing stabs of tingling and burning.

I hug myself for warmth, but I have none to give. I've been outside since the shadow sleepwalked me to the car last night—at least ten hours in the bitter cold in nothing but yoga pants and a hoodie. I don't dare take off my socks for fear of finding blackened toes ready for amputation.

I pass two wrecked cars and head toward the mangled cabin. I pass that too. I won't be welcome there. I probably won't even be allowed inside. My mother thinks I tried to kill her.

You did try to kill her.

The stress is too much. Physically. Emotionally. It's killing me. I need to figure this out. I need answers.

My body shivers so hard I can barely control it as I plod up to the shed. That's where Mom was when she first saw the fairies. She went there for firewood and they trapped her and stabbed her leg. Or so she claims. But the more I think about it, the more it doesn't make sense. The shadow manifested the fairies from my fear. I'm sure of it. There's no way my mother should have seen them before I got here. The shadow should have attacked her with something else. Whatever it is that scares *her*. I need to see for myself. I need to understand where this started so I can figure out where it ends.

I can see the shed as soon as I clear the back corner of the cabin. It's technically a free-standing one-car garage, but we kept it too full of junk to fit a vehicle inside. Sporting goods and lawn chairs and boxes of random things we didn't need but couldn't bear to get rid of. The rear wall was always stacked with split cordwood for the backyard fire pit.

The two big barn doors are closed and locked with a chain, but the smaller, human-sized door hangs wide open. My shadow spills across the floor as I step in through the shaft of sunlight pouring in behind me. Shapes come into focus as my eyes adjust to the dim light. The stacked firewood. Metal shelving units full of crap. Piles of cardboard boxes and plastic tubs. Expired gardening chemicals and badminton racquets and other random summertime junk.

A single set of Ugg boot prints disturbs the grime on the floor, tracing an in-and-out path from the doorway to a shelf covered with rusty old gardening tools. There's a clear spot in the thick layer of dust where something has been dragged off the shelf and taken away. My fingers trace the oblong shape on the bare metal. What was here? A coil of garden hose, maybe? The train of thought derails as my eyes drift over the other objects, landing on a pair of pruning shears.

"Those things trapped me in the shed and, they ... they stuck me with a pair of pruning shears." Mom said. *"Two of them, working together."*

My trembling fingers pick up the shears, leaving a clean outline of them in the filth on the shelf. I blow the dust off to reveal the faded yellow of their rubber grips.

There's not a speck of blood on them. They haven't been disturbed in years.

The implications send my mind reeling. I take a steadying step, and something squishy and soft brushes my bare calf. My leg is too numb to identify it, but my eyes instantly recognize a huge lump of brown fur lurking under a low shelf. I suck a startled breath and leap back, consciously squelching the screamed expletive trying to escape my mouth.

Fuck! It's a fucking bear cub!

The light plays across its bristly pelt. I clench the rusty shears and press myself into the opposite wall, ready to fight if I have to. Shit! I remember my parents warning me about bears around here when I was a kid. One must have wandered in and dozed off. And if there's a baby bear, mama isn't far away. I stand motionless, staring at it in the darkness, mentally begging it not to wake up. As my pupils dilate the shape gains detail but not form. I can't identify legs or feet. I can't even tell which end is the head. It's just a ball of fur.

With sleeves.

My muscles loosen as I realize what I'm looking at. It's not a bear. It's not even real fur. It's something my father and I found at a thrift store in the Valley when I was a kid. My stiffened fingers ache as I grip the fabric and pull it from under the shelf, holding it at arm's length to get a good look. It's a long, worn-out, faux-fur coat from the '70s. Claws and teeth made of corrugated cardboard are stapled to the ends of the sleeves and the edge of the hood.

I remember it instantly. It's the hide of a sasquatch, from the last summer we spent at the cabin. The last *good* summer, before the divorce. Dad and I were in the woods searching for the Lost Temple of Zamrycki when we found a clearing with wobbly stacks of rocks as high as his chest. He explained that they were "trap towers" set by a sasquatch to warn of intruders trespassing in its domain. With a grim warning to not disturb the stones, he snuck off, leaving me to cross the clearing alone.

Of course, Dad had set up the rocks the night before after he'd put me to bed. And as soon as my clumsy nine-year-old body knocked over a tower he came rushing out of the woods wearing this coat, snarling and roaring and chasing me through the trees. The game was so fun our quest stalled in that clearing for a whole summer of me "accidentally" knocking over the towers.

The memory warms my mind, but my mind isn't the thing that needs warming. I wrestle myself into the fur coat, gliding its satiny polyester lining over my dirty and bloodied clothes. The fit isn't bad. My muscles ache, but I pull up the hood and force myself to jog in place. Gently. Carefully. Pain stabs through my icy feet each time they hit the ground, but I push through the pain in my joints in an effort to fill my new layer with body heat and melt the ice in my core.

I can't believe I found this coat. What are the odds? A knee-length, hooded fur parka just when I'm on the verge of freezing to death? It's a miracle. A deus-ex-machina miracle. There is no reason I should have discovered this old thing hiding in the forgotten bottom of the shed. Except for the one that's so glaringly obvious it boils like venom in my gut.

One. Must. Kill. Another.

The shadow doesn't want me to die. It wants me to be killed. That's why it let me survive the car crash. And why it's making sure I survive the cold. And why it'll keep helping me survive every cruel abuse and injury it can come up with until one of my parents kills me.

Or you kill one of them.

The thought makes my stomach drop. I try not to let it rattle me. I acknowledge the unpleasant idea and move past it. It's natural to have dark thoughts in stressful times. The only thing to be ashamed of is acting on them.

Like you did back at the cliff.

I close my eyes and align my breathing with my stationary jogging. Lungs expand. Lungs contract. Foot up. Foot down. In. Out. Left. Right. My body is a machine in perfect balance, and I encourage my thoughts to stop racing out of control and relax into the rhythm. As it does, clarity returns to my scattered mind.

I came to the shed to figure out where the shadow came from, but the clues I've found have only added to the mystery. Why did Mom lie about being stabbed here? What was taken from the clear spot on the dusty shelf? I need context. Maybe the thing has a mate. Maybe I can figure out what's missing by looking at what's still here.

My eyes scan the shelves. Top to bottom. Left to right. It's a feast of nostalgia. A pair of jungle-hacking machetes made of cardboard tubes and aluminum foil. A worn-out softball tucked in the pocket of a little blue baseball mitt, tucked in the pocket of a big brown one. Two abused, green-and-black Super Soakers. A third "Princess" gun in glittery pink and white is still zip-tied in its packaging. I remember standing in a Toys "R" Us with Dad when I was a kid, picking this one out especially for my mother in a naïve effort to get her to come play with us.

It's a theme that repeats through a childhood's worth of stuff. Toys for two. Me and Dad. All the way around the room and down to the muddy hiking boots near the door. A men's size ten next to a child's size five next to an empty space.

Boots!

I drop to the floor and stuff my soaked feet into Dad's old boots. They're a little big, but too big is better than too small. If I lace them up tight they'll be—

A shadow blots the light coming through the door as a roaring battle cry rips the silence. Searing pain shoots from my shoulder as a wet *shik* slices the air at my ear. My head whips to the side just in time to see a bloody chef's knife unsheathe itself from my flesh.

"Aagh!" My hand claps on the wound and I tumble across the floor before the blade can connect again. I spring to my feet and whirl toward the door. My father's heavy form hunches in the sunbeam, holding the glistening knife up at his shoulder like a movie serial killer. Blood seeps through my clutching fist and slicks my fake fur coat. My vision clouds on the throbbing of my heart. "What . . . Aagh! What the fuck?"

"You're dead, you monster!"

Dad's eyes dart. His hand trembles. He's trying to act tough but he's scared shitless as he lunges toward me. I dodge his clumsy attack and he stumbles into the shelves. Before he can turn around I've plucked a baseball bat out of the corner and hefted it for a swing. It's slick in my hands, lubricated with my own blood. My father raises his knife but keeps his distance.

"You stabbed me!" I scream. I can't believe he stabbed me. Here, in the shed, surrounded by all our old playthings. The man who made cardboard machetes with me. The man who always let me win our squirt gun wars. He stabbed me. A thousand questions push toward my mouth, but only one word escapes. *"Why?"*

"You tried to kill Kim!"

In a flash I see myself as he sees me, standing here in a matted fur coat complete with pointy claws and teeth. I'm literally dressed like a monster. An out-of-control, off-the-wagon rage beast who pushed her own mother off a cliff. Regret pulls tight against the anger in my chest. I've made a mistake so unforgivable no apology can ever undo it, but I try anyway.

"I'm sorry! I lost control. It won't happen again."

"You're damn right it won't!"

My father roars and swings the knife at me. I block with the bat. It connects with a solid *thunk* against his knuckles that sends him stumbling back with a yelp. His blade clatters across the dusty floor and I hiss as pain blossoms through my stabbed shoulder. It hurts, but it still works. Thank God. The blade probably hit bone before it could do any real damage.

Dad's breath is frantic as his eyes tick between my face and my bat. He staggers toward the wood pile and grabs a long-handled splitting axe. I take two steps back and position the bat defensively in front of me.

"Dad, stop! Listen! The fairies didn't attack Mom here! She's lying!"

"Like I'm gonna believe you!"

"Look around you! Do you see any sign of a fairy fight? There's no burn marks! She's full of shit!"

Dad lurches forward, raising the axe over his shoulder. "Shut up! I know you're working for the shadow now! I know you're all screwed up! Kim told me all about how you went crazy after the divorce!"

Rashy red heat prickles up my arms and into my face. That lying bitch! I'm too smart for her manipulative bullshit so she pulled it on my lovesick father instead. Ugh! I should have seen this coming!

"If I was crazy it was because she made me that way! After she took me away from you she exploited me. She made me . . ." My jaw clenches against the memory. "She made me do horrible things."

"Don't lie to me!" Dad screeches. "Don't tell me you drove drunk because Kim wanted you to! Don't tell me she made you have sex with strangers for profit! You had the perfect life and you threw it all away! You can't blame your mother for your screw ups!"

The bat crashes into his ribs before I even realize I've swung it. Dad squeals and slams into the shelves, sending gardening tools clattering to the floor. He catches his balance and wheels on me, axe raised, eyes full of unpredictable terror.

Shit! I regret hitting him. Not because he didn't deserve it, but because I played right into Mom's game. She told him I was out of control, and now I've gone and proved her right.

I raise the bat but keep my distance and stay alert. Dad is practically hyperventilating. If I'm going to get through to him I need to keep his attention on my words and not my weapon. "Dad. Listen. I'm sorry I hit you, but you don't know what you're talking about. Nothing happened the way she told you it did. Not when I was a kid, and not now. I wasn't trying to kill her at the cliff. I just lost my temper and pushed her because she was trying to manipulate me into killing you."

He snorts. "Bullshit."

"It's not. She was laying it on thick, painting a picture of how rosy life would be if me and her managed to survive. If *somehow* a sacrifice could be made that would leave the two of us standing she'd give me money for my fitness center and I'd live happily ever after. She laid out all the dots and let me connect them to get to the answer *she* wanted. A way for her to escape this without getting blood on her pretty little hands." I nod at his axe. "I didn't fall for it, so she did the same thing to you."

Hatred chokes my father's words. "Your mother didn't ask me to hurt you. She would never do that."

I shake my head. "No. She doesn't *ask*. That's her game. She messes with your head until you think what *she* wants is actually what *you* want. Then you do it, believing it was all your idea." Bitterness creeps into my voice. "Let me guess how this went down. She came back from the woods acting like the most helpless little victim in the world. She told you how she reached out to Big Bad Rebecca and I went crazy for no reason. That I'm an inhuman Terminator who won't stop until she's dead and there's nothing *anyone* can *possibly* do about it. Then she cried. Am I right? A single tear down the cheek? It was all so heartbreaking that you vowed to kill your psycho daughter to protect her. Is that about right?" I catch his eyes. "She didn't *ask* you to hurt me. She *told* you to. And you don't even know it."

He's quiet for a long moment. His expression steams with anger, but not denial. His face tics as he thinks unknowable thoughts. Finally he speaks.

"You're sick. I don't know if it's because of the shadow in your head or whatever hard-ass life you live now, but you're not the little girl I used to know. Something has messed you up." He adjusts his grip on the axe. "I didn't come after you because your mother conned me into it. I did it because I love her."

"I know you do, Dad. But why?"

"What do you mean 'why'?" he shouts. "I don't need a reason! I love her because I do!"

I shout back. "But *why*? Name one time you two were actually happy together!"

My father's face boils red. "We were happy all the time before I screwed it all up! She loved me back then and she can love me again!"

"That's bullshit and you know it!" My grip on the bat tightens. "She's a raging sociopath who never gave a shit about either of us! She never loved you, Dad! And she never will!"

The axe comes down so fast I barely get the bat in front of my body to block it. I deflect the blade, but the force of the blow slams my own weapon into my chest. My abused legs crumple, throwing me down on my back and whipping my head against the concrete. White hot stars blast across my consciousness. A roar cuts through the agony in my skull, clearing my vision just enough to see my father silhouetted against the doorway, hefting the axe over his head for a death blow.

I throw out my palms in an impotent attempt at self-defense. As my arms push the cardboard claws of my sasquatch sleeves in front of my eyes, my concussed mind goes to a different time and place. The axe reaches the top of its swing and changes direction. My hands come together in a triangle and I scream in Swahili.

"Rafiki!"

Clarity sparks in my father's rage-blinded eyes. His muscles lock. The blade diverts and slams into the concrete inches from my head, driving a deafening *chink* into my left ear.

The brush with death slows time. Something stings my cheek. A pebble, chipped out of the floor, moving at incredible speed. My father looms over me, hands still on the axe handle. The fury on his face washes away on a wave of cold terror. He sees what he almost did. He sees the dusty crack in the floor that could have been a bloody crack in my skull. Relief and regret hit him in equal measure at unbearable volume. I know exactly what he's feeling. I felt it at the cliff when I saved Mom from falling after I tried to push her to her death.

In a flash of instinct I grab the axe handle next to my head with both hands and slam the butt up into his sternum. Dad's hands slip off the weapon and clutch his chest as he stumbles back. I pull the axe to my body and kick my feet against the concrete, scrambling into the corner.

My father coughs and falters, regaining his balance as the horror of the moment flushes the blood from his face. With an adrenalin-quick dip of his knees he grabs my dropped bat off the floor. I have the axe but I'm in no position to use it, half frozen and sprawled on my ass in a corner. He's standing. He has room to swing his arms. He has the advantage. If he tries to smash my head in there's nothing I can do to stop him.

But he doesn't try. His body shakes as he takes a step backward toward the door.

"You stay away from us. You understand?"

I move to stand. "Dad, please. Don't go. Listen, we—"

"I said stay away!"

He slams the bat into a rusty shelf, collapsing it and showering its contents to the floor in a clatter of chaos around me. I huddle in the corner for protection. A shadow blinks across me as he rushes through the sunlit door and is gone.

My heart beats so hard it forces sweat out of my icy brow. I don't get up. I stay crushed against the walls, holding the axe in both hands. A trickle of blood runs from the pebble scratch in my cheek and my left ear still rings from the impact that could have ended my life.

Everything has changed. My father tried to kill me. Not in a moment of hot-headed passion. He came looking for me, hunting me with a knife. He swung an axe at my head. It was attempted murder stopped by a lucky blurt of nostalgia.

The next time I won't be so lucky.

A groan rumbles in my throat and through my muscles as I force myself to stand and make my way to the door, kicking through the scattered debris of a happy childhood. Fury builds inside me and vents through the blood gushing from the stab wound in my back. It throbs through the bruise blossoming in my smashed shoulder.

Screams through the ringing in my left ear. My father and I used to be inseparable until Mom turned me against him. Now she's turned him against me. They're both against me. I squeeze the axe handle.

They need to be stopped.

My boots stick in the mud as I step out of the shed. The long shadows of dusk pour from the bottoms of the winter-bare trees into dark bands that stretch all the way across the backyard. Dad's footprints lead to the house. Mine lead back to where I came out of the woods. Painted over both sets is the long shadow of the gazebo farther up the hill.

Something in the shadow moves.

No. *Someone.*

I tighten my grip on the axe as my gaze follows the subtle motion back to its source. The setting sun is blinding behind the gazebo, sketching its framework in jet black against my corneas—a conical roof over vertical pillars and a horizontal railing. It sears my eyes, forcing them back to the ground. The soft mud leading to the gazebo is completely untouched.

I squint and shade my eyes, taking another look. My heart races, then stops dead. Someone is in the gazebo. Someone who's left no footprints getting there. A long, tall girl stands on the railing, swaying gently, staring at me with her head cocked to the side. Grotesquely far to the side, as if someone had snapped her neck.

I recognize her instantly.

The shadow girl has escaped my mind.

CHAPTER TWENTY-ONE

Kimberly
Twenty-Eight Years Ago

"Do you, Matthew, take Kimberly as your lawfully wedded wife, to have and to hold, to honor and cherish, to love and protect till death do you part?"

The sea breeze drifts through Matty's thick auburn hair as he looks from the officiant to me. There's an energy in his eyes as they meet mine. A love that sparks like a flint wheel whenever he looks at me. His smile pulls his face so tight over his jaw I don't think he'll be able to push the words through it. But he does.

"I do."

A joyful titter runs through the guests. I cut a subtle glance at them. It's a small ceremony, just a dozen white folding chairs near the surf on Santa Monica Beach filled with our closest friends and family. Well, Matty's family. I haven't seen my family since the second I turned eighteen. Those assholes are dead to me.

The officiant smiles and nods. "And do you, Kimberly, take Matthew as your lawfully wedded husband, to have and to hold, to honor and cherish, to love and protect till death do you part?"

Matty's intense eyes cut through my veil, through my skin, all the way down to my heart. I'm afraid he can see the fear burning in the breast of my wasp-waisted white gown.

I don't want to get married.

I can't. I didn't come to Los Angeles to get married. I came here to be a movie star. And five years later, what do I have to show for myself? Some local theater. A few regional beer commercials. One *SoCalites* walk-on where I played a non-speaking pair of tits.

I need to work harder. I need to cut out distractions. I need to focus on my career.

Matty gazes at me, hanging on my silence. Waiting for me to confirm my commitment to him. The world goes soft as tears well up in my eyes.

I can almost hear my parents laughing. Mocking me for my failure. Telling me that I'm still not a real actress. That the only reason I even got the lead in my high-school play was because I was physically overdeveloped for my age. Implying that I was banging the drama teacher behind the scenery. Har har.

I can almost see the faces of the boys. The classmates I fed off of like an emotional vampire. Using their hormone-charged simulations of affection to try to fill the emptiness. When I got to Hollywood I found the men weren't that different than the boys. Sex was a barter. A transaction to buy a moment of kindness.

Then came Matty. He was cute, if a little neurotic. After we met on the set of *SoCalites* he was convinced I was his muse. I'd heard that one before. Men who called me their muse always seemed to think inspiration flowed from between my legs. The first time Matty brought me to his condo I expected a clumsy seduction. Instead I got an unfinished screenplay. He asked me to read it. He wanted my opinions. We stayed up all night eating junk food and drinking beer and bouncing ideas off each other. Scribbling notes and getting orange fingerprints on typewritten pages. And laughing. So much laughing.

The first man who didn't try to get into my pants got into my heart.

One date turned into two. Two into four. Into ten. When I didn't get a callback for an audition, Matty comforted me. Part of me felt like getting the comfort was better than getting the job. He was a best friend first, and a lover second. Always.

Before Matty I had never known genuine affection. I'd never received it, nor given it away. It was completely foreign to me. I thought I understood what love was, but when I found myself chest-deep in the real thing it was exhilarating and terrifying all at once. When he proposed my heart said yes. My fear made him sign a pre-nup.

Then we moved in together.

Once we were in the same cramped condo I could no longer keep him at arm's length. I couldn't run away when my feelings got too scary. Matty got closer to me than any human being ever has. And he still showers me with a thousand tiny kindnesses every day. He makes me tea in the morning, exactly the way I like it. He gives me his coat when I'm cold. He spoons me when I sleep to keep away the nightmares, even though it makes his arm go numb. And he never lies to me.

I fell in love with him.

I didn't think it would happen. I didn't think it *could* happen. But I love him. I love him with my whole heart, with every fiber of my body and soul. I love him so much that I want to run away before marriage teaches us to hate each other. Before it sucks us dry and leaves us two miserable husks of our former selves, trapped with each other for life. Before I give up on my career and become resigned to being nothing but someone else's wife.

My heart hammers. No. No! Screw that. I am not my mother. Matty is not my father. Our marriage will not be a life sentence. We will not make the same mistakes they did. We'll be successful. My love for Matty won't keep me from my dreams. It will only lift me closer to them.

And we'll be happy. Forever.

Just the two of us.

I take both his hands in mine and say, "I do."

CHAPTER TWENTY-TWO

Matty

I'm still shaking as I climb the cabin's front stairs. My breath comes in short, heavy pants. Part of it is because I ran back here from the shed. Most of it is because I am freaking the fuck out.

What is even happening? I was hunting Bex. I got the biggest goddamn knife I could find and followed her footprints up to the shed to . . . I was going to kill her. This weekend has turned me into a straight-up murderer.

I wring the baseball bat in my bruised hands. I need to pull myself together. I need to man up. Just because I won't kill Bex it doesn't mean she won't try to kill us. I need to be ready to protect Kim if I have to. I need to keep her safe. I love her.

"I know you do, Dad," Bex said. *"But why? Name one time you two were actually happy together!"*

My emotions run cold. Kim and I were happy together once. Happier than two people had ever been. She was my muse. I was her rock. And then we were nothing. Bex can blame it on Kim all she wants, but I know who was really to blame. I committed an inhuman breach of my wife's trust, and she never told a soul about my sin. She just held it in, letting it slowly burn away our love like acid until it was gone.

I let myself in through the front door and close it behind me, clicking every lock and deadbolt into place. The fire is still glowing in the hearth, but Kim is gone. Panic seizes me.

"Kim?" I shout. No response. "Kim!"

I raise the bat and hustle from room to room. Kitchen. Downstairs bathroom. Dining room. All dark and cold and empty. I scream her name as I bound up the stairs. All the doors hang open except for the master bedroom. I try the knob, but it's locked.

"Kim? Are you in there?"

A weak, muffled voice pushes through the wood from the other side. "Are you alone?"

"Yes. I bolted the front door. We're safe."

The latch clicks and the door swings open. Six candles in a single candelabra light a room otherwise still darkened by its shuttered window. Kim cautiously steps back, holding the fireplace shovel at the ready. She looks past me into the hallway, scanning for danger as I step inside.

"Did you find Rebecca?" she asks quietly. "Is she ... Did you ... " The sentence dies half-finished in her mouth.

I shake my head. "She won't bother us. I scared her away."

Skepticism frosts Kim's eyes. "Scared her away?"

"I stabbed her. I ... I almost killed her. Because ... " *Because she was trying to turn me against you. Because she said you never loved me and I lost my shit because I was afraid it was true.* "Because I need to keep you safe. Because I still love you."

There. I said it. That's it. It's out. Kim lowers the shovel and sets it against the wall. She looks at it instead of me.

"No, you don't. You love who I used to be. You love your memories of me."

I set my bat next to the shovel and take her hand. "You're right. I've been loving my memories of you for thirteen years. But it's not enough anymore. I want to love *you* again. The real you. The you who you are right now." My mouth twists into a weak smile. "I want to start again, Kim."

Her eyes twinkle sadly in the candlelight. "You know we can't. If the fairies don't kill us—or Dr. Cheung, or whatever else is out there—we'll starve." She gestures at the tiny stack of health-food on the dresser next to the meager remainder of the drinking water. "One way or another we're going to die here."

I put a hand on her shoulder. "No, we're not. We're going to survive. We'll figure out some way to escape this place and go home."

She shakes her head. "We both know there's only one way the two of us can survive." Her eyes meet mine. "You have to kill her, Matty."

My stomach lurches. Her bluntness stirs up Bex's shouted words in my mind. *"She doesn't ask. That's her game. She messes with your head until you think what she wants is actually what you want."*

It may have been a game before. Now it's a flat-out demand.

I take my hand off Kim's arm and rub my smashed knuckles. "No. That's not an option."

Kim looks at the floor and bites her lip for a long, contemplative moment. "I know it's hard, but she's not our daughter anymore. She's—*it's* a demon. It's a monster wearing Bex's muscles as a weapon to slaughter us."

"No. It's not." I crush my eyes. "*She's* not. I know there's some evil thing trying to get to her." *Because it's trying to get to me too. If I can resist it . . .* "She can resist it. She won't bother us again."

"She will. The moment we let our guard down—"

"I'm not going to kill her, Kim." It comes out harsher than I expected. "She's our child. She's our flesh and blood. No matter what happens, I'll still love her."

Kim's eyes glisten and her lip trembles. "I still love her, too. I tried to make you kill her because I knew I couldn't bring myself to do it." Her words shake out on a whimper. "I'm sorry I manipulated you, but we can't all survive. I had to make a sick Sophie's choice, but I couldn't bring myself to choose who would die. Instead I chose who would *live*." She catches my eyes. "I chose you, Matty."

A tragic warmth cuts through the chill and pierces my heart, filling it with a hopeful brightness.

"Are you saying you still love me?"

Kim wipes a tear. "You don't know how many times I've wished I could go back in time and ..." She looks at me with a regret untainted by malice. "I wish I could rewrite history. Just make it so none of it ever happened and we never stopped loving each other. I want to live in a world where we grew up and grew old together, still as deeply in love as we were on our wedding day. Just the two of us."

Just the two of us. When it comes down to it that's what this all hinges on. It's what it always hinged on. Our happiness together was never able to support the weight of a third.

I rest a hand on her arm and gaze into her eyes. "We can't change the past, but we can change the present. If we're going to die here, let's live the life we have left to the fullest. Let's find our happiness, right here and right now, and hold onto it for as long as we can."

Kim smiles through a sob. "Oh, Matty!"

She throws her arms around me and her chapped lips meet mine. She's kissing me. Really kissing me, her long hands on my cheeks, pulling me closer. My stubble claws at her mouth, but I'm too caught up in the moment to be self-conscious. I can't regret the past or worry about the future. Everything is right now. Everything is this perfect moment of happiness.

She walks me backwards until the backs of my legs hit the bed and her passionate kisses push me off balance. We fall together as one, our weight forcing a creaking scream from the old mattress. Pain explodes from my fractured ribs, but I barely acknowledge it. I'm lightheaded with ecstasy.

I put my hands on Kim's slender hips and pull her close. Her long legs fold her knees onto the bed and she's straddling me, pressing the firmness of her body against the pillow of mine. It's a warmth I haven't felt in years. The warmth of the woman I love, loving me back. It seeps into me and fills every part with an incandescent euphoria.

Our lips separate, and she leans back. Her cheeks are wet with tears, but her eyes are bright with bliss.

"Thank you for still loving me, even after I treated you so badly." She caresses my face. "This is going to be a new start for us. A new 'first time.'" Her smile beams. "This time we'll get it right, and I will love you forever until the day I—"

Her thought is interrupted by the watermelon crunch of an axe blade splitting her skull.

CHAPTER TWENTY-THREE

Rebecca

The axe comes down in a smooth arc that hits that monster in the dead center of her golden scalp. With a grisly *shunk* her skull splits like firewood, ejecting a hot crown of blood and brains. It splatters up my arms and across my father's face, flushing his expression from sexual ecstasy to shell-shocked horror.

I jerk the handle back, yanking the blade free. The body slumps to the side and lands on the bed, bleeding out into the bare mattress. My father scrambles back and falls on the floor, his face wet with gore, his eyes the size of pie pans. "What! What . . . oh, fuck!" He's already crying. "Oh God! No! *No!*"

My heart is beating so fast I can barely discern the separate beats. What did I do? What have I done?

Stay strong. Keep it together, Rebecca.

I level a glare at my father. "Get away from her."

Dad's voice is a baby's anguished scream. "You killed her! You killed your mother!"

He stands by the bed, clutching the lifeless body, sobbing as her skin goes pale. I feel the thick, sticky warmth of her blood dripping down the axe and onto my hands. I see the fair stubble on the cold calves above her bare feet. I smell the final release of her bowels.

It's all so real. So viscerally real. I feel like I've awakened from a nightmare to find it's all true. Shit. Shit! It was a trick. The shadow played a mind trick on me and I fell for it!

No you didn't! This is the trick! Finish it!

My father wraps both his living hands around a cold, dead one and howls. "How could you do this! How could you—" He screeches and recoils as my axe comes down and buries itself in the body's gut. I plant my foot on her bony hip and pull my weapon free. "Bex, stop!" Dad scurries away from the bed as I hurl the blade over my shoulder for another blow. "For God's sake! Stop!"

"Go back to Hell, you fucking monster!"

A roar rips through me as I swing the axe at her heart. The instant it connects there's a *whumph* of air and the corpse disintegrates into a body-shaped pile of smoke fairies. They screech and tumble over each other, each of them battered and torn, oozing oily blood. They exist only for a confused blip of a second before collapsing into a single formless shadow on the bed.

I become aware of a high-pitched wail. It's my father. I don't know how long it's been going on. His back is pressed to the log wall almost hard enough to break through.

"Dad!" I shout. His scream continues. "Dad! Shut up! That wasn't Mom!"

"I worked that out!" he shrieks.

I gasp and jump back as the shadow slips off the bed and scuttles out the open door. "Shit! It's not dead!" My boots pound the boards as I chase the wounded monster across the hall and down the stairs, axe raised for another strike. It streaks across the living room wall and out the front door. I scamper onto the porch just in time to see it disappear into the maze of long tree shadows crisscrossing the clearing. It's gone.

"Damn it!"

Frustration burns through my arms and I bury the axe blade in the soft wood of the porch. My father comes teetering out the door behind me, flushed and winded. "Where is she? Where did she go?"

"It got away. It's still out there, somewhere."

"No, I mean . . ." His jowls bounce as his frenzied mouth tries to find words. "That thing wasn't your mother! Where is she? Where is your mother?"

Oh. Right. I look at my feet and sigh.

"I'm sorry, Dad. She's dead."

***

A knot forms in my stomach as my father and I squish through the wet mud around the side of the house. It's an uneasy truce. I just saved him from dipping his wick in the shadow monster, but he still doesn't trust me. I understand. I don't trust him either. That psycho stabbed me and attacked me with an axe. The axe I'm still carrying.

We have issues to work through, but we're in this together now.

"Dad, I'm sorry I have to do this to you, but you need to see this."

Tears glisten on his cheeks. "You . . . you didn't . . ." He gathers his courage and blurts it out. "You didn't kill her, did you?"

I shake my head. "No. I found her. She—"

A pained gasp chokes in Dad's throat, freezing his feet to the ground. I follow his gaze, but I already know what he sees. The sun has dipped below the top of the backyard rise, throwing the gazebo on the hill into soft pink light. A long, tall girl appears to stand on the railing staring at us with her head cocked to the side, but it's an illusion. My mother is actually suspended in the center of the gazebo by the coil of rope she took from the dusty shelf in the shed.

Hanging by her broken neck.

"No. No!" Dad whimpers. "No! Oh God, no!"

He runs up the hill as fast as his legs can carry him, his canvas sneakers slipping in the muck as he scrambles to the gazebo. I follow him, but I don't chase. There's no need to rush. There's nothing I can do but wait while he processes his shock and grief.

By the time I reach the broad wooden steps he's standing next to her suspended body, his face pressed into the belly of her pink pea coat, hugging her and sobbing. His stubby fingers wrap around her stiff, cold hand. My mother's eyes stare down at him, bloodshot and unblinking.

"It's my fault," he whimpers. "It's all my fault."

"You can't blame yourself. It's not your fault."

"Yes it is! She did this because of me! She said if I didn't kill one of you she'd kill both of you!"

My eyebrow raises. "Mom said that?"

"The shadow said it!" Dad cries. "That's why I came after you! I'm sorry! I'm so sorry, but there was nothing else I could do! The shadow said she would kill both of you unless I killed one of you and I couldn't do it. I couldn't kill you so the shadow killed your mother!"

He's not making sense. The poor bastard doesn't know what's happening here. I take a deep breath. "You don't understand. The girl I saw in my mind, the long, dark silhouette—it was Mom. The shadow thing was trying to look like fairies, but I saw the truth. It was posing as Mom all along. I think it attacked me with my memories to make me look crazy so you wouldn't believe me when I told you it was also a woman."

Dad squints, as if working up an argument. Finally he says, "You're wrong. I saw the shadow girl too. I saw her in the flesh and she . . . she wasn't your mother. She was someone else. A girl I know."

I nod. "I think it can take any form it wants. Anything it sees in our memories. That's why it looked like smoke fairies just like I remembered them, and why it looked like that girl you know. But mostly it looked like Mom because it was trying to manipulate us into killing each other. It knew it could get under our skin if it wore hers."

My father steps away from my mother's corpse and slumps on the creaking bench swing, his knees weak with the weight of it all. "But you're just guessing. I mean, how can you be sure about any of it?"

"I found something." My hand digs into the pocket of my fur coat and finds two rings of keys linked together. One holds the key to Mom's Lexus, house, and a few unknown locks. The other is an older set with each mismatched key meticulously labeled with tiny stickers.

Front Door - Deadbolt 1. Front Door - Deadbolt 2. Front Door - Deadbolt 3. Shed. And so on. "That thing pretending to be Mom claimed she dropped her keys when she was attacked by fairies in the shed, but they were here in her actual coat pocket all along. I used them to get in the house once I figured out what was really happening. It's all right here."

I pull out a pink, rhinestone-bedazzled smartphone tethered to my back-up battery. Dad looks at it, then me. He tips his head towards Mom's corpse without looking at her. "Is that . . . is it hers?"

"Yeah. It was in her other pocket. The battery was dead when I found it, but I used the spare from my janky phone." I wake up the screen and tap in Mom's unlock code. It wasn't hard to crack. I actually did it by accident by pure force of habit. Mom's phone has the same code as mine. My birthday. "There's an email in the outbox that she tried to send before she . . . " I don't say it. It doesn't need to be said. "It's still spinning, waiting to find signal. But it says that . . . here, just read it."

I hand him the phone and its battery and give him time to digest Mom's last words.

Carl,

I'm sorry I disappeared without telling you. I thought if I got out of the rat race for a while I'd be able to clear my head and find the strength to go on.

I know I'm a has-been. Worse than that, I'm a joke. The same late-night TV hosts who used to flirt with me across their desks now use me as fodder for their monologues. I'm never Kimberly Savage, the well-respected three-time nominee. I'm always Kimberly Savage, the gray-haired Botox beauty with the sagging tits. I sacrificed everything to become an award-winning actress. All I became was a punch line.

But now I can see that none of that matters. Since I came here I've been haunted by nightmares. Vivid and brutal, like flashbacks to the worst moments of my life. I've relived every bad choice. I've watched myself hurt the only people I ever loved. The only people who ever loved me. I've hurt them too badly to ever ask their forgiveness. I can't heal the pain I've caused. I can't live with it. I won't.

Don't bother looking for me. Just know that I left this world with dignity, from the last place I was ever truly happy.

Please tell them I'm sorry.

— Kimberly

Dad stares at the screen for a long time after I know he's finished reading. His eyelids tremble, but no tears fall. He's cried himself dry.

"I don't understand. Why would she call us here to apologize and then kill herself? It doesn't make sense."

"Her phone has no signal here. She didn't call us. She couldn't."

Dad crushes his palms over his eyes. "She said she drove into town! She called us and said she wanted to make everything right!"

I take the phone from his swollen hand—the hand I smashed with a baseball bat only an hour ago. "She didn't, Dad. Look." I pull up Mom's call log and hand it back. "I checked it before. There are no outgoing calls to our numbers. We're not even in her contacts. She didn't call us."

"But she did!"

I'm losing him behind a wall of denial. "Listen, we both think we got calls from her yesterday, right? Friday afternoon. That email has been trying to send since Wednesday." I take a breath and try to temper my voice with compassion. "I'm no forensics expert but . . . I'm sorry, she's been dead for days. And look at her face."

Dad's eyes stay locked on the kicked-over deck chair lying on the floor. "I believe you."

"No, Dad. Look. At her forehead." He reluctantly glances up to see the final confirmation that sent me running to bury an axe in my fake mother's skull. The body has a whip-crack slash across its pale forehead. Just like I do. Just like Dad does. "That *thing* got in her head before she died. It knows everything she knew. It dredged up her memories and used them to torment her into killing herself. It knows all about us, and our family and our history." I blow out a breath. "I think *it* called us."

"But how?" Dad shouts, clawing at his thin hair. "How can some kind of brain demon make a phone call? A goddamn phone can't even make a phone call from here!"

"I don't know! How can it see our memories? How does it change forms? How did it sleepwalk me into crashing Mom's car? I don't know how it does any of the bullshit things it does, but it still does them!"

Dad cools, retreating into himself and drawing his attention back to the unsent email on Mom's phone, scrolling it up and down with his thumb.

"She didn't even try to reach out to us. She didn't even send us her suicide note. She sent it to her fucking publicist!" Dad throws the phone to the ground and leans forward, elbows on his knees, eyes pressed into his palms. "I can't believe she was too scared to ask our forgiveness. There was nothing for me to forgive. I would have taken her back in a heartbeat. Even after everything, she's the only woman I ever loved."

"Oh my God, Matty. Enough with the sentimental crap. We both know where you really wanted to bury your baloney."

The voice makes me start so violently I almost fall off the steps. I whip around to see a girl leaning back on her elbows against the railing near Dad's swing. She's long and willowy with short black hair. Latina. Her subtle curves wrapped tight in flower-print shorts and a midriff-bearing T-shirt that says *¿Qué pasa?* She can't be more than fifteen years old.

I don't know who she is. I don't care. She's not real. With a scream I charge and swing the axe at her chest. She barely reacts, casually swishing a two-fingered point across her body like a flight attendant pointing out the nearest exit. The axe head follows her direction, arcing wide and embedding in a vertical support beam next to her. Pain squeezes through tweaked muscles all the way down my back.

She didn't push the blade aside. I pulled it. I forced it to change course mid-swing. Her gesture moved my arms like a puppet.

My father stumbles off the bench and pushes himself to the other end of the gazebo. "Get away from me! You're not Rosebud!"

I jerk the axe free of the beam and hop back, putting some swinging distance between myself and Not Rosebud. "Dad, who is this?"

"It's the shadow!"

"I know it's the fucking shadow! Who is Rosebud?"

The girl slowly twists her hips and nibbles her lip like a wallflower at a junior-high dance. "Tell her, Matty. Tell her who I am."

"She's my co-worker!" Dad shouts. "She works with me! That's all!"

Not Rosebud rolls her eyes. "That is *so* not all. Tell her. Or I will."

Dad huffs. "She works with me at Rex Mex, okay? I'm a fifty-year-old loser who works at a Rex Mex! Are you happy?"

My patience thins. "I don't give a shit where you work! Why are you afraid of her?"

"I'm not!"

"You are, or else she wouldn't be here!"

The girl curls a finger through her hair. "Oh, Matty's not afraid of little ol' me. He's afraid of *you*." She smiles, drawing back her glossy lips. "He's afraid of what you'll think when I tell you how much he wants to pound my little pussy."

"I don't!" Dad cries. "It's all lies! Rosebud doesn't even look like that! She's older!"

Not Rosebud shakes her little head. "Older. Ha. The real Rosebud isn't even half your age." She rolls her huge, dark eyes to me. "Didn't you know? Your daddy robs cradles to get his dick wet."

"Shut up!" Dad shouts. "It's not true!"

His denial is so shrill it comes off as a blatant lie. Guilty sweat runs down his fat face. The kid sweeps closer to him and the sight of them together ignites my whole body in fury. I know she's not a real girl, but she represents one. She's an innocent child in a tight black pencil dress that makes her look like a woman in the eyes of a sexual predator.

"Come on, Matty. Show your daughter how you kissed me up in the bedroom." Not Rosebud coos. "You don't even need pills to get hard for me."

As the girl approaches him, my father's piggish eyes turn wild behind his round, wire-rimmed spectacles. He raises his hands to ward her off and the light glints off the three golden statuettes clenched in his fists. My heart pumps lava. My grip tightens on the axe and my muscles burn to bury it in his pedophile crotch.

"I admit it! I want you!" Dad screams. He clenches his eyes. "I mean, I want her! Rosebud! I do! But I don't want to have sex with her!"

The shadow girl clicks her tongue. "Matty, don't lie to—"

"I want *her* to have sex with *me*! I want her to be attracted to me! I want her to think I'm a worthwhile human being!" The smug smile goes flat on the shadow girl's face. My father wrings his hands and his volume drops from a confessional scream to a trembling ramble. "I want to come home and have somebody there who's happy to see me. I want to sit at the kitchen table and eat dinner with another person. I want someone to talk to and laugh with. Someone to inspire me to be a better person." He turns his watery eyes to the floor. "I don't want Rosebud because she's a hot college girl. I want her because she's kind to me. She's the only woman in Los Angeles who even acknowledges I exist." He shakes his head. "To be honest, I don't really want Rosebud at all. I just don't want to be alone."

I blink and the statuettes in my father's hands are gone. The wire glasses are gone. A chill passes through my muscles, loosening them and lowering the axe. I glance from my father to the shadow and blink with surprise. She's not a teenage girl in a *¿Qué pasa?* T-shirt. She's the same person, but older. A woman around my age, wearing an ill-fitting, grease-stained Rex Mex uniform. She's cute, but not the immaculate, blushing beauty she had been. Her black pants are covered in pet fur. Her mascara is clumped and there's a pimple under her chin. She just looks . . . normal. A sad smile haunts Dad's lips, as if he's seeing an old friend clearly for the first time.

"I'm not afraid of Rosebud anymore," Dad says calmly. "And I'm not afraid of you."

I step to his side and join him, staring the shadow down. "Neither of us are afraid of you."

Shadow Rosebud's pretty face ripples and distorts, as if a swarm of insects is scuttling under her skin. "Then you're both stupider than you look. Your dumb asses are going to die here. Painfully."

"No, we're not," I say, waving my hand. "We know your game now. We know all this bullshit is just illusions in our mind. You have no power over us."

The shadow's dark eyes flutter and become a pair of glowing orange embers sunk in her face. "I have more power over you than you can even comprehend."

I heft the axe. "Listen, asshole. If you don't want your skull cracked open again, I suggest you—"

The shadow explodes in a Big Bang of smoke fairies. A staggering legion of them spontaneously blasts into existence as if fired from a cannon, hitting me and nearly knocking me unconscious. The impact blinds me with an old tactile memory. I was a little kid in Venice, playing in the ocean. I wandered out too far and got clobbered by a wave twice my size. I couldn't see or hear or think. It was like being punched in the entire body all at once and then dragged away by a rolling liquid fist.

This is worse.

Every part of me is pummeled and scraped as I'm lifted off the ground and rolled end over end inside a black storm of smoke fairies. I kick and scream but have no control. I'm drowning in chaos edged with teeth and claws. My shoulder smashes the frame of the gazebo and I spin helplessly as I'm thrown out into the backyard. I hit the ground with a bone-jarring thud and gasp for breath as the jagged swarm spins above me like a lawnmower blade.

I hear another thump against the ground nearby, accompanied by my father's pained yelp. I try to crawl over to him, but something heavy lands on top of me and pounds the breath out of my lungs. Fairies screech and scrape over my face, beating their wings against my eyes as the shadow straddles me, clumsily kicking and slapping me with long limbs. I strike out a hand and grab its neck and its head falls loose against my arm. The body goes limp as the smoke fairies retreat from us, changing their formation to form a spiraling dome overhead. The thing on top of me is not the shadow. Mom's swollen tongue lolls from her mouth and her vacant eyes glare as I squeeze her corpse's broken throat. I squeal and throw her off me, rolling over and climbing to my feet.

The fairy swarm is so dense and thick it blots out the landscape. Their bodies spiral in huge ropy formations, weaving together like a basket of horrible motion overturned above me. But I am not afraid. I know it's all just an illusion in my mind. They could only hurt me before because the shadow made me think they could hurt me. They only had power over me because I was scared of them.

I'm not scared of them anymore.

A smoke fairy lands on the axe and scuttles down onto the back of my hand. It screeches and digs in its claws. I feel the pinching pain, but I don't swat it away. I stare into its orange eyes and speak, slowly and clearly. Not for its benefit. For mine.

"You. Are. Not. Real."

The dull impacts of three more fairies pound against my battered body. One on my thigh and two on my back. Their weight hangs heavily from my cold, muddy coat as they grab onto me and jockey for position, screeching and hissing. I close my eyes and breathe. I clear my head and imagine the fairies aren't there. Because they aren't. I vocalize my thoughts.

"I am not afraid of pictures from a storybook. I am not afraid of imaginary monsters. I am not afraid of smoke fairies."

The weights hanging on my body go still. I open my eyes. All four creatures are dead quiet. They look sick, as if my disbelief in fairies has poisoned them. I'm reminded of *Peter Pan*, and I run with it.

"I *don't* believe in fairies." The creature on my hand howls and breaks out in hives. Bubbles boil from its back, like gas seeping through the La Brea Tar Pits. It's dying. "I don't believe in fairies." Its smoky black plumage goes pale with rot. A bubble on its back grows large in the foam, thick and glassy like a fishbowl. The fairy chokes and shudders as honey-colored pus fills the globe. Everything about it turns my stomach. I screech through the nausea. "I don't believe in fairies!"

The bulbous monster screeches and buries its needle teeth in my hand, clamping on like a leech. I scream and drop the axe, but the sharp pain of the bite is immediately numbed by the dull burn of my skin inflating around the wound. Liquid from the globe on its ass pumps through the fairy's fangs in hot, orgasmic spurts as it dry humps my wrist. My mind clouds. I tear the beast out of my flesh and throw it down, smashing it under my boot. It bursts into flames as the remains of its bloated reservoir splash across the ground. I recognize its stench the instant it stings my nose.

Whisky.

Almost before I understand what's happening the other mutated fairies plunge their fangs through my clothes and into my flesh. The skin screams with pain for a split second before going numb and loose with liquor pumped in from their butt flasks.

I grab the one off my thigh and tear it free. Vodka and blood dribble from its mouth as I fling it away. I claw for the two on my back but my arms don't cooperate. The bites burn with wet, pressurized warmth just below my shoulder and above my waist. Everything starts to spin lazily through my mind.

"No! They're not real! None of thizziz real!"

My stomach lurches at the sound of my slurred voice.

Fuck. Fuck! They're not real, Rebecca! The booze isn't real! Ignore it!

I can't. Fairies are just a storybook abstraction, but liquor is a physical reality my mind is too familiar with to ignore. A cold, sweating horror grips me and I claw at my shoulder and waist. Gravity is all wrong. I pitch over backwards and land on my back, smashing the fairies against the ground. Their glassy remains pierce my skin but I barely feel it. I giggle and snort. I fell down on them and killed them. Bex fall down go boom!

Flames lick from their crushed bodies up the sides of my coat and I roll over on the soggy earth, snuffing them out. Rolly! Rolly! I'm a rolly-poly! My stomach cramps with laughter but the voice in my head won't stop screaming.

It's not funny, Rebecca! You're not drunk! Stand up! Move your ass!

Something thuds into the mud next to me. Then a second thing. Then more. The clouds in my vision part long enough for me to see a half-dozen weighted-down fairies, sloshing their alcohol-filled asses and baring their teeth as they scamper toward me. I grab for the axe but I don't remember where I lost it. I don't remember where I am. A hand grabs me tight around the arm.

"Come on!" Dad's face and hands are riddled with fairy scratches. He grunts and tugs at me, trying to pull me to my feet, but his shoes slip and he falls down on his knees next to me. "Rebecca, get up! Move! God damn it, stand up!"

Dad's sad rescue attempt steadies me enough to find my balance. My arms and legs slide on the wet ground but I manage to stand. Dad grabs my hand and pulls me into a wobbling half run through the swarm. Thousands of the fairies swarming around us have mutated into those … booze fairies. The bulbous weight of their alcoholic tumors disrupts their tight formations, sending them reeling off course and crashing into each other. Liquor and glass and fire rain down on us as we escape through the flock toward the closest shelter we can find.

We blast through the open door of the shed, lost in a stream of rampaging fairies. I swing the door and throw my weight into it, pushing it against the wave of monsters coursing through like water gushing into a damaged submarine. My boots scrape the floor and my stabbed shoulder screeches with sobering pain as I pound the door closed and twist the deadbolt. It hardly matters. There are hundreds of the tiny bastards already inside, flitting across the shelves and scurrying over the walls. Dad smashes them with a chunk of split firewood—its end already soaked in fairy grease and burning like a torch.

"Die you little shits!"

He rampages around the shed, screaming and swinging, leaving a trail of flaming corpses. But even as he slaughters them, the fairies don't attack. They just sit there and take it. I stumble back to the center of the room as my eyes dart in horror.

"Dad, stop! Stop!" I grab him and wrestle the blazing log out of his hand, throwing it aside. "Stop killing them! Look!"

He catches his gasping breath and scans the room. The fairies are no longer swarming. They're just perched on the walls, slowly creeping and scuttling as the fires of their fallen companions flicker around them.

"What's happening?" Dad asks. "What are they doing?"

"They're trying to trap us! They want us to kill them and burn ourselves to death!"

Dad waves a fist and screams. "Ha! Nice try, asshats! But we're too smart for you!" He turns to me. "Come on, let's go!"

He makes a move for the door, but before he takes one step the booze fairies ripple like a great, sweeping stadium wave. One after another they raise their globed asses and smash them into the walls, shattering their own bodies to release their incendiary contents. A cascade of brilliant orange flame engulfs the interior of the shed. Dad and I stumble to the open center of the room, throwing our arms around our faces to shield them from the inferno.

"Come on!" I shriek, leaping toward the door.

I pull the sleeve of my fur coat over my hand and plunge it into the fire to grip the deadbolt. Even through the thick fabric the heat of the metal sears my fingers. Pain forces a scream from my throat, but I don't let go. The bolt won't turn. It's stuck—welded or distorted by the fairy flame. The sleeve ignites and I screech and yank it back, stuffing it under my armpit to snuff it out.

"Shit!" Dad cries. "We're trapped!"

A set of flaming shelves buckles and collapses, scattering burning debris across the floor at our feet. Dad yelps and jumps away from me. The scorching heat pushes sweat out of my face and down my back, soaking my shirt.

I was wrong. About everything. The fairies are real. The fire is real. Real things in the real world. Not illusions in my mind.

No! That's what the shadow wants you to think! Be stronger than that! You were right about it pretending to be your mother, and you're right now. Believe!

I do believe. Not in the fairies, but in myself. I step toward the door and focus on the deadbolt knob. Flame boils over it like a witch's cauldron, heating it to a glowing red. I roll my sleeve back and take a deep breath of hot, dry air. I close my eyes. I focus the Energy of the Universe. I concentrate. I grab the lock.

My heart throbs as the metal stings my skin. It's not hot. It's cold, chilled by the winter air. With my eyes closed I can clearly picture it how it really is. Not glowing with fiery heat, but frosty, hidden in the pitch-black darkness of the shed.

I knew it! Suck it, you shadowy asshole!

I turn the knob and it clunks as the bolt slides open. Keeping my eyes closed I slide my hand down the rough, cold wood to the doorknob. My fingers bump it and I grab and give it a frantic twist, but it just rattles back and forth. It won't release. Shit! I clench my eyes tighter and try to remember. Did the knob have some kind of secondary lock on it? Do I have to slide something or release a catch? I can't remember. God damn it, I can't remember!

I take a deep, calming breath. The air is bracingly cold and damp in my lungs. There is no heat. There is no smoke. All I can hear is my father's frantic, whimpering breath as he dodges flaming debris in his own mind behind me. I open my eyes.

Blazing agony sears from the red-hot doorknob through my palm and up my wrist. My scream is barely louder than the roar of blinding yellow hellfire surrounding me. I clutch my scalded hand to my chest and stumble back as pain sizzles through my blackened flesh. My father darts to my side, horror squeezing his sweat-soaked face.

"What did you do?" he shrieks. "Why did you do that?"

I force words through my pain. "The fire isn't real! It's not real!"

A burning rafter falls from the roof, smashing down on another shelving unit and collapsing it against the door. The room seems smaller, closing in on us as it feeds the flame. Dad grabs me by the shoulders and gives me a frantic shake. "Pull yourself together! We have to get out of here!"

I shove him off with my good hand. "Listen to me! The fire isn't real!"

"Look at your hand! It's real!"

It is real. My scorched fist balled at my chest sends the sickly stench of burnt flesh and hair trickling up my nose. "It's only real because we're making it real! We have to stop believing in it. We have to clear our minds!" A realization dawns on me. "We have to meditate!"

Dad throws up his hands. "Meditate? God damn it, Rebecca! This isn't time for hippie voodoo. Don't go crazy on me. Not now!"

I'm not crazy. I'm completely sane.

As the room collapses into a flaming ruin around me, I sit cross-legged in the center of the smoldering concrete floor. I straighten my back and rest my bloody hands on my knees.

I close my eyes and breathe.

CHAPTER TWENTY-FOUR

Matty

"Meditate? God damn it, Rebecca! This isn't time for hippie voodoo. Don't go crazy on me. Not now!"

I want to grab her by the shoulders and shake her until she snaps out of it. She says the fire isn't real. It's so incredibly real! She's snapped. She doesn't even care that her hand is char-broiled, dribbling sticky blood down her elbow. She just gives me a mad, moony smile, sits on the floor, and closes her eyes.

The walls groan as the roof does a crackling shimmy on its buckling supports. The shed is about to collapse on top of us and we're dead. We're fucking dead!

I need to get Bex out of here.

There's no way we're getting out the door we came in. Not with two feet of twisted, flaming shelves collapsed in front of it. The only other exit is the big barn doors. I have to break through them. I turn to the woodpile for the axe that's not there. Damn it! A quick scan of the remaining nooks and crannies of the shed for a plan B reveals nothing but flaming toys. Shit!

The intense heat is boiling the sweat off me as fast as I can pump it out, leaving my skin raw and red. Rolling black smoke packs ash into my lungs, choking my breath and brains. I feel dizzy. I'm going to pass out and never wake up.

Get your ass in gear, Matty! Save Bex! Save yourself! You can do this!

I can do this. I have to do this.

With a roar I push all my strength into my legs and rush the barn doors. My shoulder pounds the wood, and unintentionally, so does my head. A throbbing crack twists my neck and my vision flashes white. I drop to one knee against the unyielding doors, and the flames engulfing them reach out to embrace me. The demon-hot fire crawls up my thighs as I kick and fumble into a roll to snuff them out.

I start to cry.

I cry because the pain is unbearable. Because everything is unbearable. Shards of burning wooden shrapnel explode through the shed as flames devour the walls. The roof groans and shifts, bowing and showering us with fiery splinters. It's coming down. We are going to die.

I drag myself across the baking-hot concrete to where Bex is still sitting, cross-legged and motionless. Her body is placid but her face is crushed, her eyes clenched so tightly they look as if they'll burst in their sockets. Her breath is heavy and rapid—a hysterical puffing like a sitcom mom giving birth. Sweat pours from her cheeks and drips from her chin, and black blood dribbles from the shadow gash in her forehead. But she's just sitting there in the lotus position like one of those Buddhist martyrs self-immolating in protest.

I force myself to kneel on my scalded knees in front of her. An involuntary scream spills from my mouth, but Bex doesn't open her eyes. She doesn't even flinch. Her mind has gone into some primeval catatonic coping mechanism. I don't bother trying to bring her back to reality. There's no point.

I speak to her clamped-down face. "If you can hear me, I'm sorry. For everything. I wish things could have been different between us." Tears roll down my cheeks. "Good bye, Bex."

I rest my hands on her shoulders. My sweet daughter. I want to pull her in and hug her close until the end. Squeeze her tight enough to make up for all the years of lost time we'll never get back. I lean forward, tenderly touching my forehead to hers.

The instant we connect an electric chisel stabs through the gash in my scalp. I try to grab at the pain in my skull but I don't have hands. I don't have a skull. I'm nothing, drifting in a chaos of nothing, buffeted by an aether of turbulent gray nothing. It's a rolling gray storm cloud spreading to infinity in every direction. I catch glimpses of nightmarish shapes lurking just below its surface, like chunks of enormous black insects linked by sinew into mile-long tentacles. Flashes of white sparking light illuminate strange divots whacked in the vapor, like holes ripped in the fabric of this universe.

I'm dead.

The shed must have collapsed on us. My body was crushed and burned, ejecting my spirit to haunt this grim, stormy purgatory. I become vaguely aware of something that would be sound if I had ears to hear it. An otherworldly warble, like a tortured theremin. It repeats a short, flat tone, over and over, growing crisper and more distinct until I realize it's not a tone. It's a word.

Dad!

"Bex?" I shout. But I don't shout it. I just think it and it projects out, thin and reverberating in the non-air.

"Dad!"

The word makes me think of my daughter, and tiny flakes begin to sparkle on the currents of the haze. Two of them drift together and stick. Then another, then more. As the cluster grows, it seems to push down on the mist, forming a dimple with a gravity that draws in other flakes. The nucleus grows and the process accelerates, drawing in glittering light from across the void.

"Where are you?" I try to call out.

As I watch the particles coalesce I feel my own nothingness snowballing into somethingness. I have legs. I have arms and hands. A vague sense of connectedness holds them together until I am aware of my entire body between them. A voice rings into my new ears.

"Dad?"

I have eyes. I blink and focus and see I'm not alone in this bleak abyss. The gathering particles have formed a full figure drifting in front of me. Solid and muscular, with long auburn hair floating slowly on the mist like a mermaid in a tropical spring.

"Bex!" The sight of her is a comfort wrapped in uncertainty. "Wait, are you really Bex?"

She twists and kicks her legs, turning her body in the dense fog.

"For fucks sake, Dad! Stop calling me Bex!"

It's really her. My relief is muted by the larger problem at hand.

"Are we . . . dead?"

"I don't think so." She presses her fingers on her temples. "I tried to clear my head so I could see past the illusions, but something went wrong. As soon as I closed my eyes I got yanked into this . . . place. But it's not a place. I think I've been here before."

Black ropes of cartilaginous tendon as big around as bridge cables crackle as they flex and coil through the cloud, tugging on the pockets of light in the distance. They're getting closer to us. Or we're getting closer to them. It's impossible to tell. Nothing makes sense.

"It's not a place, but you've been here?" I ask. "What does that even mean?"

Rebecca scowls. "It's not a physical place. I think it's some kind of astral realm. A mind place. Last night when I meditated I got pulled into something like this. That's where I first became aware of the shadow inside my head." She looks at me suspiciously. "Wait, if this is all in my head, how are you here? You're not real!"

"Yes, I am! The last thing I knew we were in the shed and you were having some kind of panic seizure. I leaned in to hug you and as soon as we touched my forehead exploded and I was here."

Bex's face goes pale. "It wasn't your forehead. It was your ajna chakra."

"My anajawhatnow?"

"Your third eye." She taps above her brow. "You must have touched yours to mine and somehow got pulled into my astral fever dream!"

Well, that sounds batshit crazy. I try to remember what happened. I was holding her and leaning in to say goodbye, and the instant my forehead touched hers I was suddenly here. But I'm not here. There is no here. A snowball forms in the pit of my stomach.

"Oh shit! In the real world we're both blacked out in the shed! The shadow put us into brain comas so we couldn't escape! We're going to burn to death!"

"No we're not!" Bex says impatiently. "Listen to me, there is no fire!"

I huff and cross my arms. "Okay, then what did I barbecue myself on trying to break down the goddamn door so I could save—"

A ring of light passes around us. The moment we pass its gauzy threshold the aether becomes air. Gravity snares our floating bodies and slams them down on a hardwood floor.

I groan and try to roll over. Losing the sensation of weightlessness reminds me how out of shape I am. "Aaugh. What the hell?"

Rebecca is already on her feet, knees bent, arms ready to attack. Her voice is tense with unease. "It's the house. We're in our old house."

I climb to my feet and my eyes go wide. We're in my bedroom at the "old house." The house where I still live in Venice Beach. But it's too clean. Too new. The water stain on the ceiling from the leaky roof isn't there yet, and the imposing four-poster bed is actually made, with puffy, pastry-like blankets I don't even own anymore.

"It's not real," I say. "It doesn't even look like this anymore. This is some kind of bullshit brain trick."

"Obviously," Rebecca says. "It's an old memory. The shadow can make you relive them. It did this to me last night."

I soak in the surreal flashback. If this really is a memory it must be mine. Rebecca would have been too young to remember the house looking like this. The hole in reality that we fell through to get here is gone, closing off the fourth wall with a stormy view of Venice Beach through the window. The wind howls and rain batters against the window as lightning flashes through the thrashing palm trees outside.

"Cut it out, Matty. I have a headache."

The irritated voice turns my head toward the door to the hallway as a long pair of bare legs stride through it. It's Kim, wearing a fetish-short white bathrobe with a pink towel wrapped around her wet hair like a turban. My jaw drops and my heart swells. Her face is so young and smooth, unblemished by age. Just like the house, this is the Kim of a distant past, from the golden age of our relationship.

Rebecca's muscles tighten. "It's the shadow! Get out of my brain, you bitch!" She leaps forward to throw a punch, but her fist smashes against Kim's cheek as if she were a marble statue. "Aagh! Shit!"

Bex staggers back to my side, seething and rubbing her knuckles. Kim sits on the bed and grabs a tube of lotion from the nightstand, blissfully unaware of the assault. This is obviously not an interactive memory. It's a thought film of staggering sensory detail. The paint still smells new on the walls. I can almost taste the fruity bouquet of the scented cream Kim rubs on her legs. Footsteps in the hall pull my attention back to the door.

"Ah, zee mademoiselle has retired to zee boudoir! You can run, but you cannot hide, mon chéri!"

I recognize that fake French. My pulse quickens as he walks in. As *I* walk in. A young and slim version of me, wearing a baggy flannel over his broad chest.

"The hell?" I snort. "What is this, *A Christmas Carol*?" I turn to Rebecca. "Is this what happened to you last night? The shadow made you watch lame flashback sequences?"

Rebecca shakes her head. "No. This is different."

The young Matty doesn't acknowledge us. He just smiles and runs his fingers through his thick hair, leaning rakishly against the doorframe.

"Come on, baby. You know you want some of this."

Kim scowls at him and shakes her head. "I'm going to bed."

Young Matty wags his eyebrows. "Then we're on the same page."

"I'm going to *sleep*," Kim growls.

"Yeah, you are," Matty says with a sly grin. "Right after I wear you out, if you know what I'm sayin'."

My nose wrinkles as he saunters playfully into the room. Rebecca stares at the scene in progress, frozen with paralyzed disgust. I'm also disgusted. God, did I really talk like that? What a douche. Young Matty leans over Kim and kisses her long neck. She rolls her head and smirks. "Stop it."

"Stop what? Stop this?" He gives her another flirty peck on the cheek. "This? You want me to stop *this*?" He kisses her again, on the lips. Her slender hands pound his chest and he stumbles back.

"God damn it, Matty! I said no! Leave me alone!"

Young Matty's expression tightens from startled surprise to aggravated rage. The anger in his eyes pushes cold sweat from my pores.

"Don't give me that shit!" he barks. "If you wanted to be left alone you wouldn't be wearing that little fuck-me bathrobe. You wouldn't be parading around in front of me with half your ass hanging out." He grabs his belt and furiously undoes the buckle. "You're just begging for a deep dicking."

My heart explodes in panic. *What?* What the shit is happening here? Young Matty rips off his flannel shirt and throws it to the ground. For some reason it steals my full attention. Plaid flannel. This memory would have been from the mid-'90s. The heyday of grunge. It fits, but it's wrong. I clap my palms to my temples and press, trying to force clarity into my frenzied mind.

Kim drops her lotion and stands up, her eyes darting between the door and the man standing between her and it. "Matty, don't. Just leave me alone. Please."

Blood pounds in my ears. Young Matty pushes Kim onto the bed. She screams. I scream.

I never owned a flannel shirt.

"No! What the fuck?" I grab Rebecca by the arm, turning both of us away from the attack. "Listen to me, this isn't real! This never happened!" The air blisters with pained shrieks and cries for help. I look to the sky, shouting at the demon god of this world. "You lying monster! This didn't happen! This isn't my memory!"

Rebecca swallows hard. "It's mine."

"*What?*"

She doesn't flinch away from my spittle-filled exclamation, but her voice trembles. "This is my memory. I don't know exactly where or how this happened, but I know it did." Her crystal eyes are hard and defiant. "I know what happened, Dad. I know I was a rape baby."

The accusation blows out the back of my head like a shotgun blast. "You . . . *what?* No you weren't!"

Rebecca presses her palms to her ears, trying to blot out the squeaking of springs and agonized screams behind us. "I don't want to talk about it! It doesn't matter now!"

I grab her hands and yank them off her head, forcing her to hear me. "It does matter! Rebecca, this didn't happen!"

"*Something* happened! Mom always said you hurt her and gave her another mouth to feed! She said she could never forgive you for what you did!" Her face burns red. "If it wasn't this, then what? What did you do to her, Dad?"

She stops screeching and stares at me, drilling for an answer with those penetrating eyes. A crack forms in a dam that I built in my mind long ago, letting out a stinging torrent of memory. My lips quiver. "I was selfish and I betrayed her. But I did it for you."

"What? What did you do?" Rebecca howls, shoving me away. "Just say it!"

I knew this day would someday come. The moment when I am forced to tell Rebecca the truth. But I never thought it would happen like this, trapped in a twisted mental hellscape, shouting my secrets over a fictional sexual assault in progress three feet away. The humiliation of it all, seeing how my daughter imagined me for so many years, makes me explode in a rage I didn't even know I was capable of. I turn toward the bed and scream, "This! Didn't! *Happen!*"

The two grappling figures blast against the wall and explode like dried leaves, sizzling away into nothing. My hand darts to my head as pain sears across the scrape in my forehead, but it finds only smooth, sweaty flesh. I don't have the shadow scratch in this world, but it still controls me.

No! Screw that, Matty! You saw what you just did! You control *it!*

My fingers press into the agony of my invisible scar, and I feel its energy spark around me and through me. I become one with my Chaka Khan, or whatever Rebecca called it. My third eye. My teeth grind and I shove against the pressure building in my skull. It's the mental equivalent of pushing a stalled car out of the road—heaving with everything you've got until it budges an inch, then two, then begins to roll.

It feels like hot steam is screeching through my forehead like a teapot, but I feel a shift in the energy around me. I concentrate on the truth.

The walls roll and distort, closing in, shrinking around us. My eyes narrow from the tension crushing my mind, but I keep them open and force myself to remember the truth. The room wavers and sizzles, then comes back into focus as an entirely different place.

It's a different bedroom, weary and faded with a crumbling popcorn ceiling. The traffic patterns of at least a decade's worth of former tenants are etched in the brown carpet, running between the door and the closet and the tiny window. Most of the light comes from a frosted-glass globe hanging from the ceiling, its bottom littered with housefly corpses.

It's my shitty old condo in Studio City. The place I lived when Kim moved in. The place we continued to live after she blew most of her *Blood Blitz* paycheck impulse buying a cabin near Lake Arrowhead. The only evidence of Kim's newfound success is a brand-new queen-sized four-poster crowding the walls of the tiny room. Rebecca backs into the corner, her eyes narrow with confusion. She's been here before, but she doesn't know it. We moved out of this dump when she was eighteen months old.

I become aware of another presence in the room. The other me. Young Matty wears a Def Leppard T-shirt and cargo shorts as he stands next to the bed, folding a heap of laundry. Kim shuffles in. She's barefoot, wearing pink sweatpants and a white tank top. Her hair is thick and long and pulled up in a messy ponytail high at the back of her head. Despite the sadness of the memory, the sight of her like this warms my heart. This was the best version of Kim. Casual, bummin'-around-the-house Kim. The Kim the cameras never saw. Her face is flushed but firm.

"Matty, we need to talk."

"Uh oh." Young Matty recoils and jabbers with fake worry. "I didn't do it. Nobody saw me do it. You can't prove anything!"

Kim doesn't quite smile. "I'm serious, hon. This is important."

Young Matty's fake worry turns real. He gets up and goes to her. "What is it? Is everything okay?"

A sense of dread plunges in his stomach. I know because I experience it with him, as if we're two bodies sharing the same mind. At my side, Rebecca unconsciously puts a hand on her own belly. Her face is tense with his anxiety.

Kim's lips purse. "You know how I've been so exhausted lately and I always feel sick and sore and gross?"

Young Matty nods. "Yeah, but . . . you're okay, right? I mean . . ." His eyes dart as his mind races. "Oh my God, Kim. Are you sick?"

Kim frowns.

"No, Matty. I'm not sick. I'm pregnant."

A torrent of emotion surges through me, flowing from my youthful doppelgänger. The twitching expressions of relief and bewilderment battling for dominance on Rebecca's face show the wave is hitting her too.

ONE MUST KILL ANOTHER

Young Matty chews his lip. "But . . . how? I thought you were on the pill."

"I was. I am! This must have happened right around when I fired my agent. Remember how he was pressuring me so hard to do the stupid *Blood Blitz* sequel and I got all . . ." Kim swirls her fingers around her ears, giving the universal sign for "not right in the head." "I couldn't sleep. I lost track of time and days." Her lips wrinkle. "I missed a few pills. I realized later it had happened, but I hoped it wouldn't matter." She sighs. "It mattered."

The tide of the battle in my gut turns. Disorientation and surprise ebb away, and pure joy explodes through the roof like a geyser to my brain. The change of heart reflects on Young Matty's face as it goes from slack-jawed to beaming.

"Oh my God," he mutters, then shouts. "Oh my God, Kim! This is fantastic!" He takes her hands and squeezes them. "We're gonna have a baby! I'm going to be a father!"

Kim frowns and gently pulls away. "No. You're not."

"I . . . huh?"

Even though I know how this works out, the racing logic of the moment poisons my blood. Kim is pregnant but I'm not going to be a father. She's slept with someone else. My heart shatters like a coffee mug pitched into concrete. Kim's next words belay that fear but fan the flames of confusion.

"I can't have a baby, Matty. I just can't."

The intensity of the emotion again clouds my ability to reason. She's pregnant but she can't have a baby? Is this like, an obscure female biology thing? Is this what they talked about in that secret meeting when they pulled all the girls out of the fifth grade for an hour? I can't think but my mouth knows it needs to speak, so it says the only thing it can.

"What?"

Kim takes one of my hands in both of hers, but she doesn't look me in the face. "I love you. I love you with my whole heart. The two of us have our whole lives ahead of us. I can't let anything ruin that."

Her sentiment is heartfelt, but her words make no sense. "Sweetie, nothing could ever ruin what we have. I love you so much I didn't think I had any love left to share with anyone else, but just now I realized I was wrong. I have enough love for you and our little rugrat. I have enough for a whole family."

Kim's expression fills with unease. "Matty, that's sweet but . . . you don't understand what I'm telling you." Her lips tighten. "I'm not going to have the baby."

The words hit my chest like buckshot, burning scalding wormholes through my heart. "You . . . Kim, I don't think . . ." Young Matty stops and pulls a breath. "It's okay to be nervous about this. It's a big deal. But being afraid of something big is no reason not to do it. This is our next great adventure together." He softly takes her hand. "And I know you'll make an amazing mother."

Tiny muscles tic in Kim's face. "I won't. I really won't. I . . ." Her eyes roll to the side and she lets out a long breath. "I didn't have a good childhood."

She says it as if it's a secret. Young Matty and I are both aware Kim had a rough time growing up. Her parents were assholes. She's never been very open about it, but I know her father knocked up her mother at a frat party and they decided to "do the right thing" and get married. It wasn't exactly a happily-ever-after situation for either of them.

Young Matty nods tenderly. "I know, honey. But—"

"You *don't* know." Kim's voice is a blade. "My parents were happy before they had me. My mother was pre-med. She was going to be a doctor, but she had to quit school to be a mother. I was a load for her to carry, and I made her a load for my father to carry. They treated me like a pet they were sick of owning but couldn't put to sleep. Everything was an argument. Who had to feed me. Who had to clean me. Who had to take me to school. My life was a never-ending game of 'not it.' I ruined their lives, Matty! I'm not going to ruin ours!" Her anger cracks into rapid, tearful breaths. "I can't raise a child. I can't. The very idea of it turns my stomach. I'm . . . I'm damaged."

The weight of her terror is suffocating. Rebecca gapes, too stunned to move. Young Matty takes Kim's hands and holds them tight. "You're not damaged. You're perfect. And the experiences you've had will only make you a better mother. You won't make the same mistakes your parents made."

"You don't know that!" Kim pulls away from Young Matty and crosses her arms. "I'm telling you, I can't do this. I can't create a happy childhood. I don't even know what one looks like." Her shimmering eyes capture Young Matty's. "I can't be a mother. I can't. I just can't."

Emptiness fills my heart and soul. I'm at a loss for words. I want to give her a thousand reasons why the two of us will make amazing parents to amazing children, but I know she won't be convinced. Not right now. This conversation needs time to breathe.

"I understand why you're afraid, but I have confidence in you. I love you and I know you could never hurt someone else like you've been hurt," Young Matty says. "Please just think about it. I understand it might seem daunting, but I'm asking you to consider the positives."

Kim's eyebrows arch. "Do you think I haven't done that? Do you think this was a casual decision, like choosing whether or not to eat a second cookie? My God, Matty! I've made up my mind. I just wanted to pay you the respect of letting you know. I hoped you'd support me."

I want to scream and smash my fist through the shitty drywall. How could she tell me we're going to have a baby and then . . . *yoink!* Psyche! And how can she think I'd be okay with that? I understand she has some issues to work through, but who doesn't? Nobody is ever ready to be a parent when it happens. She may have had a messed-up childhood, but I didn't. My parents loved me and played with me and taught me how to be a good person. I know how to be a good father. And I love Kim and have absolute faith in her. Once she sees her own child for the first time all the old baggage will drop. Her loving instincts will take over. She'll be the best goddamn mother the world has ever seen.

Young Matty fidgets and licks his lips, trying to find the words to make Kim understand all the things I feel. He can't.

"I support you in everything you do. You are my wife and I will always stand by you. But . . . this isn't just about you. It's about us. It's about this little dude or dudette." He rests a hand on her abdomen. "I think you're making a mistake and I'm begging you to reconsider."

Kim's body trembles as she stares down her husband. I can tell she wants to fight, but at the same time, doesn't. Her voice is a bittersweet whisper of regret. "I shouldn't have told you. You would have been happier not knowing."

She turns and leaves the room. Small steps turn longer as Kim's metered exit becomes a full retreat. In retrospect I understand she was trying to get out before she started crying. In the moment, all Young Matty knows is that diplomacy has failed. He watches her go then pauses as a scheme brews in his sitcom-addled mind. Before he can think better of it, he grabs the telephone off the nightstand and lifts the receiver.

This is it. This is the choice that ruined our marriage forever. The heartache of it hits me so completely that I lose mental concentration and the whole room starts to waver and collapse. Pain pounds through my knees as the ground buckles, and I teeter off balance. Rebecca shouts and Young Matty evaporates. I swallow the pain of my decades-old decision and focus on holding this memory together even as it falls apart around me. The walls congeal. The wilting glass of the window hardens in front of a gray morning. Time has passed, but not much. A day or two, three at the most. Just long enough to swing the wrecking ball.

Young Matty is still asleep when Kim bursts in, dressed for her morning jog. Spandex and full makeup. A daily performance for the paparazzi. Her voice trembles with barely contained fury.

"Matty, how could you?"

Young Matty groggily jolts up. "What? What happened?"

"This happened!"

Kim throws a fistful of tabloids onto the mattress, fresh off the newsstand. Three of them, each with a different scandalous variation on the same headline. *Kimberly Savage is pregnant!*

"What? How did they find out?" Young Matty asks. His mixture of confusion and indignant shock is utterly unconvincing. Kim grabs one of the papers and rifles it open to a two-page spread of photos, each with a superimposed circle around her belly, supposedly highlighting a baby bump that does not yet exist. She pins a finger to a line of text and shoves it in front of his eyes.

"They found out because 'a source' told them. An 'anonymous source very close to Ms. Savage.'"

"It must have been your lady-parts doctor." Young Matty scowls. "She must have leaked your test results!"

"It was a home pregnancy test!" Kim screams. "My doctor doesn't know! Nobody knew but you! How could you do this to me?"

Young Matty blanches. "I'm sorry. I just . . . I was excited about the news."

"You selfish prick!" Kim pounds Young Matty's broad chest with her fists. "You asshole! This wasn't news! It was a secret! It was a secret I shared with you because I trusted you! Now it's all over the gossip rags! My publicist has already gotten calls from *People* and *Us Weekly*. Everyone knows, Matty!"

My heart beats against my stomach, churning up acid. I hate myself right now. Young Matty hates himself. And some part of me is still aware of Rebecca at my side, feeling the projection of my self-loathing as if it's her own.

Young Matty chooses his next words carefully. "Just tell them about your plans. They can print a correction."

I want to throttle him. That calculating, insensitive dickweed. But I also feel what he feels, and it's not pretty. Regret consumes him. It's only just happened and he already knows he's made the biggest mistake of his life. He still believes he did it for the right reasons. He'll always believe that, but that conviction will be forever overshadowed by the pain of this betrayal.

"You know I can't do that," Kim hisses. "You know the public wouldn't care what I've gone through. Or what I'm going through. They won't want an explanation! They'll just brand me as a heartless, selfish, baby-killing bitch. They'll crucify me. I'll never work again." Her anger collapses and disintegrates under the weight of her sorrow. "I confided in you and you . . . you ruined me. You ruined everything."

She cries. I made those tears, and they shred me like knives. Young Matty wants to reach out and embrace his wife, but he knows better. He knows what's done is done, but he naively believes this wound will heal in time. His mind can't fathom the depth of the treason he has committed. He doesn't yet realize the shattered vase of his relationship will eventually be glued back together, but the seams of the breaks will always remain, raised and ragged. The shape of it will someday be recognizable as repaired, but there will always be pieces missing. It will look like a vase, but it will never hold water again.

"I just . . . I didn't know what else to do. I'm sorry I called the press. I am, I really am." Young Matty steels his voice. "But I want you to know that nothing is ruined. Having a baby won't ruin your career. It'll strengthen your career, because the whole world will fall in love with you all over again when they see what a wonderful, caring mother you are. And it'll strengthen you, because you will *be* a wonderful, caring mother. And it'll strengthen our relationship, because we'll have someone else to share our love with. Everything isn't ruined. Everything is only going to keep getting better. I promise."

The passion of his speech burns me from the inside out. Young Matty is pleading for her forgiveness and his own life, and he means every word he says. He's dumped his whole heart through his mouth and let it pool at Kim's feet, hoping against hope that she'll understand why he did what he did. She just stands for a long moment, staring at him. Her hands rub her still-flat tummy through her tank top. Finally she shakes her head and exhales.

"I want to believe you."

She turns and leaves. I'm with Rebecca and my younger self, but I feel more alone than I ever have in my life. The icy chill of solitude weakens my resolve. I hate this memory. I hate that it happened, I hate that I remember it, and I hate reliving it. The room cracks and splinters into shards of gray shadow. Young Matty vaporizes. The whole illusion collapses around us and we're whisked into the swirling vapors and writhing black tentacles of the mind storm.

I sense the psychic tether between myself and Rebecca snap and recoil into my psyche like a tape measure. She doubles over and dry heaves, then comes out of it screaming. She catches her gasping breath, turning in the vapor to face me.

"You trapped her. You forced her to have a baby she didn't want." Her eyes tighten. "You forced her to have *me*! No wonder she always hated me!"

My head dips in shame. "I was young and stupid. I didn't understand how much I would hurt her. I wasn't thinking of the consequences, I only thought of the benefits." I glance up at her. "The benefit was worth the consequences."

Rebecca smirks and holds her nauseated stomach. "Mom spent years turning me against you and I never really knew why. Why didn't you ever tell me about this?"

"You were ten years old the last time I was allowed to speak to you. I wasn't about to ruin your self-esteem by telling you that you were an 'oops baby' your mother wanted to terminate." My lips wrench into a humiliated frown. "How was I supposed to tell you the reason your mother hated me was because you were born? What kind of asshole would do that to a child?" I grumble under my breath. "This was my cross to bear, not yours."

Rebecca doesn't speak. We just fall through the mist together. The sensation jars me. We're no longer drifting. We're falling. The texture of the all-encompassing gray storm is growing thinner and brighter, losing its ability to hold us aloft. The black shapes in the clouds are becoming more visible. It's all one thing. An enormous misshapen squid of gnarled bones and quills strung together with tar. A tentacle contracts, flinging another ring of light toward us, tumbling end-over-end like a coin. It's a one-way hole—a single side with depth, the other an invisible flatness against the clouds.

"Look out!" I grab Rebecca by her arm and the opening spins around us, scooping us out of the air like the net of a lacrosse stick. We both fall straight up and crash to a carpeted floor. I groan and get my bearings, realizing we actually fell *down* to the floor. I have no idea where we are, but a creeping terror kneads at my gut.

Rebecca scrambles to her knees, her eyes wide and probing. "Oh shit. Shit!" I feel her frenzied panic as clearly as if it were my own. Whatever this place is, it's posh as hell. Glassy, modern architecture with flattering soft light. The furniture has a strange duality. It's obviously expensive, yet made to look less so. A designer imposter of the slouchy leather chairs and sofas of a sports bar. One entire wall is a window, overlooking a moonlit downtown Los Angeles from a great height. Two of the others are huge, gallery-lit trophy cases full of soccer balls and jerseys.

Rebecca is already standing, ready to bolt. I grunt myself to my feet. "Where are we? Is this a museum or something?"

"We have to go. We have to go!" Rebecca screams. She puts her fingers to her temples and rubs, clenching her eyelids. "I am not here.

268

It's just a memory. I can break it." She opens her eyes and shouts at me. "Help me break it!"

Her face pinches closed in frantic concentration. I share Rebecca's hysterical desire to bust out of this flashback and I don't even know what it is. Her breath is chokingly fast and hard in my throat. Our minds are bonded as before, but I'm only connected to her emotions, not her thoughts. The silhouettes of two figures come into view in front of the illuminated display case, a narrow one and a broader one, looking at an autographed jersey branded "Beckham."

The smaller one is Rebecca. I almost do a double take when my brain places her. This is the Rebecca from the magazine clipping that's been hanging on my refrigerator for the past eight years. This is *Bex*. She's fifteen or sixteen, awkwardly adorable in a black gown with her hair pulled up in a look of award-show glamour. The tightness of the dress accentuates the pubescent skinniness of her body. She turns to her companion and smiles uncomfortably.

"Your collection is super impressive, but I think I need to . . . Let's just take a break for a second, okay?"

The man raises an eyebrow and grins. "Of course, can I, uh . . . " He seems to mull over a thought, then shrugs and goes for it. "Can I get you a drink?"

Teen Bex's revulsion washes up the back of my throat, lubricated by my own. No, you can't get her a drink, you shit! She's a kid! What the fuck, man? I turn to Rebecca. "Who is this asshole?"

She doesn't answer me. She keeps rubbing her temples, breathing and chanting. "I am not here. I am not here."

I look back at the conversation. The guy has to be my age, stocky and gray and bespectacled. His accent is foreign. I know I've seen him on TV before, but I can't place his face.

Teen Bex demurs his offer. "No, thank you. I was just thinking . . . " She picks at her thumbnail. "I'm still thinking about that movie you talked about downstairs. It just . . . It's such a perfect Kimberly Savage role. It really is."

The man smiles and rolls his eyes. "Ohh, I see how it is. You pretend to be interested in my memorabilia so you can act as your mother's agent? Is that right, you little devil?"

"No!" Teen Bex says, too emphatically. A weak smile forces its way across her mahogany-glossed lips. "No, I really wanted to see your stuff, but, I mean, I have other interests besides soccer."

The shit weasel smiles back at her, but his smile is genuine and hungry. He takes a step closer and leans on the glass beside her. "Oh? And what other things, pray tell, are you interested in?"

My heartbeat quickens on Teen Bex's behalf. She shuffles nervously and glances up at him with her darkly mascaraed eyes. "I'm interested in seeing Kimberly Savage in your next movie."

Shit weasel tips back his head and laughs. "You do have a one-track mind, don't you? Okay, I have to be honest. Your mother is a good fit for the part. But there are a lot of other women who are also a good fit. I'm just not convinced Kimberly Savage is the right pick for *Justified Killing*."

Justified Killing! The vigilante mom movie! This assbasket is the writer-director, Robert VanDuzer! The realization only makes the revulsion in my muscles burrow all the way to the bone. Why the fuck is Robert VanDuzer flirting with my underage daughter?

Bex's sweat pumps from my underarms and forehead as her heart beats like hummingbird wings in my chest.

"Well what, uh . . ." Teen Bex fidgets. "What do I have to say to convince you?"

VanDuzer's lips curl back in a predatory grin. "You don't have to say a thing."

He closes his eyes and presses his mouth to hers. She stiffens but puckers up and pushes back. I'm overwhelmed by a crushing helplessness and a strange sense of loss. This is the first time I've ever kissed a boy. I want to cry, but I hold it in, overpowered by a fierce loyalty to my mother. The emotion twists against logic in my mind.

Not my mother. Her mother. These are Bex's emotions. This is Bex's first kiss.

This is Bex's first kiss. The vulnerability sizzles away in a hellfire of fury that burns through me. I turn to the real Rebecca. Her adult face is clenched, her voice a furious scream. "I am not here! I am not here! I am not here!"

My own muscles tighten on the double dose of my rage standing on the shoulders of hers. VanDuzer moans in the back of his throat as his thick hand slides up the outside of Teen Bex's narrow thigh and under her dress. Shame smashes me apart like cracks splintering through ice. I feel his rough palm on me, grabbing my ass. I'm so angry that I have to do what I'm about to do, but I don't see any way out of it. I ruined my mother's life and I have to fix it. If I do this one thing she'll love me again.

I scream. Scream with all the fury and complicit helplessness that Teen Bex chokes down and swallows into her own maelstrom of rage. I slam my fists onto my temples and roar. "We are not here! We are not here! We are not here!"

VanDuzer eases the zipper of Teen Bex's dress down the narrow curve of her back as a crack rips across the side of the penthouse, right through the middle of the wall of windows. Where the glass remains intact, the lights of Los Angeles continue to serenely glimmer below. Where it's broken, there's nothing but churning gray mindstorm. It's not a hole in the window. It's a hole in this reality. The fault expands, splintering the ceiling and floor, sending chunks tumbling into the void.

"We broke it!" I shout. "Let's go!"

Rebecca doesn't open her eyes. She doesn't move. She just keeps screaming her chant. I hurl myself into her abs and knock her through the hole as the memory collapses into glassy shards and blows away on the current of the storm. Rebecca cries out and presses her palms to her eyes.

"Damn it! God fucking damn it!"

271

She thrashes and screams, but her torment no longer transfers to me. Her emotions are once again her own. I catch her arm and squeeze it gently.

"It's okay. It was just a fantasy."

Rebecca snaps. "It was not a fantasy!"

I wrinkle my nose. "Sorry, bad choice of words. I mean, it was an illusion. It was just another piece of nightmare theater the shadow made up to mess with us, like that thing with me and your mom. It wasn't real."

Rebecca's reddened eyes focus on mine. They tremble with argument as if she's trying to figure out if she's pissed at me or not. A tear rolls down her cheek.

"It was real, Dad. It happened."

Her statement hits a brick wall in my mind. It simply refuses to accept the words she said assembled in that order. It was all fake. It had to be. I didn't rape Kim, and VanDuzer didn't rape Bex. It didn't happen. It just didn't.

"I believe you," I say.

And I do believe her. It's too horrible to be true, but I believe her anyway. For a long moment she just stares at me.

"Thank you."

There's a weight in her words, as if . . .

"Please tell me I'm not the first person to say that."

Her cheeks redden. "He said he'd give Mom the part in his movie but only if I never told anyone what he did to me. And I never did. Except for Mom." Her jaw tightens. "She believed me, but she didn't care. She emotionally blackmailed me into having sex with him then blamed me for making poor life choices. Then she abandoned me."

I'm so rattled with furious adrenalin that my hands shake. I want to find Robert VanDuzer, tear his dick off, and then ram it up his ass before shoving it down his throat. But that anger smothers under a blanket of heartache. VanDuzer did it, but Kim let it happen. She broke our daughter then did nothing to pick up the pieces. She abused our child, just as she was terrified she'd do from the moment she learned she was pregnant. My stomach churns with self-loathing. Kim told me this would happen. I should have believed her. I should have worked harder to make sure it didn't.

Rebecca stares cloudy-eyed at the grotesque black stalks threading through the void. "Even after I stopped giving a shit what happened to Mom I still never told anyone. I was a strung-out, tatted-up burnout and VanDuzer is one of the most powerful men in Hollywood. Before I even said anything I could already hear the arguments against me. 'That slutty skank is just trying to squeeze money out of him,' and 'If this really happened, why did she wait so long to say anything?'" She shakes her head and gazes out at nothing. "I went through rehab and therapy. I was getting my life back together. By the time people actually started believing victims it was way too late. I didn't want to dredge this all up again. I just wanted it to stay buried where it couldn't hurt me."

"And the goddamn shadow dug it up to hurt you." Rage boils under my collar. "I know exactly what you went through." Rebecca's eyebrows lower, but I continue. "That's not a platitude. I felt it in the penthouse just now. Everything she ... Everything *you* felt, I felt it too. The fear and the anger and the helplessness. And I believe it really happened." Even without a psychic connection, saying it out loud still draws up her pain and pushes it shuddering through my voice. "It wasn't fair for you to have to live with this all alone. I'm sorry I ... I'm sorry that ... " I can feel the apology but I can't forge it into words. "I'm sorry I made your mother have you even though she told me she was unfit to raise you. I'm sorry I didn't believe her. I'm sorry I didn't fight harder to be a part of your life after the divorce. I just ... I'm sorry I messed up your life."

Rebecca takes my hand as we plummet through the eternal gray blankness. There's clarity in her eyes as she looks me in the face. "Don't blame yourself for what Mom did. If it wasn't for you, I wouldn't have had a life to mess up."

She half smiles and an electric happiness crackles through me. The moment is so tender and honest that I want to sit back in it like a warm bath and savor it forever. Instead I crush her hand in mine and scream, "Watch out!"

My arm whips around, flinging her weight over my shoulder. My own body flips on her momentum, spinning us out of the path of a memory hole being shoved in our way by a great black limb. I glimpse down its throat as we tumble away from it, getting an eyeful of my junior high gym locker room. I can't even imagine what childhood trauma I just dodged. This world is nightmares all the way down.

Rebecca grabs my other hand and we plunge through the void linked like two skydivers. "Shit! That was close!" she says. "We can't let the shadow catch us in another memory. We have to get out of here!"

"How? 'Here' isn't even a place! It's a . . . flashback shitstorm!"

Rebecca's hair whips in the torrent of thinning vapor rushing around us. "It seems like the more self-aware we become the less tangible this place is. I think we can break out if we clear our minds. We have to meditate."

Oh God. This again. "I can't! I don't even know what that means!"

"You can do it, Dad. Just close your eyes and focus on my voice. Follow my lead." Her eyelids drift shut and her hands relax in mine. I've always thought of meditation as some new-agey nonsense Buddhists and hippies do to get in touch with the aura of the Earth Mother or whatever. But Rebecca believes in it, and I believe in Rebecca. I close my eyes. Rebecca continues, giving commands in a lethargic stream of words.

"Let the bad memories drift away. Let the pain of them drift away. Concentrate and find your place of mental peace. Embrace it."

Despite myself, I nearly snort in derision. My place of mental peace? How am I supposed to concentrate on a thing that doesn't exist? But even as I scoff at Rebecca's suggestion, I'm distracted by the warmth of her touch. I'm reminded of a time when we used to hold hands and find joy in each other's company. Her fingers were so much smaller then.

Rebecca keeps talking and I keep listening. "Concentrate on the rushing of the wind. Feel it flowing around us. Listen to the sound of it in your ears and breathe it into your lungs and through your body."

I feel the wind. I breathe. The more I focus on the air surging around me, the more everything else ceases to exist. I become vaguely aware of a light pressure and warmth on my face. Without looking, I know it's Rebecca's forehead pressed against mine. The feeling of my daughter so close to me pushes peace through my buzzing tension. Genuine peace. It's a sensation I haven't felt in ages. I concentrate on remembering it. On going back to that place.

With my eyes closed I see the sound of the wind. It looks like smooth, ghostly streaks, like a long-exposure photograph of a peaceful waterfall. As my mind grows more tranquil, something stirs in it. A shadowy eel circles and thrashes inside my skull, trying to dig in and find a place to hold on. Rebecca feels it too. She tells me not to fight it so I don't. I just let the current of the breeze wash it away.

The darkness screeches and squirms as it's flushed from my consciousness. A molten warmth spreads in my chest and in my belly, then flares and spins in my throat and across the top of my head. I can tell it's welding-torch hot, but to me it just feels comfortable, like being in a Jacuzzi.

I feel my forehead glowing as the wind dulls and quiets. For what seems like a long time, I don't hear or see or feel anything except Rebecca's warm hands holding mine. Then I don't even feel that.

I open my eyes.

CHAPTER TWENTY-FIVE

Rebecca

I open my eyes.

The thunderstorm in my mind has cleared. I'm no longer floating. I'm holding my father's hands, lying on my belly on an unblemished surface of pleasant white light. The ground and the sky are one contiguous, unbroken membrane of it, shrouded in misty golden light. I recognize this plane of existence. I was here last night.

I push myself up onto my knees. The glow is firm and springy under me, like I'm resting on a giant, luminous sponge. As my awareness collects, I realize my body feels strangely incomplete. I put out my arms and blink at what I see. They're skinny stalks of skin and bone. My tattoos are gone. My fingers are stubby. I slide my hands down the wrinkled surface of a grass-stained soccer uniform draped over the body of a nine-year-old girl.

"What the hell?"

Dad lies face down on the light-ground in front of me. He sits up and blinks, taking in the pure, vaporous serenity. He also looks younger than he did before. Not as young as me, and not as young as he was in the painful memories we just endured. He's the soft, mid-thirties "dad bod" version of him I remember from when I was actually nine years old.

Dreamy skepticism clouds his face as he gapes at me.

"Rebecca? Is that really you?"

I nod. "Yeah. It is. I just . . ." I stand up, and it feels like I barely get taller. One of my knobby little knees is skinned and scabbed. My tiny shoes blink blue LED flashes from their heels with each step. "What's happening? Why do we look young now?"

A smile edges over Dad's face. "I did what you said."

"You . . ." I cock my head. "I don't understand."

Dad stands up, investigating his slimmed body. "You told me to remember a place of mental peace and to go to it. I didn't know what you meant by that, so I just . . . I thought about the last time I was happy. I mean, truly happy. I thought about . . ." He points at himself, and at me. "This. About us. About this us."

I can tell he's confused, but I can also tell he doesn't care. He looks so elated the grin on his face spreads all the way to mine. I run my tiny hand over my smooth cheeks. There's no scar. No tattoo on my wrist. This little body hasn't been through hell and back. It hasn't been through anything.

When I visualized my place of mental peace, I thought of it as a destination in time. A time before the accident. Before VanDuzer, and the divorce. Back when I had no worries. When I didn't know how fucked up the world really was.

My heart warms as I realize my father and I both broke out of the nightmare storm by picturing the happiness of my childhood. I just hadn't considered it in such physically concrete terms. I run my palms over my slim hips and feel a strange sadness. If only this were real. If only we could really go back, knowing what we know now, and have a do-over. How different would our lives be today?

The thought shatters half-formed as I spot a clawing lump scrambling against the tranquility. A black blob of tar and spines thrashes and scrapes, wheezing as it piles upon itself and collapses. Dad sees it too. He protectively jumps up and pulls me away from it as if I were really as young as I look.

"Get back! It's the shadow!"

"What's wrong with it?"

A flash of realization crosses Dad's face. "Nothing. This is what it really looks like."

The shape fumbles and tosses out bony feelers. I recognize them as a miniature version of the huge, snaking limbs that threw hoops of nightmare at us in the mind storm. With a sudden clarity I realize that creature of infinite size was all an illusion. This is real. This is the shadow's true form. We've opened our third eyes and seen the truth.

The monster writhes like a wounded animal. A bony clump of goo plops off of it, still connected by ropes of tar. Two more flop out, hitting the light floor like black loogies. Jagged flaps unfold from each, vibrating and twitching. They almost form grotesque little birds flapping deformed black wings. One releases a familiar screeching whimper, and I realize what they are.

"It's trying to make smoke fairies."

But for some reason it can't. The fairies bubble and ooze but don't take shape. The shadow quivers and the unformed blobs snap back on their tendrils, absorbing into its ragged lump. It ripples and churns, throwing out a skeletal arm. Shadowy oil flows around it, forming a covering of emaciated flesh. It scratches the ground as a head bubbles out of the scum, featureless except for tufts of greasy black hair. Two slits burst open in the blank face, staring us down with big, dark eyes. A third messy gash lined with glittery pink lip gloss tears across the bottom half and screams before the beast collapses into a chunky pool.

Dad squeezes my shoulder and backs us away. "Shit! That was Rosebud!"

"It can't take another form." I gasp. "We must have injured it. It's dying!"

The inky pool swirls as fibers congeal on its surface. They multiply and grow longer, like strands of golden seaweed floating in a tide pool. A large bubble forms under the threads, pushing them upwards. As it does, the blackness runs off the shape like oil, revealing a pale, fleshy scalp. The form continues to rise, piling up and congealing and blossoming with colors and textures. In an instant the festering tar is gone, replaced by my mother, exactly as she looked at the cabin. Fifty

ONE MUST KILL ANOTHER

years old, beautiful and completely human, dressed in a sweater and jeans. A whip-crack scar cuts her forehead.

She gives us a skeptical, questioning look, then smiles with relief. "Oh Matty, thank God you found me! What is this place? Where are we?" She glances at me. "Rebecca? Is that you? You're so young. Why are you both so young?"

The soft sound of her voice, Mom's voice, relaxes Dad's hand on my shoulder. I clap a palm over it and dig in my dirty little nails, piercing his misplaced sympathy.

"God, shut up. How stupid do you think we are?"

Shadow Mom keeps looking at us with its empty gaze, sizing us up. Its hands slowly rise and its fingers stiffen before they fling out at us. It's at least ten feet away, but we both feel the phantom impact of its fingertips slamming against our skulls. Dad claps his hand over his forehead and winces.

"Aagh! Damn it," he grumbles. "What the hell?"

A memory surges back to me. The last time I found my way to this golden place, the shadow girl jabbed its fingers deep into the gash in my forehead, digging out my worst memories. I slap both hands over my ajna chakra.

"Dad! Cover your forehead!" Before I can finish the thought, Shadow Mom has already thrown its hands toward us again. The strike of its distant fingers goes through the flesh of my hands like a ghost but knocks against my skull like a concrete wall. I stagger back, realizing what it's doing. "It's trying to grab onto our memories but it can't. We've blocked it out!"

Shadow Mom's gaze ticks from my forehead, to Dad's, to its hands. It rubs its long fingers curiously, and its face softens with shades of wounded vulnerability. The humanity in the expression sparks involuntary compassion in my heart. Even knowing this thing is not my mother, looking into its perfect reproduction of Mom's bright blue eyes gives me a strange feeling. Or rather, a strange lack of feeling.

I don't hate her.

Mom always let me think she hated Dad because he raped her. She never said it, but she implied it. She played her game, throwing out dots and letting me connect them. And I connected them, densely and vividly. My mind painted in details, embellishing my masterwork over the years like Michelangelo painting the ceiling of the Sistine Chapel. The house looking as it did in my earliest memories. Mom's sexy bathrobe and the flannel shirt I know my father must have worn back when grunge was cool. I wasted so much of my life perfecting the gruesome image that the shadow couldn't tell my constructed fantasy from an actual memory.

But now I know the truth. Mom didn't want me. I was a constant reminder of her husband's betrayal. A burden she knew she couldn't handle that was forced upon her anyway. I was her childhood trauma manifested in the flesh but she tried to love me anyway, as best as she could.

I finally understand why she treated me the way she did, but understanding doesn't make it right. I still don't like her. I'll never like her.

But I can forgive her.

I wrap my nine-year-old hand around Dad's big palm. "It's over. We've found our inner peace. The shadow can't hurt us anymore with its hateful bullshit."

Shadow Mom's brows lower. "Oh give me a break. You act like you're innocent victims. Like it isn't your fault I'm here."

"Well, there's actually a very good reason for that," Dad says, raising an index finger. "It's because we're innocent victims and it's not our fault you're here."

The shadow huffs. "Kimberly was right about you, Matty. You are so selfish. She was too. You're the ones who came into my woods with your auras screeching with anger and frustration. You're the ones who woke me up then left me here to starve."

"Okay, I don't know what the hell you're even—" Dad's face goes pale. "Oh my God. The fight. The last time we were here. Kim was yelling at me and I got so angry I lost control." His eyes pierce the shadow. "That was *you* wasn't it."

Shadow Mom sighs and waves a hand. "Ugh. I was too groggy to do anything but sit on you and spike your emotions. By the time I was fully awakened and ready to play the three of you had run off and abandoned me."

My heart chills as I remember the scene. Me, peeking in from the living room. Dad, blinded with rage, knocking my mother through the glass door. It's the image that gave credibility to all of Mom's stories about him being abusive. He seemed like an inhuman monster, but he wasn't. He was only being influenced by one.

Dad's face reddens and his hands close into fists. "You son of a bitch! You made me hit her! You made her leave me!"

Shadow Mom laughs. "She was going to leave you anyway, you pathetic lump. Hitting her was just the last nail in your coffin. Trust me, I know." It taps the side of its head. "Her memories don't lie."

Dad roars and lurches toward the shadow, but I throw myself in his way. "Stop! Ignore it! It's just trying to keep us angry. We have to calm down and wake up."

My father's body vibrates with tension. He talks to me, but doesn't stop glaring at the shadow. "You're right. Sorry. So what do we do? How do we get out of here?"

"Just focus," I say calmly. "Remember that this place isn't real. Imagine where we really are. In the shed. Visualize it with as much detail as you can. See it, feel it, smell it. Then close your eyes here and open them there."

I don't know if that will actually work. I'm pulling it all out of my ass. But my confidence sells it, and Dad nods and gives Shadow Mom one last biting glance before closing his eyes. I close mine. I'm in the shed. There is no fire. I'm sitting on the cold concrete floor wearing a fake fur coat. I'm not a nine-year-old child. I'm a twenty-three-year-old woman. There's a scar running through the center of my face. Right under my eyes. My large, adult eyes . . .

My eyelids crack open, squinting against the brightness of the misty yellow void. Shadow Mom stands before me, arms crossed.

"Nice try, but you can't leave. You may have taken back your memories, but I'm still deep inside your brain stems, manipulating the basest functions of your consciousness. You don't wake up until *I* say you wake up. And the only way one of you is getting out of this alive is if . . . " Mom's enormous, movie-star smile splits the shadow's face. "Well, you know."

Dad opens his eyes and glares. "Neither of us is ever going to kill the other, you bloated sack of oil-spill garbage! So you may as well just let us go or kill us both."

Shadow Mom's grin fades. "So be it." It shakes its head and clicks its tongue. "Such a tragic waste of food."

The monster swings Mom's arms in front of its body in two huge, sweeping circles, snapping them out to its sides. The action shreds its clothes, exploding them into thin, papery wisps that dissolve into nothing.

Its form changes along with its wardrobe. The shadow is no longer fifty-year-old Kimberly Savage. It's twenty-five-year-old Scarlett Bedlam, straight out of the first *Blood Blitz* film, exactly as my mother would have remembered her. Tight-bodied and sizzling with sex in her white lace corset and matching satin panties. Her legs look a mile long in her thigh-high stockings. A katana blade impossibly slings from the sleeve of her sweater as it disintegrates, shooting out over her palm until her hand snaps closed on the handle.

The whole transformation happens in a split second. Before I can even process what's happened, Scarlett Bedlam screams and launches at us, blade first. A dull weight thuds into my back, knocking me off my tiny feet. I hit the ground and roll over just in time to see Dad— his arms still outstretched from pushing me out of the way—take fifteen inches of steel through his right thigh.

Dad wails and pounds a palm into Shadow Scarlett's face. It stumbles back, pulling its blade free of his body, the motion lubricated silent with his blood. Dad tries to make a staggering retreat, but falters on his gashed leg, hitting the ground with a roar. Shadow Scarlett twirls its sword and grabs the handle with both hands, slinging it back over its head for another strike.

"Dad! No!" I shriek.

My father throws an arm in front of his face, somehow hoping it will keep the blade from cleaving his skull. My feet push under me to leap up and stop the shadow, but it's pointless. I'm wearing the body of a child. Even if I got there in time, I'm too small to take down an image of my mother in her physical prime.

Dad's terror rips from his throat in a shrieking howl. The whole world thumps as a wall blasts upward from the glowing ground between Shadow Scarlett and my father. The katana's tip hacks through, violently cracking the plaster.

I blink and rub my throbbing temples, trying to reconcile what my eyes are showing me. It's a wall from my parents' bedroom at the beach house, free-standing in the golden mist, ringed with a ragged lath-and-plaster edge as if it had been ripped out and dropped here. The blade retracts from it, scraping off flakes of debris. My father fumbles away, clutching his bloody leg, and I dart to his side.

"Dad! Are you okay?"

"Aagh! No!" he seethes. "That hurt like a motherfucker!"

"Where did that wall come from?"

"I don't know! She was coming at me and I just . . . I wanted to be someplace safe!"

My eyes flick to the monolith in the whiteness. He wanted to be someplace safe and this world made his house.

Dad flinches and screams. "Look out!"

Shadow Scarlett pounces around the side of the wall, blade raised.

"No!" I throw out a hand and think of my parents' bedroom. I think of snuggling into bed between them when I had a nightmare. I think of how safe that made me feel and a second wall pounds the air as it bursts into existence, turning the corner from the first. "Dad, help me!"

"I don't know how!"

"You do!" I scream, pointing at the wall. "Concentrate on being safe at home! Don't think about it, just do it!"

My father grunts and flings his arms toward the empty space and another wall explodes into being. I make the fourth and the ceiling. Dad slaps a palm on the ground and a hardwood floor flicks up board-by-board across the light beneath us.

All the pieces fit perfectly together, despite being a mismatched patchwork. Grimy walls flow seamlessly into fresh paint. There's furniture, alternately new and sagging with wear. Mom's mirrored vanity table flickers in and out, as if it can't decide if it's there or not. The room is a collage of our memories, jumbled snapshots of the same place cobbled into one image.

Dad wrestles himself to his feet, palm pressed to his bleeding thigh. His eyes scan the room in disbelief. "Holy shit. We made this. With our minds!"

"We didn't make anything. This place isn't real!" I grab his free hand and squeeze, capturing his attention. "Dad, we have to wake up. Concentrate on the real world and wake up."

He nods and squeezes back. "Okay."

I grit my teeth and focus.

This is not real. This is an illusion. Wake up, Rebecca!

I'm thinking it so hard. Feeling it in my third eye. Willing it to happen. But it doesn't. It feels futile, like willing myself to fly. I can imagine what flying looks like, and what it feels like, but no amount of visualization will ever launch me into the sky.

No amount of visualization will wake me up.

The room explodes with flying glass. I squeal and jump back as Shadow Scarlett leaps blade-first through the window. Its sword swings at my head and I duck as it smashes through a lamp on a bedside table and plants itself in the wall.

Dad's grip tightens on my hand. "Shit! Run!" He throws open the bedroom door and drags me into the hallway. It doesn't look like I remember it. It's dirtier, filthy with a bachelor's neglect. Dad's memory. Scarlett wrenches its sword free and leaps toward the door. Our only chance to escape is the staircase at the far end of the hall, but we'd never make it before the shadow skewered us both. I throw myself through the nearest door, pulling Dad behind me. He slams it and turns the lock.

I blink and take in the room. We're in my memory of Dad's office. Everything looks exactly as it did when I was a child. The noisy old tower PC with its big cube of monitor perched on a rickety folding table. My own little desk to the side of it, made of an overturned cardboard box covered with construction-paper art and plastic cups full of crayons.

The locked doorknob rattles for an instant before a sword hacks through the door from the other side. Dad yelps and grabs a bookcase, pulling it over sideways. The top of the heavy shelf smashes against the neighboring wall, leaving the whole thing leaning at a precarious forty-five-degree angle across the door. He throws himself against it, holding the barricade in place.

"Dad!" I shriek. "Shit!"

My father cries in agony as the shadow's pounding weight sends tremors through the bookcase, into his back, and down his wounded leg. Blood saturates his pants and his face goes deathly pale. Dad's bulky, but injured. And Shadow Scarlett is way fitter than he is. Not just physically fit, but fictionally fit. She's a character from an action movie, stronger and more badass than any actual human being. Dad can't hold that off for long.

Not that it matters. Holding the door only postpones the inevitable.

Shadow Scarlett's blade jabs through the bookcase, skewering a paperback inches from Dad's cheek. He screams and my head throbs. I need to come up with a plan. Meditation or astral projection or lucid dreaming or ... *something*. Dad wanted to be safe and it made his house. I wanted to go back in time and it gave me a child's body. This world operates on symbols and metaphor. But what does it all mean? I wish I had more time. I wish I had more options. Mostly I wish we could wake the fuck up!

Frustration tightens my tiny muscles and I roar and kick my stupid little cardboard desk, flipping it and throwing a hail of crayons at the wall. A leaf of green construction paper flips in the air and slides across the floor toward me. It's a drawing, awkward and rendered in a heavy hand, of three gemstones in a triangular setting.

The Life Stone. The Death Stone. The Wish Stone.

I just wish we could wake the fuck up!

I have an idea.

My knees hit the floor next to the overturned box and I scramble through the scattered drawings. I snap up a yellow paper with a scribbled map of jungle trails and stacked rocks and ancient ruins. The route to the Lost Temple of Zamrycki. I don't remember it, but I do. I must! My mind created this room. My mind created this paper. It's all still in my subconscious.

I need to go there.

I slow my breath and dredge the Forbidden Jungle from the depths of my memory. The image in my head doesn't look like the drawing. It never did. My clumsy fingers and dull crayons could only create the crudest version of the real place. Even the woods outside the cabin that Dad and I used to explore weren't the jungle. They were a stand-in full of fur-coat monsters and cardboard ruins.

The real jungle was always in my mind.

I visualize the lush, dense greenness of it all, shrouded in mist and mystery. The ground covered in ferns and shaggy grasses. The sun barely able to break through the heavy canopy of mossy trees. I breathe deeply, and the stagnant, dusty air of the office turns warm and moist, musky with the smells of earth and exotic flowers and distant smoke. My father's screams become the screech of tropical birds.

I open my eyes.

The construction paper map in my hands has transformed into a parchment—an explorer's work-in-progress, illustrated in exquisite sepia detail. I'm standing in a packed-dirt clearing next to a huge structure. It looks like the cabin near Lake Arrowhead, but it's made of stone and bamboo, capped with a thatched roof and hung heavy with tribal masks. There's an old truck parked alongside the building, rust eating away at its round headlights and retro fenders. Rope netting holds a stack of wooden crates on its flat bed, each one stenciled "SAVAGE EXPADISHION."

Dad gasps. "Aagh! What the hell?"

I turn and see him, still standing exactly where he was relative to me in the office. But the bookcase is gone, and so is the door. He's next to the house, backing away from the tip of a katana jabbed through its wall of woven grass and bamboo. The blade withdraws to the interior with a muffled feminine grunt.

Dad stumbles to my side, holding his bloodied leg. "What the . . . Where the hell are we?"

"Welcome to Outpost 132," I say, a little too proudly. "Base camp of the Savage Expedition to the Lost Temple of Zamrycki."

Dad's jaw drops as he scans his new surroundings. Tropical foliage surrounds us in every direction. The faint sound of tribal drums pounds rhythmically in the humid breeze from some far-off village. In the distance, barely visible over the trees, is the square crown of a crumbling, Aztec-style pyramid.

"But . . . this doesn't exist," Dad says. "It was just a game. None of this is real!"

"Neither was my memory of you assaulting Mom. But it was real in my mind." I take in the sights and smells of a place I'd dreamed of a million times in my childhood. "This jungle may have only existed in my imagination, but to me it's as real as a memory. Apparently that's all that matters." The thatched bamboo wall of the outpost cracks and buckles as a katana slashes through it from the other side. "We have to move! Come on!"

I grab Dad's hand and lead him into the jungle as fast as my tiny legs and his wounded thigh can carry us. Glittering lizards and colorful birds scurry into the underbrush as we crash through. My pace slows as we enter a broad, circular clearing, dotted with chest-high towers of crookedly stacked rocks. The same towers appear on my map. We're on the right path. Dad staggers to a stop behind me, wheezing and limping.

I let go of his hand. "Are you okay? Need a rest?"

"I'm fine." Despite his obvious agony, a dreamy smile warms his face. "This place is so weird and beautiful," he mumbles. He inspects a rock tower but is careful not to disturb it. "It's exactly how I always imagined it when we played together. But ... why? Why did you bring us here?"

I try to speak with conviction. "We have to finish the expedition."

Dad blinks. "What?"

"We have to find the Mystic Stones."

Dad looks at me as if I've lost my mind. "Now? Are you serious?"

"I am. I have an idea. It's crazy but ..." I take a deep breath. "This whole world is a dream. The flashbacks, the beach house, this jungle. All of it. We know it, but I think on some primal level our brains refuse to accept it. Our unconscious minds won't let us wake up because deep down we don't believe there's anything to wake up from. So I think our only chance is to fully accept the delusion."

Dad's eyes narrow. "I don't get it. So we're gonna just give up and play jungle expedition?"

I shake my head. "We're not giving up. We're giving our brains a metaphor for escape. Look." I bang a fist on a tree. "I know this tree isn't real, but on some base level I must believe it is. So it is. No matter what we consciously think, our unconscious minds accept this world and everything in it as real. Including the Mystic Stones." I tap a drawing of the three stones in the margin of my map. "Do you remember their powers?"

"Of course," Dad says. "The Life Stone restores health. The Death Stone causes instant death. The Wish Stone grants a wish."

"Exactly," I say, pointing at him. "The Wish Stone grants a wish. We both know it. It's in our memories of this place, and that makes it true. That makes it real." I meet my father's eyes, dead serious. "If we get the Wish Stone we can wish to go back to the real world. Our brains will accept the magic works and let it happen. We'll wake up."

A cluck of feminine laughter pulses in the humid air. We turn to see Shadow Scarlett lurking in our trodden-down path, its blade still wet with blood. Dad steps in front of me, squeezing a palm on his useless thigh.

"Aren't you two just adorable?" Shadow Scarlett says. It stalks closer, entering the field of rock towers. "This is a very cute little game you're playing, with your tiki huts and your 'magic stones.' But you must realize none of it matters. The illusion you project around us is irrelevant. I will still feed from you."

Dad and I share a cautious glance. He doesn't know what to say. I do.

"Will you just fuck off already? How many times do we have to tell you we're not going to kill each other? Are you really that stupid?"

Shadow Scarlett raises an eyebrow. "Are you? Do you still not understand what it is that I eat? An unwilling sacrifice is a feast of fear and anguish powerful enough to knock me out cold, but you refuse to oblige me. So I'm just going to nibble on your suffering. I'm going to 'pick your brains,' so to speak." It pads forward on stocking feet, grinning devilishly and brandishing its blade. "I'm going to carve you up inside your own minds. Slowly. Methodically. Cutting your tendons to cripple you. Stabbing your eyes to blind you. Slashing your genitals just for fun. Snacking on the dregs of your mental agony for as long as I can before your physical bodies die in that shed."

Dad feebly steps away from the shadow, backing into me. He lifts his bloodied hand from his wound and holds it toward her, palm out. *Stop.* The gesture is authoritative, but the trembling ruins it. "No. You won't. You can do your psycho butcher brain vampire shit on me, but you will not touch Rebecca."

Shadow Scarlett rolls its eyes at us. It looks so much like my mother it gives me an uneasy chill. "You're in no position to make demands."

"That wasn't a demand, asshole," Dad says weakly. "It was a promise." He turns his body away from the shadow, resting his sticky palm on the closest tower of rocks. He slouches into it, gasping for breath, and mutters at me. "Go. Run. I'll hold her off."

Frustration sizzles through my muscles. "You're hurt! You can't—"

"I said *run*, goddamn it!" Dad's voice is angry but his eyes are pleading. He's trying to tell me something. The tower teeters at the edge of balance as he struggles to hold himself upright. His gaze ticks to it. To me. "Go! Before I *fall*."

The message hits me with the power of a lightning strike. The playfulness melts from Shadow Scarlett's face, leaving behind only pure malice. "Nobody is going anywhere!"

The shadow leaps forward, executing a maneuver honed over countless hours of stage martial-arts training stolen from my mother's mind. Its blade swings over its shoulder for a strike, but before it can connect, Dad lurches into the stack of rocks, tackling it to the ground. I drop to the dirt as Shadow Scarlett flies over us, whiffing its sword through empty air.

Dad rolls off of the pile of stones, hissing and holding his agonized wound. The shadow's long feet silently hit the earth and it whips around, blade already raised for another strike. Adrenaline and terror flush through me, but I stay down. If the trap towers exist in this world, toppling one must summon . . .

A deep roar rumbles through the trees, trembling the earth. Shadow Scarlett's muscles tense as it takes a fighting stance, sword raised, eyes scanning for a threat it can't identify. Branches snap and birds take flight as an eight-foot-tall sasquatch bounds out of the jungle. It's as broad as a refrigerator, a man-shaped knot of bulky muscle covered in rancid, stinking hair. Claws like steak knives curl from its fingers and toes and thick drool hangs in loops between its broken yellow teeth.

An expression of equal parts surprise and horror drops Shadow Scarlett's jaw as the sasquatch throws a massive, clawed uppercut. Four parallel gashes of black blood explode across the shadow's chest and face as it shrieks and sails backwards through the clearing.

The hairy beast snarls and turns its attention to me and Dad, lying helplessly at its feet. It raises a paw to swipe at us, but we throw out our palms, fingers and thumbs forming triangles. Our voices scream out as one.

"Rafiki!"

The sasquatch's hand stops in midair. Its eyes remain dark and expressionless, but the fury leaves its leathery face. My hands tremble, but I hold my triangle steady, as does Dad. The monster crouches and sniffs at us, dripping saliva on our quivering bodies. Its hot breath reeks of rotting flesh. I grit my teeth and flinch, fighting to keep myself from vomiting.

A clattering of rocks jerks the sasquatch's attention away from us. It turns and rises to its full towering height, releasing a spittle-filled roar. Dad and I see Shadow Scarlett supporting itself against the remains of a second knocked-over tower, clutching its katana in a white-knuckle grip. Deep black claw marks divide its face from forehead to chin, cutting straight through one of its stolen blue eyes. The wounds in its chest prickle with what look like thrashing spider legs, bleeding oily tar down the front of its mangled white corset. It's barely on its feet before the sasquatch charges across the clearing to rip another set of holes in its evil monster ass.

I spring to my feet. "Dad, let's go! Let's go!"

I help him up and we plunge into the jungle, trampling a path through the primeval foliage. The sounds of beastly roaring and tearing flesh echo through the trees, painting a gruesome picture of monster-on-monster violence behind us. We don't get very far before my father staggers and tumbles to the ground.

"Dad!" I shriek.

I kneel next to him and help him upright. "I'm okay. I'm okay," he lies. His clothes are drenched in blood and his face is pale as snow, but he's giggling. "Oh, man! That was so crazy! I knocked down a trap tower and it summoned an actual sasquatch. I can't believe that worked!"

I can't help but choke out a chuckle of my own. "But you *do* believe it. You see? Our brains accept the fantasy. We believed it would work and it did."

"And if that worked, so will the Mystic Stones," Dad says. "I get it now. You're right. About everything. You beat the shadow at its own twisted game. Nice work, kid."

I smile and blush. "Well, we're not out yet. We still need to find the Wish Stone."

Dad blinks. "Do we, though? I mean, wait."

He closes his eyes and grimaces. Muscles clench in his face and one eye squints open. He holds his breath until he turns red, then blows it out, defeated.

"What was that about?" I ask.

"I don't know. I was trying to make the stone come to us. I figured if we control this world, why not? It didn't work, so I tried to make us jet packs." He gestures at his gashed leg. "That didn't work, so I tried to at least whip up a Band-Aid. But I got nothin'."

I consider it. "I guess our minds will only accept what they already believe about this place. We can't just make things magically happen, because we weren't magical in the game. We have to play by our own rules."

"Ugh. I should have been magical," Dad grumbles. "How were we live-action role playing without a wizard? Is that even possible? What's wrong with us?"

I chuckle and grip his arm. "Come on. You can make it. The Lost Temple shouldn't be far from here."

With a grunting effort, Dad gets to his feet. I tuck myself under his shoulder and we keep moving. The path is uneven and dense with overgrowth. I'm soaked in sweat and secondhand blood by the time we break through the trees in front of a towering Aztec pyramid. Six enormous stories of rock taper upwards to a squared off room at the apex, topped with an architectural crown. The two-hundred-foot-tall facade stares down at us through three glowing eyes—the sun pouring through cut-out windows in the shape of the Mystic Stones.

The temple looks exactly as I imagined it would. But to be here, to be actually standing in front of it, is still overwhelming. The pyramid dwarfs us. It dwarfs the trees. Dad gazes at the hundreds of stone steps set into its broad face and groans.

"Shit. We couldn't have just made up a ground-level lost temple . . ."

Our soaked-through clothes stick to each other as I adjust myself under his weight. "We can do this. One step at a time. Together."

Dad shakes his head. "I can't climb that. Not with my leg all jacked up." He lifts his arm off my shoulder and slumps down heavily onto the stairs. "You have to go without me. Get the stone and wish us back to the real world."

"Not by myself." I perch on the step next to him. "We need to go together."

The smile on Dad's sweaty face dims. He looks at my skinny limbs and sighs. "I wish you had your adult body right now."

I giggle. "Why, so I could carry you to the top?"

Dad shakes his head, then nods. "No. Well, yeah, but not only that. This kid I see here is nothing but a nice memory. It's not who you really are. Not anymore. You grew up. And I . . . I missed it." Guilt clouds his expression. "When I first laid eyes on you at the cabin I hated what I saw. In my mind, you were still this child. I couldn't accept that my baby was gone. But now ... now I do." He meets my eyes. "My baby is gone. But my daughter is still here."

His words rest warmly upon my chest, seeping in and drawing out an affectionate smile. I put a palm on his sweaty shoulder. "Mom made me believe you were a monster, but you aren't. You never were. You were the only person who ever showed me the slightest bit of affection." My eyes water and lose focus. "If you had been around, maybe I wouldn't have grown up to be so messed up."

Dad shakes his head. "You're not messed up. You're battle hardened. My kid grew up to be a full-on badass. And you did it all by yourself."

A blush prickles in my cheeks. "I know I did. And that's why we have to go up the pyramid together." I blow out a long breath. "I've been doing everything all by myself for years. I'm so fucking done with doing things all by myself."

Dad's pale lips curl into a smile. "So am I."

He reaches out a hand. I grasp it in both of mine and pull him to his feet, tucking in under his arm before his leg gives out. We find our balance, and we climb the uneven stairs. Slowly and roughly, but we do it together.

Step by step, up the dizzying height of the Lost Temple, my father and I fall into a rhythm. We become a team. We become one. Inseparable, just like we were when we wore these bodies in the real world. And with each step upward, our exhaustion is numbed by our momentum.

The air feels cool and thin by the time we finally reach the top of the temple. We're soaked in sweat and blood and exhaustion, but we hold our heads high as we stride through the entry arch carved in its weathered face.

The chamber is dark and foreboding, lit by flaming stone bowls held aloft by crouching wooden tiki gods. The whole place is about the size of a handball court. A reverent space, created to house the three most powerful artifacts in this world.

On the far side of the room is a cone of volcanic rock just slightly taller than my childish form. Three craters mar its face, set in a triangle. And in each divot sits a fist-sized stone. One is rough and black as midnight, flecked with pinpricks of white. The second is smooth and egg-shaped, dull and brown. The third is a glimmering white gem, faceted like a cut diamond.

My father and I stand before them, speechless, absorbing their presence. I want to approach them, but feel strangely intimidated. To anyone else this place would mean nothing. But for us, this is the end of a long-postponed quest. A quest that had started in our imaginations and was snuffed out by the real world before it could be completed.

Dad squeezes me tight. "You did it, kiddo. You found the Mystic Stones."

A Christmas-morning excitement bubbles through me. "We found them. Now let's get the hell out of here."

I untuck myself from under Dad's sweaty arm, but before I can approach the stones I'm surprised by a wet, rasping breath. Dad and I spin around to see a female shape in the entry arch, silhouetted against the bright blue jungle sky.

The shadow takes a lurching step toward us, clutching a blade red with blood and matted with fur. Firelight flows over the figure, throwing details into focus. Ragged shreds of white fabric and pink flesh hang from its gnarled black bones. Needle-like spines thrash inside its oily wounds. Its scarred head turns my mother's face to us, glaring with confused rage from a single eye.

"You ... hurt me," the shadow rasps. The words are labored, but defiant. "You can't ... hurt me." It draws a rattling breath. "Impossible."

Its sword slips as its fingers loosen on the handle. The shadow is barely strong enough to stand, let alone fight. Dad limps toward it, his face tight with vengeful energy.

"This is our world. These are our minds." His voice lowers to a growl. "We can hurt you here, and we can kill you." He crouches into an imitation of a movie martial-arts stance and waves Shadow Scarlett in. "Come get some."

The shadow raises its blade and steps forward. Dad throws a fist at its mangled face, but Scarlett makes a quick, evasive turn. My father hits only empty air as he stumbles past. The shadow's blade jabs, piercing Dad's shoulder from the rear and pushing the tip all the way through his body.

My father and I both scream as Scarlett plants a black-tar palm on his back and yanks the sword free. Dad falls to the ground, gasping for breath as his blood pools around him.

"Dad!" I cry. "No!"

I spring toward him, but the shadow is already between us. There's wildfire in its expression. It's a wounded animal scared for its life, maybe for the first time. Dad claws at the floor, coughing. He draws in a rattling gasp and shouts, "Get the stone!"

My eyes turn to the Wish Stone, sitting in its mount ten feet away. The shadow's head follows my gaze. Its eye goes wide with realization.

"Magic . . . stones . . ."

The words illuminate a memory. The shadow, spying on us talking in the jungle. *This is a very cute little game you're playing, with your tiki huts and your 'magic stones.'* We make eye contact, and in that fraction of a second, we share a frenzied understanding. The Mystic Stones are real here, and the shadow knows it.

The LEDs in my sneakers strobe as I bound toward the Stones' volcanic cradle. The shadow breaks into its own run just behind me, vaulting in a wobbly stride on my mother's long legs. Its hot breath is on my neck as I dive forward, throwing out a hand to grab the Wish Stone from its nest.

My palm hits the stone, but I don't feel it.

It takes a full second before my eyes and nerve endings can transfer the sting from my right forearm to my consciousness. Then it all hits me at once. The swish of air, the weight of the blade, the searing pain as the katana cuts through muscle and tendon and bone in one clean swipe.

When my palm hits the stone, it is no longer connected to my body.

A long hand leaves a wet, black handprint on my soccer uniform as it shoves me out of the way. I crumple to the ground, stunned beyond the capacity to fight. Blood gushes from the stump of my wrist. I can't scream. I can't stand up. I can't even clutch at my missing limb. All I can do is stare at the shadow.

Its lips pull into Mom's famous, movie-star smile, and there's something infuriatingly perverse about it all. Me and Dad, lying bloodied and beaten at the end of our own imaginary quest with this perversion of my mother about to win the game she spent my childhood refusing to play with us.

The shadow gazes reverently at the Mystic Stones and hisses through its damaged throat. "Life Stone ... restores health." Its eyes narrow at me. "I will heal. You will die."

It reaches for the stones and I register Dad's helpless, terrified scream through my delirium. I need to stop the shadow, but I'm powerless to do anything but watch as it drops its tar-slicked palm on the giant glittering diamond at the top of the formation.

The Death Stone.

A blazing light rips down the shadow's arm. White fire coils around its body, tightening like a snake, burning its simulated human flesh down to its black monster bones. The shadow recoils and wails a final, agonized scream as it's burned to a cinder, consumed by the imaginary stone's deadly curse.

Everything goes silent as the shadow crumbles to dust and the Death Stone drops to the floor. The instant it lands, tendrils of white rot begin to spread from it like creeping moss, etching cracks that race across the floor.

Dad fumbles over to me, throwing himself over the path of spreading decay. He grabs my shoulder. "Your hand! Are you all right? What's happening?"

I'm too overwhelmed to focus. The cracks of decay spread from the diamond up the walls and across the ceiling, dropping dust and gravel from the enormous rock slabs. "The Death Stone is killing the Temple! We have to get out!"

Dad doesn't say a word. He just throws his good arm under mine and hauls me to my feet. His teeth clench and his blood spurts as he carries my stunned little body to the cradle. I slap my remaining hand on the black Wish Stone and scream over the sound of the Temple collapsing around us.

"I wish we were back in the real world!"

The universe explodes in a dazzling suction of sparking light and energy. Everything I've ever seen or known or felt rages through my mind in a brutal torrent, like a flash flood punishing a dry canyon. I close my eyes and scream but I don't have a voice. I don't have eyes. My body evaporates into the throttling, rushing abyss.

Everything goes black and still.

My lungs are on fire, panting in uncontrolled panic. I become aware of it and try to slow my breathing in the darkness. Someone else's hot, stinking breath still rasps against my lips. The muscles of my face are stiff and taut, but I crack open my eyes. All I can see is another set of closed eyelids an inch away from mine. I instinctively recoil, then wince as a scab of dried blood crackles along my forehead.

The reflex action jerks a throbbing pain through my back and legs. My muscles are stiff almost to the point of immobility. Flashes of disorientation swim through my vision as my brain does a slow, lazy circle of reality. I'm sitting cross-legged on the floor of the shed. The room is dimly lit by narrow shafts of sunlight streaming in through the cracks around the barn doors, but the building is fully intact. The only shelf that's collapsed is the one Dad knocked down with the bat. There is no fire damage. There was never a fire.

Dad is kneeling in front of me, hyperventilating with his eyes crushed closed. A jagged crust of dried blood runs across his forehead. I touch my own and feel a hot wetness. I realize my scab is torn off, still attached to Dad's scar. Both scrapes must have been bleeding when he touched them together.

I blink at my bloody fingers. Attached to my hand. Attached to my wrist, as it should be. I pull a papery breath into my dried-out lungs and push out a whisper.

"Dad?"

My frigid muscles groan and I reach out and put my hand on his leg. His eyes pop open and his breathing turns choked and erratic. "Wha?"

His voice sounds like my throat feels. Dusty and raw. I gently squeeze his knee.

"It's okay. We're okay. It's over."

In time we slowly loosen our limbs and regain our wits enough to begin to process our ordeal. Coping with the physical pain comes first, then the emotional. Dad puts a hand to the crusted scar on his forehead. "So . . . is it dead?"

I nod. "I think so."

"But . . . I don't understand," Dad says vacantly. "Why did it kill itself? Why did it grab the Death Stone?"

"It didn't know any better. It didn't have our memories." A sad smile pricks at the corners of my lips. "It had Mom's, but Mom never played with us. She didn't know which stone was which."

Dad blinks slowly. "So it assumed the prettiest one was the one it wanted." He shakes his head. "Just like your mother would have."

I feel sick with a bitter sort of irony. When I was a kid, all I wanted was for Mom to play with us. In the end, it was her refusal that saved our lives.

We find the strength to stand and open the door. I shield my eyes against the morning sun, letting its warmth soak into my chilled skin. Dad blinks and stares and a quiet trickle of words flutter from his mouth.

"Son of a bitch."

My eyes go wide, taking in everything he sees. The cabin looks exactly as it did when we arrived. Weathered and abandoned, but without a hint of fairy damage. Past the corner of the house I see Dad's station wagon, fully intact, resting on the final incline of the driveway. It's not visible from here, but I know Mom's Lexus is still sitting undisturbed by the front door.

A light creaking of rope on wood whispers in my ear and I cast a glance at the gazebo. All I see is a pink pea coat suspended in the air before I look away. Dad sees it too, but his gaze lingers. Acceptance rests numbly on his face as he looks down and sighs.

"None of it really happened except the one thing that mattered."

His mourning seeps darkly to me. "I'm sorry, Dad." I raise my hand to give him a comforting touch, but hiss as a sharp pain tears through the crusted blood binding my fur coat to the scabby wound in my shoulder. "Augh. I guess some of it happened . . ."

Dad winces. "Oh God. I'm sorry. I'm so sorry I stabbed you. I was . . . I was all messed up."

I look at his swollen hand tenderly holding his smashed ribs—both wounds sustained at the business end of a baseball bat I was swinging. I frown and shake my head. "We both were. That was the shadow's game." I run my fingers over my leg, remembering the charred flesh and bloody fairy bites that no longer exist. "It couldn't hurt us. It could only trick us into hurting each other."

"I'm just glad we got our shit sorted out before . . ." Dad looks at the ground, struck by the chill of what could have been.

I nod. "I'm glad too."

We stand and look, listening to the wind in the pines, taking it all in for a long, still moment.

"So what do we do now?" Dad asks.

What do we do? What *can* we do? It's all too absurd. My instinct is to tell the authorities about Mom's suicide, but I know that would be a disaster. What are we supposed to say? The truth makes us sound insane, and any version of the story without the shadow would land us in prison.

Yes, officer. My estranged mother mysteriously disappeared and ended up dead. Her ex-husband and I, her disowned daughter, just happened to be in the neighborhood of our old abandoned, secluded cabin and found her body, totally already dead. We definitely had nothing to do with it, honest.

I draw in a long, chill breath. "We leave. It's all we can do. We clean up any sign we were ever here and just go back to our lives like this never happened."

"But it did happen," Dad says. He considers his words. "Something happened, and I don't want to pretend it didn't. I can't just go back to my old life." A hopeful look fills his eyes as he looks to me. "After all we've been through together I just . . . Would it be okay if we keep in touch? I'd like to get to know you better, Rebecca."

I smile and give his arm a gentle squeeze.

"Call me Bex."

CHAPTER TWENTY-SIX

Matty
Four Years Later

"If you really want to have fun, come with me."

"Where are we going?"

"The Lost Temple of Zamrycki!" Becca cheered. "Once we recover the Wish Stone, we can do anything we want! It's just on the other side of these weird rock piles."

"You'd better be careful," said Marty the Wizard. "I don't like the look of this. Those towers might be a trap!"

Becca cracked her knuckles and smiled. "Don't be such a scaredy cat. They're only rocks. What could go wrong?"

I lean back from my keyboard and smile at the blinking cursor on the screen. Once again, the headstrong pre-teen explorer Becca Wild is about to make a poor choice that will lead her and her magical sidekick to valuable life lessons. I can't wait to show my latest work-in-progress to my creative writing teacher tonight.

Quest for the Wish Stone is the third novel in my *Chronicles of the Forbidden Jungle* series of children's books. The first two titles weren't exactly best-sellers, but they do all right for small-press offerings. The royalties aren't enough to quit my day job, but it's not about the money. I write these stories for my own enjoyment. And to keep my mind occupied. To keep it from straying to places I don't want it to go.

The second I think it, the cabin flashes in my subconscious. Fairies and shadow. Blood and fire. A nightmare montage of insanity and violence hits me all at once like a sucker punch to the brain. My heart races and sweat beads on my upper lip. I close my eyes and I breathe. I meditate. I remind myself that I'm safe. That it's over. It's been over for a long time.

Whatever it was.

When we got back to civilization I was consumed with sorting it all out. Finding the logic, and making it all make sense. I thought I'd never find closure until I knew what the "shadow" really was, where it came from, and why.

I spent that first year scouring books on various brain ghouls and astral demons, desperate for answers. As I fell deeper down the rabbit hole, my research led me to murder statistics in the Lake Arrowhead area. Records only went back about a hundred years, but there were nine reports of people "going crazy" in the woods and murdering someone close to them.

I don't know what the shadow was or where it came from, but I know what it did. It fed and it slept. When we had our little "family reunion," it had been twenty-seven years since Dr. Laurie Cheung sacrificed her husband to save her son. The monster had slept through me and Kim forming our happy newlywed memories, and through Bex's childhood games in the woods. It might still be asleep now if my family hadn't awoken it with our drama. But at least we made sure it will never wake up again. Because it's dead.

We killed the motherfucker.

At least that's my theory. A "based on true events" story that I made up to help myself sleep at night. I continue my meditative breathing until I believe it's true. Because believing it's true makes it true. The old nightmare fades away and I slowly open my eyes, calmed and ready to face the world.

I shuffle across the hall to the cozy little bathroom. My thin face is like a welcome stranger in the mirror. I run my razor under hot water and drag it over my bristly scalp. I've made peace with the fact my hair is never coming back, so screw it. I traded in the budding comb-over for a whole Bruce Willis thing. It works with the new shape of my head. I pat the back of my hand under my jaw. I've heard weight in the face is the hardest to lose, but even the double chin has faded away.

Lookin' good, Matty!

Getting myself back in shape hasn't been easy, but luckily I have a very patient personal trainer.

I bend to brush my teeth, and my butt bumps against the back wall of the bathroom. My apartment is small, but it's homey and warm. And, most importantly, not haunted by ghosts of the past.

A few years ago I sold the Venice Beach house and everything in it. My overblown ergonomic desk, the sagging four-poster bed, the refrigerator with its decade-old grocery list. All of it. Surviving the incident at the cabin felt like a sign, an opportunity to start over. It was time to stop being such a sentimental schmuck and make a clean break with the past.

But before I could start a new life, I had to put the old one properly to rest. Bex was initially opposed to my plan, but after enough time passed without fallout, she agreed it had been the right thing to do.

We knew we couldn't tell anyone where Kim was, but I couldn't just leave her there to rot and feed the scavengers. It was too cruel and undignified an end to the woman I loved. So, before we returned to civilization, we put everything at the cabin back as Kim had left it with one exception—her phone. I took it and kept it turned off until I could do an inconspicuous drive-by of her house in the Hollywood Hills. Only then did I turn it on for a single minute. Just long enough for it to catch signal and send her final email. Later I soaked it in bleach, destroyed it with a hammer, wrapped it in a trash bag, and tossed it in a dumpster behind a CVS Pharmacy in Tujunga.

Sure enough, the detectives involved in Kim's missing-person case only ever got one ping on the location of her phone, apparently from her own house. The device was never recovered, but the email effectively closed the investigation. In her suicide note, Kim didn't say where she had done the deed, but it didn't take long for them to find her once the lawyers started breaking up her estate and examining her assets. The secret cabin near Lake Arrowhead was discovered, and along with it, her missing car and her final remains. Despite the mystery of the disappearing phone, after the coroner confirmed the death was a suicide the detectives decided it was Miller Time and closed the case.

I knew Kim had never really been at the cabin with us that weekend. I knew all the kind things she'd said about missing me and wanting to get back together were just a demon toying with my emotions to get me to hurt Bex. But something still nagged at my mind and heart. The shadow knew everything Kim knew. It could feel everything she felt. So was its ruse completely fabricated, or were its gestures of reconciliation for me and Bex based on genuine feelings it took from the real Kim?

It's impossible to say for sure, but Kim's final wishes spoke volumes. She willed her entire fortune to various charities for abused children and victims of sex crimes. It was an extreme case of "too little, too late," but at least I know she wasn't a monster. She clearly had deep regret for what she'd put our daughter through. If only Kim had been brave enough to reach out to Bex, maybe they could have patched things up. Maybe we all could have. Maybe she would still be alive now.

I try not to think too much about what could have been.

In a sad bit of irony, Kim's death finally earned her the respect she so craved in life. When Hollywood made their tributes, the *Blood Blitz* franchise was a footnote to her oeuvre of "notable and tragically underrated" performances. She never did win her golden statuette, but that year her glimmering face was the showcase finale of the ceremony's "In Memoriam" segment. Every A-lister in the theater was on their feet in a solemn, tearful ovation to her genius.

I wish she could have been there to see it.

My fumbling hands grab a towel and I dry my face and pull on a branded uniform polo.

Time to go to work.

CHAPTER TWENTY-SEVEN

Rebecca

Upbeat music echoes through the warehouse from the cardio class in progress at its far end. Between me and it, encouraging voices banter and fitness machines whirr their wheels and clank their weights. I stand beside my client in front of a wall of mirrors, carefully watching her motions as she does slow squats with an empty weight bar over her shoulders.

"Okay, that's good. Like really good," I say. "Your form is looking so much better than last time. How's that feeling?"

"Feeling good!"

"All right. Keep your chest up. There you go. I want you to do five more reps. Do you have five more for me, Shirley?"

"I can do ten."

I chuckle. "That's my girl! Just don't overdo it. Keep your knees parallel with your feet."

Shirley Jacobs is a sixty-seven-year-old ex-smoker with joint problems. The first time I saw her she told me her fitness goal was to be able to play with her grandchildren without getting winded. After a year with me she's running a charity 5K this weekend. I couldn't be prouder.

I step back to get a look at her body mechanics from behind. Every time she squats her pants ride down to reveal a faded lower-back tattoo with a little red devil and pointed script reading *Bad Ass*. It seems totally out of place on this sweet grandmother, but I'm not one to judge other people's expired ink.

My eyes tick to the wall of mirrors in front of us. The tank top I'm wearing leaves my arms and shoulders completely exposed, but I am no longer self-conscious about showing them. With business booming, I finally felt justified spending the dough to get my own unfortunate tats removed. After a long, painful, expensive romance with medical-grade lasers, the barbed wire heart on my left arm professing love to "Nobody" is nothing but a fading memory, as is the TOXIC warning on my back.

The cherry blossoms creeping over my right shoulder, however, are still there. They're supposed to be a symbol of fragile beauty that dies too soon. That's why I kept them. Not as a memorial to the old Bex, but to my mother. As twisted as our relationship was, I still think she died too soon. I found reconciliation with Dad. In time, I know we both could have found it together with Mom.

Then again, Dad and I never would have been reunited at all had it not been for her suicide and the ensuing supernatural clusterfuck. Still, sometimes I wish I could talk to her again. Not a monster impersonating her, but the real woman. I wonder what she'd say if she could see me now.

The thought runs my fingers over the tattoo on my wrist. *Fuck the World* was the mission statement of the self-destructive life she'd helped forge. It was too deep an emotional scar to just erase. It needed to be amended. The laser and needle worked together to create a new message. *Fix the World.*

"And that's ten!" I say. "Great job, that was perfect!"

I step up behind Shirley and take the bar from her. She lowers her arms and rolls her shoulders and neck. Her eyes catch on the muted TV screen attached to a nearby exercise bike and she harrumphs. "Oh God, that guy is such a dirtbag."

"What guy?" I ask.

She tosses a nod at the screen. "That VonDoozeler guy. He makes me sick."

I look, knowing what I'll see. It's a 24-hour news channel, gnawing away at the ongoing Robert VanDuzer trial. A few months ago a fourteen-year-old girl publicly accused him of rape. At least a dozen more women and girls came forward after her, dating back to the '80s.

When the story first broke it made me sick to my stomach, knowing I wasn't VanDuzer's first victim, or his last. The courage of the women who spoke up inspired me to add Bex Savage's name to the list of his accusers, albeit a decade too late. It kills me to think if I had spoken out at the time maybe I could have made the list that much shorter. But the world is finally listening to victims of Hollywood predators, and we are screaming. Knowing I've done my part to ensure he'll never ruin another life helps fight the guilt of not doing it sooner.

I shake my head and turn off the bike screen before my name splashes up among the others.

"I just hope this helps all his victims find closure."

Ever since I got out of therapy after my accident I've been trying to put my damaged past behind me and choose the best road to move forward. But no matter what road I chose, I was plagued with an always-smoldering rage. My rage against my mother, VanDuzer, and most importantly, myself. I couldn't drive far enough down the road of life to get away from my anger. I now realize why. It was trapped in the car with me. Only by opening the door to let Dad in did I finally let my anger out. Since then it's been growing ever smaller in my rearview mirror.

I finish guiding Shirley through the rest of her session, take notes on her progress chart, and send her on her way. She's a gold brick in my new road forward. She is, and all the fitness clients I work for are, and so are all the instructors and coaches who work for me. I breathe in the sweet smell of fresh air and fresh sweat mingled by the warehouse's ventilation system as I wind through the collection of machines and workout gear toward the main entrance. The place is busy today, with a half-dozen personal trainers working as well as the group cardio and yoga classes going on.

"Yo, Rebecca!"

The deep voice turns my head. One of my staff is on a break, loitering near a water cooler. Sean is fit as hell, but not 'roid-ripped. Just sturdy and tall, with a mop of black hair that he gels straight up like a shark fin. It's kind of adorable. A yoga instructor, Jessica, is with him. Petite and blonde and radiantly gorgeous, she purses her lips and stretches her triceps, pushing her perky boobs up to attention in Sean's direction. I try not to roll my eyes as I tuck my clipboard under my arm and join them.

"Hey guys, what's up?"

"Nothing much. I just got done teaching a class and I'm all gross and sweaty and *blaaagh*," Jessica says, wagging her tongue. This time I do roll my eyes. She's incapable of looking '*blaaagh*' and she knows it. She nods to Sean. "We were just talking about hitting a movie tonight."

"You wanna join us?" he asks.

I glance at Jessica, then back at Sean. "I, uh ... No, I can't. I wouldn't want to be a third wheel."

"Ha!" Jessica snorts. "Please. It's not like that. I don't date trainers."

Sean doesn't look broken up about it. I blink and shake my head. "Oh, okay. Duh. Sorry. Yeah! A movie sounds fun. I'm in."

"Sweet," Sean says. "I'll text you later. Maybe we can all go out and do something before."

I nod. "Cool. I'm down." I check my watch. "I gotta go. I've got another client coming in a few minutes."

"Sure, I see how it is." Jessica smiles and shoos me off. "Busy busy boss lady, always too busy to hang with the small people."

I chuckle and excuse myself, making a bee line for the front desk. "Boss lady." She's obnoxious, but I have to admit, I secretly like it when she calls me that. But this place isn't just about me. It's about all of us. We're a family here. We have to be or it will all fall apart. This fitness center is way bigger than what I had originally envisioned when I made my business plan, but a large cash infusion made a bigger dream possible. Too big for me to manage alone.

After all of my failed attempts to get a start-up loan, in the end it turned out what I really needed was a partner. My feet slow as I proudly brush a fuzz of dust off a set of huge plastic letters that dominate the front entrance.

Strong & Savage Fitness

I glide up behind the long, tall reception counter. My receptionist doesn't notice me over his shoulder. He's busy working on appointment reminder emails and humming to himself. I recognize the tune as a Van Halen song, but can't identify it.

"You're in a good mood today," I say.

Dad jumps and spins in his chair, grabbing his chest. "Aagh! Dang, kid! You trying to give me a heart attack?"

I smile and shake my head. "Give it up, Dad. You're too fit for that shtick now."

He smooths down his Strong & Savage polo over his flat belly and smiles proudly. I can't get over how much I've accomplished with him. There's still work to be done, but he's surpassed his original fitness goal of "not being a fat disgusting blob anymore."

His words, not mine.

After he sold the beach house he insisted on giving me the money to start Strong Fitness. I knew his heart was in the right place, but I didn't want his charity. I told him I'd only accept a loan, with interest. We eventually compromised and formed a partnership. Even after we bought the warehouse and equipment, he still had enough left over to retire comfortably, but he's too proud to live off the spoils of his divorce. He wants to work here to earn his own keep. Or so he claims. I think he just wants an excuse to hang with me all day. Which, honestly, I don't mind at all.

At any rate, I'm pretty sure he's the only millionaire receptionist in Pomona.

I lean on the desk next to him. "Hey, Sean and Jessica invited me to the movies tonight. Want to come with us?"

"What, do you kids need a chaperone or something?" Dad shakes his head. "You don't want an old man tagging along. Besides, I have a meeting with Judy. I'm going to show her what I've got so far on the new book." He grins and rubs his hands. "Oh man, I put in that thing you came up with about the poison dart trap. It was genius. It really got me out of a jam at the end of the first act. I can't wait till you read it."

His praise tickles me. He may be the official scribe of the Forbidden Jungle, but it's still *our* made-up world. Our regular vegan pizza and expedition brainstorming sessions are one of the highlights of my week. Even so, that's not the part that piqued my interest.

"Oh, it's *Judy* now, is it?" I raise a scandalous eyebrow. "When did it stop being Professor Adams?"

Dad's creative writing teacher is a horn-rimmed-glasses librarian type with a truly impressive body of published work. For someone over fifty, her actual body is pretty damn impressive as well.

Dad blushes. "I don't know. She's really taken an interest in my writing. We've been spending a lot more time together out of class, and . . . whatever."

Whatever. *And all that implies.* The name of the song Dad was humming finally comes to me. "Hot for Teacher."

I tap his arm with the back of my hand. "Looks like someone's gunning for some extra credit, eh?"

Dad smirks and pretends to busy himself at his computer. "Shut up."

I gear up to needle him some more, but I'm interrupted by Sean sidling up to the other side of the counter. "Oh, Rebecca. Hey. Listen, Jessica bailed on the movie tonight. Do you still, uh . . . " He clears his throat and drags his finger distractedly across the countertop. "Would you still want to go out if it was just the two of us?"

He looks up at me and his eyes glimmer with nerves and hope. Warmth blossoms through my skin, drawing redness up my neck and across my scarred cheeks.

"I . . . yeah. That would be fine. I'm cool with that."

Sean blinks. "Yeah?"

I nod and smile. "Yeah."

A grin brightens his face. "Yeah! Okay. Cool. So, I'll find you after my next session and we'll work it all out."

"Sounds good," I say.

"Right on." He waits for an awkwardly long moment before darting back into the gym with a spring in his step. A fluttering heat settles in my stomach and I turn to Dad. He's just staring at me with a cheeky grin on his face. I scowl at him.

"Don't even start."

He shakes his head in mock judgment, speaking in a high pitched voice. "Oooh, Dad! You're so naughty dating your teacher! It's much more ethical to make kissy-kissy eyes at my own employee."

"I said don't start!"

I give him a sharp, playful slap to his bicep. He recoils and laughs, throwing his hands up in self-defense. "Whoa whoa! Don't get violent. I was just messing with ya. You know I love you, kid."

His goofy smile draws a matching smile out of me.

"I love you too, Dad."

THANK YOU

Hello, reader!

Thank you for spending these three-hundred-and-something pages of supernatural family drama with me and the Savages. I hope you enjoyed reading *One Must Kill Another* as much as I enjoyed writing it. And I hope that doesn't mean we're all psychopaths.

If you liked this book, I'd really appreciate a quick review on Amazon.com and/or Goodreads. Just a few words and a bunch of stars is all it takes to get the 'ol algorithms to share my work with awesome new readers like you.

This handy URL will take you directly to the review pages:

OldPalMarcus.com/review-omka/

(Note: Tapping the link does not work here. This is paper.)

Also, you can get three of my ebooks for free when you join my "Army of Marcness" mailing list at OldPalMarcus.com.

Thanks again for reading and reviewing! You're the best!

Your old pal,
Marcus

ALSO THANK YOU

Thank you to my beta readers, Gary Fixler, Ben Jerred, Robyn Kralik, Austin McKinley, John Walsh, and everyone at Portland Writer's Workshop. Each of you made this book slightly less ridiculous. In a good way.

Thank you to Michael Greenholt for coming up with the concept of "Rex Mex," and then allowing me to blatantly steal it.

Thank you to Rebecca Essenpreis (*née* Zamrycki) for having a name that sounded so perfect I had to appropriate it. Apologies to Addie VanDuzer for the same reason.

Thank you to my mentor Lauren Smith for her endless knowledge, encouragement, and generosity.

Thank you to my family, for not inspiring the Savages.

Thank you to my amazing editor Noah Chinn, fantastic cover designers Shaela Odd and Kitty Cook, heroic blurb writer Jennifer Jakes, meticulous proofreader Alexa, and the whole team at Canaby Press. You've made publishing more fun than it's supposed to be.

And most of all, thank you to my wife, Amanda. Thank you for your patience, and for never giving up on me, even when I did. I couldn't do this, or anything, without you.

ABOUT THE AUTHOR

Marcus Alexander Hart has written for stage and screen, including projects for Disney Channel and Disney XD. In past lives he's been a computer animator, internet humorist, and contributing editor to the lifestyle/tech magazine *Geek Monthly*. Marcus lives near Portland, Oregon with his wife and two imaginary children.

Visit Marcus online at OldPalMarcus.com.

CPSIA information can be obtained
at www.ICGtesting.com
Printed in the USA
LVHW081639220920
666793LV00029B/944